Nige...
World Champion

The Full Story

The road was long and as it unfolded it kept twisting back on itself across dangerous terrain. Often – too often – it dipped into dark valleys, ascended, dipped again . . . Then, very quickly, it straightened and led to a summit wreathed in sunlight. Nigel Ernest Mansell reached that summit on 16 August 1992, safely home at last, Champion of the World.

Three times he'd seen the summit already. The first time, 1986, he nearly died, the second, 1987, he nearly broke his back, the third, 1991, he ran off the road and skidded away into a dust-cloud. Now, this fourth time – at the Hungaroring near Budapest – he resisted the familiar ravages of misfortune, crossed the dangerous terrain and completed the ascension.

He'd beaten them all, the doubters and critics, beaten his own early impoverished years when only he and his wife truly believed in him, beaten the accidents and hospital wards, beaten 12 years of waiting. And 12 years of Formula One is an extremely long road.

His story is supercharged, no less, all the way through.

Nigel Mansell
World Champion

The Full Story

SIMON & SCHUSTER

LONDON·SYDNEY·NEW YORK·TOKYO·SINGAPORE·TORONTO

First published in Great Britain
in this edition in 1992
by Simon & Schuster Ltd
A Paramount Communications Company

Simon & Schuster Ltd
West Garden Place
Kendal Street
London W2 2AQ

Simon & Schuster of Australia Pty Ltd
Sydney

A CIP catalogue record for this book is
available from the British Library
ISBN 0-671-85099-7

Typeset in 10/13 Plantin by
Hewer Text Composition Services, Edinburgh
Printed and bound in Great Britain by
HarperCollinsManufacturing, Glasgow

Contents

Nigel Mansell: World Champion

Edited by: David Emery, Sports Editor of
Daily Express
Written by: Bob McKenzie, Motor Racing
Correspondent of *Daily Express*
(and the *Daily Express* Sports Team)

Drivers in Action

How they lined up for the 1992 Season

No.	Name	Team	Age	Country
1	Ayrton Senna	McLaren-Honda	32	Brazil
2	Gerhard Berger	McLaren-Honda	33	Austria
3	Olivier Grouillard	Tyrrell-Ford	34	France
4	Andrea de Cesaris	Tyrrell-Ford	33	Italy
5	Nigel Mansell	Williams-Renault	39	Britain
6	Ricardo Patrese	Williams-Reanult	38	Italy
9	Michele Alborelo	Footwork-Mugen Honda	35	Italy
10	Aguri Suzuki	Footwork-Mugen Honda	32	Japan
11	Mika Hakkinen	Lotus-Ford	24	Finland
12	Johnny Herbert	Lotus-Ford	28	Britain
16	Jan Lammers	March-Ilmor	36	Holland
17	Emanuele Naspetti	March-Ilmor	24	Italy
19	Michael Schumacher	Benetton-Ford	23	Germany
20	Martin Brundle	Benetton-Ford	33	Britain
21	JJ Lehto	Dallara-Ferrari	26	Finland
22	Plerluigi Martini	Dallara-Ferrari	31	Italy
23	Christian Fittipaldi	Minardi-Lamborghini	21	Brazil
24	Gianni Morbldelli	Minardi-Lamborghini	24	Italy
25	Thierry Boutsen	Ligier-Renault	35	Belgium
26	Erik Comas	Ligier-Renault	29	France
27	Jean Alesi	Ferrari	28	France
28	Nicola Larini	Ferrari	28	Italy
29	Bertrand Gachot	Venturi-Lamborghini	22	France
30	Ukyo Katayama	Venturi-Lamborghini	29	Japan
32	Stefano Modena	Jordan-Yamaha	29	Italy
33	Mauricio Gugelmin	Jordan-Yamaha	29	Brazil
34	Alex Caffi	Andrea Moda-Judd	27	Italy
35	Enrico Bortaggia	Andrea Moda-Judd	27	Italy

Best of British

The road was long and as it unfolded it kept twisting back on itself across dangerous terrain. Often too often – it dipped into dark valleys, ascended, dipped again as if some terrible, endless torment was being enacted along the way. Then, very quickly, the road straightened and led to a summit wreathed in sunlight. Nigel Ernest Mansell reached that summit on 16 August 1992, safely home at last, Champion of the World.

Three times he'd seen the summit already. The first time, 1986, he nearly died, the second, 1987, he nearly broke his back, the third, 1991, he ran off the road and skidded away into a dust-cloud. Now, this fourth time – at the Hungaroring near Budapest – he resisted the familiar ravages of misfortune, crossed the dangerous terrain and completed the ascension.

He'd beaten them all, the doubters and critics, beaten his own early impoverished years when only he and his wife truly believed in him, beaten the accidents and hospital wards, beaten 12 years of waiting. And 12 years of Formula One is an extremely long road.

His story is supercharged, no less, all the way through.

Nigel Mansell was born at Upton-on-Severn in deepest Worcestershire on 8 August 1953, the third of four children. His father, Eric, an aerospace engineer, had raced karts around the Midlands so, however humbly, racing ran in the blood. As Mansell reached towards the summit through the late 1980s and early 1990s there were two drivers he had to beat: Ayrton Senna and Alain Prost. Senna's father was a farmer, Prost's father a carpenter who evidently showed no interest in motor sport until little Alain started karting.

For Mansell the first real taste of the intoxication of speed came at what seems now a most improbable place: Aintree, home of the Grand National. The British Grand Prix was held there five times from 1955 to 1962. Eric Mansell took Nigel there to watch on 21 July 1962 and they saw three British World Champions drive in the race: Jim Clark (Lotus), Graham Hill (BRM) and John Surtees (Lola). It's a sobering perspective: only four other Britons had been or would become World Champion: Mike Hawthorn, Jackie Stewart, James Hunt and the nine-year-old spectator at Aintree that day.

Clark won the race from Surtees and Hill was fourth. By their nature they were very different drivers, Hill a determined slogger, Surtees enveloped by a self-belief nobody and nothing could shake, Clark born with extra-ordinary gifts of balance, sensitivity and completely instinctive co-ordination. In time one aspect of the nine-year-old would resemble Hill, another would mirror Surtees very precisely and a third would lead people into comparisons with Clark himself.

Nigel Mansell was an ordinary schoolboy who liked football and cricket and disliked Latin. Although the family moved to Birmingham he spent happy hours at a friend's farm, where they drove a battered old Austin Seven round the fields. Mansell subsequently said that he and his pal were so small they couldn't see through the long grass to gauge where they were going, and anyway they didn't know anything about brakes. They used stone walls to stop the car.

A couple of years after Aintree Mansell happened to notice an ancient go-kart for sale in a garage at Hall Green. They wanted £25 for it. Mansell persuaded Dad to go along and have a look. Eric discovered that its mighty powerhouse was in fact a lawn mower engine, but he did allow Nigel a tentative run round the garage forecourt. Legend insists that Nigel ran into a petrol pump and Eric had to buy it because he'd damaged it. Perhaps that's where the story really begins.

Mansell used the kart as a toy, driving it round and round some allotments, delighted that he could go fast (well, relatively fast) without having to pedal, and he became so keen he thought he'd like to race it. He was ten, and although strictly speaking he had to be 11 to obtain a licence, ten-year-olds rarely weigh such niceties. He took the kart to Shenington, a former airbase near Edge Hill, Banbury, entered for a race and was quite certain he would win it.

This particular legend is misty. Some say he hit a kerb on the warm-up lap and rolled the kart, he insists that during practice he was hammering along the straight as fast as he could and inexplicably the kart slowed and rolled to a complete halt. A marshall rushed up to see if he was all right and Mansell muttered, "Yes, but my chain's fallen off." "Chain?" the marshall said. "Your engine's fallen off!" The mountings on the ancient kart had snapped. He looked and – no engine.

Even when the engine was welded back on and he competed in other races Mansell discovered that most frustrating thing in motor sport, lack of speed. He strongly objected to being lapped, as he constantly was, so he persuaded Dad to pay £34 for a more powerful engine. He had embarked on the long road, however much he remained unaware of that.

3

If you're being lapped and by inclination you're a true racer you face a decision. Either you accept that the machinery is slow and simply enjoy yourself, or you do something about it. The investment of £34 represented the outcome of that decision for Mansell, and from that moment on there would be no turning back.

Motor sport is a strange, eccentric, egotistical and far-flung fraternity, but a fraternity none the less. People in it know people in it, know people in it. The fraternity embraces little kart meetings at places few have heard of as well as the summit so far, far away and the same impulses literally drive them all: they talk the same language (coded and specialised), they're all at differing staging posts along the same road. Inevitably, for reasons of cost and availability, karts are where a lot of youngsters get in.

Most current Formula One drivers did this – Senna, Prost and Riccardo Patrese as well as Mansell, to name but four – although paradoxically Patrese is the only man to have won the World Karting Championship. Mansell was drawn further and further into the fraternity (it happens), spent more and more time tinkering with his engines and eventually was able to buy a Birel 100cc kart. On that you could win, and he might have taken the British Junior Championships had the engine not blown up when he was in second place.

There were journeys to meetings on the Continent accompanied by the family and organised on a humble scale. They camped (it also happens). Legend has it that driving for the British junior team in Holland he plunged off and came to rest in a tree . . .

At 15 he raced in a meeting in Heysham, a track so small that two sections of it ran parallel and were divided by a stout wooden fence set in concrete, wooden boards

4

and then straw bales. Mansell says his steering snapped and he somersaulted into the barrier. Bert Hesketh, an organiser of the meeting, didn't see that but did see the aftermath. "We ran over. He hadn't gone completely through the barrier although his legs were in it. He was unconscious. We pulled him out the way he had gone in and put him in an ambulance. He had a broken thigh."

From this moment on mighty and fearsome crashes punctuated his career, each adding to the legend. In hospital he was given the Last Rites.

In 1968 he reached the World Senior Championships, run in Milan over two heats. He won the first but the second was drowned by heavy rain. He had no wet tyres and managed eighth place, third overall. This little forgotten heat is a key. Whether you're in a kart or a racing car the wet alters everything, braking points, acceleration, deceleration, visibility. In a taut, highly-strung machine, if you lack sensitivity, if you can't feel every nuance of movement, you'll be flung off. Mansell felt the nuances, and on dry smooth tyres, offering the most minimal of grip, he wasn't flung off.

In 1970 he studied at Solihull Technical College as part of an engineering apprenticeship with Lucas. Outside the college one day he glimpsed a very short mini-skirt and cheekily asked the girl inside it if she wanted a lift. She naturally hesitated, but she was going to the college, too, she recognised him and finally accepted.

Rosanne Perry was a year younger than Mansell and knew nothing whatsoever about kart racing. She started to go to meetings with him – she was at Heysham the day he crashed – so that she came to know both the man and the risks inherent in what he did.

By 1975 Mansell had won a great deal in karting:

seven Midlands Championships and a couple of Welsh titles and he was voted Driver of the Year at a meeting at Shenington. In the spring of 1975 he married Rosanne. He made another decision. You can stay in karts indefinitely but the big world is single seaters, and a friend had been doing well in the lowest rung of that, Formula Ford 1600. Mansell and Rosanne saved £15 and he took a lesson at Mallory Park. They could afford only this one lesson, not the full course.

Single seaters are completely unlike karts. You have to learn how to change gear, the racing lines where you take up position for corners differ because karts have staggering adhesion, the braking points differ – they're further back in cars. In sum a car is a more sophisticated, more complicated piece of machinery even at Formula Ford 1600 level, and the fact that you're a good karter does not mean you will instantly be a good driver.

He wasn't outstanding during the lesson. Virtually nobody is. The first lesson discourages flair in favour of mastering the very basics of how and why you actually make the car go forward. This is explained fully, often on blackboards as well as on the track (brake in straight lines before a corner not in the corner, change down to the right gear before the corner, not when you're in it). He could do the basics. He and Rosanne scraped together £1500 for a car with a Ford engine called a Hawke – she describes it as "elderly" – and a trailer to get it to and from races.

Mansell entered the Hawke for a race at Mallory Park. It was 29 May 1976. He set the fastest lap and won, although reportedly there wasn't much opposition. Six weeks later he won a heat of the Dunlop Star of Tomorrow 1600cc race at Castle Combe, a month after that he won another 1600cc race, again at Castle Combe . . .

To finance this Rosanne worked for the West Midlands Gas Board and Mansell cleaned windows and made picture frames. If this was the price of a career in motor racing they were prepared to pay it because Mansell now regarded himself as a professional. When he told his father he was leaving Lucas to pursue this career they had a monumental row and the fall-out lasted for months, Eric insisting that if that was what Mansell wanted he'd have to finance it himself.

That season of 1976 has passed into legend. Some say he drove 11 times; he thinks it was nine, but the noted statistician John Taylor could find only five races. It depends how you care to enumerate them because, for example, there were two Dunlop Star of Tomorrow meetings each involving a heat and a final. But we don't need to be pedantic about this because, counting these heats, he drove seven times and won five, with a second place and a sixth for good measure. It is evidence enough of promise.

In 1977 he and Rosanne raised enough money to launch a full frontal assault on Formula Ford 1600. In something approaching a frenzy of activity he drove virtually every weekend, managed to get his hands on four types of car and won a batch of races.

The legend was growing in another way, too. At Brands Hatch in June he touched wheels with another car and was launched into a series of somersaults. Marshals prised him carefully from the wreckage, his neck badly injured in two places. He was taken to Sidcup Hospital where specialists said he'd need to lie flat for several months if he didn't want to risk permanent damage. Lying there Mansell became despondent, thinking that his career was over already and he might as well get up and go home. He did. And he raced again within weeks . . .

Overall 1977 had been good, if you can draw that kind of balance after nearly paralysing yourself and already, here and there, people murmured about another Jim Clark. How many other young drivers have had to bear that heavy comparison? Plenty, probably, as they begin to emerge, their shortcomings not yet exposed. In the jostle of Formula Ford 1600 a man's full range, his full potential, is not revealed: it is too early for that.

But Formula Ford is a useful touchstone because the engine power of all the cars is similar. What Mansell needed was Formula Three, the next staging post along the road, and to get into that what Mansell needed was money. He and Rosanne made a savage, far-reaching decision. They sold their flat near Solihull for £6000, moved into a rented house and used the £6000 to strike a deal with a famous manufacturer of racing cars, March. It bought Mansell just five races, and these against drivers like Nelson Piquet and Derek Warwick, who were already regarded as good Formula One material.

Mansell described the background as: "Hell, we had no money." He spent his hours either window cleaning or exercising in a little gym he'd created in the garage of the house. In that garage he arranged a montage of his crash at Brands Hatch along one wall. The montage served several purposes. It constantly reminded him of the danger and thus, as he exercised, posed the question: do you really want to go on with this? The exercising was his answer: yes, I do.

Moreover a very fit body absorbs an accident much better than an unfit one and recovers more quickly from an accident, too. You need to be fit, anyway, to drive. It is true that the lesser formulae do not make the same depth of demands as Formula One, where the G-loading tries to pull your head off your shoulders, but the lesser formulae do make demands, particularly if you're racing a lot. Counting heats and finals, for example, Mansell drove 50 times in 1977.

His first Formula Three race of 1978 was at Silverstone, where he finished second. He'd taken pole and in the race beat Piquet and Warwick, but the car wasn't particularly competitive and in his four remaining races before the £6000 ran out he was seventh three times and fourth once. He found what ought to have been some consolation when, in recognition of what he had achieved so far in difficult circumstances, he received a British Drivers' Award of a Formula Two drive at Donington Park with the ICI Chevron team.

This might have been and perhaps ought to have been a real chance. Formula Two was the last staging post before Formula One and the road to the summit. Not that he'd vault straight into Formula One, of course, but at least he could demonstrate in front of important people that he could handle a Formula Two car and was maybe worth a full and proper season of that.

The weekend went disastrously wrong. Mansell partnered Derek Daly, an affable Irishman who himself would reach Formula One, and the team had a spare car in case of emergencies. During practice some errant driver spilled oil on the track and by bad fortune Mansell ran into it just after the oil had been spilled, lost control and hit a wall – hard. Worse, a rich and ambitious young Italian, Elio de Angelis, arrived and bought a drive with the team. They put him in the spare car, which meant Mansell had to make do with the race car he'd crashed. It was repaired, but in the time available that could be only makeshift. The handling was wrong and he didn't qualify for the race.

The long road dipped into one of the dark valleys,

perhaps none darker than this. He was armed with a determination so ferocious that not even passing strangers could doubt it, but he had no money and he had no car; and this when the years were already moving by. In 1979 he would be 26, not old in a Formula One context, but starting to get old if you've done no more than a Formula Two meeting and failed, for whatever reason, to qualify.

At last, unexpectedly, a real chance to ascend loomed from the depths of the valley. A man called Dave Price was due to run a Unipart-backed Formula Three team in 1979 and already had a driver signed, Brett Riley. It would be a two-car team and Price had no thought of Mansell for the other seat. He'd interviewed several drivers for that, Mansell not among them. Mansell rang Price, journeyed to Twickenham where the team was based and by force of character persuaded Price he was the man.

With Unipart money, Price found himself in a position to pay his drivers, a most astonishing thing in Formula Three then. Mansell could stop cleaning windows and dreaming. The cars were Marches but powered by Triumph Dolomite engines. The problem soon revealed itself; not enough power. There is virtually no way round this, even for a very great driver, never mind someone only beginnning to explore greatness. However much you caress and goad and squeeze a car to its limit, however superior your judgement, nerve and technique in corners, you'll be blown away on the straights. All the other guys have to do is dip their accelerators and they're gone.

Mansell was 11th at Silverstone in the opening race, second at Thruxton and won the third at Silverstone again, although only because an Italian, Andrea de Cesaris, was penalised for missing out the chicane.

10

Mansell settled into a sort of rhythm, bringing the March Triumph into fourth and sixth and seventh places regularly, which perhaps was all it was really capable of anyway. That is particularly significant to people who know, however infuriating it has to be for the driver who loathes being beaten and feels sixth place is the wilderness.

Those who know evaluate this in a completely different way. Team managers from Formula Three to Formula One fully understand that great disparities exist from car to car in each formula except 1600, and furthermore that each season one or two or three young drivers will dominate because they have the machinery to do that. These young drivers will be good, they'll be ticking off the victories. Further down the grid the context alters. The people who know fully understand how bad some of the cars may be and if a driver can cajole a bad car towards respectable results he might be as good, if not better, than those romping away at the front.

Such judgements can turn on fleeting moments. Formula Three provided one of the British Grand Prix support races at Silverstone in July 1979, and here Mansell was introduced to Colin Chapman, creator of Lotus and among the most important people in motor sport. Chapman knew every nook and cranny of the business. He had taken Clark to World Championships and memorably a victory at the Indianapolis 500. In 1978 Mario Andretti walked the World Championship in a Lotus, a car so good he said publicly that a monkey would have won in it.

Now, in midsummer 1979, Mansell had struck up a friendship with a journalist, Peter Windsor, who liked his determination, liked his whole approach. Windsor, an extremely astute and informed observer, was among those who knew. During the Formula Three race he

11

persuaded Chapman and assistant Lotus team manager Peter Collins to wander over to the chicane to have a look. The Silverstone 2 chicane (now long gone into memory) was a very interesting place.

Approached at high speed under the Daily Express bridge it lay like a tight, narrow snake and demanded bravery and finesse in equal measure. Chapman pointed out that Mansell was running sixth in the race. Windsor and Collins pointed out that the car was good for only sixth place, but told Chapman to watch how late Mansell braked for the chicane, how much car control he had threading through, how early he was getting onto the power as he came out. Chapman was impressed. Chapman did not forget.

The Formula Three season churned on into September and a race at Oulton Park. There Mansell became involved in a duel with Eddie Jordan (who now runs his own Formula One team) and de Cesaris became involved, too. De Cesaris tried to overtake Mansell in a corner – something neither Mansell nor Jordan, who was watching in his mirrors, anticipated. De Cesaris and Mansell collided, Mansell barrel-rolled and the car came to rest upside down. He was taken to hospital with broken vertebrae.

A few weeks later, while he was still recovering, the phone rang. It was Lotus, who wondered if he'd be available to do a Formula One test at the Paul Ricard circuit in the South of France. Mansell said yes immediately, but the voice at the other end mused that hadn't he had a bad accident at Oulton? Legend insists Mansell replied that it must have been someone else and he'd be at the test all right.

He would not be alone at Ricard, itself a kind of test. Chapman had invited Stephen South, then a promising

British driver going well in Formula Two, de Angelis, Eddie Cheever, a European-based American, and Jan Lammers, a neat and talented Dutchman. All were much more experienced than Mansell. Cheever had driven Formula One in 1978, albeit only once and for the Hesketh team; de Angelis was in a full season with the Shadow Ford team.

Mansell flew to Marseilles dosing himself with pain killers, found the circuit (itself a feat because it's in the hills in the middle of nowhere) and prepared to prove what he could do.

The test was conducted on Ricard's short circuit as opposed to the full Grand Prix panorama and in British-style weather, wind and showers. Mansell covered 35 laps and spun only once. That's significant because he was handling so much more power than he ever had before. It comes at you extremely fast and despite the width of the tyres, despite the amazing adhesion of a Formula One chassis, losing control is very, very easy. It's a vivid thought the first-timer keeps at the forefront of his mind: don't damage the car.

But he must also strike a balance, because if he travels slowly and is governed by total prudence the team might well wonder what he's doing there. Anyway, Mansell got the balance right and although de Angelis was hired to partner Andretti in 1980, Chapman offered Mansell a testing contract and three races.

In a sense he had come to this very quickly, virtually straight from Formula Three and with only a single win in that, the one he had inherited after de Cesaris had been penalised at Silverstone. In another sense he was much nearer 30 than 20 and if he didn't do it soon the years would run hard against him. It would be too late.

He stayed in Formula Three in 1980, finishing fourth,

fifth, sixth again, while he waited for his first Grand Prix, Austria on 17 August. To run three cars at a Grand Prix meeting – Andretti and de Angelis in the other two, of course – traditionally stretches a Formula One team and is rarely tried. However it can be done, particularly when the third car is only to give a chap a feel of it and the outcome is not crucial either way.

Mansell had tested the Lotus well since Ricard and initially felt confident. That confidence turned to nervousness when he arrived at the Osterreichring, a fast circuit of awe-inspiring swoops set into undulating countryside. He qualified on the back row of the grid, which is more or less where reality dictates you will be on your debut in the third car. The legend was poised to grow.

On the grid waiting for the start the mechanics topped up the fuel. Some of it spilt down onto the seat and it began to burn through his overalls. The mechanics poured water over it and over Mansell but the fuel burned through that, too. They said he could get out if he wanted, miss the race, no shame, not his fault, but in his dogged way Mansell explained that he'd waited years for this and he'd race, thank you. He lasted 42 laps until the engine went and by then he had third degree burns. He could barely walk when he reached Heathrow (his tendons seized), couldn't sleep and went to a hospital accident unit in Birmingham for treatment.

Two weeks later he drove in the Dutch Grand Prix at Zandvoort, qualifying on the eighth row, but spun off when the brakes went. Two weeks after that he failed to qualify for the Italian Grand Prix at Imola. And that was his season.

Andretti now left to join Alfa Romeo and Chapman gave his place to Mansell. He found himself in a leading Formula One team and one rich in the history of what

14

it had achieved, power-driven by the genius of Chapman and heavy with expectations. Nobody could know that Lotus were descending into the darkest of dark valleys.

As Mansell prepared for the 1981 season Lotus had not won a race since Holland in 1978, and soon enough, when the rush for turbo power began in earnest, Chapman would be untypically, almost unbelievably, off the pace in joining it. The coveted drive which Mansell now held securely in both hands might not be coveted at all.

At Long Beach, a street circuit lined by concrete walls and thus a place where any small error involved large consequences, he hit a kerb which volleyed him into one of the walls. In the next race, Brazil, he finished 11th and in the race after that, Argentina, didn't finish at all – engine problems. However impetuous a driver is at the start of his Formula One career he will almost certainly have to learn the art of waiting, a contradiction but a necessary one. Experience can be bought only with time, each track is different, each situation is different and you're competing against drivers who have been mastering every facet for perhaps a decade or more.

To finish in the top six – a points finish, as they say – remains awkwardly elusive while you're waiting, but Mansell did it in the fifth race of 1981, at Zolder in Belgium. The background was sad and disturbing. A mechanic rushed onto the grid to work on a stalled car just before the green light went on and was run over. Mansell, who saw this clearly although he wasn't involved, thought instantly the mechanic must be dead. The race was naturally stopped and Mansell, badly shaken and with tears in his eyes, stayed in the cockpit because he feared if he got out he'd never get back in again. He took part in the re-started race only when he was given categorical assurances that the mechanic had not been killed.

From this alarming sequence of events he produced a storming drive, bringing the Lotus in third, and in the process held off the ultimate charger, Gilles Villeneuve (Ferrari turbo). Mansell launched a career and launched it decisively, although the rest of 1981 drifted. He picked up a point in Spain, was seventh in France and, amid a frenetic and frantic squabble between Lotus, Chapman and officialdom, did not qualify for the British Grand Prix at Silverstone.

Chapman, who specialised in original thinking which from time to time caught the opposition totally by surprise, created a 'twin-chassis' car – one chassis moving within the other – but it was declared illegal early in the season. However the RAC, who had jurisdiction over Silverstone, pronounced it legal for the British Grand Prix. But after the first day's qualifying session several teams protested and the stewards at the meeting upheld this. The Lotus was illegal again.

Mansell's time was taken from him. Chapman stalked around enraged making savage statements, but the team had to convert the car to a normal chassis overnight for the second qualifying session. They struggled to do so, but in an echo of Donington 1978 there simply wasn't enough time. Mansell tried – he was always going to do that – but he couldn't make it go fast enough to force his way onto the grid. He felt 'blazing anger' but it wasn't directed towards Lotus, it was aimed at officialdom: "I can't find words to express my utter misery and humiliation at the bloody fiasco of the last few days."

He retired in the next five races but came fourth at Caesar's Palace, Las Vegas in the last of the season. Eight points and 14th in the Championship table (de Angelis had 14 points for eighth place) represented at least a foundation. Retrospectively it represented a solid foundation, the opening lessons in what Formula One calls the learning curve.

For 1982 Chapman hired Peter Warr as team manager. The relationship between Warr, tall and sometimes scholarly, and Mansell was to become very strained although that wasn't evident as the season began. Mansell retired in South Africa and finished a strong third in Brazil, but turbo engines were now what you had to have and Chapman hadn't.

The turbo, introduced to general scepticism by Renault as far back as 1977, worked on a simple theory: if you can trap and recycle the gasses a normal engine gives out you gain a big increase in power. Making the simple theory work, and work reliably, proved extremely complex and brought with it associated problems. If you braked and then pumped the throttle you had a 'time-lag' before the power came on which enabled what were now called 'normally-aspirated' cars to be quicker on twisty circuits, but by 1982 turbos had so much power they could compensate.

Between them Renault, Brabham and Ferrari, who all had turbos, set the pace and that was reflected in Mansell's season as he struggled along behind them: he was fourth at Monaco, so twisty it negated some of the turbo's advantage, but of the remaining races he finished ninth in Germany, eighth in the Swiss, seventh in Italy and didn't finish any of the other five.

He sensed, however, that he was a match for De Angelis and Chapman began to talk of another Clark. How sincere Chapman was about this we will never know. Some astute and seasoned judges construct a case for Clark being the greatest driver who ever lived, others go for Juan-Manuel Fangio but, whoever you favour, it's exalted company. Clark drove 72 races between

1960 and 1968, all for Lotus, and won 25 of them, an utterly astonishing strike rate; not to mention that he freely competed in many other categories and won consummately in those, too.

Chapman must have known the dangers of comparing Mansell to Clark, indeed, of comparing anyone to Clark. By the end of 1982 Mansell had competed in 18 Grands Prix with that third place at Zolder his best result. By the end of his third season Clark had driven 22 times, won three races, been on pole position six times and set fastest laps in races six times; in his fourth season he had won seven times and become World Champion.

It may be that Chapman saw this, or something of it, in Mansell, it may be that Chapman, a natural publicist, thought he's stir up some publicity, but it is beyond dispute that Chapman believed in Mansell and showed him many kindnesses as well as his faith that Mansell was more than very good.

In December 1982 Colin Chapman died of a heart attack.

Warr inherited the running of the team and the friction between him and Mansell rubbed hard. They didn't like each other. Lotus now had Renault turbo engines but de Angelis was given preference – Mansell didn't get his until the British Grand Prix at Silverstone – and he totalled only ten points for the whole season. De Angelis recorded only two points.

Mansell retired in the first four races of 1984 but managed third place in France. That was something, not a huge amount but something. And at Monaco it rained. There he led a race for the first time in his life. Because Monaco is a place where people live rather than a custom-built circuit the road is an ordinary one, with a white line down the middle, used for conventional traffic when the Grand Prix is not there.

Going up the hill towards the Casino Square Mansell brushed over the white line, which was extremely slippery. He lost adhesion and thundered into the barrier. "When that happens you're just a passenger", he would say. The incident (or accident) became a fierce controversy in its own right because, as some people insisted, Mansell was moving away from Prost, in second place, at a much faster rate than he needed to. Overtaking is all but impossible at Monaco, particularly in the wet. It's too narrow.

Many, many felt Mansell was a loser . . .

At the Dutch Grand Prix in August Warr announced that Mansell was being replaced by a Brazilian driver graced by genius. Ayrton Senna. Mansell put on his best stoical face and in any case had had enough of Lotus. Complete retirement tempted him but Frank Williams showed positive interest. Williams already had Keke Rosberg who – without a turbo engine – had been consistent enough in 1982 to win the World Championship, the last time a non-turbo engine had done so.

Williams himself saw Mansell as a good 'journeyman' who would back Rosberg and no doubt pick up points here and there, giving the team a good balance. That's how it unfolded into 1985, a couple of fifth places, three sixth places and a seventh – albeit with a monumental crash at Paul Ricard thrown in. A tyre went at 200mph, the car veered and battered a concrete post, wrenching off a wheel which struck him and knocked him out. From his hospital bed he said he'd be in the British Grand Prix in two weeks' time and he was – but the clutch went.

The Belgian Grand Prix at Spa on 15 September changed everything, although that was scarcely evident at

19

the time. Senna won, with Mansell safely in second place behind him, the best result of his career. Psychologically as well as physically he'd joined the front runners. It is worth re-stating how long the wait for this may be, how much experience you need to accumulate, how invaluable that experience proves when you have a data bank of it to draw on. For many years – in fact until Michael Schumacher, the 23-year-old German, won the Belgian Grand Prix in 1992 – drivers under 30 did not win races.

Three weeks after Mansell's second place at Spa the European Grand Prix was held at Brands Hatch. He felt good, the psychology was nicely reinforced because the team had tested at Brands and the car handled better and better, went faster and faster. An immense crowd came and most had a single question: can he do it?

He ran fourth behind Senna, Rosberg and Piquet but the loops and curves of Brands, bathed in autumnal sunshine, would fashion a tumultuous Grand Prix. Rosberg, a very determined man, had been trying to get past Senna and Senna didn't like that, fending him away, or more accurately, blocking. Rosberg didn't appreciate that. He harried, and on lap seven he spun. Piquet couldn't avoid him and they crashed. Piquet was out and Rosberg limped back to the pits. That hoisted Mansell to second.

By an exquisite irony Rosberg emerged from the pits with new tyres and regained the track just as Senna approached – Senna was, of course, a complete lap ahead in the race but physically behind Rosberg, who now proceeded to give him a taste of his own medicine.

While Rosberg and Senna locked horns Mansell stole through into the lead and never lost it. Monaco and the white line was a long, long way away now. Mansell controlled himself and the race for 66 laps, and towards the end the crowd, deeply intoxicated, counted down those laps by holding up their fingers. Still Mansell controlled himself and crossed the line 21.396 seconds ahead of Senna. In the pit lane Eric Mansell burst into tears and Rosanne murmured that she wished Colin Chapman had been able to see it.

The loser had become a winner who hadn't got lucky with his win but had learned the art of constructing it. This, truly, had happened very quickly, virtually since Belgium. To emphasise his graduation Mansell won the next race, South Africa, from Rosberg and Prost and put the car on the front row in Australia, seizing the lead before he crashed with Senna.

Mansell was sixth in the Championship with 31 points, but that meant little or nothing. Of the possible 36 points from the previous four races he had taken 26 – and had led Adelaide. That meant everything in terms of his career and the future.

The next season, 1986, began very, very badly. Leaving the Ricard circuit after a test session, Frank Williams rolled his hire car and was paralysed. For long weeks and months the sure hand which had guided the team was missing. Mansell, who'd known the trauma of Chapman's death, said he felt sure that "the whole team will pull together."

Nelson Piquet came to Williams for 1986, Rosberg having decided that he wanted to sample Marlboro McLaren before he retired. Piquet, World Champion in 1981 and 1983, had obvious stature as a driver but he lost no time in trying to niggle Mansell, who resolutely refused to react except once, when, exasperated, he informed Piquet of what would happen if he didn't stop. Piquet came to Williams as the team's Number One, which befitted a double World Champion. The team had Honda turbo power, and although Piquet won Brazil, Mansell came on strongly with second in Spain, fourth at Monaco, wins in Belgium and Canada, fifth in Detroit and a win in France. That perfectly set up the British Grand Prix at Brands Hatch.

Piquet took pole, Mansell alongside him on the front row. At the green light Mansell was away fast but as he changed gear he felt the drive shaft give way and drifted slowly down the incline after the first corner. It was over virtually before it had begun. Because Mansell had started at the front he had no way of knowing that an extensive crash had engulfed the cars in mid-grid – engulfed them so badly the race had to be stopped. It allowed Mansell time to move to the spare car, set up of course for Piquet as the Number One.

Hasty adjustments were made, frantic hands worked and at the re-start Piquet surged off into the lead, with Mansell third and biding his time, exploring the spare car. When he was ready he flicked past Gerhard Berger (Benetton) and stalked Piquet, closing and closing. On lap 23 Piquet missed a gear and Mansell went through swiftly, incisively. A monumental, breathless battle developed, Piquet hammering away at Mansell and his own spare car. Mansell resisted this raw, relentless pressure as the two cars shrieked round Brands, always close, Piquet sustaining the pressure and trying to build more of it.

At no stage was Frank Williams tempted to put out the traditional pit board sign ordering Mansell to slow down to allow his Number One to overtake, something of a standard practice in the ethos of Grand Prix racing. "After all, you can't stamp on a man's career, and in any case we would have held the sport up to ridicule" Williams was to say afterwards. Lap after lap Piquet hammered and Mansell resisted, until towards the very end Piquet backed off as if the sheer, concentrated effort of it had defeated him. The winning margin, 5.571 seconds, was nearly academic. Prost (third) finished a lap behind the two Williams, Rene Arnoux (fourth) at two laps and Martin Brundle (fifth) at three laps. Mansell and Piquet burned them all off and finally Mansell burned off Piquet, too.

You cannot maintain that sort of frenetic pace or frenetic race, and in the second half of the season Mansell proved consistent while Piquet put together a run, winning Germany, Hungary and Italy. Mansell took Portugal and might have become World Champion in Mexico had he not blown the start – "a nightmare" – to come in fifth. The Championship would be decided at Adelaide, where numerically Piquet and Prost could win it but only if Mansell finished lower than third.

Superficially this took a great deal of pressure off Mansell, particularly since Frank Williams had said there would be no team orders. In reality it made Mansell's choice of race tactics difficult. Do you go for the win, which of necessity involves stretching your machinery and brings the consequent risks? Do you play the percentages and risk the percentages going wrong? Neither Prost nor Piquet needed trouble themselves about this. They had to win whatever Mansell did.

Rosberg, now partnering Prost at Marlboro McLaren, took the lead. Prost and Piquet were locked into their own personal struggle and Mansell ran fourth. Gently does it. On lap 32 Prost came into the pits with a puncture which shifted the whole balance of the race – and the Championship – but in a way nobody could have foreseen. Goodyear examined Prost's tyre and concluded that the puncture was no more than a racing puncture (possibly caused by running over some debris). They examined Prost's other tyres and pronounced that they would have been able to last the race. By definition this meant that the other Goodyear runners – Rosberg, Piquet and Mansell among them – ought to be able to run to the end without pit stops. Goodyear informed the MacLaren and Williams teams of this.

It seemed of marginal importance in the broad scheme of a street race with a shoal of cars darting and rushing round, and anyway Prost now faced the task of battling through the shoal to regain all he had lost while he'd been in the pits. As Prost re-emerged Piquet vainly pursued Rosberg, while Mansell was comfortable and safe in third, just where he wanted to be. The percentages had played themselves out beautifully.

Prost charged and caught Mansell, who had drawn up to Piquet, but Rosberg held a huge lead and was winning the race so easily that he asked himself why he was retiring after it. If it was this easy why not stay? On lap 63 and without warning Rosberg heard an ominous growling and thought that the engine must have gone. He tucked his MacLaren into the side of the track, got out and walked away, unaware that the growl had been a rear tyre which, broken up, flapped urgently against the bodywork. Goodyear, watching their television monitors in the pits, saw this instantly and moved very, very fast. The tyres wouldn't last the distance. They told the Williams team so that they could signal Piquet and Mansell in for new ones immediately.

It was too late.

Prost was past Mansell, but with Rosberg out Mansell still rode along in third place. Mansell moved onto the long straight and accelerated. The Williams, straining under the impetus of this acceleration, neared its absolute limit of 200mph. In a single moment the left rear tyre exploded and disintegrated, the chassis dipping against the surface of the track and churning a maelstrom of molten sparks.

Mansell physically fought a car which was now a bronco. The three wheels tugged and hauled it left and right in a sequence of terrible twitches and convulsions. Somehow he corrected every one by instinct and strength, somehow he wrestled the bronco broadly straight ahead – still it hauled and tugged – somehow he smoothed it into the run-off road at the end of the straight where, the speed gone from it, it gently bumped into a wall. The Championship had perished but he was alive.

The televised images of all this were so potent, so horrifying, so stark that they made Mansell globally famous, a very great paradox. And that was the first view of the summit.

By 1987 the Honda engine delivered enormous power. Williams designed a car to complement it and the whole season lay between Piquet and Mansell. Piquet set his own personal tone for this in an interview with *Playboy* in which he said some extremely pungent things about Senna and Mansell's family. (A British driver was moved to comment: "Tell Nigel I'll hold Piquet while he hits him. Families are definitely off limits.")

As it happened Prost won Brazil from Piquet, with Mansell sixth, but Piquet crashed very heavily in qualifying at Imola for the San Marino Grand Prix, missed the race and Mansell won it. Mansell gripped the mid-season, winning France, Britain and Austria, was third in Italy as autumn came in, then retired in Portugal (electrics) but won Spain and Mexico.

Going into Japan, the penultimate race, Piquet's consistency had brought him 76 points of which he could count 73 – he'd already fulfilled his quota under the 11-best-finishes-to-count rule. Mansell had 61 points. He needed to win Japan and needed surely to win Australia after it.

Disaster struck. In the first qualifying session, negotiating a section where the track turned hard right and then hard left after a mini-straight he ran wide, churned dust and the car lost its adhesion, rotated across the track into a tyre wall, was pitched into the air and almost flipped. It came down on kerbing, a battering shock wave travelling up Mansell's spine. When the car stopped he sat with his head cast back in agony, a prisoner in the cockpit, while the rescue services came. And that was the second view of the summit.

He spent the night in hospital, heard the screams of someone dying in a nearby ward, flew home to the Isle of Man and watched the race on television just like everybody else. The moment he crashed Nelson Piquet became World Champion for the third time.

Honda and Williams fell into dispute in this year of 1987 so that for 1988 the team had British Judd engines and Piquet departed for Lotus to be replaced by the Italian Riccardo Patrese. There were two problems for Mansell: the team experimented with a special 'reactive' suspension system which had major teething troubles and the Honda turbo, now with Marlboro McLaren, proved devastatingly fast. Over at McLaren Prost or Senna won every race except the Italian while Mansell didn't actually finish a race until the British in July, when he was second. At that meeting he finally announced that he would be driving for Ferrari in 1989, a move which had long been rumoured. He spoke of Ferrari's offer as an honour, a privilege, and it remains true that every driver wants to have at least one season with Ferrari. A career is almost incomplete without it, whatever happens when a driver does get to Ferrari.

He slogged out the rest of 1988, retiring in every remaining race except Spain, where he was second. It was, as he said, time to move on and there had been friction between him and the Williams designer Patrick Head. Frank Williams said: "I'll miss him as a driver, not as a bloke."

At Ferrari he joined Berger. They liked and respected each other and had socialised in the past. The problem here was never going to be Berger but Ferrari itself. Enzo Ferrari, who had died the year before (Mansell was the last driver he signed), had habitually stoked and stirred internal politics. The squabbles he provoked survived him. Worse, the car wasn't anything like reliable and Mansell didn't speak Italian. From this bleak landscape he created something entirely typical: in a car which wouldn't, couldn't, last five laps he took the lead in the first race, Brazil, and – miracle of miracles – the car survived to the end. Church bells rang at Modena, home of the Ferrari factory, local priests offered benedictions and the Italian fans (called *tifosi*) found their own name for Mansell *Il leone*. The lion.

Much of 1989 was frankly frustrating. Four times the gearbox failed. He nursed the car home second in France and Britain, was third in Germany and created one of the great moments of the whole season in Hungary, overtaking Senna by harnessing power and car control to go inside the Brazilian. It was the kind of move only he could – or would – contemplate and it was in its execution so certain that it seemed no risk at all. He won Hungary and finished the season fourth in the table with 38 points. At Williams Patrese had 40, but it was all light years away from the

Marlboro McLarens: Prost had 81 points (76 counting), Senna 60.

Prost and Senna did not co-exist easily and now Prost left for Ferrari. He and Mansell would not co-exist easily either. Prost spoke Italian (which is an advantage as big as it is obvious, especially if internal politics grip) and Prost knew all about looking after himself, let us say.

That second season at Ferrari was so unhappy that Mansell decided after yet another mechanical failure at Silverstone to retire. He said he'd been considering it for a while and he was going to devote more time to his family. He certainly had enough money and the golf courses of the world beckoned. He finished 1990 in fifth place with 37 points. So it was over and done, a solid career with outstanding moments but not really a great one. He'd seen the summit but never scaled it and now, reasonably enough, he could savour the rewards he had earned.

Frank Williams was grappling with a difficulty, and it pressed more and more. He had Renault engines and Renault, who were committed to winning the Championship, would put in whatever resources they judged necessary to achieve that, and would not be seen to fail. He had a technical team eminently capable of producing a car to win the Championship. He had two pleasant and extremely competent drivers – Patrese and the Belgian Thierry Boutsen – but neither, as it seemed, were likely to beat Senna at McLaren or Prost at Ferrari over a season. Frank Williams needed the one man who certainly could, the man entering retirement on the Isle of Man.

It's a paradox that just when Nigel Mansell didn't want Formula One it wanted him so badly: another paradox that at the moment of his leaving he had become one of the best three drivers in Formula One, and the determination alone had not made him into that. He had glorious ability. He could be genuinely thrilling, inspiring the global audience to hold its breath. He feared no man, including Senna.

Frank Williams grappled, decided and made Mansell an offer he couldn't refuse: within the boundaries of sanity name what you want and you can have it. In return, Frank said, we'll give you the thing you want: the Championship. Mansell was more than tempted. He said yes. Exit Boutsen.

Initially, Williams' decision assumed the proportions of a nightmarish mistake. Senna, thundering forward with all that Honda technology could give him, won the first four races of 1991 and surely threatened to win the rest. But this was entirely deceptive and nobody knew that better than Senna. He sensed that the Williams was quite some car and urged everyone associated with McLaren to work even harder because if they were on the pace now they wouldn't be for long. But it is difficult to hammer this home when you've just won the first four races . . .

Mansell ought to have won Canada, the race after Monaco, but the car stopped on the last lap virtually within sight of the finishing line. Mystery surrounds that still – did the car stall, did the electrics fail? – and it would cost Mansell dear later on.

For the moment he seized the season: second behind Patrese in Mexico, a clear win in France, pole and a thunderous win at Silverstone, pole and a clean win in Germany, second to Senna in Hungary; but the electrics did go at Spa and Senna won that. Mansell was being squeezed for the title. He responded by storming the Italian Grand Prix at Monza but, tantalisingly, Senna finished second and he had six points for that.

Bitter controversy lingered over Portugal. Mansell

came in for tyres and was so far in front that he could afford a sedate stop. It became a catastrophe because of an understandable misunderstanding (if it can be phrased in such a way). A wheel nut cross-threaded and while the mechanics used the pneumatic gun to wrench it off and replace it the signaller at the front of the car assumed that the pneumatic gun was coming out because the wheel was safely on.

Mansell, who could not know any of this, was waved away, and as he moved along the pit lane the wheel came off completely, and bounded away. He beat his fists in fury against the cockpit while the team galloped up and re-fitted the wheel. The team could do nothing else because Mansell's car stood in an extremely dangerous position – namely, in the pit lane where other cars would be arriving and departing, and at no negligible speed either. The rules, however, are clear: if you work on a car outside your carefully delineated pit area you are disqualified.

Mansell, on four wheels again, rejoined the race and mounted a great assault to haul it all back, travelling so quickly that by journey's end a podium place was not beyond him. But he was black flagged. A black flag is extremely final. Come directly to the pits and stop. Mansell obeyed. When he realised he was so distraught that he cut a path through the throng of people in the pit to the rear door and kept on going, saying nothing. In the sharpest terms the situation squeezed the Championship much harder, Patrese winning but Senna coming second.

Spain provided a moment which epitomised the whole of Formula One, although not before Mansell and Senna had exchanged pungent words at the drivers' briefing. On the straight Mansell and Senna jousted, moving closer and closer as they screamed towards the corner at the end of the straight, their wheels a yard apart, a foot apart, inches apart and, in the blink of an eye, almost in contact. At such speed any contact might produce any reaction.

To go so close depends on how much you want it, who you are, how deep your car control is, how you evaluate your life against the moment. Mansell won Spain.

The mathematics of the season had simplified themselves. If Senna won or finished second in the next race, Japan, he had his third Championship. The odds against Mansell were longer than that. If he won Japan and Senna was no higher than third the battle went on to Australia, where Mansell had to win again and needed Senna to get no points. The mystery of Canada and the wheel which had come off in Portugal both punished Mansell now and punished him mercilessly. He'd go to Japan and give it his best shot, as they say, and just like Prost and Piquet at Adelaide in 1986 he didn't have to concern himself with tactics. He had to win.

To counter this Marlboro McLaren evolved a neat strategy. Berger had pole, with Senna alongside him, and at the green light Berger fled into the distance while Senna positioned himself in front of Mansell and held him back, both of them going a good deal slower than Berger. Mansell absolutely needed to overtake Senna and get after Berger before Berger became uncatchable. The summit receded.

Mansell radioed to the pits that he was backing off for a moment, no panic. He did so and then re-caught Senna. The race was not yet a quarter run and he tracked Senna into the corner at the end of the start-finish straight, a right-hander. All at once Mansell ran wide, the car scrabbled over the kerbing and kept on into the dusty run-off area to sink there, beached. The brake pedal, he said later, had gone soft, although the turbulent air flowing back from Senna's car – every car creates that and when you follow closely you're in it – can hardly have helped. The summit had gone.

Adelaide, the last race of the season, might have meant simply going through the motions, but it didn't. In a storm cars crashed and bashed, Mansell among them, and the thing was halted forever on lap 17. It was all anti-climax, all somehow the story of a life: nearly but not quite. The summit. Could he ever scale it now?

South African Grand Prix

Kyalami

Even as the sceptics were lining up his epitaph as a man who was destined to be second in life, Nigel Mansell was preparing to prove them wrong. As he contemplated another season as the 'nearly man', second in the World Championship for the third time in his career, Mansell knew that the moment of truth was arriving. After a terrible start to the 1991 season, Mansell had begun a love affair with the Williams Renault car.

Mansell had not troubled the scorers until Monaco in May, when he was second, and then won three races on the run, France, Britain and Germany, before adding Italy and Germany.

But again the luck seemed to desert him at crucial moments.

In Canada he was cruising to victory when the engine stalled after a gear change went wrong. He ended with only one point. In Portugal the pit crew waved him out with a loose wheel which flew off after a few yards, and he was disqualified. In Japan he needed to win to have a chance in the final race but his hopes disappeared into a gravel trap.

He was, claimed doubters, destined to be the modern equivalent of Stirling Moss, another great driver who was never to win the drivers' title. But Mansell launched a two-pronged attack on the World Championship even before his stealthy enemy, Father Time, had ushered in 1992.

In his 38th year, Mansell realised that time was running out for his dream of standing on the podium with the crowds acclaiming him as World Champion. As he headed to his new mansion in Clearwater, Florida, he felt major changes were needed not only in the Williams Renault FW14 but in his own human chassis.

Mansell is not like the others in Formula One in physical form. Most of the men who slide into the confinement of the monocoque are little more than motorised jockeys: thin, wiry men who battle with their weights and diets, emulating the car designers in their attempts to find the perfect power-to-weight ratio to cope with extraordinary G-forces.

Mansell is of a chunkier, more solid build than his contemporaries. The difference is obvious as they walk through the pits in their one-piece racing suits. They are all of a similar height, around 5ft 8ins or 5ft 9ins, but Ayrton Senna is noticeably thinner than Mansell, as is his team-mate Riccardo Patrese. Mansell, who loves playing football and golf, looks like the average robust English sportsman, although his fondness for basic foods, particularly sweets, tends to push his weight up.

With a year of his contract with Williams to run and the added incentive of a marvellous run of success which showed the car's real potential, he began a radical change in lifestyle. The move to the United States had been planned for a while but it worked perfectly.

The reason for moving was more than a basic desire to feel sun on his back during the winter. A catalogue of crashes in his career had left his bones with chips, breaks and fractures – hidden, almost forgotten injuries which failed to halt the man, but occasionally, after a hard day's driving, left him aching or limping.

In the close season, he headed home to Ballaman House at Port Erin on the Isle of Man to relax with the family and recuperate. But even with the aid of the Gulfstream, the Isle of Man is not exactly Bermuda in mid-winter.

The Atlantic winds blow hard, sweeping in the rain and damp chill which soon awaken old wounds, stiffening limbs, stirring the memories of the whirlwind crashes.

"I feel like a man of 90 some days, everything creaks and I really suffer," said Mansell. "I love the place and I will always keep a home there, but now I need somewhere during the winter which helps me to live the way I must. Basically I am an old crock. I have broken my neck, my back twice, smashed toes, fractured wrists and a whole lot of other stuff. Florida just allows me to escape some of that pain in the winter and it allows me to train in good conditions. Getting up on a wet, cold, windy morning to go for a run is not easy. When the sun is up, the temperature is good and the day is warm, you just cannot wait to get out."

Mansell was relentless, determined to hone his body to peak fitness, realising that the young lions in other cars would have age and natural fitness to their advantage.

When he arrived in Florida, he intended to have a break before getting down to hard work and winter testing with the team. That had been agreed, but within a couple of days the telephone was ringing. Williams were testing – but this was different. It was not a new engine, a change in chassis design or new aerofoils.

They had developed an active suspension system, designed to keep the car as close to the ground as possible at all times, thus improving its handling and making it quicker through corners and on bumpy circuits.

It was not brand new, for other teams, led by Lotus, who developed the first similar system, had been toying with it. But the brilliance of Patrick Head, the team's technical director, had made the system a workable reality for the Williams car.

Everyone knew that if they could iron out the problems of making the active system work in harness with the car, there would be huge advantages. It required supreme technical back-up from all concerned. An inordinate amount of test work to prove its worth, capability, limits and reliability would be needed before the first race on 1 March in South Africa.

Soon Mansell and Patrese were hard at work with test driver Damon Hill coming to grips with the system, which changed the feel of the car enormously for the driver. Around Europe they went, testing the cars at Estoril in Portugal, the Paul Ricard circuit in the south of France, Jerez in southern Spain and at Silverstone in Britain.

Hill, the son of former World Champion Graham Hill, is the hidden man of the Williams set-up but he was a crucial figure in the winter work, as Mansell was the first to admit.

Back home in Florida, Mansell continued his own aerodynamic improvements, working out in the gym and boosting his upper body strength by playing around on a 750bhp jet-ski. "Open it up and it takes off even more fiercely than the car," said Mansell. "It feels as if it is going to pull the arms out of their sockets. It is great fun but it also serves a useful purpose."

With an American friend, he was also doing 14 miles a day on a mountain bike. In addition he launched himself on a diet, cutting out white sugar – difficult for a man who loves his chocolate biscuits and Mars bars.

At 5ft 9¹/₂ins, Mansell is a stocky man, and with every pound in weight worth a fraction of a second, he knew he had to slim down. It went well: the pounds were shed and the fitness went up as the weight went down.

The new way was a rigorous fitness schedule allied to a stricter diet, and as Mansell admitted: "In Florida, I wanted to get out into the sunshine. I felt great. There was no point in just being on a diet. It had to be used in conjunction with exercise."

The new way was constant work. A regime entered his life of gym circuits at his home, swimming, jogging and cycling on and off roads on his mountain bike. There were no trainers, no dieticians, no fitness gurus. Mansell summed up his attitude to it: "I have had these people but they just cost you money. At the end of the day, it is up to you. If you are honest with yourself, you can do a far better job.

"The secret of dieting is willpower and exercise. If you need someone to tell you whether to eat something or not, it won't work. I set targets and tried to keep to a fat-free diet. I ate my three main meals all at set times. If I was hungry in between, I loaded myself up with carrots, celery, anything like that which is low on calories but makes you feel full.

"I drank gallons of water, too. At first I was in a shocking state with stomach cramps and constant hunger. It was not easy, but I knew that if I broke my routine, I would destroy my diet."

But when Christmas came along Mansell shocked himself. "I enjoyed all the good things, as you do – turkey and stuffing, Christmas pudding and cake – and when I went to the scales I was horrified to find I had put on 8lbs. Instead of having to lose half a stone, I had to lose about 16lbs."

So it was back on the diet, back to the 50 miles a day on the bike, back to playing tennis, and back to the dedication and single-mindedness which typify the man. Sure enough, by the time he stepped onto the scales for the compulsory drivers' weigh-in in South Africa for the opening race, he was 76 kilos, half a stone lighter than he had been a year earlier.

Now Mauricio Gugelmin was heaviest at 81 kilos, Karl Wendlinger and Bertrand Gachot were next at 79 and Riccardo Patrese weighed 78. Mansell was gleeful that he had beaten his Italian team-mate. "The weight was a personal goal for me. It meant more than winning some races when I hit 76 kilos," he insisted.

More testing followed and by now Williams were convinced that their active suspension was going to be a success. As pleasing were the tests which showed that the the FW14 was faster and more powerful. Renault had been working extensively on their engine, a V10 RS3C, and Elf had also been trying various fuel mixes.

At the end of February, the Grand Prix circus finally quit the northern hemisphere winter and headed for South Africa for the first time since 1985. The last occasion they had taken their roaring cars to the Republic had been in 1985, when Nigel Mansell, driving a Williams Honda, won the race. Ayrton Senna had been in a Lotus Renault, Gerhard Berger in an Arrows BMW and Alain Prost in a McLaren Porsche. But, like South Africa, the times had changed.

The political climate now allowed the world's sportsmen to return and for the Grand Prix men it was a delight: without Africa a World Championship could not be considered complete.

It also unlocked the doors for some of South Africa's rand to flow their way. Eddie Jordan had been quick off the mark to capture the backing of the Sasol company.

Only traces of the old Kyalami circuit near Johannesburg remained. The old names had also disappeared under new tarmac and sponsorship. Out went such romantic corners as Barbecue Bend and Jukskei Kink, and in came Budget and Yellow Page Corners.

It was tight, hardly ideal for overtaking, but the drivers gave it the thumbs-up and Mansell was very keen. "It is very demanding and I wish there was a good long straight for overtaking, but they have done a fantastic job on it," he said.

Senna also liked the track, and with Prost absent on sabbatical after being removed from Ferrari and failing to find a drive, it looked like being a duel between him and Mansell.

Mansell had arrived lean and mean and it showed in his attitude. "My state of mind, my focus, health and fitness and my weight, offer the chance for me to start the season better than at any time in my career," he said. "This season I have a genuine chance of winning the World Championship.

"Senna will be committed to winning for a fourth time because he wants to emulate Juan Fangio's record of five Championships. He will believe it is his God-given right to win the Championship and that no one should challenge him. We saw that in Spain last year when I beat him and he had a real go at me. But it was a fight I wanted no part of.

"Senna and I know that we are the only two drivers who can do certain things on the track and we have to have a higher respect for each other."

Mansell was well aware that it was more than just man versus man. The machinery was crucial, and although

Williams Renault were confident and comfortable with their combination, little was known about the mighty McLaren Honda.

"They have opted not to train alongside anyone this winter," said Mansell. "I have never known that happen in my Formula One career. Either they are being a bit arrogant or a little complacent. We will know soon. This weekend is going to set the pattern for the year."

Mansell was also quick to deny that race orders would give him an advantage over his team-mate, Patrese, who had finished third in the 1991 Championship. It was to be every man for himself. Mansell relaxed with his friend, South African golfer Mark McNulty, at a barbecue.

For the first time, there were to be no qualifying tyres. With only Goodyear left as the Formula One supplier, the idea of having soft compound tyres which allowed the drivers two eyeballs-out laps to get the fastest times had been scrapped. Now there would be two sets of more conventional tyres, which would give the drivers longer on the circuit.

An extra problem was the number of young, inexperienced drivers new to Formula One who were trying to come to grips with the power of the machines they were now attempting to steer.

Giovanna Amati, Formula One's first woman driver, was struggling in her Brabham Judd. There were others, too, such as Austria's Karl Wendlinger, veteran of two races, Andrea Chiesa of Switzerland, Paul Belmondo of France, Brazil's Christian Fittipaldi and Japan's Ukyo Katayama.

Even Germany's Michael Schumacher had only six Grand Prix starts behind him – but he was a bit special compared to the others.

Sadly, a talent for raising money rather than earning

it as a quick driver can buy a seat in a car. Britain's up-and-coming drivers are as cash-strapped as the country and are silent just now while money talks.

The top drivers now had to get to grips with a new track and new kids on the block.

Mansell had the look of invincibility after two days of qualifying. On the Friday, he had set 1 minute 15.576 seconds, and after the night's brilliant electrical storm, was ready for early action on Saturday. Again he led the free practice but left it a little late to head out onto the circuit after lunch for the final qualifying run.

It was the 11th hour when he sallied forth – and Senna went with him. But the Brazilian could not live with the pace – and for a brief but heart-stopping moment, neither could Mansell.

At the Nashau Corner, he abruptly departed from the tarmac. There was little damage and Mansell admitted that either there had been something on the track or he was just going too fast. Businesslike, he hurried to the pits and swept out in the spare car, which he did not believe was as quick as his racing machine.

Gradually he wound up the pace again, and after 12 laps set the fastest time so far, 1 minute 15.486 seconds.

It was a time no one could get close to. In fact, only Berger, Senna and Patrese could climb into the 1.16s.

Mansell denied that there was a huge gap between Williams and McLaren. "That is false," he declared. "It is a complete package we are looking at, gentlemen. I am lighter, fitter and more focused that ever before.

"Renault have done a fantastic job on the engine, Elf have come up with new fuels and the Williams team has doubled its efforts. I am here to do a job and nothing will be left to chance. I am pushing myself to the limit. Maybe that is part of the reason I went off."

When the race day arrived, Mansell was quickest in the morning warm-up, although again he had to use his spare car while an electrical fault was fixed in the semi-automatic gearbox of his race car.

On the grid, with the weather overcast and slightly cooler than on the previous searingly hot days, he looked determined, with 72 laps of the 2.663 circuit to come.

On the green light, he powered away and found team-mate Patrese behind on the first corner. The Italian had squeezed past the McLarens which had been ahead of him in second and third. Mansell, however, was using his early strike tactics, and after one lap he held a 2.4-second lead over Patrese.

After two laps it was a shade under four seconds and he was gone.

His only problem came in mid-race as he attempted to lap Olivier Grouillard. The Frenchman set his standard for the season, too, by blocking Mansell, but it was no more than a temporary hold-up.

Soon Mansell was past and rocketing round the circuit. Just two laps from the end, he did the unexpected – which has become his trademark. With a lead of nearly half a minute, he set his fastest time of the day, 1 minute 17.578 seconds.

Eventually he finished in 1 hour 36 minutes 45.320 seconds. Patrese, having held off a sustained challenge from Senna, was second in 1 hour 37 minutes 09.680 seconds. Senna took third place and Schumacher confirmed his talent with a fourth place ahead of Berger.

Another Briton, Lotus driver Johnny Herbert, was almost as pleased as Mansell: he had nursed the team's veteran car to sixth place. Sadly, Martin Brundle, back in Formula One with Camel Benetton Ford, had gone out after only one lap with clutch failure.

Mansell was less happy at suggestions that the race had been easy because he was in technically superior equipment. "We don't have a great advantage," he insisted. "We have done a tremendous amount of work on the car and it is paying off – but let's wait and see what the opposition comes up with. I have done what I came here to do, to win the first race and get us off to a great start."

It was victory number 22 in his career, ten points in the Championship, and now it was on to Mexico.

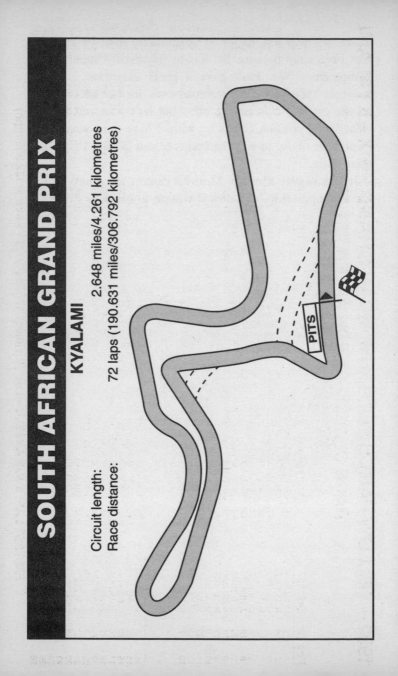

SOUTH AFRICAN GRAND PRIX

KYALAMI

Circuit length: 2.648 miles/4.261 kilometres
Race distance: 72 laps (190.631 miles/306.792 kilometres)

1992 – YELLOW PAGES SOUTH AFRICAN GRAND PRIX – KYALAMI

RACE CLASSIFICATION AFTER 72 LAPS
(306.792 km = 190.631 mls)

Pos	Nr	Driver		Team Make	Make	Total Time	km/h	mph	Diff
1	5	N. MANSELL	GBR	CANON WILLIAMS TEAM	WILLIAMS RENAULT	1:36:45.320	190.248	118.215	
2	6	R. PATRESE	ITA	CANON WILLIAMS TEAM	WILLIAMS RENAULT	1:37:09.680	189.453	117.721	24.360
3	1	A. SENNA	BRA	HONDA MARLBORO McLAREN	McLAREN HONDA	1:37:19.995	189.119	117.513	34.675
4	19	M. SCHUMACHER	GER	CAMEL BENETTON FORD	BENETTON FORD	1:37:33.183	188.692	117.248	47.863
5	2	G. BERGER	AUT	HONDA MARLBORO McLAREN	McLAREN HONDA	1:37:58.954	187.665	116.734	1:13.634
6	12	J. HERBERT	GBR	TEAM LOTUS	LOTUS FORD	1:37:12.749	186.724	116.025	1 LAP
7	26	E. COMAS	FRA	LIGIER GITANES BLONDES	LIGIER RENAULT	1:37:41.558	185.806	115.454	1 LAP
8	10	A. SUZUKI	JPN	FOOTWORK MUGEN-HONDA	FOOTWORK MUGEN-HONDA	1:37:41.026	184.148	114.424	2 LAPS
9	11	M. HAKKINEN	FIN	TEAM LOTUS	LOTUS FORD	1:37:20.233	183.858	114.244	2 LAPS
10	9	M. ALBORETO	ITA	FOOTWORK MUGEN-HONDA	FOOTWORK MUGEN-HONDA	1:37:27.654	183.624	114.099	2 LAPS
11	33	M. GUGELMIN	BRA	SASOL JORDAN YAMAHA	JORDAN YAMAHA	1:37:50.054	182.924	113.664	2 LAPS
12	30	U. KATAYAMA	JPN	CENTRAL PARK-VEN.LARR.	VENTURI LAMBORGHINI	1:36:49.840	179.539	111.560	4 LAPS
13	7	E. VAN DE POELE	BEL	MOTOR RACING DEV.	BRABHAM JUDD	1:37:21.272	178.573	110.960	4 LAPS

NOT CLASSIFIED

									COVERED
14	3	O. GROUILLARD	FRA	TYRRELL RAC. ORG.	TYRRELL ILMOR	1:26:10.590	183.936	114.292	62 LAPS
15	25	T. BOUTSEN	BEL	LIGIER GITANES BLONDES	LIGIER RENAULT	1:22:31.572	185.876	115.498	60 LAPS
16	22	P. MARTINI	ITA	SCUDERIA ITALIA	BMS DALLARA-FERRARI	1:20:37.090	177.590	110.349	56 LAPS
17	24	G. MORBIDELLI	ITA	MINARDI TEAM	MINARDI LAMBORGHINI	1:17:02.213	182.527	113.417	55 LAPS
18	21	J. LEHTO	FIN	SCUDERIA ITALIA	BMS DALLARA-FERRARI	1:04:05.859	183.476	114.007	46 LAPS
19	23	C. FITTIPALDI	BRA	MINARDI TEAM	MINARDI LAMBORGHINI	1:00:16.659	182.379	113.325	43 LAPS
20	4	A. DE CESARIS	ITA	TYRRELL RAC. ORG.	TYRRELL ILMOR	56:43.011	184.814	114.838	41 LAPS
21	27	J. ALESI	FRA	FERRARI	FERRARI	54:54.396	186.251	115.731	40 LAPS
22	28	I. CAPELLI	ITA	FERRARI	FERRARI	38:44.682	184.805	114.805	28 LAPS
23	15	G. TARQUINI	ITA	FONDMETAL F1	FONDMETAL FORD	32:17.100	182.133	113.173	23 LAPS
24	16	K. WENDLINGER	AUT	MARCH F.1	MARCH ILMOR	18:21.592	181.024	112.483	13 LAPS
25	29	B. GACHOT	FRA	CENTRAL PARK-VEN. LARR.	VENTURI LAMBORGHINI	17:32.720	116.571	72.434	8 LAPS
26	20	M. BRUNDLE	GBR	CAMEL BENETTON FORD	BENETTON FORD	1:51.189	137.960	85.724	1 LAP

FASTEST LAP: 5 N. MANSELL – Lap 70 Time: 1'17.578 (197.731 Km/h = 122.865 mph)

Mexican Grand Prix

Mexico City

Most drivers have a love-hate relationship with Mexico and its Autodromo Hermanos Rodriguez. . . mainly it is the circuit they love to hate. Mansell held off as long as possible before flying over from his home in Florida to join the team in the heat, dust and smells of Mexico.

Earlier in the week, as the Grand Prix circus was starting to gather, the air pollution hanging over the city had reached dangerous levels. A city about to stage an event featuring the most exotic collection of expensive and fuel-guzzling racing cars then put emergency traffic control measures into effect.

At the circuit, there had also been attempts at traffic control: controversial changes had been made to the famed Peraltada Curve. This 180-degree sweeping bend, which sends the cars hurtling down the pit lane straight, is celebrated.

A year earlier, Ayrton Senna had rolled in qualifying and there had been calls for changes. The authorities had reduced the banking from 12 to five degrees to slow speeds but still managed to leave a nasty dip as drivers accelerated out.

The track is also incredibly bumpy, a test of nerve, car suspension systems, tyres and teeth. It has a good lay-out but the lack of real investment is obvious, and over the years the circuit, named after two local racing brothers, one of whom was killed in practice for the first Mexican Grand Prix, has provided plenty of unexpected excitement.

Crowds have been known to swarm onto the track and people wander about aimlessly, oblivious to the dangers of the 200mph projectiles inches away.

In 1970 the race was stopped after spectators clambered over fences and barriers for a closer view, and Scotsman Jackie Stewart once retired with broken suspension after hitting a dog on the circuit.

Each driver has his own way of dealing with the tumultuous Mexican set-up. Mansell's way was to concentrate totally on winning for the second time.

He was at the circuit early on Friday morning and soon it became obvious that in the three weeks between South Africa and Mexico little had changed in the way things were likely to go.

Senna, however, held court in the paddock.

He was concerned that drivers were becoming robots, men being pushed into programmed machines which would soon have automatic gearboxes.

"Maybe all we will do is just guide the car," he suggested. "I think that changing the gear is part of the skill of driving a race car. You might change gear 3,000 times in one race and it is the skill of the driver in being able to change on a bend or in a tight situation that can make the difference between winning and losing. If we keep on going along the road of technology then drivers will not have much to do."

Yet he could see, as do others, the problems the manufacturers face, for Formula One cars are the technological cutting edge of motoring and many innovations will turn up in road cars in the years ahead.

Engine suppliers such as Ford, Renault and Honda,

petrol companies like Elf and BP and other big sponsors use the sport for development work. The idea of a computerised throttle, for example, with no cable, simply a sensor which revs according to the signal it is sent, is one which will surely be seen in saloon cars soon.

Whether Senna was also troubled by the technological advances which appeared to be weighing in Williams' favour was open to question.

Mansell roared round in the free practice on the Friday morning under a burning sun, easily quickest, setting a top speed of 190.38mph. He tried both his race car and his back-up but was less than impressed with the reduced banking.

"We may have lost five or so degrees assistance of the banking," he said, "but it has probably made the circuit tougher. The track is also still very bumpy and quite slippery, although the surface is not breaking up.

"The cars went very well and in some places the track felt smoother than it did last year. In others it feels as if the wheels are off the ground. But it is dusty and dirty."

All interest was on how the Williams' active suspension, which was meant to ride the bumps, would cope. "Too early to tell," insisted Mansell whose team-mate, Patrese was second in practice.

The McLaren Hondas finished fourth and fifth, finding the German Michael Schumacher ahead, but team boss Ron Dennis was optimistic. "We have a few slight set-up problems but I think we can go a second quicker," he said.

Senna agreed with Mansell that the Peraltada changes made life tougher and was more guarded about how the McLaren MP4/6 would improve. His desperation to catch Mansell saw the season's first big shunt on the Friday afternoon, 18 minutes into the qualifying session.

A silence had fallen over the track, always an ominous sign during a session for it means that there has been an accident bad enough to stop the cars running. Sometimes it is simply in an awkward spot, sometimes there has been damage to the barriers or oil has been liberally sprayed onto the track.

Mansell, sitting in his car waiting to go out, eventually saw on a television screen what the media were watching.

Senna had been coming through the Esses, and as he swept through the last curve, the red and white McLaren suddenly went away with him. The car did a complete 360-degree turn, ignored Senna's efforts at control and slid across the grass, slamming sideways into the wall in a curtain of soil and stones.

It looked as if he had clipped a kerb as he came through but Britain's Johnny Herbert, following behind, claimed that the McLaren had lost its line on a bump. Whatever had happened, at something around 150mph, even a Formula One car, built with safety in mind, cannot cushion the driver completely from such a shuddering collision.

At first Senna raised a hand, a signal to show that he was all right, then he hit his helmet in exasperation. Seconds later, however, he realised that he could not haul himself out of the cockpit and his face twisted in agony. The pain had begun to surge through as the shock eased.

He had to wait. The stewards were there to offer help but there was no movement until Professor Sid Watkins, the British doctor who travels the world as FISA's trackside specialist, arrived. Ten anxious minutes passed before Senna was eased gently from the car and taken to the hospital.

The session continued and eventually the other drivers were relieved to hear that Senna's injury was no worse than a heavily bruised left leg. Considering the impact and proximity of a wishbone strut which had burst into the cockpit, he had been fortunate to escape without real injury.

If the incident made some drivers wary of a track for which they have little enthusiasm, it appeared to make no difference to the driving of Mansell or Schumacher, who were soon duelling in the sun.

Schumacher was settling into the Camel Benetton Ford like a veteran, and when the session resumed, he was soon setting the pace.

He powered the car round in 1 minute 18.336 seconds, trimmed that and broke through to the 1.17s, putting himself less than a tenth of a second behind Mansell.

The Englishman was watching and waiting in the garage, and within minutes he was out again, hurtling round in response to the German's challenge to take his time down to 1 minute 17.130 seconds.

It is one of the joys of watching Mansell that once he begins to enjoy himself behind the wheel, usually when he has wound the car up, he keeps the excitement going. Soon he was into the 1.16s, and finally called a halt only when he had reduced the time to 1 minute 16.346 seconds, hitting the fastest speed of 189.61mph. He had made the quickest time on his 20th lap.

"It was a hard session this afternoon," said Mansell. "It was also upsetting as it is not nice to see anybody hurt, least of all the main opposition, Ayrton.

"I understand that he has not broken anything but is

only badly bruised, and I sincerely hope he will be able to drive during the rest of the weekend.

"I have to admit that after the break following Ayrton's accident, it was quite hard to get back into the car and motivate myself. I had to push exceedingly hard as Schumacher was driving very well and it was a struggle to get back to pole position.

"My last lap was a good one and I am happy. The credit must go to the Williams team and to Renault and Elf."

He went off to the hotel happy with the time, less delighted with the track.

Elsewhere there was less than joy. Mansell's team-mate, Riccardo Patrese, was 1.6 seconds behind and complaining of poor handling because of the active suspension.

Sounds of discord were heard in other pits. Already Ferrari's car was being labelled a 'pig' and Jean Alesi and Ivan Capelli had both been on off-track excursions.

Saturday was even hotter but at least the traffic jams which made travelling between the city centre and the track difficult, were lessened. This allowed every Mexican taxi driver who thinks he is Senna or Mansell a little extra scope for daredevil acts on the road, for which he expects a few pesos more.

At the track was Senna, heavily bandaged and limping badly. But his just being there along with the car was a testament to the strength of the construction of the chassis. Senna had not qualified the previous day so it was imperative that he drive, even in pain, and on his 32nd birthday he was determined to give himself a present.

Around the track the colourful Mexicans were enjoying themselves but in the pits the early-season strain was beginning to tell. Britain's Martin Brundle was struggling to come to terms with his Benetton Ford and the challenge of team-mate Schumacher. Already rumours were that Brundle, who had lasted only a lap in South Africa, might be replaced by Alexandro Zanardi.

Ferrari qualified 10th and 20th and the McLarens continued their nightmare weekend. Gerhard Berger suffered the indignity of being lifted in the car by a crane to be taken back to the track for a bump start in the morning. Later he copied Senna by slamming into the same wall in the spare car after an earlier spin forced him to abandon his own vehicle.

Senna pushed hard and bravely for his place on the grid but had to survive a spin which did nothing for his nerves. The Brazilian was none too impressed with the circuit or the car. "I am sore but it is nothing serious," he said. "The main problem is that you do not know what the car is going to do next. It is so unpredictable in the qualifying set-up.

"It gives us not enough grip, and on a surface as bumpy and dirty as this, that is not good. Also the track has insufficient run-off areas. I have nothing against Mexico but I do not think we should be coming here until the track is re-surfaced and run-off areas are improved. We go to street circuits with better sur-faces."

Mansell was not to be moved, despite a challenge from Patrese, who appeared to be responding to outside criticism that if Mansell could do it, why couldn't he. The Italian hauled himself to number two on the grid with 1 minute 16.362 seconds, just 16 hundredths behind Mansell, who was less satisfied with his Saturday performance.

But the Benettons were also flying and Schumacher lowered his time again to take third spot while Brundle nipped ahead of Berger by one thousandth of a second to take fourth.

"I am happy to be on pole but I would be much happier if I did not have some problems," he said. "We had a complete computer failure as I was about to go out this afternoon and the engine in my race car is better than the one in the back-up. It is noticeable that when the clouds come over, the track gets maybe upwards of a second quicker. You have to be running well at that moment to do a quick time and I am pleased to see that my team-mate did a very good lap.

"But the big problem is so many cars going off the circuit. When they return they bring so much dust. I went into one fast corner and it was fine but in the middle my car just went sideways. That's what makes the track difficult. It is incredibly slippery.

"The environment for the computers is much harder than it was in South Africa. With the bumps and the speed of the corners, cars are constantly spinning off. It is the same for everyone, not just the cars with computers.

"The main factor which worries me is reliability. We have to pay very great attention. It is not as easy as some people think to be reliable, I am more concerned that my car is completely correct in the morning session tomorrow so that I can go into the race completely confident."

Mansell is rarely a man to mince his words and he said: "Normally you would expect the McLarens to be after us on the grid, so all I can say is that the Benetton team is doing a much better job than them at the moment.

"My aim now is just to finish. During the race the track will get slippery in places. The way it changes from minute to minute is just incredible. It is going to be very unpredictable and we must all pay attention to this in the first 20 laps or so."

The Williams Renaults were also using a new traction control system to prevent wheelspin at the start and to allow a faster take-off, but Mansell left the decision on using it to his technical team.

Come the day, again sunny with a few squadrons of white clouds around, Mansell eased through the warm-up session and was relaxed before going to the grid. From the moment he took the lead off the grid Mansell was charging, but this time he found Patrese with him all the way.

After ten laps, Mansell had a lead of almost three seconds, with Senna a valiant third, Schumacher fourth and Brundle in fifth. The German was giving Senna little breathing space, and on the 12th lap, the World Champion departed, the victim of a transmission problem.

Mansell set the fastest time on lap 9, another on 16, and as the procession continued round he broke into the 1.18s on lap 35.

For the crowd, the real action was between Brundle and Berger as they jousted for the fourth spot. They battled it out until a fluke disaster for Brundle forced him off on the 48th lap. A tear-off visor strip from Theirry Boutsen, who had been about to be lapped in his Ligier, lodged in Brundle's radiator and the engine overheated, forcing him out. A disconsolate Brundle walked around shaking his head.

Mansell continued to drive faultlessly at the front and by the end of the 69 laps, covering 189 miles, he took the chequered flag by 13 seconds from Patrese.

There were just 13 finishers, and Lotus were almost as pleased as Mansell, their cars finishing sixth with Mika Haakinen and seventh with Herbert at the wheel. But the talk was all of Williams' dominance, their second one-two of the season and the ease with which it was achieved.

Mansell, however was quick to counter the post-race euphoria. He had won with style and ease, and a technological barrier had been set up between Williams and the other teams. Surely he could not be happier, surely the Championship was looking good already?

He bristled at suggestions that it had been easy. "My team-mate was never far away and he pushed me really hard in qualifying and in the race. You don't think he is simply going to let me run away with it when he is in a similar car, do you?

"We don't have team orders and, I tell you, we were really racing out there. He has his own ambitions and I cannot afford to relax with Riccardo around."

Patrese confirmed that he was out to win but acknowledged: "Nigel drove very carefully at the start and deserved to win. He drove a marvellous race."

Mansell, with memories of other Championship failures fresh in his mind, did not even consider talk of the title. "Yeah, it has been a great start and you like to think it will continue just as smoothly for the rest of the year, but I know better than that.

"We have worked really hard as a team to achieve this kind of start but we know that we have a lot of work ahead. McLaren are not going to take this lying down. They have been working to catch up and I know there is new machinery coming along. They are planning to take half a dozen cars to Brazil and Senna will be demanding big things for the next race.

"They don't like being down and they will throw everything at us. I hear a lot about their new car and it will be interesting to see what comes of it, but it ensures that we will be keyed up for the fightback.

"Our car worked beautifully here although it was difficult to drive. I had a problem after the warm-up lap with oversteer and the team had to do a lot of work on the grid. That was worrying, but it ran perfectly afterwards.

"There was also a moment in the race when pieces of debris flew up from another car. One piece just missed my head and smashed the wing mirror – things like that can be a bit disconcerting.

"There were an awful lot of drivers going off the track and at the drivers' meeting the switch from qualifying tyres was mentioned by Ayrton Senna. I expressed my doubts before the season, but you have to sympathise with Goodyear, who had to look at the financial side of producing these tyres. But it does not make life easier for us. Instead of a couple of really flying laps, you can stay out for a while and have more attempts and that causes a lot of traffic and more pressures.

"Fortunately, it worked out well for me over the weekend, but despite what everyone says, I think we had a better ride here last year than with the active suspension system. Certainly our lap times were slower, so we need to look at that."

But there could be no better start for Mansell, could there?

"Three wins," he said, and left for Florida within a couple of hours of the trophy presentation.

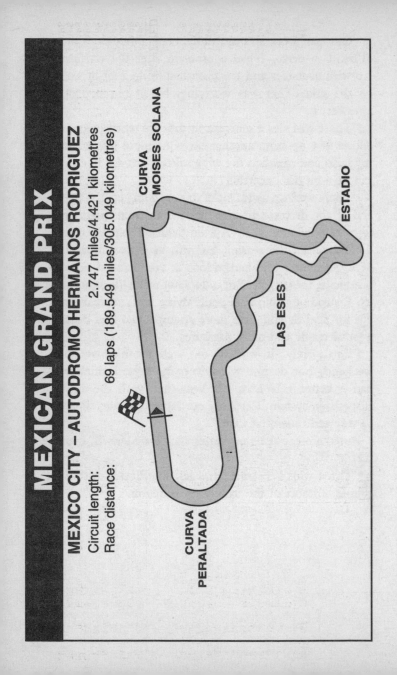

MEXICAN GRAND PRIX

MEXICO CITY – AUTODROMO HERMANOS RODRIGUEZ

Circuit length: 2.747 miles/4.421 kilometres
Race distance: 69 laps (189.549 miles/305.049 kilometres)

CURVA
MOISES SOLANA

ESTADIO

LAS ESES

CURVA
PERALTADA

1992 – MEXICAN GRAND PRIX – MEXICO CITY

RACE CLASSIFICATION AFTER 69 LAPS

(305.049 km = 189.548 mls)

Pos Nr	Driver		Team Make	Make	Total Time	km/h	mph	Diff
1	5	N. MANSELL	GBR	CANON WILLIAMS TEAM	WILLIAMS RENAULT	1:31'53.587	199.176	123.762	
2	6	R. PATRESE	ITA	CANON WILLIAMS TEAM	WILLIAMS RENAULT	1:32'06.558	198.709	123.472	12.971
3	19	M. SCHUMACHER	GER	CAMEL BENETTON FORD	BENETTON FORD	1:32'15.016	198.405	123.283	21.429
4	2	G. BERGER	AUT	HONDA MARLBORO McLAREN	McLAREN HONDA	1:32'26.934	197.979	123.018	33.347
5	4	A. DE CESARIS	ITA	TYRRELL RAC. ORG.	TYRRELL ILMOR	1:32'05.970	195.850	121.695	1 LAP
6	11	M. HAKKINEN	FIN	TEAM LOTUS	LOTUS FORD	1:32'10.983	195.672	121.585	1 LAP
7	12	J. HERBERT	GBR	TEAM LOTUS	LOTUS FORD	1:32'33.413	194.882	121.094	1 LAP
8	21	J. LEHTO	FIN	SCUDERIA ITALIA	BMS DALLARA FERRARI	1:33'10.155	193.601	120.298	1 LAP
9	26	E. COMAS	FRA	LIGIER GITANES BLONDES	LIGIER RENAULT	1:31'54.205	193.381	120.162	2 LAPS
10	25	T. BOUTSEN	BEL	LIGIER GITANES BLONDES	LIGIER RENAULT	1:31'55.083	193.351	120.143	2 LAPS
11	29	B. GACHOT	FRA	CENTRAL PARK-VEN. LARR.	VENTURI LAMBORGHINI	1:32'04.047	190.156	118.157	3 LAPS
12	30	U. KATAYAMA	JPN	CENTRAL PARK-VEN. LARR.	VENTURI LAMBORGHINI	1:32'24.267	189.462	117.726	3 LAPS
13	9	M. ALBORETO	ITA	FOOTWORK MUGEN-HONDA	FOOTWORK MUGEN-HONDA	1:32'03.852	187.281	116.371	4 LAPS

NOT CLASSIFIED

Pos Nr	Driver		Team Make	Make	Total Time	km/h	mph	COVERED
14	20	M. BRUNDLE	GBR	CAMEL BENETTON FORD	BENETTON FORD	1:03'35.732	196.039	121.813	47 LAPS
15	15	G. TARQUINI	ITA	FONDMETAL F1	FONDMETAL FORD	1:03'29.842	187.987	116.810	45 LAPS
16	14	A. CHIESA	SUI	FONDMETAL F1	FONDMETAL FORD	52'15.503	187.809	116.699	37 LAPS
17	22	P. MARTINI	ITA	SCUDERIA ITALIA	BMS DALLARA FERRARI	51'58.493	183.730	114.165	36 LAPS
18	27	J. ALESI	FRA	FERRARI	FERRARI	42'33.682	193.205	120.052	31 LAPS
19	24	G. MORBIDELLI	ITA	MINARDI TEAM	MINARDI LAMBORGHINI	40'04.181	191.979	119.290	29 LAPS
20	32	S. MODENA	ITA	SASOL JORDAN YAMAHA	JORDAN YAMAHA	24'18.916	185.456	115.237	17 LAPS
21	3	O. GROUILLARD	FRA	TYRRELL RAC. ORG.	TYRRELL ILMOR	17'14.915	184.544	114.670	12 LAPS
22	1	A. SENNA	BRA	HONDA MALRBO McLAREN	McLAREN HONDA	15'10.190	192.346	119.518	11 LAPS
23	23	C. FITTIPALDI	BRA	MINARDI TEAM	MINARDI LAMBORGHINI	3'04.737	172.305	107.066	2 LAPS

FASTEST LAP: 2. G. BERGER – Lap 60 Time: 1'17.711 (204.805 Km/h = 127.260 mph)

Brazilian Grand Prix

Interlagos

The Autodromo José Carlos Pace is set in a natural hillside amphitheatre, offering a marvellous view as it swoops around the Interlagos area on the edge of São Paulo. Those who have enjoyed the regular trip to Brazil lament the switch from Rio down to the coast. At times it is difficult to justify racing in a country where you drive past the *favellos*, sprawling estates of pathetic homes made from cardboard, wood, tin and any old junk lying around. One weekend's Formula One budget would house a few thousand people.

The first Brazilian Grand Prix was held at Interlagos in 1973 and was duly won by their own man, Emerson Fittipaldi, in a Lotus Ford. The great man races on in the American Indycar circuit, but his name returned to Grand Prix racing with his nephew, Christian Fittipaldi, in the Minardi Lamborghini in his first season of Formula One.

Mansell was in Brazil in questioning mood. São Paulo is Senna's home town, his home track. McLaren were there in force, smarting and desperate for a reversal of fortunes. The three Canon Williams Renualt FW14B cars were taken direct from Mexico to Brazil, giving no chance of test work. The faultless performances of Mansell and Riccardo Patrese in their one-two finishes in the opening two races had also brought the team 32 points in the constructors' Championship. Patrese was the only driver left in Formula One who was participating when the Grand Prix was held at Interlagos on the old track. "It is a nice track," he said, "but not as challenging as the old one."

Mansell was more enthusiastic: "It is a great circuit which has been imaginatively designed, making good use of the rolling terrain and providing a good test for the driver." Yet it was not a good track for the Englishman. His best finish had been fourth, and he was lying second in 1991 when he had to retire with 11 laps to go. Interest was high: could the Williams Renaults perform as well at a track which, unlike Kyalami in South Africa and Mexico, was much nearer sea-level? Could Mansell maintain his fault-free driving? Could McLaren's new weapon strike back?

At last, the Woking-based team had rolled out their updated MP4/7A. It had a lot to live up to as previous models had all won first time out of the box. The McLaren effort was so big in Brazil that it had the look of a military airlift. They·took six cars, three of the old M4/6Bs and three of the new M4/7As, plus 17 engines. To look after this small car park they also had 47 of their own staff and 23 Honda men, not to mention the caterers. Soon they were calling it the McLaren Army. Their garages looked like Victoria Station in the Monday morning rush hour. Still, the inspiration was the new car with its more aerodynamic lines, extra high-tech spec and a new, lighter Honda engine.

Ron Dennis, the McLaren team boss, had ridden high for four years and now he was set to embark on a new era after a brief spell of domination by Williams . . . or so the theory went. Honda had come up with their new V12 power unit, lighter, more compact and designed to be part of an aerodynamic package. A new compact exhaust system was included and it was designed to work with McLaren's revolutionary 'fly-by-wire' system which replaced throttle cable with sensor. That also controlled engine speed during gear changes so that the driver could keep his foot on the pedal while changing gear. Dennis said: "It is a technically significant step for us. You cannot win races unless you finish them, and that is why we tend to be conservative about changes. The new car is different, it looks different and, combined with a new engine, it should really get the job done."

This was a key point of the season, as everyone realised, and McLaren, who act with the cold efficiency of a big company in a sport which still mixes corner-shop friendliness with fierce rivalry, really put on a show. The only doubt was that they had had little time to test the whole new package and even Senna admitted: "We have very little experience of this new car. We do not know how it will run and we have no idea of the possible problems. We will just have to wait and see and hope. I feel positive, I want to win, especially here in Brazil, and I hope this car gives me the chance." Senna had won the first four races of 1991 and he was quick to insist that "Mansell has a good advantage but not a decisive one. We will see what it is after this weekend. The quality of our new car will decide the title and it looks as if it will be between McLaren and Williams."

Considering that the Benettons had crushed the McLarens in Mexico, it was a bold statement. Mansell arrived looking relaxed after spending time at home with his family in Florida. "Being just up the road, so to speak, is much better for me," he said. "It has been great to get home and keep my feet on the ground with Rosanne and the kids. I've only seen the McLarens – there are a lot of them, aren't there? But we will not worry about them. It is what we can do that matters."

Senna was very aware of his responsibility to his home support. "Deep down the desire to win is very great because when you see and feel the applause of thousands it moves you. No matter how cold and calculating you are, it does get to you. But you must be careful, for when the heart and emotion take over reason suffers." Even then, however, the possibility of a change of team at the end of the season on the expiry of his contract seemed to be on his mind. Ferrari had hinted that they would love to have him. "I would be dishonest if I said that it does not touch or interest me," said Senna. "But the future and what will happen will have to be thought about at the right time."

Mansell barely gave Senna time to think about anything other than the immediate future. He never shirks a challenge, on or off the track, and perhaps the huge presence of McLaren's red and white battalion fired him up. Whatever inspired him, he could hardly wait for the first qualifying session to begin on the Friday afternoon. Barely had the motorhomes stopped serving lunch before Mansell eased his car out of the garage and onto the track. He warmed his tyres, eased himself into the feel of the track and then unleashed just under 76 seconds of brilliance. In the pits and the stands, everyone suddenly began checking their watches as he grilled the track in 1 minute 15.703 seconds.

It was exhilarating, sudden, early and lightning quick at an average of 127mph, and too much for everyone else. Out they went to try: Senna, Patrese, Berger, Schumacher, Alesi. Their times were good – but none could compare with Mansell, who had the pleasure of watching the rest of the best beating their heads in frustration. Mansell not only finished with the best time but also with four laps quicker than anyone else. "That was one of the best laps of my career," he announced afterwards. "Even I will say that it was a good lap. But you must not be taken in by McLaren and Honda. They have the ability to jump straight back at a moment's notice. I felt that the Renault engine was working perfectly and the whole Williams team is working very well. We have also got a new fuel from Elf, and that seems to be working well, too."

It was not an overstatement. You only had to look at everyone else's times. Mansell's closest rival was Patrese, who clocked 1 minute 16.894 seconds, over a second slower. Mansell pondered why Patrese was so far off the pace and then asked: "Why is everyone else so much slower? I wonder what they are doing when I look at the timesheets. I had a great lap where everything went well, there was no traffic and it was fantastic, but I expected others to be closer."

Senna was short on pace and even shorter on words. Having managed to squeeze 1 minute 19.358 seconds out of his new car, he said tersely: "I feel it is premature to make any comment now. Let's see what happens tomorrow." Berger's time was slightly better but he was fifth and Senna seventh. As the circus dispersed to hotels and motorhomes for the night, the talk was of McLaren's fall from grace. Still, they were in good company. Ferrari continued to perform just as badly, and both Benettons were struggling to find the flow they had in Mexico. But such are McLaren's standards, gained over years of success, that the mood was sombre. Even if they did not really believe it, secretly everyone had hoped that the new cars would react like Popeye on spinach. Dennis said: "We have obviously not reached a situation where we are happy with the new car's performance, and naturally what we need right now is more miles under our belt."

For another Briton it was a heart-breaking weekend. Perry McCarthy, whose dream was to be in Formula One, flew to Brazil to accept a drive with the Andrea Moda team. McCarthy was given a superlicence after he and Roberto Moreno were nominated to replace the men listed by the small Italian team. But on presenting himself at Interlagos he was told that the licence had been withdrawn. For a man who had had his house repossessed by the bank a few weeks earlier and had had to scrape together the cash for the air fare, it was a bitter blow. He had to spectate on the Saturday when he had hoped to be driving. However, there was plenty to watch.

In the morning session, Mansell was again fastest, using Patrese's car. The Italian had complained of feeling uncomfortable with it on the Friday. Mansell took it into the 1.17s and delivered a sharp message for his team-mate. "I don't think the car is bad. Riccardo is a great driver, but sometimes he has a problem on some circuits." Perhaps the word got to Patrese, for in the afternoon he applied more power and got down to 1 minute 16.894 seconds – still 1.2 seconds off Mansell's hot lap. But the real drama was being played out by Mansell, who made his first mistake of the season. He was near the end of the final qualifying session when he came upon Senna going into a right-hand corner. There seemed little danger, but quite abruptly Mansell was off the track and hit the nearby wall with a shuddering crash.

A startled Senna is reported to have told his pit on the radio: "The stupid bugger has just driven into the wall." Mansell had to be prised from the car and taken straight to the medical centre. He emerged limping, being helped along, but happily only bruised and shaken. "I don't blame Ayrton at all," said Mansell. "It was a bit of a misunderstanding. I thought he had pulled over to let me pass and then we almost touched. There was no opportunity to come back and I got into a half-spin and hit the wall. I was winded and felt sick. It was just as well it was near the end." His tonic was the news that he had his third pole position of the season while the new McLarens were struggling, although they had pulled up to third and fourth.

Senna and Berger had both been forced into the old cars to finish after agonies with the new model including a blown engine and a fire. As Mansell headed to his hotel to recuperate, his team got to work rebuilding his car, corners and sidepods. Senna also left the track feeling sore, his face set like thunder. Ron Dennis was several paces behind as Senna stalked into the distance. He already feared that while Mansell's troubles would heal, it might take a miracle worker to cure the McLaren cars' problems.

Mansell arrived at the track early on Sunday, always a good idea in São Paulo which, it is said, will one day join up with Rio to become the world's first mega-opolis. Life is one big traffic jam. He was sore, aching in all sorts of places, he said, and his night's sleep had been short and restless due to pain and noise. Behind him were Patrese, Berger, Senna, Jean Alesi and Michael Schumacher. The race start was hardly encouraging, either, as Mansell anticipated the lights, braked and found Patrese screaming past into the lead. Mansell quickly tucked in behind his team-mate and began a real scrap for the lead which was the highlight of the season so far. It was clear that there were no team orders as both men battled at high speed for the first place. In the pits, wheelchair-bound team owner Frank Williams must have wondered if he should ask one of them to ease off, but both drivers were too wise to go over the top. Mansell set the fastest lap on the tenth as he hurtled along behind Patrese. Senna and Schumacher were third and fourth, but the Williams cars were pulling away at astonishing speed.

By the tenth lap they were 38 seconds ahead, a country mile in Formula One. Senna was leading a convoy and there was no team help – Berger had been forced to start from the pits and lasted only four laps. The crowds, waving their Brazilian flags and Senna banners, saw Schumacher pass their hero only to be retaken almost immediately. But the end was nigh for Senna, and on the fateful 18th lap he headed into the pits, climbed out of the MP4/7A, glared at the car and walked to the back of the garage to cool down. "We have a problem now but it did not start here, it began last year when we had to put so much effort into winning the Championship that it hurt us," explained Senna. "The effort to keep winning was enormous. McLaren were more content to hold their level while Williams were building for the future. It is very difficult for us now."

Just to make Senna's day, Schumacher, who finished third, then had a verbal hack at him at the post-race press conference. "He was slowing down and speeding up. If he had a problem he should have got out of the way," said the bold 22-year-old German. "I don't know what game he was playing but it was not a game I like. He is the World Champion and he should behave better."

On the track, Mansell and Patrese had swept to their third one-two and again the Italian had been forced to give way to the British ace. Tyre stops were to prove crucial. Mansell dived in on his 29th lap, was held for just 8.5

seconds and was on his way again. Patrese stayed on the go for another two laps and his stop was only half a second longer, but Mansell had broken through to the mental and physical plane where he operates with brilliance. He was on the charge, and despite his stop and having to get back to racing speed, he had the lead. Eventually, in a race which had just ten finishers, Mansell came home 30 seconds ahead of Patrese, who set the fastest lap. His average speed had been 118mph over the 190 miles.

Mansell was delighted with his third win as the Senna army trooped away as dispirited as their local hero. "I made a really duff start, probably one of my worst ever," said Mansell. "I was just pleased that I did not stall the engine and managed to get going. But the first 29 laps were fantastic and Riccardo drove absolutely brilliantly. When I was behind him he did not make one mistake, and I was there all the time in case of a slip. It was a big fight and a great race, and in the end I think I lucked in with the pit stop, as I went in before we hit traffic. We did have some problems, but compared with everyone else's these were insignificant. I don't think people realise what a great job Renault have done for us over the winter. Not only have they supplied us with reliable engines but with much more power than last year, which goes cap in hand with the Elf fuel as well. The combination of the engine, the fuel, the car and Riccardo and myself, who worked hard over the winter, is showing now. But it is a long, long season and we just have to keep the momentum going. It is a great start to have won the first three races but I am having a job taking it all in. One thing I won't be is complacent."

All around him were angry men, it seemed. Senna was very down at the McLarens' debut, Martin Brundle raged at Jean Alesi for putting him off on lap 30, an action which earned the Frenchman an official censure, and Johnny Herbert was none too happy at being caught in an inter-team war. Thierry Boutsen and Erik Comas had a strained relationship which came to a head when Boutsen tried to pass the Belgian. Herbert's Lotus, which had only just made the grid in 26th spot, was caught in the squeeze and off he went. "I was Boutsened," quipped Herbert, who at least could cheer himself that the new Lotus was close to roll-out. Mansell, with 30 World Championship points tucked away, now led from Patrese (18), Schumacher (11), Berger (5), Senna (4) and Alesi (3).

"The Championship?" queried Mansell as he headed for the airport. "I remember last year very well. I did not pick up a point from the first four races and I was still able to challenge strongly. There is no let-up. Now I am going home to Florida for 36 hours and then I am off to England for testing."

Significantly, Renault were delighted, a rare admission for a man such as their technical director, Bernard Dudot. "We are very satisfied," said Dudot, the master technician behind the Renault charge. "For the first time this season the Williams Renault team has totally dominated every session and the race. The victory is very encouraging for the rest of the season as Interlagos is more representative of the remaining circuits, apart from Monaco."

Senna said simply: "My car had an intermittent engine cut-out and I had to retire. I am disappointed. There is much work to do." They were wise words from the three-times World Champion.

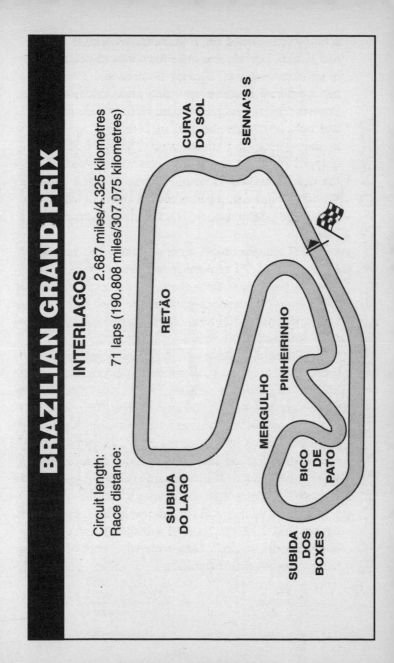

BRAZILIAN GRAND PRIX

INTERLAGOS

Circuit length: 2.687 miles/4.325 kilometres
Race distance: 71 laps (190.808 miles/307.075 kilometres)

SUBIDA
DO LAGO

RETÃO

CURVA
DO SOL

SENNA'S S

MERGULHO

PINHEIRINHO

BICO DE
PATO

SUBIDA
DOS
BOXES

1992 – BRAZILIAN GRAND PRIX – SAO PAULO

RACE CLASSIFICATION AFTER 71 LAPS

(307.075 km = 190.807 mls)

Pos	Nr	Driver		Team Make	Make	Total Time	km/h	mph	Diff
1	5	N. MANSELL	GBR	CANON WILLIAMS TEAM	WILLIAMS RENAULT	1:36'51.856	190.209	118.191	
2	6	R. PATRESE	ITA	CANON WILLIAMS TEAM	WILLIAMS RENAULT	1:37'21.186	189.254	117.597	29.330
3	19	M. SCHUMACHER	GER	CAMEL BENETTON FORD	BENETTON FORD	1:37'10.816	186.921	116.147	1 LAP
4	27	J. ALESI	FRA	FERRARI	FERRARI	1:37'35.222	186.142	115.663	1 LAP
5	28	I. CAPELLI	ITA	FERRARI	FERRARI	1:38'05.313	185.190	115.072	1 LAP
6	9	M. ALBORETO	ITA	FOOTWORK MUGEN-HONDA	FOOTWORK MUGEN-HONDA	1:38'06.994	185.137	115.039	1 LAP
7	24	G. MORBIDELLI	ITA	MINARDI TEAM	MINARDI LAMBORGHINI	1:37'04.980	184.435	114.603	2 LAPS
8	21	J. LEHTO	FIN	SCUDERIA ITALIA	BMS DALLARA FERRARI	1:38'12.414	182.324	113.291	2 LAPS
9	30	U. KATAYAMA	JPN	CENTRAL PARK-VEN. LARR.	VENTURI LAMBORGHINI	1:36'52.344	182.157	113.187	3 LAPS
10	11	M. HAKKINEN	FIN	TEAM LOTUS	LOTUS FORD	1:37'42.460	177.944	110.569	4 LAPS

NOT CLASSIFIED

Pos	Nr	Driver		Team Make	Make	Total Time	km/h	mph	COVERED
11	15	G. TARQUINI	ITA	FONDMETAL F1	FONDMETAL FORD	1:32'51.476	173.265	107.662	62 LAPS
12	16	K. WENDLINGER	AUT	MARCH F.1	MARCH ILMOR	1:18'14.949	182.398	113.337	55 LAPS
13	23	C. FITTIPALDI	BRA	MINARDI TEAM	MINARDI LAMBORGHINI	1:16'38.839	182.824	113.602	54 LAPS
14	3	O. GROUILLARD	FRA	TYRRELL	TYRRELL ILMOR	1:14'24.088	181.367	112.696	52 LAPS
15	26	E. COMAS	FRA	LIGIER GITANES BLONDES	LIGIER RENAULT	59'16.074	183.894	114.266	42 LAPS
16	12	J. HERBERT	GBR	TEAM LOTUS	LOTUS FORD	50'57.200	183.344	113.925	36 LAPS
17	25	T. BOUTSEN	BEL	LIGIER GITANES BLONDES	LIGIER RENAULT	50'57.580	183.321	113.911	36 LAPS
18	33	M. GUGELMIN	BRA	SASOL JORDAN YAMAHA	JORDAN YAMAHA	51'51.260	180.159	111.946	36 LAPS
19	20	M. BRUNDLE	GBR	CAMEL BENETTON FORD	BENETTON FORD	42'11.388	184.523	114.657	30 LAPS
20	22	P. MARTINI	ITA	SCUDERIA ITALIA	BMS DALLARA FERRARI	33'51.935	183.904	114.272	24 LAPS
21	29	B. GACHOT	FRA	CENTRAL PARK-VEN. LARR.	VENTURI LAMBORGHINI	32'28.004	183.834	114.229	23 LAPS
22	4	A. DE CESARIS	ITA	TYRRELL	TYRRELL ILMOR	29'33.408	184.374	114.565	21 LAPS
23	1	A. SENNA	BRA	HONDA MARLBORO McLAREN	McLAREN HONDA	24'02.599	183.481	114.010	17 LAPS
24	2	G. BERGER	AUT	HONDA MARLBORO McLAREN	McLAREN HONDA	7'48.664	132.888	82.573	4 LAPS
25	10	A. SUZUKI	JPN	FOOTWORK MUGEN-HONDA	FOOTWORK MUGEN-HONDA	3'26.817	150.568	93.559	2 LAPS
26	32	S. MODENA	ITA	SASOL JORDAN YAMAHA	JORDAN YAMAHA	2'08.611	121.063	75.225	1 LAP

FASTEST LAP: 6 R. PATRESE – Lap 34 Time: 1'19.490 (195.874 km/h = 121.710 mph)

Spanish Grand Prix

Catalunya

Life had been hectic for the Formula One teams before they set up camp just north of Barcelona for the Spanish Grand Prix on 5 May. The month between Brazil and Spain allowed the teams a breathing space to try to sort out their problems, develop new cars and engines, and test, test, test. It was hectic, detailed and raised optimism levels all round. It was like starting all over again. McLaren had been working flat out to try to break in their MP4/7A after its ill-starred debut. Camel Benetton Ford had also been busy after rolling out their dramatic new-look B192 with a raised shark nose. Even Williams Renault, despite their hat-trick of runaway successes, had been working non-stop. They were keen to introduce a new engine, the Renault RS4.

The Gran Premio de España at the Circuit de Cataluña was the opening battle of the European campaign which would be waged across the Continent until late September. The first three races are jet-set affairs, long-distance hauls which occasionally make for upset results and strange performances from man and machine. For Spain, the race was also an important piece of a jigsaw which was designed to raise the status and image of the country during the year. Seville had Expo 92, Madrid was the European city of culture and Barcelona had the Olympics. Certainly, the amount of work on roads and buildings around the Catalan city was impressive, and moving around was easier than ever from arrival at the airport to track access. It was only the second year of the circuit's existence and on gathering day, the Thursday prior to the race, it was looking good in the warm glow of the early summer sunshine.

In official testing at Silverstone the previous week, Mansell had proved fastest by over a second. He worked with the Williams test driver Damon Hill, who was third in the work-out. Mansell, having survived a crash in Brazil, had startled himself and the team again on the Monday at Silverstone when he emerged unscathed from another high-speed scare. A front tyre had punctured at around 150mph and he fought to control the car as it swung away, smashing against a kerb. There was a great impact to the car and damage to the undertray, but he managed to bring it back to the pits. It was a heavy workload: Mansell piled on the laps to test the RS4 engine to race distance and he did so at some speed.

Williams had been to Italy to test at Imola, where Riccardo Patrese had also survived a heavy shunt but still had the satisfaction of being the fastest man there. Ferrari struggled on with their new but obstinately troublesome F192, which looked the part but acted like something else.

Meanwhile, Benetton and Martin Brundle were pounding round and Brundle was delighted with the new car. "It is good – very good," said the man from King's Lynn. "It is superior aerodynamically." McLaren, desperately seeking the key to unlock the magic of their new box of tricks, had some measure of comfort with improved test times but nowhere near as much as they had hoped.

At this point we should look at where the Williams and McLarens were coming from. McLaren had won the first four races of 1991 with an updated car while Williams, after signing Mansell and undertaking a severe winter of testing, had introduced a new car. They had come up with their six-speed, semi-automatic gearbox, which allowed the driver to change gear without taking his hands off the wheel to reach for a lever. The gear selector was behind the steering wheel and the clutch was required only at the start of a race. This eased some driver pressure and helped on corners. Now they had added the active suspension which was computer operated, giving a regular height ride on corners, in braking and over bumps. By improving the aerodynamic shape of the car, maintaining its optimum angle, the speed was increased as air resistance decreased. Carbon brakes also allowed tougher braking.

McLaren, with TAG Electronics building engine management systems, tried to go one better with their 'fly-by-wire' car which virtually cut out direct mechanical connection between driver and engine. "He is left free to drive," said Ron Dennis, McLaren's owner.

Both teams had achieved technological heights undreamed of by Stirling Moss or even James Hunt, Britain's last World Champion in 1976. With computers and sensors sending signals back to the pits, the engineers could monitor everything from oil consumption to tyre wear, even if there was a puncture. Mansell was to rue that little light in the cockpit later in the season, and for the drivers, the feeling that their teams were listening more to the computer than to their experienced pilots was frustrating at times.

A battle of technology was now beginning to take over and that troubled many, not least other teams who lacked the finance to go to war. Spain was to prove, however, that no matter what is in the car, it is the man of flesh and blood with skill and bravery who will win the day.

The weekend began with Renault announcing that they would use the RS4 during qualifying practice and that as a result Williams would have four cars at Cataluña. The race cars would be fitted with the RS3C engine while two others would have the new unit, an all-new engine in which the main difference was a cylinder head housing an innovative timing system. For the other teams, it was a psychological blow as much as anything else to learn that the engine which was currently blowing them away was about to be superseded by an even better version.

Elsewhere the good news was that Damon Hill had at last got himself another Formula One drive, at the expense of the sport's only woman driver. Italy's Giovanna Amati, a 29-year-old Roman, had turned heads with her looks but her drives in the Brabham Judd had attracted the wrong kind of attention. Not that it was a fair contest, for the current Brabham team was a pale shadow of the one that had been a front-runner. Every week brought a new crisis, and 29-year-old Hill was invited to take over. "I am proud to carry the name forward to Formula One," said Hill, whose father won the World title in 1968 and 1971. "It doesn't bring extra pressure. If my presence helps the team, either because my name attracts money or through results, then that is fine."

Money was certainly needed. On the way to Spain, the Brabham cars had been impounded at the French border on the instructions of an aggrieved creditor, who claimed £15000 for catering bills from the previous season. They left a car as security to free the other two for the race.

Another Briton, Perry McCarthy, had finally obtained his superlicence and was now set to drive for Andrea Moda.

Mansell started the Friday with the RS4 car but then switched to an RS3C. When he found that the throttle was sticking, he returned to the new engine but then set the fastest time in the morning practice with the old unit. "The track is very slippery," complained Mansell, "and we are fighting for balance. I could not drive a race distance with the car handling like that so we need to make some improvements in that respect."

In qualifying, with the weather overcast and warm, Mansell was soon exploiting the power and reliability of the RS3C engine to set the fastest time of 1 minute 20.190 seconds. Michael Schumacher was next, a full second behind. Senna was happier for a while with third, 1.1 off the pace, and disgruntled Patrese settled for fourth. Schumacher was delighted with the feel of his new Benetton 192 but it was not long before he bent one, going into a wall after a tyre blistered at speed. The nose came off and the chassis broke but the driver was unscathed. Brundle admitted that he had been fighting the car and was clearly not in best humour.

McCarthy's sense of humour was tested to the limit when he climbed into the black Moda car for his free practice run. Team-mate Roberto Moreno had already returned to the pits without his car. A fired-up McCarthy was told he would be allowed just one lap. Unfortunately, the man from Essex stalled the car at the end of the pit lane as he headed onto the circuit, and his lap came to an end after 30 feet. The car was eventually hauled back to the garage and Moreno headed out only for the engine to blow up after one lap. Moda would not qualify, and neither would Brabham.

The Friday times were to be more significant than anyone realised, for the rain began to fall in Spain on the plain, the hills, the coast and the circuit. On the coast, Saturday dawned to the sound of a river in spate – but there was no river nearby. So torrential was the rain that the steep road was now two feet deep in water roaring down off the hills. Further inland at the circuit it was as bad, and extortionate prices were being asked and paid for umbrellas and rain jackets. The relentless rain was to fall until the circus departed on Monday. With streams of brown, muddy water pouring across the track, Saturday was going to be a test of nothing except patience and nerves.

The track drained well enough but the sheer volume of rain kept it awash. Some teams skipped the Saturday morning session. Not Ferrari's Jean Alesi, however; he revelled in the monsoon. He had been bested on the Friday by team-mate Ivan Capelli, who took fifth on the grid, but he was first out in the rain, and although everyone knew that they would not get near Friday's times, some were keen to try.

As for Mansell, he pondered whether he should have brought one of his boats over from Florida. But the weather was a challenge and, of course, Mansell is the man for that. Soon he had the Williams, with the RS4 engine, howling around, slipping and sliding as he came to terms with the conditions which were bound to prevail on the Sunday. Mansell had complained on the dry Friday that the track was "like a moving target with grip on one lap, none on another." In the wet, it was a place for none but the brave. He spun off in the morning but avoided any damage, as did Schumacher. The times, of course, were irrelevant and the forecast was for more of the same, but Mansell had no doubt that the race would go ahead. "Unlike Adelaide last year, which was affected by this kind of weather, this track has space and run-off areas," he said.

Mansell was happy. The 20th pole of his career was secure and he had felt good in the wet, even though Alesi had been quickest, albeit at 1 minute 45.903 seconds. Berger and Senna had also gone faster in the wet than Mansell, who had run the RS4 but it was only a fraction of a second and he was unworried. Alesi ventured: "If it rains Ferrari have a chance," and even Senna admitted: "We would prefer it to be wet as that might be favourable to our position." Mansell congratulated Ferrari on their revival and talked fondly of the team he had left two years previously. "If it rains like this tomorrow, it will be a battle for survival," he said as he left.

Next morning the rain had eased but it was cool, threatening and very damp. Then just before the 2.00 pm start it began to drizzle again – not on many people, though, for only 28000 attended. This was hardly surprising in view of the conditions, but those who were there were given a brilliant driving display by Mansell. Just two minutes before the green light, the race was officially declared 'wet'. Most had already switched to rain tyres when the drizzle began. The Footwork team were eventually fined $5000 dollars for a late change on the grid while others waited until the race had started before making a pit stop.

As Mansell sat on the grid he must have contemplated the value of the race. Victory would equal Senna's four in a row at the start of the previous season and would give him an enormous advantage in the drivers' Championship over his great rival. A win would also equal the record set by Jim Clark and Niki Lauda for 25 Grand Prix successes. By the time the red light changed to green, his mind was fully focused on the race. He hit the hammer hard and flew to the first corner safely in first place. Patrese executed another searing start, propelling himself from fourth to second. Behind him, Alesi was even faster, blazing away from eighth spot on the grid past a startled pack of drivers to whip into the first bend in third behind the two Williams Renaults.

Gerhard Berger was not impressed as Alesi's red Ferrari shot past his McLaren. "I was surprised to find Alesi beside me with the lights still at red," commented the Austrian wryly.

Mansell powered into the misty rain and after ten laps he was three seconds ahead of Patrese, 16 clear of Schumacher, 19 in front of Senna and 21 away from Alesi. He set the fastest lap of the race on this lap, 1 minute 42.503 seconds, an average speed of 103.594mph, and at this stage it was fairly dry. Already the race had claimed the scalp of Martin Brundle, who had retired on lap five. Brundle, who had clutch problems, was clipped on the inside by Erik Comas and spun off. Such was his luck that the car, engine still running, straddled the kerb with the rear wheels spinning in the gravel. He was out.

The first blow of the season to Williams domination came on the 19th lap when, with the rain falling heavily, Patrese suddenly came upon a backmarker in the chicane, lost downforce as he slowed and went off. Mansell was left out on his own with a 22-second lead from Schumacher. All around, they were slipping, sliding, skidding and spinning. The field was an élite gathering now, and Mansell found himself slowed by traffic ahead, a group containing Olivier Grouillard, J.J. Lehto, Pierluigi Martini and Gabriele Tarquini. That slowed him, and Schumacher closed to 12 seconds at one point. Once clear, however, Mansell was off again, disappearing in a curtain of water.

At the halfway stage of the 69-lap race, many were forecasting an early stop as the rain fell and the water level rose. Mansell was lapping at around 100mph, remaining comfortably ahead of the young German, who was driving with remarkable efficiency despite his inexperience in these conditions in a Formula One car. With 40 laps gone, Mansell was 15 seconds in front of the Benetton Ford car and just over 19 in front of Senna. He had lapped everyone except the five behind him. So it continued, but as spectators peered through the rain to spot the cars, quite suddenly Schumacher's bright yellow car was closing on Mansell.

Mansell was lapping a shade slower, Schumacher going a touch quicker, and by lap 51 the gap was down to 4.4 seconds. Senna was just 11 seconds away.

Schumacher was as surprised as anyone when he saw Mansell's car ahead. "I thought he must have had a spin," said Schumacher. Mansell gave the credit to the German: "Michael must have found a short cut. It was just like when José Maria Olazabal shot a 62 at Jack Nicklaus's course. For about 15 laps I did not know where this son-of-a-gun had come from. It was fabulous to watch but not to be caught. I was driving flat out but the gap kept coming down. I altered my line through three corners and found more grip by changing my direction."

Whatever the reason, and it looked as if he had eased for a while, Mansell the matador then took over again almost immediately. Having lured the young bull, Mansell delivered the killing thrust, increasing his lead to 6, 9, 12, and 14 seconds and finally sweeping home in a plume of spray which rose like a victory salute. He was 23.914 seconds ahead, a remarkable margin after being almost caught 14 laps earlier. Had he used traction control to help avoid aquaplaning? "At times today I did not think it existed," he replied.

His joy at a fourth victory was merely heightened when

he heard that once again Senna had failed to finish. Having battled with his team-mate, Berger, for much of the race, Senna had finally lost the car three laps from the end when, under pressure from Alesi, he went off. The Frenchman in the Ferrari had run a race second only to Mansell in driving skill, giving it everything in the latter stages despite a spin and tyre stop on the 33rd lap.

Mansell had 40 points from four races but he admitted: "It was one of the hardest races of my career. I cannot remember having had to drive so hard for so long. I was fighting to stay on the circuit so I have got to be happy that I won. I went out with the car on a compromise set-up in case it dried up so we suffered a bit in the rain. But you can never be perfect in these conditions. I lost time, but let's face it, everybody who was out there drove fantastically just to stay on the circuit. Every driver who finished deserves a medal. I think the marshals also did a brilliant job in that weather, and they have to be complimented. Getting four wins in a row is fantastic. To be alongside a driver as great as Jim Clark in wins is wonderful."

As usual he declined to talk about the Championship, and that led to the nastiest part of the weekend. Australian journalist Mark Fogarty asked Mansell: "Why do you continually play down the technical advantage your car clearly has?" Mansell, perhaps feeling that his driving ability was being questioned after a superbly controlled race in appalling conditions, blew up like an engine. "Are you serious? Are you on the same planet? If you are, you should see a psychiatrist. You must be on drugs or something . . . You are stupid. Can we have a serious press conference, please?"

It was a sour note on which to finish, but it showed that Mansell was tiring of the car being given all the credit by those who doubted him. When he was coming second, the critics suggested that he could not be a winner. Now he was winning everything, and that seemed as hard for them to take. They would have to stomach a lot more.

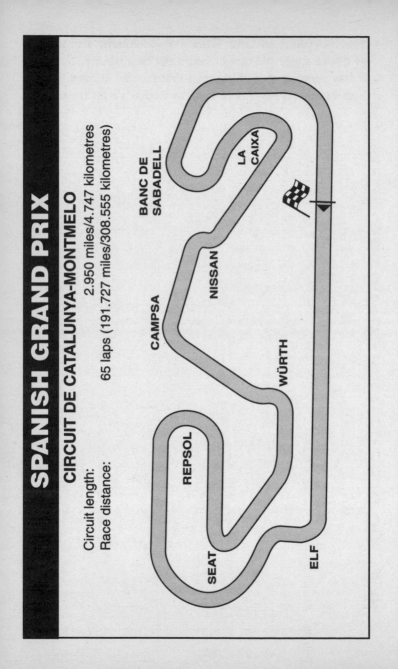

1992 – TIO PEPE SPANISH GRAND PRIX – CATALUNYA

RACE CLASSIFICATION AFTER 65 LAPS

(308.555 km = 191.727 mls)

Pos	Nr	Driver		Team Make	Make	Total Time	km/h	mph	Diff
1	5	N. MANSELL	GBR	CANON WILLIAMS TEAM	WILLIAMS RENAULT	1:56'10.674	159.353	99.017	
2	19	M. SCHUMACHER	GER	CAMEL BENETTON FORD	BENETTON FORD	1:56'34.588	158.808	98.679	23.914
3	27	J. ALESI	FRA	FERRARI	FERRARI	1:56'37.136	158.750	98.643	26.482
4	2	G. BERGER	AUT	HONDA MARLBORO McLAREN	McLAREN HONDA	1:57'31.321	157.530	97.885	1'20.647
5	9	M. ALBORETO	ITA	FOOTWORK MUGEN-HONDA	FOOTWORK MUGEN-HONDA	1:57'52.448	154.544	96.091	1 LAP
6	22	P. MARTINI	ITA	SCUDERIA ITALIA	BMS DALLARA FERRARI	1:56'55.310	153.467	95.380	2 LAPS
7	10	A. SUZUKI	JPN	FOOTWORK MUGEN-HONDA	FOOTWORK MUGEN-HONDA	1:57'15.005	153.037	95.093	2 LAPS
8	16	K. WENDLINGER	AUT	MARCH F.1	MARCH ILMOR	1:57'47.901	152.325	94.650	2 LAPS
9	1	A. SENNA	BRA	HONDA MARLBORO McLAREN	McLAREN HONDA	1:50'55.939	159.135	96.913	3 LAPS
10	28	I. CAPELLI	ITA	FERRARI	FERRARI	1:52'58.459	156.355	97.154	3 LAPS
11	23	C. FITTIPALDI	BRA	MINARDI TEAM	MINARDI LAMBORGHINI	1:56'36.905	148.988	92.578	4 LAPS
12	17	P. BELMONDO	FRA	MARCH F.1	MARCH ILMOR	1:57'16.645	148.145	92.053	4 LAPS

NOT CLASSIFIED

Pos	Nr	Driver		Team Make	Make	Total Time	km/h	mph	COVERED
13	21	J. LEHTO	FIN	SCUDERIA ITALIA	BMS DALLARA FERRARI	1:42'39.305	156.374	95.545	56 LAPS
14	15	G. TARQUINI	ITA	FONDMETAL F1	FONDMETAL FORD	1:43'16.472	154.442	95.986	58 LAPS
15	11	M. HAKKINEN	FIN	TEAM LOTUS	LOTUS FORD	1:43'48.806	153.616	95.452	58 LAPS
16	26	E. COMAS	FRA	LIGIER GITANES BLONDES	LIGIER RENAULT	1:42'33.817	152.735	94.905	55 LAPS
17	29	B. GACHOT	FRA	CENTRAL PARK-VEN. LARR.	VENTURI LAMBORGHINI	1:04'29.073	154.591	96.058	35 LAPS
18	3	O. GROUILLARD	FRA	TYRRELL	TYRRELL ILMOR	55'14.281	154.687	96.116	30 LAPS
19	24	G. MORBIDELLI	ITA	MINARDI TEAM	MINARDI LAMBORGHINI	50'45.385	145.899	90.658	25 LAPS
20	33	M. GUGELMIN	BRA	SASOL JORDAN YAMAHA	JORDAN YAMAHA	44'29.931	153.672	95.488	24 LAPS
21	14	A. CHIESA	SUI	FONDMETAL F1	FONDMETAL FORD	43'10.637	145.124	90.176	22 LAPS
22	6	R. PATRESE	ITA	CANON WILLIAMS TEAM	WILLIAMS RENAULT	33'32.024	151.377	100.275	19 LAPS
23	12	J. HERBERT	GBR	TEAM LOTUS	LOTUS FORD	24'21.465	152.012	94.456	13 LAPS
24	25	T. BOUTSEN	BEL	LIGIER GITANES BLONDES	LIGIER RENAULT	25'51.597	121.153	75.281	11 LAPS
25	20	M. BRUNDLE	GBR	CAMEL BENETTON FORD	BENETTON FORD	7'38.343	148.814	92.459	4 LAPS
26	4	A. DE CESARIS	ITA	TYRRELL	TYRRELL ILMOR	4'29.589	126.730	78.777	2 LAP

FASTEST LAP: 5 N. MANSELL – Lap 10 Time: 1'42.503 (166.719 km/h = 103.594 mph)

San Marino Grand Prix

Imola

The pressure was on without a doubt as Nigel Mansell, now operating from his Isle of Man home, headed for Imola and the San Marino Grand Prix on 17 May. A fifth first would give him a world record: he would become the first driver to win the opening five rounds of the World Championship. It would also put him in such a favourable position in the title race that Senna would struggle to get back into the contest.

There was no rest after the fourth win in Spain. The cars were transported direct to Imola for an official test session and after scarcely two days at home, Mansell followed them. Even the total dominance he had enjoyed so far had not eased Mansell's or Williams' search for perfection. "We know there will be a backlash," said Mansell. "McLaren will be back. The more time goes on, the more they will learn about the new car and they will be close soon."

Sure enough, the three-day test programme proved Mansell right. He set the fastest time on the Thursday, 1 minute 22.236 seconds, but he found Senna just over three hundredths of a second behind. Riccardo Patrese was third a fraction slower, but he was lucky to escape from a big shunt on the Friday when, in a repeat of Mansell's test accident at Silverstone, a rear tyre punctured. The Italian driver was on a full Grand Prix distance test when his tyre deflated and the car smashed into a left-hand wall. Patrese suffered concussion, neck strain and heavy bruising, but declared himself fit for San Marino the following week.

But the test had shown that under certain conditions, Senna and Alesi in the Ferrari, admittedly on its home track, could be close. Williams had set their times with full fuel tanks but it was not known whether the opposition were running less fuel to lighten their cars. Schumacher was up there as well and the *wunderkind* of Formula One admitted: "My only target this season is to win a Grand Prix. I have to accept this as a learning period as well as a great adventure. In normal circumstances we cannot beat the Williams cars but I am sure we can get closer. With all the extra top-end power we will have from the new engine, it is my aim to put some pressure on Patrese and Mansell at Imola. It is going to be a big race for us."

The extra power for the new Camel Benetton Ford was coming from an improved engine, the Series VII 3.5 litre Ford F1V8. The engine developed more than 700 horsepower and was designed to develop substantially more power at engine speeds in excess of 13000rpm. McLaren, with their apparently improving MP4/7A, had new Shell fuel to try. Lotus had finally unveiled their 107 model to replaced the aged and heavier car which had at least been reliable enough to earn some valuable points in the first four races. Ferrari had also modified their 1992 car. The hunters were closing in with their tweaked engines, aerodynamic cars and fierce ambition.

Mansell arrived in Imola and immediately pleaded for a speed-up in the Williams development programme. "Unless we make improvements we could be behind in a couple of races," he said. "It would be good for the sport but not for me." While testing on the Renault RS4 engine continued apace, there was no sign of the new Williams FW15 chassis and Mansell showed slight impatience. "Ask Frank," he said when questioned about its arrival on the scene. "I need it now and I hope they can give it to me soon. The others are catching up, they are here now."

It showed Mansell's deep-seated fear of another campaign going wrong. Three times he had ended as runner-up in the Championship, twice when the trophy seemed in his grasp, and he was not ready to lose his dream after four wins. Even Williams' technical director, Patrick Head, the man responsible for the development of the FW14, admitted: "I think that we will see a real motor race in Imola."

There was a further challenge, too, from team-mate Patrese, born not far away in Padova. He confirmed before San Marino: "I want to win this race. It is like my home race. I consider the track my own. Not scoring any points in Spain was bad because until then I was still quite close to Nigel and now I have Schumacher right behind me. I think our cars will be competitive at Imola, but McLaren and Benetton have made progress since Brazil and I don't think we have a big advantage over them. It is very competitive now and it is going to be very tough. I feel I can go faster on the European circuits than Nigel. Thanks to the three second places I have had the gap between us is not unbridgeable. I am still fighting to be World Champion. What gives me great pride after 15 years in Formula One is that I belong to one of the finest teams in the field, if not the finest, and that I am racing for the title."

Mansell was quick to recognise the threat from his friend and colleague. "Riccardo will be really fired up in Imola," he agreed. "He always goes well here and won two years ago. He will be determined to come back strongly. He knows the track well and was very quick in testing. You can't discount him from the Championship. There are still 12 races and 120 points to go, and I know he wants to win it."

Imola is a superb circuit with fans to match. From its romantic name, Autodromo Dino & Enzo Ferrari, to the setting in low, rolling hills half an hour from Bologna, it is a must for motor racing fans. This is no flat, featureless circuit with sponsors' names for bends. Here they honour their history, acknowledge the debt to the past. There is an air of enjoyment, goodwill and comradeship.

In the Emilio Romagna, near the Apennines, in May it is green and lush with fruit trees and vineyards and old, rambling houses. The *tifosi*, the car-crazy Italian motor racing fans, come early and pitch camp on the heights of the circuit. The favourite area for the die-hards is the Rivazza hill, where the cars sweep down and into the long, flat run past the pits. They come with their small tents, pieces of polythene, blankets, straw, wood and scaffolding and build their own stands and temporary homes. Those who do not want to pay or cannot afford it bring their own custom-built seats which hook neatly over the top of the wall surrounding one side of the circuit and allow them a grandstand view. Houses overlooking the circuit have scaffolding towers built right up the front and onto the roofs.

The authorities, normally keen to block every chink at a track for fear that someone may see something that does not cost a £50 ticket, turn a blind eye at Imola. It is part of the atmosphere. The supporters jeer and cheer, roar encouragement and whistle in derision at drivers. The brave and the quick are well-regarded.

That is why Mansell, an out-and-out Englishman in looks and attitude, is such a huge star in Italy. The man they dubbed *Il Leone* – the lion – had won only one race in his two years with Ferrari but his all-out, aggressive driving thrilled the Italians.

There is sympathy for those who appear to be trying in lesser equipment, but those unfortunate enough to depart the track within sight of the *tifosi* and who have to walk back can expect a noisy stroll. At least here they could promenade in the sunshine: the early summer sun was a delight after the rain in Spain and it was not long before the racing matched the sparkling weather.

The morning practice session, officially termed as untimed, gave everyone plenty to talk about at lunch. Mansell had been just a tenth of a second faster than Senna. The Briton had clocked 202mph in Red Five with the RS4 engine for the fastest lap, but Senna had set the quickest average speed of 162.11mph. After constant Williams domination, it offered hope to those looking for a tightly-fought race. "I told you McLaren were catching us," said Mansell, who was having trouble with his hay fever.

Unlike in Spain, Perry McCarthy had managed seven laps in the pre-qualifying battle but again the Moda team failed. Senna threw down the gauntlet early, setting the fastest time 20 minutes into the one-hour qualifying session. Mansell's response was almost immediate, and as Senna headed for the pits he went six tenths of a second faster. That stood for a while until Mansell reappeared and went for it again, blazing round, bringing roars of approval from the *tifosi* – and rightly so. He had beaten Senna's 1991 pole position record with a time of 1 minute 21.842 seconds and declared it "a very special lap. I am really happy. It was half a second quicker than any other lap I did. I knew I was on a hot lap out there. I was ready for it, the tyres came in just at the right time and, most importantly, there was no traffic to hold me up.

"You have to remember that without the qualifying tyres, the C tyres have to brought in carefully because there is only a short time when they are worth half a second a lap. But it was like musical chairs in our garage. I qualified in the race car with my race engine, the RS3C. The RS4 was in my spare car, which I let Riccardo have to qualify, and he had a great drive considering everything."

What Renault had discovered was that they needed more time to change an RS4 for an RS3C, and when Patrese's car developed a problem in the morning, they struggled. He eventually took over Mansell's spare car with five minutes to go and qualified fifth. But Mansell was again looking over his shoulder at the two McLaren drivers, Senna and Berger, in second and third, even though they were over a second behind. Schumacher had finished fourth, but trouble had erupted between his team-mate Martin Brundle and Jean Alesi. "He is crazy," said an angry Brundle after the session in which he ended up a disappointing 11th on the grid.

Alesi, fired up for the race in front of his home crowd, had tangled with Brundle. "He overtook me, pushed me onto the grass and then slowed," said the English driver. "I passed him and he came racing alongside and dropped a wheel inside mine. I went flying into the air. It was crazy, I cannot believe he did a thing like that." Later the two met in the pits and Alesi, who believed that Brundle had deliberately slowed to block him, made his message plain. "If you try to **** with me, I will **** you," he told Brundle. At speeds reaching 203mph, it added another dimension to an already dangerous game.

Damon Hill, after spending the morning sitting around while Brabham fought out their latest money problem, this time with engine supplier Judd, eventually had his qualifying times scrubbed as the car was found to be underweight. Saturday morning found Mansell bright and early at the circuit which he clearly loves. "I have happy memories here. It is good to be around it," he said. The temperature was even higher and this time the Williams drivers used the RS4 engines. Mansell had even gone off at one corner onto the grass at Tosa.

Only Patrese and Brundle among the top drivers could improve their Friday times after their troubles. Patrese took up his regular position at number two on the grid while Brundle leaped to sixth ahead of Alesi and alongside Schumacher. It was a welcome relief for Brundle, who admitted that he felt under intense pressure from his German team-mate, poor results and rumours of a replacement. So they lined up on the grid two-by-two at the front. Williams, McLaren, Benetton, Ferrari and Lotus continued to have problems, Johnny Herbert just making it into the race at 26th in the new car, Mika Haakinen failing in the old one.

Race day dawned in Sunday best and as the time for the race start approached, the temperature soared into the 80s. Luck, the key ingredient in any sporting year and so often missing from the Mansell armoury, was with him.

On the warm-up lap, he found problems with his clutch and the revs were hitting the limiter. There would be no time to fix it on the grid. He would need either to head into the pits and miss the grid start or to run in hope and make a stop. He was saved by Austria's brilliant young driver, Karl Wendlinger, who stalled his March car as they waited for the green light. For safety reasons, the start was aborted and that gave Mansell time to talk to his engineers who told him what to do. "I floored the clutch at the second start and, fortunately, it grabbed and away I went. After that it was fine." From then on the others saw Mansell only as he went past and it was just 88 minutes before the red rivers of the *tifosi* were pouring down from the Rivazza to pay homage to *Il Leone*. What had been expected to be a tough, wheel-to-wheel battle had been turned into a parade by Mansell.

Mansell was flying from the start and after ten laps had five-second lead on Patrese and 18 seconds on Senna. After 20 laps it was 26 and 30 seconds. It was the cushion he required on a very hot day which was tough on drivers, engines and tyres. Conservation of all three was essential to last the 60 laps covering 187 miles. He had managed to retain the lead even with a 23rd-lap tyre stop, such was his domination.

There was a scare when Berger and Alesi hit each other on lap 40 and crashed, spilling oil and water on a bend, and a marshal ran across in front of Mansell, giving him a 'wake up call'. Schumacher, admitting that it was his own fault, had had a poor day, losing his place to Brundle at the start, spinning off and retiring on lap 21. Brundle lasted the pace to finish fourth, Senna third, but even as Mansell was celebrating his win on the podium with the champagne shower, the Brazilian was receiving medical treatment in his car. He had suffered cramp and heat exhaustion. Patrese had taken second place but Mansell had won his world record fifth race.

"It is fantastic . . . probably the happiest day of my life," he declared. "Winning five in a row at the start of the season is an historic achievement and it is a great tribute to the team. It has never been done before and I dedicate this to the designers, the engineers, the sponsors. Easy? You have to be joking. It was very tough and I finished the race with cramp and muscle spasms on my right side. It was 32 degrees and I must have lost about eight pounds in weight in the car. I was really glad I trained so hard in the winter. It was not a simple race, although I was always at the front. But what a day, it feels like a dream."

By now the *tifosi*, bedecked in Ferrari red, had long since switched their allegiance to Mansell. They flowed to the pit lane and called for his appearance. It was a fitting way to celebrate a little piece of motor racing history.

Already, however, the future was beginning to intrude. There had been tentative talks with Frank Williams about the 1993 contract, and with only five races of 16 gone Ferrari, extremely unhappy with their own showing, were looking at Mansell with envious eyes. Their car would need big improvements, but even simply having the lion-hearted Mansell back would be a reward for their loyal fans. "We would pay whatever he wanted," said one Ferrari executive, "but at the moment we cannot offer him the car he wants."

Mansell's only appetite now was for more work. He headed back to Silverstone to continue to search for the problems which could yet ruin his five-star season. In moments of doubt, however, he could always comfort himself with a look at the drivers' Championship chart. Mansell led with a perfect 50 points, Patrese was second on 24, Schumacher third with 17 and Senna, the three-times World Champion defending his title, had just 8. Even if Senna won the next five races and Mansell was second, the man from the Midlands would still lead by 30 points. Williams as a team was in an even better situation, for they led the constructors' Championship with 74 points from Benetton Ford on 20 while McLaren Honda took up third on a mere 16.

What about Monaco, the next race? came the question. "I only want to enjoy thinking about having won five in a row," replied Mansell. "That is enough for now. We have earned that. It was very moving to stand on the podium and think about what we have achieved, and, apart from Silverstone, it could not have happened at a better place than Imola. They really like me here, and, believe me, I like them. I have a wonderful relationship with Italian fans."

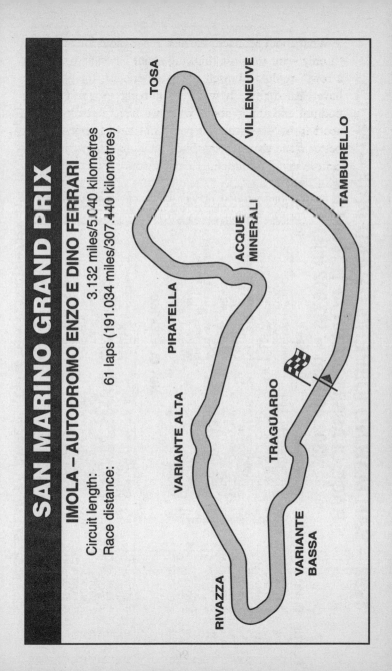

SAN MARINO GRAND PRIX

IMOLA – AUTODROMO ENZO E DINO FERRARI

Circuit length: 3.132 miles/5.040 kilometres
Race distance: 61 laps (191.034 miles/307.440 kilometres)

TOSA

VILLENEUVE

TAMBURELLO

ACQUE MINERALI

PIRATELLA

VARIANTE ALTA

TRAGUARDO

VARIANTE BASSA

RIVAZZA

1992 – SAN MARINO ICEBERG GRAND PRIX – IMOLA

RACE CLASSIFICATION AFTER 60 LAPS

(302.400 km = 187.902 mls)

Pos Nr	Driver		Team Make	Make	Total Time	km/h	mph	Diff
1	5	N. MANSELL	GBR	CANON WILLIAMS TEAM	WILLIAMS RENAULT	1:28'40.927	204.596	127.130	
2	6	R. PATRESE	ITA	CANON WILLIAMS TEAM	WILLIAMS RENAULT	1:28'50.378	204.233	126.905	9.451
3	1	A. SENNA	BRA	HONDA MARLBORO McLAREN	McLAREN HONDA	1:29'29.911	202.730	125.970	48.984
4	20	M. BRUNDLE	GBR	CAMEL BENETTON FORD	BENETTON FORD	1:29'33.934	202.578	125.875	53.007
5	9	M. ALBORETO	ITA	FOOTWORK MUGEN-HONDA	FOOTWORK MUGEN-HONDA	1:29'03.416	200.339	124.485	1 LAP
6	22	P. MARTINI	ITA	SCUDERIA ITALIA	BMS DALLARA FERRARI	1:29'05.964	200.244	124.426	1 LAP
7	33	M. GUGELMIN	BRA	SASOL JORDAN YAMAHA	JORDAN YAMAHA	1:28'46.624	197.565	122.761	2 LAPS
8	3	O. GROUILLARD	FRA	TYRRELL	TYRRELL ILMOR	1:28'56.302	197.206	122.538	2 LAPS
9	26	E. COMAS	FRA	LIGIER GITANES BLONDES	LIGIER RENAULT	1:29'00.360	197.056	122.445	2 LAPS
10	10	A. SUZUKI	JPN	FOOTWORK MUGEN-HONDA	FOOTWORK MUGEN-HONDA	1:29'05.060	196.883	122.337	2 LAPS
11	21	J. LEHTO	FIN	SCUDERIA ITALIA	BMS DALLARA FERRARI	1:26'07.751	200.127	124.353	3 LAPS
12	16	K. WENDLINGER	AUT	MARCH F.1	MARCH ILMOR	1:28'44.703	194.228	120.688	3 LAPS
13	17	P. BELMONDO	FRA	MARCH F.1	MARCH ILMOR	1:29'55.028	191.697	119.115	3 LAPS
14	4	A. DE CESARIS	ITA	TYRRELL	TYRRELL ILMOR	1:23'57.839	198.085	123.084	5 LAPS

NOT CLASSIFIED

								COVERED
15	30	U. KATAYAMA	JPN	CENTRAL PARK-VEN. LARR.	VENTURI LAMBORGHINI	1:01'29.393	196.715	122.233	40 LAPS
16	27	J. ALESI	FRA	FERRARI	FERRARI	58'19.558	202.202	125.642	39 LAPS
17	2	G. BERGER	AUT	HONDA MARLBORO McLAREN	McLAREN HONDA	58'20.384	202.154	125.613	39 LAPS
18	29	B. GACHOT	FRA	CENTRAL PARK-VEN. LARR.	VENTURI LAMBORGHINI	49'11.887	196.690	122.218	32 LAPS
19	25	T. BOUTSEN	BEL	LIGIER GITANES BLONDES	LIGIER RENAULT	44'08.026	198.705	123.470	29 LAPS
20	32	S. MODENA	ITA	SASOL JORDAN YAMAHA	JORDAN YAMAHA	39'00.421	193.811	120.429	25 LAPS
21	24	G. MORBIDELLI	ITA	MINARDI TEAM	MINARDI LAMBORGHINI	37'04.119	195.788	121.657	24 LAPS
22	15	G. TARQUINI	ITA	FONDMETAL F1	FONDMETAL FORD	37'35.797	193.039	119.949	24 LAPS
23	19	M. SCHUMACHER	GER	CAMEL BENETTON FORD	BENETTON FORD	33'43.754	179.310	111.418	20 LAPS
24	28	I. CAPELLI	ITA	FERRARI	FERRARI	16'44.279	198.734	123.487	11 LAPS
25	23	C. FITTIPALDI	BRA	MINARDI TEAM	MINARDI LAMBORGHINI	12'35.077	192.235	119.449	8 LAPS
26	12	J. HERBERT	GBR	TEAM LOTUS	LOTUS FORD	14'59.254	181.414	100.298	8 LAPS

FASTEST LAP: 6 R. PATRESE – Lap 60 Time: 1'26.100 (210.732 km/h = 130.943 mph)

Monaco Grand Prix

Monte Carlo

Nigel Mansell gazed out across the harbour at Monte
Carlo where cruisers and yachts laden with champagne
and caviar rolled lazily in the afternoon sun. The 39-
year-old Englishman was not looking at the multi-million
floating palaces, however; instead he focused on the
circuit he feared could end his victory roll. "I like Monte
Carlo but the track does not like me," he said.

"I have never won here and it would be nice to break
my duck, but it is a lottery – a casino, as the Italians say
– because the streets are so tight. If you have a problem
in qualifying or a bad start you are in a terrible situation
because it is almost impossible to overtake. This is a
one-off race. There is nowhere else like it."

For the second time in the season, Mansell had to take
on Ayrton Senna on his home territory. The Brazilian
had made the Principality his base in Europe. In 1988,
when he crashed out of the race while well in the lead, he
nipped straight home to his flat. He knew every bump
and curve of the streets round the town, having walked
them often.

Mansell had been cruelly treated by Monte Carlo. In
11 attempts to conquer the world's most glamorous race,
Mansell had crashed four times and finished in the points
in only four races. Twice he had been in the lead by
around 30 seconds when something had gone wrong.

Senna had much more to look forward to; he had made the race his own, winning the last three in a row. That gave him four wins in five years with two second places.

Senna knew that the power of the Williams would not matter as much on the winding streets in high temperatures, with tyres and metal being tested by up to 3000 gear changes. As Goodyear boss Barry Griffin explained: "The track surface is also a challenge to a tyre company and this year Goodyear, who have a monopoly in Grand Prix racing, and have won 268 Grands Prix, 19 drivers' World Championships and 20 constructors' World Championships, will be supplying only one type of dry racing tyre, the softest D compound.

"The streets, which are normally busy with everyday traffic, become very polished and slick during the previous 12 months, with traffic grime and oil drippings helping to make the road surface very slippery. It provides little mechanical grip for the tyres to interact with. There is only one type of tyre that will provide acceptable performance and it is one with a very soft tread compound, the D tyre."

Monaco sticks to the tradition of using Thursday as the first qualifying day and having Friday as a day off. This stems from the time when those who came – spectators, drivers, teams – visited in holiday mood. There was plenty of time, and the casinos, shows and bars were there for Friday night adventure.

Even these days, when cities everywhere tend to look the same, Marks and Spencer, C&A, McDonalds and other universal conglomerates crowding the high streets, Monaco retains a certain charm. A fading charm, certainly; but the Grand Prix adds to the colour, history and romance of the place, while the grand old lady of Monte Carlo offers much the same to Formula One.

Many now question, however, whether the Grand Prix circus will be able to continue to come to the tiny state. The non-stop rise in the power and speed of the cars and the inability of the circuit to change accordingly – a strength and a failing in one – make racing more and more dangerous. The facilities are now very stretched as the teams come in bigger numbers with more motorhomes and mobile garages. And for those who attend, the prices being asked for hotel rooms, food and drink have reached meltdown stage for plastic cards.

Still they flock here in all manner of transport, the beautiful people in helicopters and yachts, Rolls Royces and Ferraris. Outside the casino you can still see the finest line-up of Ferraris, interspersed with the odd Maserati and Lamborghini. Other people, just as beautiful but without the money, come in everything else from mini-buses to scooters. The streets are crowded and so is every restaurant, but the mood is good and the only drunks are usually loud-mouthed Brits draped in Union Jacks and making a nuisance of themselves.

On the quayside, only the top teams get a harbour view. The others are forced up onto the road above to use a multi-storey car park. Even here, where access is controlled by special passes, the crowds besiege the motorhomes. The only place of refuge is one of the yachts that the teams occasionally hire.

Early on the Thursday morning, Mansell was in a reflective mood. For the first time in the season he had brought along his whole family. They had come over from Florida for the summer and his pleasure was obvious as he watched wife Rosanne and his children, Chloe, Greg and Leo, playing around.

"I wouldn't say that this is the happiest time of my life," he said. "It is not. I no longer have any time to myself. I have compromised my family life, my own life, everything to do what I possibly can. I have put heart and soul and total commitment into this year and, no matter what happens, I will be able to live with myself as a driver and know that I gave it my best shot.

"To have won the first five races is a great tribute to Renault, Elf and the Williams team. It is a fantastic feat. I would have liked more time off in the winter, but we had major decisions to make with the team. We had to decide whether or not to go with the active suspension. Riccardo and I had to work with the system and then advise on whether we thought we should go ahead with it. We did, and it meant a tremendous amount of time, but we were prepared to put that in. Now we are benefiting from all that winter work."

Mansell had led in qualifying and races since the start of the season but he admitted: "It is harder to drive at the front. There is more pressure. You are setting the pace and everyone is shooting at you. To maintain this level is difficult."

He played down his improved performances at the wheel which had beaten the rest in all types of conditions. Surely he was driving at the peak of his career? "I am the same guy doing the same job, but I did train extremely hard in the winter and I put in a lot of mileage. We're talking hours per day, not minutes."

Mansell was perhaps contemplating his life as he looked around at so many citizens of Monte Carlo, affluent like himself, but enjoying their lives with their families. But of course, he was not the only one to have spent a long time away from home: so had the mechanics, the engineers – even the reporters – and this fact seemed to fuel a growing tide of apathy towards Mansell among a group of Grand Prix devotees.

It was a strange thing. Those new to the circuit and those who dealt with Mansell on a day-to-day basis found him good to deal with: usually polite, even under pressure; usually approachable, always newsworthy. But the technical press were less impressed; so too were others who seemed unable to accept that the man they thought would never be a winner was now apparently unbeatable.

They pointed to the technology, the car, the back-up, the team. If some hung onto Mansell's every word, there were others who sneered at every syllable. Mainly they were the people who had never had to deal with top sportsmen in other areas, many of whom are often not available, not polite, not coherent or not helpful.

To add to the pressure, FISA and other associated parties were now debating openly about the domination of Grand Prix by one team. Too much technology, said the men who had followed the circuit since Stirling Moss was a boy. But director general of Renault Raymond Levy insisted: "What better way can there be to demonstrate our expertise than with success in Formula One?

"The immediate consequence for teams and manufacturers of the current technical evolution is that it is forever pushing up costs at an alarming rate. But ongoing technical innovation is the very essence of Formula One.

"For example, I am convinced that the technology behind the automatic gearboxes that are currently making their mark in Formula One will one day be applied to the standard car."

It was a relief for everyone when the cars fired up and snarling and roaring could be heard from V10 and V8 engines. Then, for Mansell, it was down to breaking his duck in Monte Carlo's 50th race. Victory would also mean 27 wins, which would put him alongside Jackie Stewart as Britain's top race-winning driver.

The qualifying session was to prove eventful. Having run extensively in the morning free practice, Mansell appeared after lunch and ploughed through another 25 laps. On his 19th, he finally found the lap he had been seeking to depose Senna, howling round the streets in the hot sun to record 1 minute 20.714 seconds, the only man under the 1.21 mark.

Senna split the Williams drivers, finishing just 0.753 seconds behind Mansell. The word 'just' is relative – it was still a big gap in Formula One terms, but nonetheless narrower than in other races.

Mansell had a moment to remember when he skidded out of the tunnel and headed backwards for the chicane. He entered the chicane sideways, charging hard and fast for the sea wall. "I was waiting for the impact but I dropped the clutch and the car did a 360-degree turn – there was tyre smoke everywhere – and off we went again. I was very lucky, but I was more relieved to get a clear lap on my second set of tyres. As usual, traffic here was a problem, as we expected."

The difference in speeds compared with other circuits is what keeps Monte Carlo safe: Mansell's average was 92mph.

On Friday, Mansell played golf and enjoyed some time with his family. McLaren took time off from trying to solve the mysteries of their MP4/7A engine to unveil their very exclusive Formula One road car, a magnificent £535,000 gull-winged three seater.

There was another boost for Mansell when Senna conceded the World Championship to his rival. "Count me out," he said. "It is a fight between the Williams cars.

Mansell will probably win but Patrese has a chance. The rest of us will have some fun and suffer a bit, but Williams are in another league."

Saturday was another fine, warm day and once again Mansell was hungry for work, packing in 26 laps, more than anyone else. Senna quit when he beat his previous pole time, clocking 1 minute 20.608 seconds on his 14th lap. Patrese beat that by just under three tenths of a second to move up alongside Mansell at the front of the grid. The Englishman, however, bettered Senna's time on three laps, and even after he became the only driver to break into the 1.19s he carried on. Finally, he called a halt just under half a second ahead of Patrese at 1 minute 19.945 seconds.

Not surprisingly, the forecast was for a processional race with the Williams cars blasting off the grid to lead the 72 laps from start to finish. But Senna began rewriting the script from the start.

Mansell held the lead from the green light but Senna edged alongside Patrese and outbraked the Italian to get into the first corner in second place. Any hope Mansell had of keeping his team-mate as a buffer evaporated, but there seemed little danger for Mansell, who mounted his charge immediately. He was almost a second ahead after one run round the 2.068 miles. After ten laps he was a blink of an eye under nine seconds in the lead with Patrese another second away from Senna.

After 20 laps and 41 miles, he was 13.6 seconds clear of Senna, 16 from Patrese and 24 ahead of Alesi and Schumacher, who were battling for fourth. Already the list of casualties was high and the causes were commonplace, broken engines or broken gearboxes being the main problems.

Wisely, Mansell had settled to a steady pace, pulling away inexorably. He added only a second between laps 40 and 50 to go 22 seconds clear, but he had stretched this to 30 by the 60th lap. In the press room, situated on two floors below ground level in a car park, the race was being treated as a foregone conclusion. With just eight laps to go, Mansell had a 28-second lead.

It was boring, repetitive, predictable . . . Quite suddenly, it became dramatic, stunning, confusing: Mansell had disappeared from millions of television screens and from the view of thousands on the circuit.

In a few moments he was back in sight, but moving slowly on lap 71 – agonisingly slowly. Red Five had been to the pits alongside the harbour where it seemed to take an age to get him going again. While he was there Senna flashed past, and Mansell rejoined the circuit 5.1 seconds behind. He admitted later: "When Senna went past I knew it was probably going to be impossible to get ahead again on this circuit."

Mansell chased and harried as the crowds went wild. He had fresh tyres, Senna's were gone and after another lap the gap was down to 4.3 seconds, then 1.9 on 73. He was right on Senna's tail for the last four enthralling laps, diving one way, then another, looking for a gap, trying to cover any error that Senna might make. Mansell had long insisted that the McLaren had better straight line speed and it looked possible as Senna always managed to urge enough yardage between his McLaren and the Williams at every overtaking area.

On the 73rd and 74th laps Mansell set the fastest times, his 12th and 13th quickest laps of the race. Only Martin Brundle, who was to be fifth, had broken the sequence with two hot laps earlier on.

Senna's skill held off Mansell. There was no way through, no debut win in Monte Carlo, no equality with Jackie Stewart.

Mansell staggered from the car in dramatic style. He was exhausted, drained, disappointed, barely able to stand. Eventually he dragged himself to the podium and was held up as he shook hands with Prince Rainier. The champagne bottle seemed to revive him but eventually he sat on the road and let the realisation of defeat wash over him along with the champagne.

So what had happened? At first, even Mansell was unsure. "Coming through the tunnel I almost lost it. The back end went down and I felt immediately that I had a puncture," he said after limping into the press conference on the shoulder of Patrese.

"I was halfway from the pits and had to drive so slowly that I lost 15 seconds or so just getting there. They could not find a puncture and it took a little longer to check and get me going again."

After rumours of a television switch-off and cancelled contracts because of Mansell's dominance, all denied by FOCA, it could not have been a better finish to the race if it had been planned. And, this being Monaco, there were many ready to suggest that the result *had* been pre-arranged.

Mansell had been ordered to let Senna win, it was said. A deal had been done between McLaren, Williams and FISA; someone had seen someone else shoot Mansell's rear tyre; another claimed that Mansell had deliberately slowed down to let Senna catch up for the finish but it had gone wrong. All this was incredible and completely untrue. The truth, however was to take a week to emerge and a lot of investigative work by Williams, who shipped the cars back to Britain. But they were able to confirm, before they left, along with Goodyear, that there had been no puncture.

After extensive checks, Williams found that a wheel-nut had loosened through a freak combination of thread wear and vibration. The wheel had worked loose, rubbed against a brake caliper and the car had felt 'washy' at the back. When Mansell had hollered on the radio to the pits: "Puncture, puncture. I am coming in", he had done the right thing. He could have ended up with a three wheeler.

"Ayrton drove fantastically well," said Mansell later. "I tried everything I knew but he second-guessed me every time. I tried to get past whenever possible but he held me off. I don't blame him. It was a fantastic finish.

"I think we were both probably driving over the limit in the end, but his car was just too wide to get past. And, as I said before, the McLaren did not exactly seem to be short of straight line power to keep ahead.

"People continue to say that we have the most powerful engine, but I was right on his gearbox several times in the tunnel and coming out I was a car length behind."

Senna could not help retorting: "Maybe, Nigel, you should try a little less wing the next time so you go faster on the straight."

"Monaco for Ayrton is like Silverstone for me," said Mansell. "He has won five times here and I have not won at all. You have to have an element of luck here. As we saw today, so many things can happen. You can say that it is not a fair race, but then, is motor racing fair in general? Many things can go wrong, but fortunately there is only one Monaco on the calendar. If there were more like Monte Carlo, then perhaps I would be upset. But I don't have a problem with Monaco."

Mansell looked drained by the final 15 minutes of high drama and he admitted: "It is the most important second place of my life – tinged with disappointment."

Yet for all that happened at Monaco, the Championship scoreboard was still heavily in favour of Mansell – hence his comment about his most valuable second place. He now had 56 points, Patrese, who had quietly finished third, was on 28, Schumacher, who was fourth in the race, had 20 and Senna 18.

Yet it was a very significant weekend, on and off the track. For the first time, contract talk had surfaced. One story was that Mansell was about to re-sign with Williams for two more years; more significantly, another suggested that three-times World Champion Alain Prost, having a year out, would sign for Williams as Mansell's partner.

Senna went home with the trophy for winning five Monaco Grands Prix, named after the man who first achieved the feat, Graham Hill. Mansell contemplated the end of his winning streak but, as it turned out, it was not so much the end of the beginning as the beginning of a bitter sweet end.

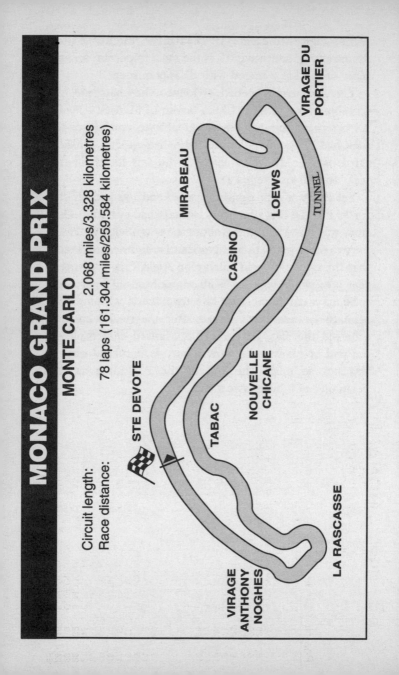

1992 – MONACO GRAND PRIX – MONTECARLO

RACE CLASSIFICATION AFTER 78 LAPS

(259.584 km = 161.298 mls)

Pos	Nr	Driver		Make	Team Make		Total Time	km/h	mph	Diff
1	1	A. SENNA	BRA	McLAREN HONDA	HONDA MARLBORO McLAREN		1:50'59.372	140.329	87.196	
2	5	N. MANSELL	GBR	WILLIAMS RENAULT	CANON WILLIAMS TEAM		1:50'59.587	140.324	87.194	0.215
3	6	R. PATRESE	ITA	WILLIAMS RENAULT	CANON WILLIAMS TEAM		1:51'31.215	139.661	86.781	31.843
4	19	M. SCHUMACHER	GER	BENETTON FORD	CAMEL BENETTON FORD		1:51'38.666	139.506	86.685	39.204
5	20	M. BRUNDLE	GBR	BENETTON FORD	CAMEL BENETTON FORD		1:52'20.719	138.635	80.144	1'21.347
6	29	B. GACHOT	FRA	VENTURI LAMBORGHINI	CENTRAL PARK-VEN. LARR.		1:51'23.958	138.020	85.762	1 LAP
7	9	M. ALBORETO	ITA	FOOTWORK MUGEN-HONDA	FOOTWORK MUGEN-HONDA		1:51'45.533	137.576	86.486	1 LAP
8	23	C. FITTIPALDI	BRA	MINARDI LAMBORGHINI	MINARDI TEAM		1:52'19.665	136.879	85.053	1 LAP
9	21	J. LEHTO	FIN	BMS DALLARA FERRARI	SCUDERIA ITALIA		1:51'08.976	136.534	84.838	2 LAPS
10	26	E. COMAS	FRA	LIGIER GITANES BLONDES	LIGIER GITANES BLONDES		1:51'17.'21	136.355	84.727	2 LAPS
11	10	A. SUZUKI	JPN	FOOTWORK MUGEN-HONDA	FOOTWORK MUGEN-HONDA		1:51'19.200	136.325	84.708	2 LAPS
12	25	T. BOUTSEN	BEL	LIGIER RENAULT	LIGIER GITANES BLONDES		1:51'49.764	133.918	83.213	3 LAPS

NOT CLASSIFIED

Pos	Nr	Driver		Make	Team Make		Total Time	km/h	mph	COVERED
13	28	I. CAPELLI	ITA	FERRARI	FERRARI		1:26'30.427	138.495	86.067	60 LAPS
14	2	G. BERGER	AUT	McLAREN HONDA	HONDA MARLBORO McLAREN		46'15.942	138.110	85.818	32 LAPS
15	11	M. HAKKINEN	FIN	LOTUS FORD	TEAM LOTUS		43'45.876	136.878	85.062	30 LAPS
16	27	J. ALESI	FRA	FERRARI	FERRARI		40'30.381	138.029	85.767	28 LAPS
17	33	M. GUGELMIN	BRA	JORDAN YAMAHA	SASOL JORDAN YAMAHA		26'41.475	134.660	83.674	18 LAPS
18	12	J. HERBERT	GBR	LOTUS FORD	TEAM LOTUS		24'53.571	136.367	84.734	17 LAPS
19	34	R. MORENO	BRA	ANDREA MODA FORMULA	ANDREA MODA FORMULA		17'16.217	127.183	79.028	11 LAPS
20	4	A. DE CESARIS	ITA	TYRRELL	TYRRELL		13'22.464	134.370	83.494	9 LAPS
21	15	G. TARQUINI	ITA	FONDMETAL FORD	FONDMETAL F1		14'09.693	126.901	78.853	9 LAPS
22	32	S. MODENA	ITA	JORDAN YAMAHA	SASOL JORDAN YAMAHA		9'15.498	129.406	80.409	6 LAPS
23	3	O. GROUILLARD	FRA	TYRRELL ILMOR	TYRRELL		6'21.532	125.607	78.049	4 LAPS
24	16	K. WENDLINGER	AUT	MARCH ILMOR	MARCH F.1		1'44.613	114.525	71.163	1 LAP
25	24	G. MORBIDELLI	ITA	MINARDI LAMBORGHINI	MINARDI TEAM		5'34.500	35.817	22.256	1 LAP

FASTEST LAP: 5 N. MANSELL – Lap 74 Time: 1'21.598 (146.827 km/h = 91.234 mph)

Canadian Grand Prix

Montreal

By the time the Canadian Grand Prix rolled along, all attention was on the row over FISA's proposed rule changes. It would have to be an extraordinary race to compensate for the threat of two leading companies to pull out and the radical ideas being floated. It was.

Perversity or good marketing? No one in Grand Prix racing can quite make up their minds about the switch back across the Atlantic after three races in Europe to tackle the Canadian race in Montreal. It rekindles interest in North America but upsets the routine on the European circuit and adds to costs.

Mansell and company packed in another test session at the scene of July's French Grand Prix before jumping the pond. As usual, the Williams car performed like a cat on cream and was a second ahead of the opposition.

After the drama of Monaco it was surely too much to hope for another blockbuster race, but this was to be another controversial two hours. The heat on the track was almost as fierce as the controversy off it. FISA finally cracked under the strain of seeing their golden cow being milked by Williams.

It seemed odd to many that there had been no panic for change when McLaren was winning race after race, but now the rule changes came in with a vengeance. Pace cars were to be introduced à la Indycar series, where after a race stoppage the cars would keep their time differentials but line up behind the lead car and make a moving start rather than another standing start. This was reasonably popular, but Goodyear were as displeased as the drivers to learn that narrower tyres were to be introduced, three inches slimmer with smaller 'footprints'. The tyre company was less than delighted that the decision had been taken without consultation. A spokesman said: "Drivers are complaining now about lack of grip. If you reduce the width by 25 per cent you won't have seen anything yet. We are in business to produce good, safe tyres and if we have a lot more spins with narrower tyres, it will not reflect well on us."

A change in tyres was also going to cost the company money. Moulds would have to be changed, and more tyres would be required because the narrower, harder versions would mean more pit stops. Cornering speeds would be lowered but drivers complained that the safety measures offered by the wider rear tyres would be reduced. The aim was to improve and increase overtaking chances and end the processional races. Ironically, as fate was to prove for Mansell, it would make the Formula One cars more like Indycars.

Another unhappy company was French fuel producer Elf, the Williams supplier. A standard fuel would be used, which would have to be 'green', but Elf had developed a range of mixtures for the Renault engines, used by Williams and Ligier. If the rule is in, we are out, they insisted – although you can expect to see them next season.

Montreal followed the style of Monte Carlo. The circuit, honed from the street of the old Olympic Village, is narrow and twisty but lacks the romance of the old European Principality. Yet is it unique, for the Circuit

Gilles Villeneuve, a 2.7-mile track, sits on a small island, Ile Nôtre Dame, in the St Lawrence river.

Mansell stood on the victory podium in 1986 but twice since then Ayrton Senna had enjoyed the same experience. The previous year's winner, Nelson Piquet, was recovering in hospital after smashing both legs horribly in a crash during the build-up to the Indianapolis 500.

Senna arrived in Canada claiming that it would take another fluke to prevent Mansell and the Canon Williams Renault team from winning their sixth race of the season. He had better feelings towards his Marlboro McLaren Honda after the Monte Carlo success, but he said: "What happened there means nothing here. There is no way we can stop Williams in this race. The only thing that can stop them is a problem with the car. If they break down we have a chance. We need to make three or four big changes to our car, but that will not happen for two or three races."

For Mansell Canada held bad memories. A year earlier, his title charge had stumbled when he led from the start only for his engine to cut out on the final lap.

The first shock came in the opening qualifying session. For the first time in the season, Mansell failed to take provisional pole. A fault in a suspension component had got him off to a poor start in the free practice on Friday morning. Many went for a spin, Mansell among them, but he was second by lunchtime and went back to the motorhome for some pasta.

In the official session in the afternoon he was frustrated by heavy traffic on the circuit, complained of lack of grip and found that the Renault RS4 engine had less power than it should have had and than his older engine normally offered.

The top two drivers were out early to take advantage of

slightly cooler conditions. Mansell was quickest, but this time it was Senna who pressed on, building momentum. Mansell even tried switching off his traction control to find stability in the car's performance. "I have been saying all along that McLaren are improving and Honda are getting more power," said Mansell. "Now it looks worse than I feared. We are struggling."

More frustratingly, Friday morning's sunshine faded at lunchtime, when a breeze sprang up and the weather cooled. The waters of the surrounding river began to ruffle and sure enough, by evening, it was raining heavily. The grey clouds suited Mansell's mood as he returned to a wet circuit in the morning. But in the free practice, like the weather, he brightened and suddenly he was flying again, lapping in 1 minute 19.638 seconds, the best time of the weekend.

"We have got the set-up right now and it feels good," said Nigel as he emerged from the garage. "We will just have to hope for decent weather this afternoon." As is his wont, he was in the car and ready to go before the session began. Barely two minutes had gone by before Red Five was barrelling down the pit lane and into the action. Mansell spun as he wound up the speed but was quickly on the pace again and broke through to 1 minute 19.948 seconds, third fastest.

Senna then went one worse than his rival, spinning off but having to leave the car in a gravel trap and make the long, lonely walk back to the pits to take out the spare. Others were sliding, too; even a safety car rushing to an accident in which J. J. Lehto's Dallara lost a wheel and swept into a gravel trap.

In the closing minutes, Mansell reappeared to have one last lunge at the pole position. Such was the expectation of Mansell after his first six races that few doubted that he would find the time. It was not to be. Senna found himself at his first pole press conference of the season. Yes, he agreed, there had been a huge improvement in Honda's engine, things were getting better. Yet he still believed that if Mansell was first to the corner in the race it would all be over, such was his regard for the Williams Renault combination.

It seemed barely credible that Mansell was not only missing from pole but absent from the front row of the grid, but at least the weather was hot and sunny again for the 69-lap race. Patrese was in second place to Senna and Berger was behind him, alongside Mansell. When the lights changed, Mansell rocketed past Patrese but had to tuck in behind Senna.

No fewer than 11 cars followed each other round – and round and round and round. So on it went, an unremarkable procession, everyone waiting for an error, a mechanical failure, the unexpected. What happened next was due to a combination of several factors.

Everyone had had a thought about overtaking but suddenly it was Mansell who went for it at the end of lap 15. Senna went wide into the bend, Mansell went inside and was off the clean line alongside in what they call 'the marbles', the dirty area where grip is less certain. Senna held his line and Mansell could not turn in. He had nowhere to go. His car careered across the kerb, lost a wing in the sand trap, crossed the chicane in front of Senna, and came spinning back onto the track.

Senna almost caught the Williams car, which was shedding debris as he came past. Everyone else steered their way round Mansell who sat in his car for another half minute. Eventually he allowed himself to be helped from the car and carried over the track wall. As Senna sailed past seconds later, Mansell shook his fist angrily at the Brazilian.

Now he went in search of targets, finding first the McLaren boss Ron Dennis in the pits. Mansell made his views known in forcible terms to a man who has never been his greatest ally, and then turned his attention to Peter Warr, a FISA steward and a former colleague at Lotus. He registered his complaints but there was to be no official help. Mansell, face red, veins sticking out, was raging and he let fly: "I got inside Senna and he pushed me off." Later he issued a short statement, saying: "I have always been told that if you cannot say something good about somebody then it is best to say nothing at all. That is all I have to say."

But he had said a lot more to Dennis. It was reported that he had suggested that the McLaren boss take action against his star. Dennis, as sardonic as usual, claimed later that Mansell had said: "Ron, I made a mistake, I hope Ayrton wins." More seriously, he added: "It is understandable how Nigel should react but the cars definitely did not touch. He made a mistake."

Senna, hardly surprisingly, saw it differently from Mansell, explaining: "He realised he could not brake in time for the corner, so he lined up the car for the middle of the kerb and hoped to clear it. But he hit it with such force that he appeared to land on the car's nose."

Senna retired himself on the 38th lap, engine trouble caused by an electrical fault forcing him out. He walked back to the pits, stopping for what looked like a reasonably friendly chat with Frank Williams on the way to the McLaren garage. That allowed his team-mate, Gerhard Berger, who had moved up to second when Patrese had eased slightly to avoid Mansell, to go on to victory.

Berger, who had been running behind Mansell when

the great drama had exploded, then gave his eye-witness view of events. "In the early part of the race it was a question of discipline, I think. Everyone knows that if you want to overtake you must go off line, and off line the track is dirty and you lose grip. It was early in the race, and there was no reason for anybody to do it. The first was Mansell, at the same place where I had tried to overtake Patrese, and if I am honest, I had thought there was no way it was going to work. When I saw Nigel go for it I thought the same thing, that it was not going to work. Nigel had to go onto the dirty surface and he lost it."

Patrese saw his hopes of points to close up on Mansell disappear with his gearbox selections, which finally ran out on the 43rd lap. He was reticent at first but later said: "Nigel decided to take the inside line, which was dirty and slippery. Ayrton did not help him but he was not unfair. The cars did not touch. I think Nigel made a mistake."

Frank Williams gave Mansell a vote of confidence, insisting: "I certainly have no thoughts that Nigel might have tried to overtake too early or have done anything risky. He is a terrific driver. After this, any complacency in the team has been blown away."

Williams team manager Peter Windsor, a friend and colleague of Mansell's for years, said: "Too many people have been too quick to condemn Nigel. This is not an area of the circuit where you would overtake. There is a quick S-bend, a short straight and a slow chicane with single file entry. Senna may have slowed slightly on his approach to the corner – it has happened before – and Nigel was so close that he had to move across. Senna moved to his right and Nigel was forced off line and had nowhere to go except into the sand.

The incident totally dominated the race, leaving the

podium celebrations with a new look and new men. Berger enjoyed the sound of the Austrian anthem for the first time in the season and the 26th of his career. Amazingly, in his first full season, Michael Schumacher had a second place and was now on 26 points, just two fewer than Patrese, Grand Prix's most experienced driver. Ferrari were also given a night of delight – rare in Montreal or anywhere in 1992 – Jean Alesi having nursed his Prancing Horse to third place.

Mansell packed up and left to return to his family for a week before another test programme. Once again, he was the subject of everyone's conversation as they scattered among the smart restaurants, bars and clubs of Montreal. Why had he not been content to sit tight and wait for something to happen? Even if he had not got past Senna, he would have earned six more points.

Mansell's early move was inexplicable. Either it was a foolhardy piece of adventure, a red-mist manoeuvre or a piece of cunning by Senna to lure the Englishman into an error. There is no doubt that one of the thrilling aspects of Mansell the driver is his innate spirit as a racer. He has often been criticised for punishing the car needlessly, putting in fast laps near the end when he could cruise. These are not complaints you hear from the paying customers or television directors.

Mansell is at his most thrilling when he slips into race mode. It puts everyone on edge, team members, other drivers, journalists, because something special can be seen. He is, as the Americans say, a balls-out driver. The problem is that when you walk on the edge occasionally you fall over it, but the danger is a wonderful sensation for the watchers and the walker.

What makes Mansell great can also be his failing, then, but as long as the balance is in his favour, he is highly employable. The employment talk continued to bubble off the track in Canada. There was further mention of Mansell re-signing, but no clues from the man himself.

Around the pits were two young Americans from Indycar racing, Michael Andretti and Al Unser Jr. Andretti revealed that he had turned down a Ferrari drive for 1992. His name was to surface again before the end of the season, linked to those of Senna and Mansell. Already tiny pieces of the 1993 jigsaw were appearing, although not yet being put in place.

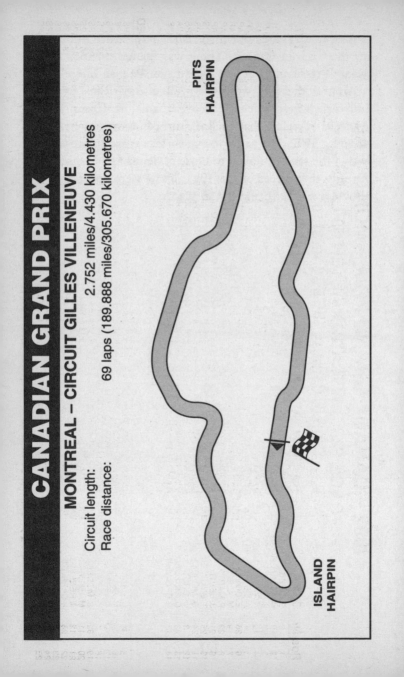

1992 – CANADA GRAND PRIX – MONTREAL

RACE CLASSIFICATION AFTER 69 LAPS

(305.670 km = 189.934 mls)

Pos	Nr	Driver		Team Make	Make	Total Time	km/h	mph	Diff
1	2	G. BERGER	AUT	HONDA MARLBORO McLAREN	McLAREN HONDA	1:37'08.299	188.805	117.318	
2	19	M. SCHUMACHER	GER	CAMEL BENETTON FORD	BENETTON FORD	1:37'20.700	188.404	117.069	12.401
3	27	J. ALESI	FRA	FERRARI	FERRARI	1:38'15.626	188.649	115.978	1'07.327
4	16	K. WENDLINGER	AUT	MARCH F.1	MARCH ILMOR	1:37'15.022	185.111	115.022	1 LAP
5	4	A. DE CESARIS	ITA	TYRRELL	TYRRELL ILMOR	1:37'45.620	184.853	114.863	1 LAP
6	26	E. COMAS	FRA	LIGIER GITANES BLONDES	LIGIER RENAULT	1:37'47.876	184.814	114.838	1 LAP
7	9	M. ALBORETO	ITA	FOOTWORK MUGEN-HONDA	FOOTWORK MUGEN-HONDA	1:37'48.065	184.808	114.834	1 LAP
8	22	P. MARTINI	ITA	SCUDERIA ITALIA	BMS DALLARA FERRARI	1:36'17.842	183.875	114.254	1 LAP
9	21	J. LEHTO	FIN	SCUDERIA ITALIA	BMS DALLARA FERRARI	1:36'20.371	183.796	114.205	1 LAP
10	25	T. BOUTSEN	BEL	LIGIER GITANES BLONDES	LIGIER RENAULT	1:37'25.099	182.868	113.629	2 LAPS
11	24	G. MORBIDELLI	ITA	MINARDI TEAM	MINARDI LAMBORGHINI	1:37'32.615	182.821	113.599	2 LAPS
12	3	O. GROUILLARD	FRA	TYRRELL	TYRRELL ILMOR	1:37'33.977	182.528	113.418	2 LAPS
13	23	C. FITTIPALDI	BRA	MINARDI TEAM	MINARDI LAMBORGHINI	1:34'46.532	182.230	113.232	4 LAPA
14	17	P. BELMONDO	FRA	MARCH F.1	MARCH ILMOR	1:37'43.557	174.070	108.162	5 LAPS

NOT CLASSIFIED

									COVERED
15	30	U. KATAYAMA	JPN	CENTRAL PARK-VEN. LARR.	VENTURI LAMBORGHINI	1:27'42.563	184.858	114.866	61 LAPS
16	20	M. BRUNDLE	GBR	CAMEL BENETTON FORD	BENETTON FORD	1:03'57.338	187.020	116.209	45 LAPS
17	6	R. PATRESE	ITA	CANON WILLIAMS TEAM	WILLIAMS RENAULT	1:01'09.553	186.879	116.121	43 LAPS
18	1	A. SENNA	BRA	HONDA MARLBORO McLAREN	McLAREN HONDA	53'24.428	186.472	115.868	37 LAPS
19	32	S. MODENA	ITA	SASOL JORDAN YAMAHA	JORDAN YAMAHA	53'13.294	179.792	111.717	36 LAPS
20	11	M. HAKKINEN	FIN	TEAM LOTUS	LOTUS FORD	50'15.921	185.078	115.002	35 LAPS
21	12	J. HERBERT	GBR	TEAM LOTUS	LOTUS FORD	48'46.594	185.277	115.126	34 LAPS
22	28	I. CAPELLI	ITA	FERRARI	FERRARI	26'10.057	182.837	113.609	18 LAPS
23	5	N. MANSELL	GBR	CANON WILLIAMS TEAM	WILLIAMS RENAULT	20'13.518	183.987	114.324	14 LAPS
24	33	M. GUGELMIN	BRA	SASOL JORDAN YAMAHA	JORDAN YAMAHA	21'37.750	176.117	109.434	14 LAPS
25	29	B. GACHOT	FRA	CENTRAL PARK-VEN. LARR.	VENTURI LAMBORGHINI	24'27.961	152.097	94.508	14 LAPS

FASTEST LAP: 2 G. BERGER – Lap 61 Time:1'22.325 (193.720 km/h = 120.372 mph)

French Grand Prix

Magny-Cours

The scene was idyllic and very French. In the middle of Fontainebleau Forest, a group of old men sat at a picnic table discussing life over a bottle of wine while nearby another group played *boules*. The only difference was that they were picnicking on the N7, the main route which runs through the scenic town, and they were in the middle of a 300-lorry jam.

France was almost paralysed and a big fat question-mark hung over the French Grand Prix at Nevers Magny-Cours in the centre of the country. The truckers were protesting about a new road traffic law which would put them off the road if they collected a small number of points. Formula One's drivers were desperate to race to collect as many points as possible.

Mansell was still chasing his 27th win to equal the record of Jackie Stewart, who said: "Good luck to Nigel. If he does break the record then he does so with my best wishes. Records are made to be broken, and to have held it for 19 years is very nice, but I really felt it had been broken when Alain Prost and then Ayrton Senna moved ahead of me with more wins. I had not considered it in British terms.

"Mansell has an edge with the Williams Renault, but no more so than Senna has had with the McLaren Honda set-up in the last three years. Senna and Prost had what I call the unfair advantage – now Nigel has that. This year Senna does not have the world-beating machinery, and for the first time he does not look like the bullet-proof superman any more. When you don't have that advantage you drive a bit harder, and that is tough on the car and on yourself – you wear out the machinery and your body faster."

Mansell, however, had been wearing out parts pretty quickly himself in the previous two races in Monte Carlo and Canada. France offered him a more straightforward chance to get back on top in that the track was a change from the twisting, narrow circuits of the previous two races. But neither of the Williams drivers was completely happy. Riccardo Patrese was blunt about the two-year-old circuit, which was built with public funds to help revitalise the region. "I don't like it," said the Italian. "The track is nearly impossible for overtaking. Maybe there is a place at the end of the straight near the hairpin, but it is not easy."

Mansell said: "The new circuits tend to be too narrow. I know that the organisers at Magny-Cours have tried to do something about this, so I hope it will be better this year. Apart from that, I am very happy in France as I won here last year and twice at the Paul Ricard circuit. It is always a good warm-up for my home Grand Prix a week later."

Getting to the circuit was to prove more of a headache than actually driving on it. Those heading down from the coast or Paris found that what was usually a two-hour journey took four times longer. The huge fleet of team trucks and motorhomes somehow got there, surviving threats, blackmail, road blocks, petrol shortages and a thousand signs saying 'deviation'.

Perry McCarthy's Andrea Moda team added to their

catalogue of troubles by managing to be the only team to fail to get through. Yet again McCarthy was a spectator. On Friday morning there were only 30 cars, so no pre-qualifying was necessary. Some of the Vauxhall Euro series teams failed to make it and there were scares for the Formula One teams, but come Thursday, the paddock was full and the circus was ready to stage its spectacular show once again.

Whether any spectators would get through to see it was another matter, but the television cameras were there so, barring the rumoured track invasion by the truckers, the show would go on.

Mansell and Patrese had already set their mark before the race in three days' testing at Silverstone. Nigel's best time was 1 minute 20.5 seconds, faster than his pole time for the 1991 British Grand Prix.

For some, fuel was a problem. The lorry drivers' strike took a ten-minute bite out of the Benetton Ford session as Martin Brundle and Michael Schumacher had to wait for the late arrival of their fuel tanker, and Johnny Herbert, in the new Lotus, had to borrow a few gallons of petrol as the BP tanker was also held up in the blockades. Agip had used helicopters to fly in 88 drums of fuel for their customers, including Ferrari, and Mobil arrived just 15 minutes before the free practice session began.

The only fuel problem for Mansell was getting it from the tank into the key areas of the engine. Mansell and Patrese had wheeled out their cars with Renault RS4 engines. Soon Mansell was walking home, his car stricken by a sudden loss of fuel pressure. To the rescue came the trusty RS3C powered version, and he set fastest time of the morning, nearly a second ahead of Senna, who was third behind Patrese. Mansell was adamant: "We are not quite sure what caused the problem but the engine has to come out."

Early in the official qualifying session, Mansell went out and shot round in 1 minute 15.047 seconds and the day finished in the regular order – at least the regular order prior to Canada – of Mansell first, Patrese second, Senna third, and Berger and Schumacher following on. The gap was significant, however. There were 1.8 seconds between Mansell and Senna, a lifetime in motor racing, but again the spectre of McLaren rose in Mansell's thoughts. "I used my race car with the RS4 engine to set my best time," he said, "but I expect a much stronger challenge from the opposition than we got today. I am bewildered by their performance. I don't think it is a real reflection of what they can do. There is no way their times are realistic."

But again events off the track stole the show. McLaren boss Ron Dennis held a pre-British mid-season press lunch which proved interesting in several ways. He was asked if he thought McLaren could still win the World Championship and replied: "I must choose my words carefully. In normal circumstances, no. But I don't think we are in a normal situation. I think there is an emotional inconsistency of performance in some people." Could he enlarge, was he talking of someone in particular? "Let's just say . . . there is a police expression 'aided and abetted'."

It seemed a thinly-veiled attack on Mansell after his behaviour in Montreal, where he had berated Dennis about Senna's driving. Mansell was less than impressed and replied: "The guy is jealous as hell. It is good to see them rattled. Why else would he say something like that? The red and white team have been on top of the world for years and they don't like it now that Williams and Renault

128

are doing such a magnificent job. We made history by winning five races in a row, and it should have been six had it not been for someone in a McLaren. He can say what he likes but it doesn't bother me. The opposition were on top in Montreal but where are they now?"

The gloves were off without a doubt, and the fists were not flying in only one direction. Dennis also had a swing at FISA's newly-published race calendar for 1993. "I am absolutely disgusted with it," said Dennis. "It was imposed on every single team without consultation. The concept of finishing one Grand Prix season in the second week of November and starting again at the end of February demonstrates a total lack of understanding of what Grand Prix racing is all about. There is no breathing space."

The level of insularity within motor racing was also shown in sharp relief at the lunch when Dennis announced that he had recently been at a function in the company of Nick Faldo. He had been 'astounded' to find that Faldo had as much commitment to winning as any of his drivers. Shocked motor sport die-hards reeled at the news that other sports people could be as dedicated to victory – some for a touch less than £10 million a year.

The real world is another world for those who live in Formula One and the weekend was spent worrying about how to get round the truckers to get back in time for the British Grand Prix. They had a point, however, as a man had appeared at the media office looking for a press kit with a circuit map and had been asked if he was a journalist. "I am Albert, a truck driver," he replied. "I only need the map to work out which entrances we are going to block."

Heavy rain fell overnight on a track that according to

Mansell lacked grip, washing off any rubber that had been laid down in the first session. On a cloudy Saturday morning, it made little difference as Mansell hot-footed round in 1 minute 14.117 seconds before sliding off the track with his foot jammed between the brake and the accelerator.

Christian Fittipaldi became the first victim of the track when he crashed his Minardi and was flown to hospital with neck problems.

Senna and Berger had taken third and fifth places in the morning with the World Champion closing up on Mansell, and they were optimistic about getting closer in the afternoon session. Mansell, however, had other plans. While most sought to get into the 1.15 bracket and only Mansell, Patrese and Senna had achieved the 1.14s, the man in Red Five suddenly burst through into the 1.13s. It was a spectacular way to achieve the 24th pole position of his career, and he hoisted himself alongside Niki Lauda and Nelson Piquet.

Mansell was 1.335 seconds ahead of Senna, and nearly half a second in front of Patrese, with an average speed of 128mph. He was pleased with his 1 minute 13.864, but now wondered which car to use in the race. "We still don't know what caused the problem in my race car on Friday and I would really like to be sure that it is not going to happen again in the race. We have to make a major decision. I qualified in the spare car because I am not happy with the race car."

That night a soggy rock concert with fireworks was held but the race was anything but a damp squib. Mansell was back to his dominating best, leading the times in the warm-up session on Sunday morning, and had decided to race in his spare car with the RS3C engine. "We just seem to be off the pace," said Senna, while Schumacher admitted: "We are closer to McLaren but Williams still remain out of reach."

Once more the grid had the early-season look: Williams were on the front row, and the McLarens on the second, with Schumacher in fifth place, Jean Alesi sixth and Martin Brundle seventh. The forecast was far from cheery and the black rain clouds were gathering like vultures over a body. The track was dry as the drivers lined up and the cars exploded down the straight on the green light – but Patrese had the drop on Mansell again.

Strong rumours had again suggested that Alain Prost, who was in evidence at Magny-Cours in his role as a television commentator, would be in a Williams in 1993 – and that would oust Patrese. Perhaps it was this that fired the Italian, who held off Mansell's occasional thrust to take over the lead. But even as Mansell was staring down Patrese's tailpipe, Senna was gazing at the wreck of his car after less than a lap. At the Adelaide hairpin, Michael Schumacher had taken a run at Senna, misjudged it and smashed into the rear of the McLaren, heaving it off the track.

Schumacher limped to the pits and rejoined a lap later after a new nose had been fitted to his Benetton but Senna's race was over. The German lasted another 16 laps but in his haste to climb back up the field he climbed over the top of Stefan Modena's Jordan and this time he was the victim.

By now, the McLaren challenge had failed with Berger's engine. Martin Brundle moved to third. On they charged, but now the rain was falling and on the back straight the weather was worse. The race had been started as a 'dry' event with more than 50 per cent of the field on slicks, and as the new circuit is particularly slippery, the clerk of the course halted proceedings.

Almost immediately the rain eased and most teams started out on slick tyres again, although they changed soon afterwards when it really began to pour. While they were lined up on the grid during the 15-minute halt, Senna stalked down the track and had an animated conversation with Schumacher, presumably pointing out to him the error of his ways on the first lap. "I thought it was right to approach him personally," said Senna. "I asked what he thought he was doing and he apologised and admitted his mistake."

When the race re-started Patrese took the lead again off his 'pole' position. This time it was short-lived – but it was not Patrese's doing. He and Mansell had duelled fiercely before the stoppage and on lap 19 they were at it again. Mansell swooped past half-way round but then Patrese brilliantly re-took his team leader. It was great stuff, but what if they took each other off?

Perish the thought. But Frank Williams had already dealt with the matter, and as they came along in front of the pits and the stands, Patrese's arm came up and he waved Mansell through. It was as quick as it was unexpected, but Mansell was given free road and zoomed into the lead and on to victory.

Behind him Patrese drove on faultlessly but without any real challenge to take second place 46 seconds behind. Afterwards, Patrese was asked about the ding-dong at the start of the second race. "I would say we were dancing, maybe the twist," he replied. But he was in a dark mood, and there was an edge to another comment he made in response to a question about how he felt about being in second place.

"I feel very well. I think the team did a fantastic job, first and second places again. I am very pleased for Nigel and for myself, for everybody. It is my usual place and I am very comfortable with it."

Had he actually waved Mansell through? Patrese looked at the questioner and said nothing. Mansell jumped in to answer, with a laugh: "I can confirm that, yes, he waved me through. But I don't know why." Patrese was asked why he did not want to talk about it and replied: "Because there is not really much to say about it from my point of view. Let's just say that Nigel was pressing me hard and I thought that it was best for the team to let him go." Had there been team orders? Mansell and Patrese were not forthcoming and there was no enlightenment either from Frank Williams, who said: "While we are competing for the Championship how I run the team is my business."

What had happened was that the team's technical director, Patrick Head, had spoken to Patrese during the stoppage and pointed out that Mansell should not be held up in his charge to the Championship. Unless he thought he could win and hold Mansell off, Patrese should let him go. Mansell said later: "Riccardo drove brilliantly. He got a great start and we had a lot of fun. He waved me through, admitting that he knew I was faster. Riccardo is fine. We spoke after the race about the car, which is private, but we have no problems. He is very professional. We get on great together and I really hope the team stays as it is for next season."

This was the first mention made by Mansell of doubts that the personnel might remain the same, but it was not to be the last.

Mansell also had the satisfaction of having equalled Stewart's record and he stated: "I am very proud to be alongside a driver like Jackie. He was a triple World Champion, one of the greatest drivers in the history of the sport."

Mansell was equally delighted that Martin Brundle had finished third in his Camel Benetton Ford while Johnny Herbert's Lotus had finally come good. It was the first time in three years that Britain had managed to get three drivers in the points together. Brundle had been about to retire from the race when he was saved by the rain. He had been passed by Jean Alesi, who drove a remarkable race in his Ferrari, ploughing through the wet on slicks almost as fast as those on rain tyres, until his engine blew.

Mika Haakinen had also led Brundle, whose engine was cutting out in right-hand corners, but when the rain came on, the speed and the G-forces in the corners dropped and the problem cured itself. Even a spin near the end could not halt Brundle who at last had the result he deserved.

"Three Britons in the top six shows the strength in depth we have," said Mansell. "Now they won't have just me to cheer on at Silverstone next week but three of us."

Once Mansell and Patrese had escaped the road blocks and were safely back in Britain, they turned again to the question of team orders. "There were no team orders and there are none for the British," insisted Mansell, while Patrese said: "My action was best for the team." Head, however, while never ordering Patrese to let Mansell go, had said: "Let's not damage both cars. If he is quicker let him go." Patrese, in his helmet and with a lot of noise around him at the re-start of the race, may have misunderstood, hence his attitude, but that day in France cleared the last real obstacle from Mansell's path for it effectively shattered the fragments of the Italian's title dream.

Now Mansell had 66 points, Patrese 34, Schumacher 26, Senna 18, Berger 18, Alesi 11 and Brundle 9. Between them the Williams drivers had amassed 100 points, exactly the same total as the team had in the constructors' World Championship in which McLaren were now second by a single point from Benetton Ford, 36 to 35. Together they were no match for Williams Renault.

Mansell could hardly wait to get home. It was, as he said excitedly, the best week of his year . . . the British Grand Prix.

FRENCH GRAND PRIX

MAGNY-COURS

Circuit length: 2.641 miles/4.250 kilometres
Race distance: 72 laps (190.152 miles/306.000 kilometres)

ADELAIDE

GOLF

IMOLA

CHICANE

LYCÉE

NÜRBURGRING

ESTORIL

GRANDE COURBE

1992 – RHONE POULENC FRENCH GRAND PRIX – MAGNY COURS

RACE CLASSIFICATION AFTER 69 LAPS
(293.250 km = 182.217 mls)

Pos	Nr	Driver		Team Make		Make	Total Time	km/h	mph	Diff
1	5	N. MANSELL	GBR	CANON WILLIAMS TEAM		WILLIAMS RENAULT	1:38'08.459	179.283	111.401	
2	6	R. PATRESE	ITA	CANON WILLIAMS TEAM		WILLIAMS RENAULT	1:38'54.906	177.880	110.529	46.447
3	20	M. BRUNDLE	GBR	CAMEL BENETTON FORD		BENETTON FORD	1:39'21.038	177.100	110.045	1:12.579
4	11	M. HAKKINEN	FIN	TEAM LOTUS		LOTUS FORD	1:38'53.992	175.329	108.944	1 LAP
5	26	E. COMAS	FRA	LIGIER GITANES BLONDES		LIGIER FORD	1:38'57.596	175.222	108.878	1 LAP
6	12	J. HERBERT	GBR	TEAM LOTUS		LOTUS FORD	1:38'59.666	175.161	108.840	1 LAP
7	9	M. ALBORETO	ITA	FOOTWORK MUGEN-HONDA		FOOTWORK MUGEN-HONDA	1:39'28.457	174.316	108.315	1 LAP
8	24	G. MORBIDELLI	ITA	MINARDI TEAM		MINARDI LAMBORGHINI	1:40'19.263	172.845	107.401	1 LAP
9	21	J. LEHTO	FIN	SCUDERIA ITALIA		BMS DALLARA FERRARI	1:40'01.842	170.798	106.129	2 LAPS
10	22	P. MARTINI	ITA	SCUDERIA ITALIA		BMS DALLARA FERRARI	1:40'49.760	169.445	105.288	2 LAPS
11	3	O. GROUILLARD	FRA	TYRRELL		TYRRELL ILMOR	1:39'09.141	169.739	105.471	3 LAPS

NOT CLASSIFIED

Pos	Nr	Driver		Team Make		Make	Total Time	km/h	mph	COVERED
12	27	J. ALESI	FRA	FERRARI		FERRARI	1:26'36.008	179.550	111.567	61 LAPS
13	4	A. DE CESARIS	ITA	TYRRELL		TYRRELL ILMOR	1:11'49.648	181.059	112.505	51 LAPS
14	30	U. KATAYAMA	JPN	CENTRAL PARK-VEN. LARR.		VENTURI LAMBORGHINI	1:08'27.542	182.518	113.411	49 LAPS
15	25	T. BOUTSEN	BEL	LIGIER GITANES BLONDES		LIGIER RENAULT	1:02'32.254	187.567	116.549	46 LAPS
16	28	I. CAPELLI	ITA	FERRARI		FERRARI	52'51.085	183.344	113.925	38 LAPS
17	16	K. WENDLINGER	AUT	MARCH F.1		MARCH ILMOR	46'53.778	179.438	111.498	33 LAPS
18	32	S. MODENA	ITA	SASOL JORDAN YAMAHA		JORDAN YAMAHA	35'42.170	178.557	110.950	25 LAPS
19	10	M. SCHUMACHER	GER	FOOTWORK MUGEN-HONDA		FOOTWORK MUGEN-HONDA	28'07.020	181.385	112.707	20 LAPS
20	19	M. SCHUMACHER	GER	CAMEL BENETTON FORD		BENETTON FORD	24'57.501	173.689	107.926	17 LAPS
21	2	G. BERGER	AUT	HONDA MARLBORO McLAREN		McLAREN HONDA	13'34.452	187.856	116.729	10 LAPS
22	15	G. TARQUINI	ITA	FONDMETAL F1		FONDMETAL FORD	8'34.366	178.472	110.897	6 LAPS

FASTEST LAP: 5 N. MANSELL – Lap 37 Time: 1'17.070 (198.521 km/h = 123.355 mph)

British Grand Prix

Silverstone

Nigel Mansell and Silverstone: a combination so exciting that it should carry a health warning. He gets positively euphoric about the old airfield. It is the hardest, fastest, most exciting, most atmospheric, best circuit in the world with the greatest fans, says Mansell, who might be just a touch biased.

Nothing stirs his racing blood as much as the British Grand Prix in July. He looks forward to the visit for months, as if it were a call on a long-lost lover – and Silverstone, in the beautiful dress of an English summer, greets him with a passionate embrace.

Other drivers helicopter in and out and stay in five-star hotels or rented mansions. Mansell sets up camp with family and friends in a caravan in the centre of Silverstone among the other mobile people. From there he walks around or uses a motorbike to criss-cross the old British airfield, stopping to talk to fans, pose for photographs and sign autograph books, T-shirts, arms and legs.

Mansell had said at Silverstone testing two weeks earlier, when he was easily the quickest man around, "Woe betide anyone who does anything he shouldn't – he won't get out alive." He was half-joking, but his words reflected the man's thinking about Silverstone and the pressures he faced as he fought his World title campaign. His complete faith and confidence in his oft-criticised army of fans and his continued feeling that he had been hard done by in Canada, where he claimed he had been forced off by Senna, were juxtaposed.

This was his holy ground and he was the prophet. The trek to the tiny hamlet in Northamptonshire was more like a pilgrimage for many, some of whom chose to drape themselves with Union Jacks and appeared to be walking pubs. "I love the atmosphere, I don't feel pressure here," said Mansell. "I have been looking forward to coming here for months. It is the highlight of the season and having backing like this is fantastic.

"Last year, when I won, was one of the most remarkable times of my life. From the start of the race the supporters stood up at every part of the circuit as I came round. By the final few laps I could actually hear the cheering at times, despite the helmet and all the engine noise. I cannot tell you what it means to have this kind of support. I feel I own this place. It is my special place, my comfort zone."

Mansell had won four Grands Prix in England: the European Grand Prix, his first ever, at Brands Hatch and three British races at Silverstone in 1986, 1987 and 1991. There had also been second places in 1988 and 1989. No wonder he has a love affair with the circuit. The crowd of over 120,000 in 1991 – official figures are hard to come by for various reasons – was certainly due to him.

Of course, Mansell is not the only one on home ground. There are other British drivers who also get an enormous kick from Silverstone, and this year Martin Brundle, Johnny Herbert, Damon Hill and Perry McCarthy all hoped to benefit from varying degrees of Silverstone magic.

Many of the teams are also British-based with British

designers, engineers and mechanics. Canon Williams Renault, Marlboro McLaren Honda, Camel Benetton Ford, Team Castrol Lotus, Brabham, Tyrrell, Sasol Jordan Yamaha, March and Footwork Mugen Honda may all have international commerce sponsorship but they are rooted in England.

Of 42 British races, 15 have been won by home drivers, a superb record which many believe could be even better if the country's major companies put more cash behind young drivers as happens on the Continent and in the USA. For the moment there was Nigel Mansell OBE, a 39-year-old born little more than a high-speed dash from Silverstone, to fulfil the demands and potential of Britain's motor industry and its devotees.

In the build-up to Silverstone, Mansell had spoken deeply and at length about his rise and rise, surrounded by the luxuries acquired by 13 years of putting his life on the line. He was honest and open. "World Champion," he said. "Yes, that is what it is all about. That's the only reason I am here, the only reason I am in the game. But no, I don't go around thinking about being World Champion all the time. The title is the only thing that drew me back after retiring. I am not in it for the rewards because, quite honestly, I don't like some of the rewards.

"I prefer anonymity, the company of my own family. That is one reason why I prefer to spend the winter in Florida now – I am not so well known over there. We can go out as a family shopping or to McDonalds without any hassle. Not that I am moaning about the fans; they're great, I love them, but it is nice to be on your own.

"One of the things I don't like is that it is open season for people to write anything they like about you and some of it is shocking. My career has not been easy and there are a lot of people, particularly in sections of the press, who have a grudging respect at best.

"Why? A lot of people wrote me off years ago or just never fancied me from the start. They had their own favourites, other drivers who are no longer around. They said I could never do this, never do that, never win. I have proved them wrong time and again, and they are not man enough to admit that they were wrong and say, 'you are doing a great job now.' It is too pathetic for words.

"I have nothing to prove to myself or anyone. I don't need to prove one little thing to a single person. That is the nice thing, and that is why I am so comfortable with the world. I don't know what the outcome will be at Silverstone or in the Championship, but even if we don't win another race this season, it will have been a fantastic year."

His straightforward approach is, he believes, what makes him so popular with the man in the street. "They know I am one of them, they can identify with me. What is wrong with that? I give them the time of day and at Silverstone I will do as many walkabouts as possible and sign as many autographs as I can. They also know that I give 100 per cent all the time, and that is all you can do. Some of my contemporaries get glowing reports yet they don't have quite the same concern. I have seen how some other people treat the fans and I don't like it."

They talk of his lack of charisma, lack of a sense of humour, lack of proportion, but Mansell says: "Charisma is only a matter of opinion, really. I have been to lots of places and have met lots of people and even had the privilege of dining with the Queen on a one-to-one basis. Those people seem to think I have something to offer. I certainly carry a presence when I want. Anyway, being complimented in the biggest way by my country, being awarded the OBE and meeting the Queen, is enough for me."

That award followed his retirement in 1990 before he was talked back by Frank Williams. He had finished as runner-up in the Championship three times in painful circumstances.

Mansell was quick to deny that he was putting in vast amounts of time and effort because he saw this as his last chance of winning the title. "I am just not prepared to be compromised this time," he said. "There are no passengers this year. Everyone is working their backsides off – me, Riccardo, Williams, Renault and Elf. Whatever it takes to get the job done, I will do it."

As he talked, his sons Greg and Leo played nearby, but spectating is as close to the Formula One business as he wants them to get. "I want them to be tennis players or golfers and, fortunately, it looks as if they will be too tall to be racing drivers," said Mansell. "I would love to have been a professional golfer rather than a racing driver. They can play whenever they want in any tournament. If they want to miss one out, they can. Not like in this sport. And the great thing is that they don't risk their lives every time they go out."

He loves having his family around. "It is certainly not a distraction. We are a very tight-knit family and when we have to leave the children with someone else it is not worth the worry. When I do my job I like to be completely worry-free."

He was certainly unworried about Silverstone, but contract negotiations had begun again and they bring pressures of their own. Mansell, reputed to be somewhere around the £6 million mark, defends the salaries fiercely. "Drivers are worth every penny they can get and they are probably underpaid," he said firmly. "I am obviously in an élite club now and I am not complaining. In my opinion no one should begrudge drivers whatever they can get.

"The money side is only what you get for doing the job, it is not the motivation. There is no other sport where you risk the ultimate every time you go out. You may do everything right and something else may go wrong. How can anyone put a price on a man's life? When I get into the car at Silverstone it is for everything except money."

Even before the engines roared in anger, Mansell found himself embroiled in team politics. The rumour that Patrese might not be around in the Williams car in 1993 was now running strongly, and there were no denials coming from the team. Mansell had now told Frank Williams that he would refuse to sign a new deal until he knew who was going to be his team-mate the following season. He feared that his two great rivals, Ayrton Senna and Alain Prost, might move in.

Senna was now publicly voicing his unhappiness with the uncompetitive McLaren while Prost, who had taken a year out after being fired by Ferrari, was saying that he would be back. Mansell told Frank Williams to stick with Patrese and said: "We are close to sorting out a contract but I want to firm up on who the other driver is for next year. Until then I am not prepared to commit myself. Frank and I have agreed almost everything except who will be the other driver."

On the Thursday before Silverstone, Mansell went off to play golf while Patrese tried his hand at cricket for the first time, taking a few friendly deliveries from England pace bowler David 'Syd' Lawrence. Patrese had the same worry on his mind and he was happy to have Mansell as an ally. "I agree with Nigel, and I have told Frank that I want to stay. It is a nice atmosphere and a base for success. Look how well we have done this season working as a team. There is not much more we could have done. Frank is aware of this, but like any good team manager he is looking at all the options."

Williams, playing his cards close to his chest, said simply: "The situation is fluid and I cannot comment. I always listen to what Nigel says."

On Thursday Mansell confessed that something was worrying him – the weather. "We don't want it like Spain," he said. "It would be nice to have a dry race. Given the choice I would go 99 per cent of the time for dry conditions, 1 per cent for rain. You get ideal laps with clear skies and good vision, but I can foresee this weekend being bad.

"I will have to work hard to win. This could be my 28th win, which would be fantastic – Jackie Stewart is one of my heroes. But I don't think about the numbers. What I think about most is the World Championship. You need to keep reliability, to keep finishing to keep scoring. Anyone can still do it. It is a long way from being over. So far Spain has been the hardest to win in the toughest conditions at the end. France was more awkward, moving from slicks to wets as the weather changed a few times."

Again he was challenged about Patrese's wave through. Would it happen again if they were in a similar position at Silverstone? "There were no team orders. It was his decision," said Mansell, who obviously believed that Patrick Head's message to Patrese came into the category of 'advice'. "It was up to Riccardo, but no one should be under any illusion: there is no way he could have stopped me winning the race. I was pressurising him all the way, and if he had continued as he was going at high revs he would have run out of fuel."

It was blunt and to the point, and a less than diplomatic statement. His self-confidence is one of the traits which have not endeared him to some, but it has seen him through many a crisis.

Patrese sounded like a man who was resigned to his fate as runner-up. "I am the only man who can catch Mansell, and I don't have a chance. He is very strong and he is backed by a very good car. I gave up my thoughts of the Championship after four or five races when I saw how well Nigel was going. He has a very good chance this season and I cannot see him being caught."

As Friday morning dawned the roads were drying after a night's heavy rain and lines of cars and caravans streamed back from Silverstone's woefully inadequate entrance and exit facilities. Perry McCarthy was the first Briton to disappear, a victim of Andrea Moda's lack of cash, car spares and ability to cope with pre-qualifying.

The hordes of Mansell maniacs did not have long to wait to see their hero and he was soon living up to his reputation as the most exciting driver to watch. In free practice, Mansell quickly found the right set-up and before it was over he had already ripped apart the 1991 pole position time. A 1 minute 20.246 second lap sliced off half a second. He was over a second quicker than his team-mate and 2.48 seconds out of sight of Senna. He and his followers went cheerfully for lunch in the knowledge that the first qualifying session could be even tastier.

Barely had the high-priced hamburgers and sandwiches slipped down the throat when Mansell fired up his famed car and headed for the open road. It wasn't too open for everyone had decided to go out early and beat the threat of rain. But when Mansell went out he conjured visions of a wolf moving among sheep. Quickly he scattered all comers to the winds, lapping in the 1.20s. Patrese was next, but everyone else seemed to be driving with the brakes on.

Senna rose to the challenge, forcing his car round in the 1.22s, but no sooner had he managed that than Mansell disappeared into the 1.19s. He hit 1 minute 19.161 seconds and admitted: "I was really pleased with that, but I thought I would give it another go because of the fans – have you ever seen so many here on a Friday?"

Mansell moved into hyper-drive, delivering the car from start to finish line in just 1 minute 18.965 seconds on his 20th lap. Patrese was 1.9 seconds behind, Senna 2.7, Schumacher 3.1, Berger 3.3 and Brundle 4.5. If it had been a boxing match they would have awarded Mansell all the points and called it off to save the rest from further punishment.

"That was a spectacular session with the perfect lap," said a delighted Mansell later. "I cannot imagine going any quicker than that. This is the meanest, most physical circuit in the world and I really gave it everything. I thought 1.19 was optimistic, but to get down to 1.18 . . . I did not think it was for real. I am suffering now, though. I am aching all over, including my teeth, which are sore from being clenched in the corners because of the G-forces.

"My quickest lap was quite something. I could hardly believe the speed at which I was going through Copse Corner. At one point I got into a huge slide which gave me quite a moment, but that time will make people think. I'm not surprised, feeling as good as I do here. But we have to do the business in the race now."

No one doubted that Mansell's lap would stand until Sunday as pole time. Only one man in the Williams Renault was capable of beating it . . . Mansell himself.

Even Marlboro's newsletter announced 'Mansell by a mile' and declared: "Mansell should have no trouble taking his 28th Grand Prix win and his seventh of the season in Sunday's race." By Saturday morning there were already banners bearing messages such as 'Mansell magic – now you see him, now you don't' and 'Give Senna a chance, Nige – give him a tow.'

Now the spectators were really rolling in, drawn like crowds to the Coliseum to see the Mansell the Lion, *Il Leone*, eat the Christians. A weather change meant that they would not see the times of the previous day, but Mansell was happy. It was a showery day, guaranteeing that the Friday times would not be beaten. Mansell tried and topped the lists yet again, but had to settle for a 1 minute 24.968 second lap.

"To be honest," he admitted "even if it had been dry I don't think I would have been able to match my time or to get anywhere near it. I found out this morning out there that I could not get the same commitment. I could not get myself to go through at the same speed."

A little more light was shed on the mysteries of the active suspension system when Mansell explained that while it may give the car a smoother run over bumps, the driver does not always enjoy the same benefit. "It changes on you," he said. "The ride can change as you go along because the hydraulic fluid warms up and things change . . . but that is as much as I am allowed to say." Patrese, too, agreed that it was not an easy car to drive because the active suspension and the traction control allowed much higher speeds. Higher limits on the car meant that the drivers had to push more to find their own limits to match the car.

Patrese was involved in the day's big moment when

he slowed at yellow warning flags and was hammered by Erik Comas, who tried to overtake. Patrese's car was sent flying into the wall and Comas's Ligier was also wrecked. Yet both drivers survived without much damage, although Comas missed the second qualifying session because he was having his legs massaged and was later fined $5000 for his pains.

By late afternoon, a huge thunderstorm had reduced Silverstone to a giant mud puddle, but some people were happy, notably Damon Hill, who had qualified in 26th place on the Friday in his Brabham and was in his first British. "My father retired from Formula One after his last race here in 1975, so it is fitting that I should make my start here," said Hill.

Mansell went off to a Camel-sponsored quiz night but was not really in the mood. Martin Brundle's team won and Mansell retired to his camp, although he admitted the next morning that the noise of fireworks and early celebrations from the thousands roaming the circuit had disrupted his sleep. Not that he seemed bothered, for soon he was leading the morning warm-up times with Patrese second. Mika Haakinen was absent – he had been arrested for pulling out of a traffic jam and driving on the wrong side of the road in an attempt to make it to Silverstone on time.

The grid was bathed in sunshine as they lined up, the Williams cars in front again. Senna and Schumacher filled the second row with Berger and Brundle in the third. Another British boost was the sight of Johnny Herbert in seventh place. Mansell's anxiety to get away first caused him his first and only problem in the race as he gunned the engine and found himself with too much wheel-spin. Patrese pulled alongside and nipped into Copse first. It was a very brief upset for the Mansell army. Within seconds, Mansell had pulled past Patrese – without an invitation – and was gone.

He then set about building a lead as handsome as anyone could remember. After just one lap Mansell was 3.2 ahead, which shouldn't happen in Formula One. With two laps gone he was 5.9 seconds ahead, on four it was 10.1 seconds and after ten it was an astounding 20.5.

The next four were enjoying their own race. Brundle, also inspired by the crowd and in a car which allowed him to exhibit his skills, had made a dynamic start, passing Schumacher and Senna. He tracked Patrese and was followed by his old rival from their Formula Three days, Ayrton Senna. Schumacher came next and, to add to the huge crowd's delight, Herbert was in sixth.

Mansell eased slightly to be a mere 22 seconds clear after 20 laps but extended the gap to 32 seconds after 30 trips round the track. That was when he made his planned pit stop for tyres in a relaxed fashion. No rush, no errors, and he was back on the track in 12 seconds, with no one in sight. Herbert became a casualty of gearbox trouble as Mansell swept onwards. He drew cheers and flags on his every solo lap, but the real excitement was Brundle's brilliant battle to hold off Senna, who was trying everything he knew to pass.

They were never more than a second apart, but the man from King's Lynn held on to join Mansell on the podium – although only after some amazing scenes. After Mansell completed his 59 laps, he was 39 seconds ahead of Patrese who was in turn seven clear of Brundle. As Mansell set off on his final lap the fans began lining up for a charge, and as soon as he had taken the chequered flag they began their invasion. Most ran down the grass verge but some got onto the track, racing towards him,

1. Nigel Mansell eases himself into the tight cockpit as team members busy around with final checks in the garage.

2. Flowers for victory. Before the race,
well-wishers present Mansell with a Red
Five replica made from carnations.

3. Mansell and his young son arriving at
Silverstone for the British Grand Prix.

4. Intense and determined, Mansell prepares to leave the pit garage for what he calls "the meanest, most physical circuit in the world."

5. On his own, just as he was for most of the season, Mansell pilots Red Five to a stunning victory in the British Grand Prix.

6. Royal fan Prince William smiles with delight as Mansell races to glory.

7. The pride of Britain – Mansell fans celebrate national success.

8. A break with Formula One.
Mansell at the 85th anniversary of
Brooklands with the 1902 Renault
which raced from Paris to Vienna.

9. Out of his racing overalls and helmet,
a debonair Mansell enjoys a day at the
famous Brooklands circuit.

10. World Champion – Nigel Mansell salutes his fans.

and were still there when the other cars came round. It was wild, over the top, and it was condemned by many drivers and officials.

Mansell had to abandon his car in the press of fans on his victory lap and was rescued by an emergency vehicle. Yet he declined to censure the supporters, saying: "I am not going to knock them. As long as no one was injured, I hope they enjoyed themselves. Today has been the most wonderful day for the sport in the history of Formula One at Silverstone. I dedicate this victory to the fans."

It confounded everyone that he would not at least warn the crowds of the dangers of running onto the track when cars were still racing. Mansell admitted that on his victory lap he had even run down a man, a big man, while not travelling very fast. The man had apologised to Mansell – "he loved it" said the hero – and the victim had! "The fans are unbelievable," insisted Mansell. "The 28 wins have not yet sunk in."

McLaren boss Ron Dennis said flatly: "I knew it was going to be hard – but not this hard." Mansell's figures for the race are worth studying. He set the 11 fastest laps, including two near the end – "for the fans" – and, inevitably, the quickest lap of the day, 1 minute 22.539 seconds. That was nearly four seconds faster than his fastest lap the previous year. His average speed was 141mph. The win made him Britain's most successful driver in terms of race wins with 28 from 174 races. It was also Britain's most successful day at the home Grand Prix since 1965.

That night, a calm, mild evening, Mansell invited a few people into his camp, a small collection of caravans housing friends and relatives, drawn up in a circle in the centre of the track he had made his own. This was no wild celebration awash with drink, just a quiet time. Tea was on offer, someone had to go for champagne and he talked of the great day as his friends sat at their caravans and his children played happily. Across at the paddock, where he had been earlier, the pit crews and other team workers enjoyed a barbecue with their own rock band blasting away.

The king was savouring the moment in his castle, locking away the memories, while his army, who had beaten the security but not the traffic jams, slowly dispersed, some singing, some drinking, all celebrating.

Yet even in his moment of glory Mansell warned that unless he got the guarantees he was seeking in his contract he would quit. "The time in my career when I needed to do what I didn't want to has long gone," he said as he sat under the night sky. 'I won't do anything next year unless I get my guarantees.

"I think it would be a real pity to break up a team which has done so well. I would even drive alongside Ayrton Senna if I had to. He does not daunt me, but you would need to guarantee me the same car and the same engine. Ayrton is a great driver but he does not surprise me in anything – except his tactics at times."

His big problem was with Alain Prost, France's three-times World Champion. Renault had quietly made it clear during the weekend that they would like a Frenchman with Mansell in their record-breaking car. Prost said: "I will be back in Formula One next season. I would drive with Mansell – it is not a problem."

But it most certainly was a problem for Mansell. Some were to doubt his threat to quit: they learned to their cost later just how serious he was.

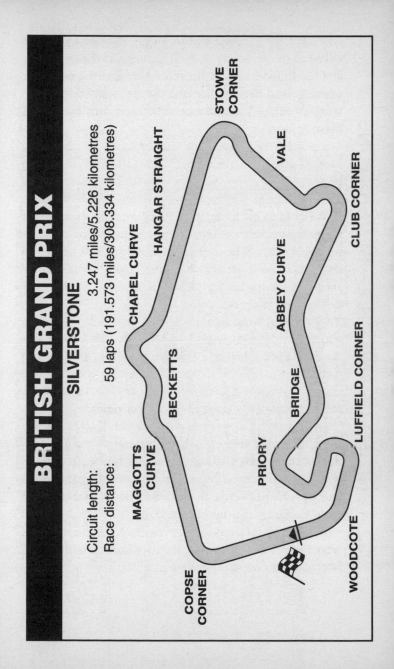

BRITISH GRAND PRIX

SILVERSTONE

Circuit length: 3.247 miles/5.226 kilometres
Race distance: 59 laps (191.573 miles/308.334 kilometres)

COPSE CORNER

MAGGOTTS CURVE

CHAPEL CURVE

HANGAR STRAIGHT

BECKETTS

PRIORY

BRIDGE

ABBEY CURVE

STOWE CORNER

VALE

CLUB CORNER

LUFFIELD CORNER

WOODCOTE

1992 – BRITISH GRAND PRIX – SILVERSTONE

RACE CLASSIFICATION AFTER 59 LAPS

(308.334 km = 191.589 mls)

Pos	Nr	Driver		Team Make	Make	Total Time	km/h	mph	Diff
1	5	N. MANSELL	GBR	CANON WILLIAMS TEAM	WILLIAMS RENAULT	1:25'42.991	215.828	134.109	
2	6	R. PATRESE	ITA	CANON WILLIAMS TEAM	WILLIAMS RENAULT	1:26'22.085	214.200	133.038	39.094
3	20	M. BRUNDLE	GBR	CAMEL BENETTON FORD	BENETTON FORD	1:26'31.386	213.818	132.859	48.395
4	19	M. SCHUMACHER	GER	CAMEL BENETTON FORD	BENETTON FORD	1:26'36.258	213.616	132.735	53.267
5	2	G. BERGER	AUT	HONDA MARLBORO McLAREN	McLAREN HONDA	1:26'38.788	213.512	132.370	55.795
6	11	M. HAKKINEN	FIN	TEAM CASTROL LOTUS	LOTUS FORD	1:27'03.129	212.517	132.052	1'20.138
7	9	M. ALBORETO	ITA	FOOTWORK MUGEN-HONDA	FOOTWORK MUGEN-HONDA	1:26'53.950	209.283	130.042	1 LAP
8	26	E. COMAS	FRA	LIGIER GITANES BLONDES	LIGIER RENAULT	1:26'54.483	209.261	130.029	1 LAP
9	28	I. CAPELLI	ITA	FERRARI	FERRARI	1:26'55.074	209.237	130.014	1 LAP
10	25	T. BOUTSEN	BEL	LIGIER GITANES BLONDES	LIGIER RENAULT	1:26'07.117	207.538	128.955	2 LAPS
11	3	O. GROUILLARD	FRA	TYRRELL	TYRRELL FORD	1:26'07.258	207.533	128.955	2 LAPS
12	10	A. SUZUKI	JPN	FOOTWORK MUGEN-HONDA	FOOTWORK MUGEN-HONDA	1:26'07.769	207.512	128.942	2 LAPS
13	21	J. LEHTO	FIN	SCUDERIA ITALIA	BMS DALLARA FERRARI	1:26'08.374	207.488	128.927	2 LAPS
14	15	G. TARQUINI	ITA	FONDMETAL F1	FONDMETAL F1	1:26'28.000	206.703	128.439	2 LAPS
15	22	P. MARTINI	ITA	SCUDERIA ITALIA	BMS DALLARA FERRARI	1:25'85.262	204.366	126.887	3 LAPS
16	8	D. HILL	GBR	MOTOR RACING DEV.	BRABHAM JUDD	1:25'48.260	200.990	124.889	4 LAPS
17	24	G. MORBIDELLI	ITA	MINARDI TEAM	MINARDI LAMBORGHINI	1:20'35.158	206.223	128.141	6 LAPS

NOT CLASSIFIED

Pos	Nr	Driver		Team Make	Make	Total Time	km/h	mph	COVERED
18	1	A. SENNA	BRA	HONDA MARLBORO McLAREN	McLAREN HONDA	1:16'12.505	213.954	132.945	52 LAPS
19	4	A. DE CESARIS	ITA	TYRRELL	TYRRELL ILMOR	1:11'26.090	201.915	125.464	46 LAPS
20	27	J. ALESI	FRA	FERRARI	FERRARI	1:03'59.522	210.699	130.923	43 LAPS
21	32	S. MODENA	ITA	SASOL JORDAN YAMAHA	JORDAN YAMAHA	1:05'18.339	206.461	128.209	43 LAPS
22	33	M. GUGELMIN	BRA	SASOL JORDAN YAMAHA	JORDAN YAMAHA	56'42.840	204.565	127.111	37 LAPS
23	29	B. GACHOT	FRA	CENTRAL PARK-VEN. LARR.	VENTURI LAMBORGHINI	48'37.214	206.373	128.234	32 LAPS
24	12	J. HERBERT	GBR	TEAM CASTROL LOTUS	LOTUS FORD	46'18.250	209.924	130.441	30 LAPS
25	16	K. WENDLINGER	AUT	MARCH F.1	MARCH ILMOR	41'31.657	203.857	126.677	27 LAPS
26	30	U. KATAYAMA	JPN	CENTRAL PARK-VEN. LARR.	VENTURI LAMBORGHINI	41'38.448	203.313	126.333	27 LAPS

FASTEST LAP: 5 N. MANSELL – Lap 57 Time: 1'22.539 (227.936 km/h = 141.633 mph)

German Grand Prix

Hockenheim

Nigel Mansell took the puritanical approach to getting over the high drama of Silverstone and avoiding all the razzmattazz. He went to work. He did so in a confused state of mind. Contract negotiations were going on and on, and all around drivers were looking at the Williams supercar with envious eyes.

Ayrton Senna had now declared that unless he found a competitive car for 1993 he would take a sabbatical for a season. He had learned that Honda were now almost certain to quit Formula One, taking away its engines. "I have worked with Honda for several years now and enjoy working with them," he said. "We have had tremendous success. Without any doubt, if they decide not to continue that decision would have a great impact, not only on any decisions I have to make, but also on McLaren's future and the competitiveness of Formula One.

"For myself, I think that once you have the experience of winning the World Championship three times, of being very competitive for years, a season like this is too frustrating. I am not sure that it is really worth the effort that we all, as drivers, put in when you know you have no chance of winning. I might take a season out if I do not find a car that will allow me to be competitive next year. Who knows? I am only 32 and have a long way to go. We will have to wait and see what happens."

This first salvo was designed to wake everyone up to the idea that he was available for hire if they had a car which would give him a real crack at a fourth World title. His frustration was understandable but it raised questions about his loyalty. Having had the good years with McLaren, perhaps he should have showed himself willing to stay and help them through a harder time.

Patrese was now being linked with Camel Benetton Ford and Ferrari, and Gerhard Berger was said to be on the verge of a deal with Ferrari. By now questions were openly being asked about Mansell's situation. Why had the outstanding driver of the season not been re-signed already? Why had Britain's top team not quickly ensured that they had the leading British driver? For the first time it seemed that there were problems.

Mansell was watching the goings-on with increasing interest and some disquiet. "I know certain things that McLaren are trying which, if they take place, will totally destabilise this team," he said cryptically. His worry was that McLaren, with the huge financial muscle of Marlboro, would try to lure Renault to their team.

The Williams team took itself to Hockenheim to begin testing in preparation for the German Grand Prix on 26 July. The 22-year-old circuit is carved into a flat, woodland area south-west of the university town of Heidelberg in the Rhine Valley. It is a power circuit, 4.226 miles in length with a long straight and very fast bends, which allow cars to reach almost 210mph, testing man and machine to the limit of their endurance.

This was the place, said some, where the McLaren Honda power would come good, blasting them to victory over the Williams cars. Amazingly, some clung to their theory even after the test session in which Mansell and Patrese continued their total domination.

The strain was getting to some people, and after Michael Schumacher had tangled on the track with Ayrton Senna, the Brazilian had a real set-to with him on the circuit. Later, team officials had to calm things down when the World Champion met the German in the pits.

There had been talk of Williams finally rolling out their new car, the FW15, which had been expected to appear in France or Britain. It was not seen at Hockenheim; in fact it was not seen at all during the season. Already it may have been superseded by a 15B. The Williams drivers put a lot more work into honing the RS4 engines in test, doing full race distance to check reliability. Mansell was impressed.

A year earlier, Mansell and Patrese had enjoyed a one-two finish which had given the Englishman his first ever hat-trick of victories. A win this time would equal Senna's record of eight in a row. When Mansell arrived in sunny Germany there was the first hint that he was moving on from his original negotiating position of "no Prost, no way." He still wanted Patrese as his team-mate, he stressed. There was no need to change the most successful team in motor racing, no need to upset the goodwill and wonderful working arrangements with the team.

But "Frank Williams has acted totally professionally and he is giving all avenues serious consideration," said Mansell. "What I want for the team is not unreasonable but this is the most expensive sport in the world and if another commercial element comes in, you have to look at it." Basically, Mansell seemed to be saying that Williams was a small team compared to some and needed to hang on to the biggest sponsors it could get – and they don't come much bigger than Canon, Camel and Renault.

The French engine company now seemed to be exercising some commercial thoughts of their own. Their top man, Patrick Faure, had said before Silverstone that it was not necessary for drivers to be in absolute harmony as Mansell and Patrese were. "Look how Senna and Prost won 15 of the 16 races when they were together at McLaren in 1988," he reasoned. His words seemed prophetic now. Mansell and Prost would never be friends after their year at Ferrari when the Englishman had felt totally usurped by what he claimed was Prost's politicking.

Mansell was scathing when talking of the little Frenchman. "I don't object to good drivers in the team. Riccardo is a great driver, so is Senna, but the thing I object to is an incredibly political driver who starts orchestrating things. The biggest question-mark I have over the possibility of even considering working with Prost is how things soured at Ferrari."

Mansell arrived to find immediate problems with his race car. It had an oil leak which meant it had to be replaced overnight and worked on. In Friday morning's free practice he led from Senna and Berger with Patrese fourth.

But it did not take long in the qualifying session in high temperatures for Mansell to prove that McLaren's hopes and his problems were to be left in his slipstream. While the others were still sorting themselves out, Mansell headed onto the circuit. Gerhard Berger had said that the circuit required the perfect set-up to balance the downforce needed on the infield section while at the same time allowing the best possible top speed on the long straights.

Mansell was second out and quickly found the balance and pace. On only his third lap he was round in 1 minute

38.340 seconds. His average speed was 155mph and he had topped 209 at the fastest point. Before most of the other cars had even come to life, Mansell had caught the beast of Hockenheim as it slumbered in the sun before waking to savage his rivals.

His time was much too good for the rest. "My secret was going out early when the track was clear and clean and there was no traffic," said Mansell. "I wanted to go out right at the beginning and I was lucky. I got my time straight away when there was no one spinning and leaving debris out there. Then I was able to concentrate on doing some homework for the race. I cannot remember a session like that for conditions changing so quickly. It was pretty bumpy."

For those without the Williams' active suspension system, the ride must have been agony. Mansell was delighted with the power of his car. "The RS4 engine in my car was the best I have had and I would be delighted if we were racing it on Sunday! But my race car has the RS3C engine." He headed for the pits after his flying lap and watched a stock car derby in progress with cars flying off everywhere.

Herbert, Schumacher, Brundle, Hill and Modena were just some of the dozen drivers who went careering off. The chicanes had been modified to allow run-off areas, and the Ostkurve was even sharper on the way in. The effect was dramatic and perverse. So many cars crossed the kerbs, bouncing and sliding, rocking and rolling, that gravel and sand were soon coating the circuit.

The session was eventually halted for 20 minutes as the track, looking more like a desert, was swept by teams of workers with brushes and road-sweeping trucks. At the end, Mansell had provisional pole by 1.9 seconds from Senna, who commented drily: "Nearly two seconds behind Nigel? It is all down to driving style."

Senna had already been involved in an angry exchange at the circuit, going out to point out the raised kerbing and demanding improvements on the grounds of safety. The work was done. But Mansell went to his hotel safe in the knowledge that he again looked uncatchable. The followers were the usual band, except that Patrese was third, hampered by car problems. Berger, Schumacher and Alesi were there, but Brundle was ninth after an off-road excursion.

Saturday offered more sunshine, more flags urging Schumacher to victory in his home Grand Prix . . . and more speed from Mansell. Naturally, he was fastest in free practice, and kept the rhythm going. On lap two of his afternoon session he did the tour in 1 minute 37.960 seconds from another early start. Again, he had dealt a blow to those who felt that the conditions would allow them to catch up.

Most were quicker than they had been, but the target had moved. Mansell then gave his spare car, which he had been using for qualifying, to Patrese, who had suffered an engine failure. It made for an interesting comparision: same machinery, different driver. Patrese took full advantage, getting round just 0.350 seconds behind Mansell. He got his own car back for the end of the session, but he must have wished he had not bothered. As he swept round, he and Brundle had a mix-up and Patrese piloted his car into a wall.

Senna worked hard to take his McLaren to third place but was still over a second behind Mansell while Schumacher, in sixth place, was over three seconds down. "I don't know how often one team has been able to qualify one car in first and second position on the grid," said

Mansell. "We have been a fantastic team today. I had no doubts about giving Riccardo the car. He needed it and I had set my time. I did get a bit anxious when Ayrton got down into the 1.39s because the McLarens are usually able to find more revs from somewhere, but there was nothing I could do then because Riccardo was in the car."

In the morning he had lost 50 minutes of running because of a sensor problem but he had not pushed for the car to ease the pressure on his hard-worked mechanics. "We could afford to relax a little," he said, but warned: "We need reliability here and you must stay on the track. One of the problems is that some people don't allow for the fact that even the slow cars are doing more than 200mph. If drivers make a mistake, you can see how much debris comes onto the track. I just hope it does not happen in the race, because the track has to be cleaned. If we are behind a pace car, the slow speeds reduce tyre pressure and temperatures. When you have to go so fast here, that is a problem."

At a reception on the eve of the race, McLaren boss Ron Dennis had even found time to smile about his troubles, saying that he had intended to make a joke but he had decided not to mention the MP4/7A. Yet it was Mansell who was complaining about the handling of his car after the warm-up session, even though he had led the way as usual.

When the race began Patrese's foot was once again faster in putting the pedal to the metal, and he streaked into the first corner in the lead. Mansell's gearbox, possibly inspired by wheel-spin, had thought it was time to go from first to third, costing him the start. But Mansell had read this script before, and as they roared down the straight to the first chicane, he pulled alongside Patrese and took the line into the corner. "I did not have time to sort out what had happened," said Mansell. "I just left it in third and went after Riccardo. He went in a bit deep and I managed to get a good tow down the straight and was able to get past."

Senna had also done the same to his team-mate, Berger, while Brundle had leapt from ninth to sixth. The scene had an all-too familiar look. Mansell was building up his lead slowly but surely with a hot streak which saw him set the fastest laps on 1, 2, 4, 8, 11, 12 and 13. But he was about to be kidded by technology.

To cope with the active suspension, which made it more difficult for the drivers to tell what was really happening by the feel of the car, Williams had developed a sensor which alerted them to punctures. A warning light came on in the cockpit on lap 14 and Mansell, fearing that he was about to suffer a tyre problem, went in to change tyres with another 31 laps to go. "I think I was conned," he said. "I picked up a lot of debris on the tyre, the car began handling really badly and I had a couple of big spins. The warning light came on at the same time and I was convinced I had a puncture."

The tyre change went smoothly but Mansell returned to the chase in third place behind Patrese and Senna. Mansell did take Senna but was quickly passed again. The Brazilian had Mansell where he wanted him – except in the pits – and he knew from experience as recent as Canada that Mansell could be lured into trouble.

Sure enough, as they came into the Ostkurve, Mansell went for the inside. Senna slammed the door and Mansell, off line, powered over a cone, through the exit and back behind the Brazilian. This time Senna realised that on fresh tyres and in a Williams Renault, Mansell was going to make life very uncomfortable indeed for the rest of the afternoon, and for the second time in three races the Englishman was waved through.

That sent Mansell off on his own to victory number eight and left Senna to do battle with Patrese, and a crowd-pleasing, cut-and-thrust fight it was, too. Patrese was determined to make it another Williams one-two but his enthusiasm changed to desperation and on the last lap, in sight of the finish straight, he went for a last-gasp lunge. Senna held the line and the Italian went straight through onto the grass. The engine stalled as he tried to bring the car round to get back to the track.

That was significant for Michael Schumacher, who had been fourth. Now he was on the podium, to the noisy delight of the German crowd who could not have been more jubilant if he had won. The winner, though, was Mansell, but by just four seconds – he had fought his own private battle in the closing stages.

"I was really worried that I would not finish," he said later. "It was not a nice race, very difficult really. I had to come in too early for tyres and I had to try to conserve them near the end. I had terrible vibrations and the tyres were blistered and holed with the heat and the speed but they held out. All I am thinking about now is seeing a dentist. If you don't keep your mouth slightly open you suffer because your teeth crack together with the vibration of the car. It has been a tough one."

Now he needed only one more win to guarantee the World title – surely he could talk of it now? He brought groans from the assembled press by replying: "No. I know what you want me to say but I won't. I have been runner-up three times and I don't want to tempt fate. None of you were in my position in Australia in 1986 when I was 16 laps from the Championship only to have it taken away. I will approach the race in Hungary in the same way I have approached the other ten, and if I do that, I hope that everything else will fall into place."

As Schumacher celebrated his new status as the first German on the podium of his home race since 1977 and Martin Brundle added to Benetton's joy with fourth, the least joyful place was at the Williams motorhome, where Mansell prepared to depart. He was now troubled by the contract situation as rumour after rumour bubbled to the surface. On the final leg of his journey to the holy grail, he was feeling down.

"I feel a bit deflated at times that I am in this position of uncertainty over my contract for next season," he said glumly. "It should be my finest hour, but I don't know what is happening. I just try to concentrate on getting the job done. It goes without saying that I would like this sorted out by the time we get to Hungary. I want to concentrate totally on the race there. There is a great air of uncertainty at the moment." During the weekend, team owner Frank Williams had asked Mansell to make no further comment on the contract negotiations, but things were coming to a head.

Events on and off the track in Budapest were to settle all issues once and for all.

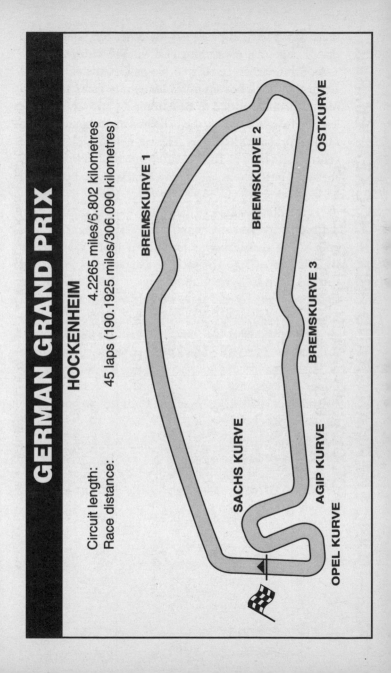

GERMAN GRAND PRIX

HOCKENHEIM

Circuit length: 4.2265 miles/6.802 kilometres
Race distance: 45 laps (190.1925 miles/306.090 kilometres)

BREMSKURVE 1

BREMSKURVE 2

OSTKURVE

BREMSKURVE 3

SACHS KURVE

AGIP KURVE

OPEL KURVE

1992 – MOBIL 1 GERMAN GRAND PRIX – HOCKENHEIMRING

RACE CLASSIFICATION AFTER 45 LAPS

(306.675 km = 190.559 mls)

Pos	Nr	Driver		Make	Team Make		Total Time	km/h	mph	Diff
1	5	N. MANSELL	GBR	WILLIAMS RENAULT	CANON WILLIAMS TEAM		1:18'22.032	234.798	145.897	
2	1	A. SENNA	BRA	McLAREN HONDA	HONDA MARLBORO McLAREN		1:18'26.532	234.574	145.758	4.500
3	19	M. SCHUMACHER	GER	BENETTON FORD	CAMEL BENETTON FORD		1:18'56.494	233.090	144.835	34.462
4	20	M. BRUNDLE	GBR	BENETTON FORD	CAMEL BENETTON FORD		1:18'58.991	232.967	144.759	36.959
5	27	J. ALESI	FRA	FERRARI	FERRARI		1:19'34.639	231.228	143.678	1:12.607
6	26	E. COMAS	FRA	LIGIER RENAULT	LIGIER GITANES BLONDES		1:19'58.530	230.077	142.963	1'36.498
7	25	T. BOUTSEN	BEL	LIGIER RENAULT	LIGIER GITANES BLONDES		1:19'59.212	230.044	142.943	1'37.180
8	6	R. PATRESE	ITA	WILLIAMS RENAULT	CANON WILLIAMS TEAM		1:16'43.147	234.513	145.719	1 LAP
9	9	M. ALBORETO	ITA	FOOTWORK MUGEN-HONDA	FOOTWORK MUGEN-HONDA		1:19'04.176	227.581	141.388	1 LAP
10	21	J. LEHTO	FIN	BMS DALLARA FERRARI	SCUDERIA ITALIA		1:19'18.317	226.866	140.967	1 LAP
11	22	P. MARTINI	ITA	BMS DALLARA FERRARI	SCUDERIA ITALIA		1:19'19.817	226.794	140.923	1 LAP
12	24	G. MORBIDELLI	ITA	MINARDI LAMBORGHINI	MINARDI TEAM		1:19'30.943	226.265	140.594	1 LAP
13	17	P. BELMONDO	FRA	MARCH ILMOR	MARCH F.1		1:19'31.776	226.225	140.570	1 LAP
14	29	B. GACHOT	FRA	VENTURI LAMBORGHINI	CENTRAL PARK-VEN. LARR.		1:19'33.241	226.156	140.527	1 LAP
15	33	M. GUGELMIN	BRA	JORDAN YAMAHA	SASOL JORDAN YAMAHA		1:19'58.013	219.875	136.624	2 LAPS
16	16	K. WENDLINGER	AUT	MARCH ILMOR	MARCH F.1		1:19'03.021	217.251	134.994	3 LAPS

NOT CLASSIFIED

Pos	Nr	Driver		Make	Team Make		Total Time	km/h	mph	COVERED
17	15	G. TARQUINI	ITA	FONDMETAL FORD	FONDMETAL F.1		1:00'00.282	224.877	139.732	33 LAPS
18	4	A. DE CESARIS	ITA	TYRRELL ILMOR	TYRRELL		46'03.810	221.922	137.896	25 LAPS
19	12	J. HERBERT	GBR	LOTUS FORD	TEAM CASTROL LOTUS		41'40.032	225.710	140.250	23 LAPS
20	28	I. CAPELLI	ITA	FERRARI	FERRARI		37'48.091	227.158	141.149	21 LAPS
21	11	M. HAKKINEN	FIN	LOTUS FORD	TEAM CASTROL LOTUS		37'54.866	226.481	140.729	21 LAPS
22	2	G. BERGER	AUT	McLAREN HONDA	HONDA MARLBORO McLAREN		38'34.919	169.571	105.367	16 LAPS
23	3	O. GROUILLARD	FRA	TYRRELL ILMOR	TYRRELL		14'53.128	219.750	136.551	8 LAPS
24	30	U. KATAYAMA	JPN	VENTURI LAMBORGHINI	CENTRAL PARK-VEN. LARR.		14'57.129	218.778	135.942	8 LAPS
25	10	A. SUZUKI	JPN	FOOTWORK MUGEN-HONDA	FOOTWORK MUGEN-HONDA		2:03.333	198.925	123.606	1 LAP
26	23	A. ZANARDI	ITA	MINARDI LAMBORGHINI	MINARDI TEAM		2'33.902	159.406	99.050	1 LAP

FASTEST LAP: 6 R. PATRESE – Lap 36 Time: 1'41.591 (241.498 Km/h = 150.060 mph)

Hungarian Grand Prix

Budapest

Nigel Mansell laughed long and easily as he sat in the sun in Budapest. He slowly repeated the statement which had been made to him: "All I need to do is win. It's that simple, eh?" He was in relaxed mood, trying to shut out the memories of having been through this before: memories of 'only' needing to win in Adelaide in 1986; of 'only' needing to keep winning in 1987 and again in 1991. "All I need to do is just get in the car and make it go round for a couple of hours," he said.

He was on the doorstep of his destiny again, knocking loudly at the hall of greatness. Nigel Ernest James Mansell, winner of 29 Grands Prix, just turned 39 years old, veteran of 175 Formula One races, wished to join the immortals such as Jim Clark, Graham Hill, Jackie Stewart. Time was not yet running out. Failure in the Hungarian Grand Prix would not be fatal to his hopes, it would merely prolong what everyone except Mansell believed was inevitable.

"So many things can happen, believe me, gentlemen, I know only too well," he told the press men sitting in the shade with him. "Don't forget that there are a lot of other drivers who want to win this race. I will talk about the Championship when it is over. Until then I will talk about the race."

The simple fact was that if Mansell won the race, he

would be World Champion. It would be his ninth win of the season, a world record. Such was his dominance after eight wins that there were other permutations which would give him the title. He had 86 points, his nearest rival, Riccardo Patrese, had 40, Michael Schumacher 33 and Ayrton Senna just 20. Including Hungary there were six races left. Senna, the defending World Champion, could not catch Mansell.

Schumacher, the remarkable 23-year-old German, in his first full season, could theoretically overhaul Mansell but he would need the Englishman to score no more points while he won five races and scored at least four points in another.

That left Patrese, Mansell's team-mate at Williams Renault, who had been second six times to Mansell. He, too, would have to hope for a spectacular collapse by Mansell. Mansell knew that if he finished ahead of his rivals in the points he would be Champion. Patrese was not about to lie down for him, and FISA had already sown a few seeds of doubt in Mansell's mind. Formula One's governing body had decreed that only regular fuel could be used from this race on.

Pump fuel, they called it, although if anyone had filled a V10 engine with four-star from the local garage it would have been interesting to watch the engineers trying to make it work. Ostensibly, the teams should all have been using a regular mix but over the years, as FISA overlooked the strange smells around the pits, some remarkable concoctions had been brewed.

It was hardly surprising, because of course the petrol giants were in Formula One for the same reasons as engine suppliers – to advertise and develop their wares in the front line of motor sport. As the engines became more refined, so did their diets and Shell, Elf and BP had worked hard to come up with blends which suited the different tracks and temperatures.

To Mansell and the Williams team the ruling seemed like another hurried change to put the brakes on their all-out assault on the Championship: "It amazes me that the sport can be dominated for four years by one team, who win 15 of 16 races in one season, and nothing is said, nothing changed," said Mansell. "Suddenly, we are winning and this happens. Some of the rule changes have been beneficial, some extraordinary."

Pace cars had also arrived and Goodyear had lost the battle to retain the width of tyres. They would definitely be down by three inches to 15 inches in 1993. Williams looked at the legal position and Mansell warned: "It is a big step backwards on performance. Now we will see who had the best fuel and who will be hurt most. I am pretty sure we had the best fuel thanks to Elf. There could be a 50 horsepower difference – and not for the better. We could be struggling."

In the build-up to the race Mansell had relaxed with the family, had done some work with his Canon sponsors, who were planning a major advertising campaign featuring him, and had enjoyed a day with Brian Clough at Nottingham Forest, also backed by Labatt's Brewery. He had also gone testing at Silverstone, running the RS4 engine over half race distance. A final decision was yet to be made as to whether the engine would be run in action for the first time in the Grand Prix.

Renault had had to put all their engines on test to calibrate them for the new fuel. "It has meant a fantastic amount of work for everyone," said Mansell. All this plus a circuit which was slow, tight and offered little opportunity for overtaking. "The race is won or lost in the first five seconds," said Mansell. "It is all about qualifying, getting in front on the grid and staying there."

There were also the inevitable contract questions. Mansell was relaxed about it: "Nothing will be happening in the near future. I have not made up my mind," he said. "I am ready to sign a new contract under the right conditions. My motivation is to get the right package and if I can do that I will drive again next year." Little did Mansell know that everything would change within five days.

But for the moment none of these many pressures seemed to be affecting him. He was remarkably laid back. Wife Rosanne was around and the children were back in the Isle of Man. Sunday would be Chloe's tenth birthday. Irrespective of the result of the race, Mansell had arranged a private plane to whisk him back to his home for *the* celebration.

Mansell headed out to the track early, driving himself from his hotel overlooking the Danube in the heart of Budapest, a city that is rapidly shaking off its Communist greyness. The day was hot and sunny but it was not long before Mansell was really feeling the heat. The free practice on the Friday is always of interest as it gives heavy clues to who has the best set-up for the track and who is adapting best.

As Mansell had forecast a loss of power from the change in fuel, everyone watched and waited to see what would happen. Mansell hardly had time to find out: a small flash fire in his engine bay forced him to switch to the spare car. That stranded him with an electrical failure. He switched back to the repaired race car and then tried the spare car before the end. He finished the session fourth.

"We still have a lot of work to do. There are improvements we can make," said Mansell, who had watched team-mate Patrese finally prove that despite the fuel changes the pattern could remain the same. The McLarens of Senna and Gerhard Berger had been first and second but Patrese got his act together after 27 laps and was the only man into the 1.15s, a second and a half ahead of Mansell. Yet again, the cars were indulging in some spectacular synchronised spinning, the problem being that the kerbs had been lifted for a motorcycle Grand Prix and drivers were cutting corners and bringing dirt onto the track.

Lunch was served and Mansell came back to find that his army was now in evidence, somewhat prematurely flying flags and banners proclaiming 'Nigel the King'. He welcomed them ten minutes into the session with a hot lap. He went round in 1 minute 15.959 seconds, and that was the signal for the McLarens to growl into action. Patrese struck first, however, with 1 minute 15.476 seconds. Mansell responded with a lap which was two tenths slower, tried again and went off, setting the dry grass alight as he started off once more. He came out for another try later but locked up his brakes again avoiding another incident and ruined his tyres.

He was smiling at the end. Neither McLaren man had been able to get closer than eight tenths of a second and Mansell admitted: "I almost T-boned someone out there. We have had some excitement with traffic today. I am just happy to be on the front row. We will have to improve again tomorrow to stay clear. The big problem is the lack of kerbs – there are no apexes, people are putting their wheels off and you can come across dust clouds on flying laps. As long as you are at the front, it is OK.

"Let's face it, though, this is not a proper race circuit. It is Mickey Mouse. I can hit a one iron further than the straight. It is tough going and I had a little mishap when

I went off. It was my fault - I was pushing on tyres that I thought had come in and they had not. At the end of the day, I have to say that on 16-lap tyres I was happy to do a 1 minute 15.7."

He denied any pressure. "I am taking it calmer here. If Riccardo goes steaming into the distance and I get second then I will be happy. I have already been told that there will be no team orders, but that does not surprise me as there have not been any all season." This was just as well, for Patrese was busy saying: "It would be nice for me to win a race this season. For once I have had no problems and I am confident that I can stay on pole."

Martin Brundle, who finished the day in seventh position, said: "There were cars spinning all over the place. I have never seen anything like it."

A breeze easing through the surrounding hills made Saturday's heat more bearable, but soon some drivers were blaming it for adding to the handling problems. Patrese held his position as quickest as Mansell pointed out: "Track conditions are unbelievably slippery. It seems as though there is virtually no grip."

Brabham continued to struggle on, surviving another crisis which kept Damon Hill, now their only driver after the loss of Eric van de Poele, in the pits. He showed his form when, without morning practice, he emerged to pilot the aged Brabham onto the last row of the grid before piling it into a barrier.

Perry McCarthy had already been eliminated at the pre-qualifying stage after his Moda team earned themselves a FISA warning by restricting the man from Romford to 45 seconds. McCarthy had finally exploded with rage, and so had the officials.

At the top end of the pits, Mansell put his faith in the second qualifying session. He gave it plenty of boot but the best he could manage on a day of mayhem was 1 minute 15.950, which was not enough to improve his position to first. Oddly enough, most other drivers did improve their times, but not by enough to change their grid ranking significantly, apart from Brundle, who moved to sixth, and Michele Alboreto, an outstandingly consistent driver, in his Footwork: he moved from 18th to seventh. Cars were spinning like jugglers' plates and Mansell was not immune, waltzing off on a quick run and testing the barrier strength.

Patrese, the main threat, had pole position for the second time in Hungary but Mansell said: "I am just happy to be on the front row. This afternoon was just a big lottery, with everyone trying to get clear laps, and there were many, many accidents. I came round on a quick lap and there was dust. I had to brake because of another accident and I lost it – it was as simple as that. The race is going to be very difficult."

Renault confirmed that for the first time, the RS4 engine would be raced.

So the grid had a familiar look: two Williams, followed by Senna, whose McLaren now also had traction control, and Schumacher on second row with Berger and Brundle filling the third. There was an atmosphere of impatience in Sunday's warm-up and Patrese again emphasised his determination: "Today I am going for a win."

After the warm-up, Mansell attended the usual drivers' briefing where ideas are discussed and argued among them. Then he headed for the motorhome for a lunch of pasta and parmesan cheese and plenty to drink. He needed to keep up his heavy intake of fluid to compensate for weight loss and dehydration during the race.

Then he had 40 minutes of quiet rest, finding sleep impossible. He walked to the pits and had a quick chat with Frank Williams and his race engineer David Brown. His wife, Rosanne, came across, wished him well and kissed him before he pulled on his asbestos hood, zipped up his racing suit, forced his head inside his helmet and climbed into the car. Mansell sat on the grid in the shade of the footbridge as final adjustments were made. All around him was organised bedlam, with mechanics, photographers, hangers-on – even parachutists who landed very nearby – milling about. He closed his eyes for some quiet contemplation, focusing on what the next two hours meant, the sacrifices, the pain, the scares. Now was the time.

A look at the watch of his friend and team manager Peter Windsor and he was on his feet. He took a long swig of water from a bottle as someone kept the sun off him with an umbrella and then he poured it round his thick, powerful neck and onto his white T-shirt before fastening his racing suit.

Then it was into the car, ready to go. One warm-up lap and suddenly he was propelled into the big race. Red turned to green at 2.00pm and Mansell got a calmer, more controlled start than previously, but when he reached the first corner, Patrese held him off from taking the inside line.

As Mansell backed off, both McLarens took him on the outside. Mansell expected no team favours but he was a touch aggrieved at Patrese. "I think you saw that there were no team orders – that was demonstrated when he pushed me sideways into the barrier," said Mansell later.

This was the time for Patrese to show his paces. He gave it full blast, building a solid lead of almost seven seconds after five laps. Senna seemed content to let Patrese disappear over the horizon while he held second and controlled the rest of the race from there on the tight track. There were already only 22 cars, for at the very first bend another team with no orders, Ligier, lost both cars as they went for it together. Sadly for Johnny Herbert, he was caught up in the mess, as was Gabriele Tarquini.

Lap 8 proved eventful. Benetton team-mates Brundle and Schumacher were doing battle and the Norfolk man's fist was definitely shaken in the German's direction after one manoeuvre.

Ahead, Mansell swooped on Berger, passing the Austrian at the end of the pit straight. On lap 12 he tried to take Senna at the same place as Patrese's lead increased to 19 seconds. By the 18th lap the Italian was lapping backmarkers. Ferrari, who had displayed a stunning line-up of their famous cars in a parade to celebrate their 500th Grand Prix, must have wished that they had one of them on the track, for Jean Alesi spun off, one of five cars to depart on laps 14 and 15. After 20 laps, 11 cars had gone.

Mansell was now blatantly held up lapping Pierluigi Martini, who earned himself a ten second penalty for his pains. As he chased Senna, Mansell set the fastest lap, 1 minute 21.023 seconds. On lap 30, Patrese was almost as many seconds ahead, and one tour later Berger took advantage of Mansell running wide on a bend and dived through. It was three laps before Mansell took him again. This was certainly no procession, for behind Mansell Berger was fighting off the Benettons and Mika Haakinen in the Lotus.

As is the way in Formula One, the race changed in the blink of an eye on lap 39. Coming through a left-hand bend, the leading Williams car suddenly went into a spin, finishing up straddled over the kerb. It was a dangerous position and the marshals were allowed to push Patrese back on . . . but by that time he was seventh, and his dream had been devoured by the pack.

Senna led, Mansell was second and the Brazilian manufactured a ten-second cushion, the British driver apparently deciding to settle for the six points and the title. Suddenly the memories of 1986 flooded Mansell's mind as the voice of technical director Patrick Head burst through on the radio. "Come in, come in, you have a problem," he said.

Mansell's heart sank and he headed for the pits on lap 61. After Germany, the team had taped over the cockpit light that gave warning of a puncture as it had been wrong, but in the pits their computer read-outs told them he had a slow puncture. The tyre change, often not one of Williams' strong points, was quick and smooth. Nearby, the red army of McLaren mechanics watched with bated breath. Mansell went back in a screaming, angry cloud of dust.

Although it was a quick stop he rejoined the pack in sixth place. Minutes later it was fifth as Schumacher's race came to a dramatic end. The German's complete rear wing unit flew off as he hurtled down the straight, and in a stunning demonstration of how these cars cannot run without downforce, his Benetton went into a series of spins. Fortunately, it came to rest safely in a huge sand trap and the wing unit, which had flown over the barrier, miraculously missed the spectators.

Even excellent drivers such as Mika Haakinen, Martin Brundle and Gerhard Berger were no match for Mansell on fresh tyres. He passed them all, Berger for the third time. Now he was second, but Senna had shown his wisdom by using up some of his 50-second cushion to pop in for tyres. Even that had taken only 6.6 seconds.

There was to be no catching the Brazilian. It was the

reigning World Champion's last act of defiance before the crown slipped into the grasp of a man who had been stretching out for it for six years. Mansell swept over the line 40.139 seconds behind Senna and probably for the first time in his life was delighted to be there.

He had not won the race – he had 'only' come second – but it was the greatest second of his competitive life and now he was Britain's seventh Formula One World Champion. The lifelong quest had been to follow Mike Hawthorn (1958), Graham Hill (1962 and 1968), Jim Clark (1963 and 1965), John Surtees (1964), Jackie Stewart (1969, 1971 and 1973) and James Hunt (1976).

A small contingent of Mansell maniacs climbed the walls and the fences to dance around with flags, one holding a banner which proclaimed: 'Mansell – the ultimate driving machine.' This delayed his entry to the *parc ferme* where the cars must be taken after the race for regulation checks.

There were congratulations from all sides as he climbed out and then it was up onto the podium. The national anthem was played for Brazil, but the fans sang 'God Save the Queen', replacing Her Majesty's name with Nigel's for the moment. They basked in the sunshine and in the reflected glory of Mansell's victory, and soon they were bathing in the champagne which sprayed from the podium.

Mansell then began the walk along an open passageway between the podium and the press room for his post-race conference, and it was fitting that there, in the full public gaze, his wife finally caught up with him. They embraced and kissed and there were tears of joy at having overcome so much. The crowd roared their approval and Mansell invited Rosanne to sit with him at the press conference.

She admitted: "I walked up and down behind the pit

garages, popping in to look at the monitors now and again. I must have walked miles." Mansell, caught up in the whole thing, had been so bewildered that he thought he had come third. He had asked his pit crew on the radio twice after the descent of the chequered flag to confirm that he was World Champion.

"I just could not grasp it. I just kept asking 'is it true?' and they kept saying it was. I don't want it to sink in quickly. It has been a long time coming but now it is the most amazing feeling. I dedicate this win to my fans, my fantastic Canon Williams Renault team, Elf and everyone who has helped, but mostly to my lovely wife who has stood by me all the way. I could not have done this without her. We are a team.

"It felt like I had 100 tons on my shoulders. I put on a smile and tried to be cheerful all the while, but I'm glad it is all over now. I had a bad moment when they radioed that I had a puncture. I did not really need the radio – Patrick Head's voice was that loud."

Everybody wanted to congratulate him, but he was sticking to his plan: interviews, handshakes and then a dash for the jet back to the Isle of Man. At Ballaman House his daughter Chloe had celebrated her birthday with her brothers Leo and Greg and her grandfather by watching the race. When it was over the boys went to play football in the garden while Chloe watched for more shots of her dad. "It is Chloe's birthday and I hope I am taking her back the greatest present she could ever have," said Mansell.

He departed, firing angry words at James Hunt for his latest television comments suggesting that Mansell was asking around $23 million to drive the next season and that he would need to moderate his demands. Senna, said Hunt, had offered to drive the Williams for nothing.

Frank Williams' response was wry. "If he said that, get him on the telephone."

Mansell's reply was more forthright: "I am fed up with hearing what James Hunt has to say. He is the ex-Champion. I am the Champion now. Frank and I are very close to agreement." Mansell left saying that he wanted to defend the title in 1993. "I will be talking with Frank on Monday or Tuesday and I hope that we can come to a sensible agreement. We are close. We know each other's position."

On Tuesday he called a press conference at a golf club hotel near his home on the Isle of Man. He arrived in a top-line Renault sportscar with Rosanne and was promptly encouraged to ride a bike near the beach by photographers.

He had spent the day and the previous night opening letters and reading faxes of congratulation. "The postman should get overtime. He's carrying so much stuff to our house. It is unbelievable," said Mansell. Rock stars and motor sport enthusiasts Chris Rea and Chris de Burgh had been on the phone, as had some of his superstar golfing buddies such as Mark McNulty and Greg Norman.

Mansell was in a good mood but determined about the future when he spoke. The contract situation had not been sorted, far from it, but he could confirm that Alain Prost would definitely be in a Williams car in 1993. Riccardo Patrese had been told to offer his services elsewhere for the next season. Mansell said: "I don't know how Prost has done it, but to be out for a year and to come back and get into the best team and the best drive is some achievement. On paper, Alain is the greatest driver in Formula One with 44 wins, but his reputation has not done him proud. Being fired from the most historic team, Ferrari, is not exactly the best way to leave motor racing."

He gave Prost a good working over in his usual direct manner. "I am a better and more courageous racer than he will be if he is in Formula One for a lifetime or another ten years. He will be more of a chauffeur, making the car work for him. I can carry a car round but it is much more tiring." The chauffeur comment made a dozen headlines the following day but it had been made with some respect, offering a contrast between styles.

Williams must have rubbed his eyes with some disbelief when he read Mansell's forthright comments, but the Englishman was clearing the ground for a future relationship. The duo had first teamed up in 1990 when Prost had joined Ferrari. Mansell had enjoyed his first season with the team, but by mid-season he had had enough and retired.

"When we were together at Ferrari I was very uncomfortable. I could not compete on a technical level. Now he would underestimate me at his peril. I have learned a lot more and I am a much better driver. Prost disrupted things at Ferrari and upset what was a good team. This time he is in an English team, and I have had a total of six years with them. Alain has more to lose. If anything goes on, all the engineers will come running to tell me in a second."

That put down the markers for Prost, but Mansell was also anxious to make it known that, given the opportunities for equal status in the team, he would defend the title 'vigorously'. If the opportunity was not made he would consider retirement, but he added: "I do not want to leave a team which I have helped create with hard work. I have now won 26 races with Frank Williams and three with Ferrari. My future is with Williams or not at all."

Rosanne agreed that they would make a joint decision about whether he would drive, but she added: "He deserves the chance to enjoy it." Mansell retorted: "Whether or not we get it is another thing. Who says life is fair?"

Within hours, his words would be haunting him. A Williams director, Sheridan Thynne, telephoned from the Didcot headquarters. The offer made to him in Hungary had been greatly reduced – Ayrton Senna had said that he would drive for nothing. "If you do not accept the new offer, Senna is ready to sign tonight," was the message.

Newly arrived at the summit of his achievement, Mansell could already see the end of the road.

HUNGARIAN GRAND PRIX

HUNGARORING

Circuit length: 2.465 miles/3.968 kilometres

Race distance: 77 laps (189.805 miles/305.536 kilometres)

1992 – MARLBORO HUNGARIAN GRAND PRIX – BUDAPEST

RACE CLASSIFICATION AFTER 77 LAPS
(305.536 km = 189.851 mls)

Pos	Nr	Driver	Nat	Make	Team Make	Nat	Total Time	km/h	mph	Diff
1	1	A. SENNA	BRA	McLaren Honda	HONDA MARLBORO McLAREN		1:45'19.216	172.424	107.139	
2	5	N. MANSELL	GBR	Williams Renault	CANON WILLIAMS TEAM		1:45'59.355	171.346	106.469	40.139
3	2	G. BERGER	AUT	McLaren Honda	HONDA MARLBORO McLAREN		1:46'09.998	171.062	106.293	50.782
4	11	M. HAKKINEN	FIN	Lotus Ford	TEAM CASTROL LOTUS		1:46'13.529	170.968	106.235	54.313
5	20	M. BRUNDLE	GBR	Benetton Ford	CAMEL BENETTON FORD		1:46'16.714	170.884	106.182	57.498
6	28	I. CAPELLI	ITA	Ferrari	FERRARI		1:46'09.430	168.856	104.922	1 LAP
7	4	M. ALBORETO	ITA	Footwork Mugen-Honda	FOOTWORK MUGEN-HONDA		1:45'27.400	167.730	104.223	2 LAPS
8	9	A. DE CESARIS	ITA	Tyrrell Ilmor	TYRRELL		1:45'34.023	167.556	104.115	2 LAPS
9	17	P. BELMONDO	FRA	March Ilmor	MARCH F.1		1:47'21.960	164.092	101.962	3 LAPS
10	33	M. GUGELMIN	BRA	Jordan Yamaha	SASOL JORDAN YAMAHA		1:46'45.780	162.789	101.152	4 LAPS
11	8	D. HILL	GBR	Brabham Judd	MOTOR RACING DEV.		1:46'55.406	162.545	101.001	4 LAPS

NOT CLASSIFIED

Pos	Nr	Driver	Nat	Make	Team Make	Nat	Total Time	km/h	mph	COVERED
12	19	M. SCHUMACHER	GER	Benetton Ford	CAMEL BENETTON FORD		1:27'27.678	171.493	106.561	63 LAPS
13	6	R. PATRESE	ITA	Williams Renault	CANON WILLIAMS TEAM		1:17'01.735	169.991	105.628	55 LAPS
14	22	P. MARTINI	ITA	BMS Dallara Ferrari	SCUDERIA ITALIA		58'57.103	161.542	100.378	40 LAPS
15	30	U. KATAYAMA	JPN	Venturi Lamborghini	CENTRAL PARK-VEN. LARR.		50'48.428	164.008	101.910	35 LAPS
16	27	J. ALESI	FRA	Ferrari	FERRARI		19'54.332	167.440	104.042	14 LAPS
17	29	B. GACHOT	FRA	Venturi Lamborghini	CENTRAL PARK-VEN. LARR.		18'59.963	162.902	101.223	14 LAPS
18	10	A. SUZUKI	JPN	Footwork Mugen-Honda	FOOTWORK MUGEN-HONDA		19'00.251	162.861	101.197	13 LAPS
19	3	O. GROUILLARD	FRA	Tyrrell Ilmor	TYRRELL		19'19.336	160.180	99.531	13 LAPS
20	16	K. WENDLINGER	AUT	March Ilmor	MARCH F.1		19'19.807	160.115	89.491	13 LAPS
21	32	S. MODENA	ITA	Jordan Yamaha	SASOL JORDAN YAMAHA		19'21.039	159.945	99.385	13 LAPS
22	14	E. VAN DE POELE	BEL	Fondmetal Ford	FONDMETAL F1		3'13.643	147.537	91.676	2 LAPS

FASTEST LAP: 5 N. MANSELL – Lap 63 Time: 1'18.308 (182.418 km/h = 113.349 mph)

Belgium Grand Prix

Spa

Nigel Mansell arrived at the village of Spa-Francor-champs, situated among pine forests in the hills of the Ardennes, with much on his mind after his celebrations had been torpedoed by that telephone call. By the time the Grand Prix circus rolled into town, the race on one of the world's great tracks was the last topic of conversation.

The talk was of where Mansell, Senna and Prost would end up and whether Lotus employee James Gilbey, whose telephone conversation with Princess Diana had made him infamous, would turn up. Gilbey's situation was the easiest to solve. He stayed at home puzzling how to beat the media, leaving Formula One to cope with the great mathematical problem – how to divide three into two.

It was now clear that Mansell, Senna and Prost were engaged in a battle for the two Williams cars for 1993. Even though Prost had already signed, the only certainty in Grand Prix racing is that there are no certainties. The Ides of March plotters could take lessons from Formula One. The only definite news on drivers was that Gerhard Berger would be quitting Marlboro McLaren and rejoining Ferrari in 1993 to team up with Jean Alesi. Ivan Capelli was out. That left a McLaren seat open and, apart from the big three, everyone seemed interested even though it now seemed certain that Honda would be quitting.

Mansell had had his telephone call but, when spurning the Williams team's ultimatum, he had told them: "If these are the terms you are offering me, you had better go ahead and sign Senna." What was now clear was that the possibility of defending the title with Williams Renault was now eclipsed by the serious threat of losing his seat beforehand. He had not signed a contract and his negotiations with Frank Williams had ground to a halt. He arrived in Belgium philosophic about events.

"There are things I know now which would shock. I have not had any direct contact with Frank Williams since winning the title. He has not been on the phone to congratulate me. There are things going on which shock me, even after all this time in the sport. I do not know what is happening with the contract. They haven't even told me officially that Prost is joining the team. Anything could happen but I know one thing – for the first time in my career I will decide what is best for me and my family. I will not be rushed."

He had his financial adviser with him but Frank Williams, the team owner, was also adopting a 'wait and see' attitude. Williams is an articulate man who chooses his words carefully, and his comments seemed to carry even more of a message than their face value offered. "There is no date I can give you," said Williams. "I have always said I wanted Nigel to stay. I know which two drivers I want. As a Briton I would like to see Nigel here next year but there have to be many considerations."

Surely public opinion would be outraged if the top British driver were not to be involved with the leading British team after a season like this? Williams was as blunt and logical as usual, saying: "We get no money from Britain. None of our sponsorship is British. They do not pay for the running of the team. It might be different if everyone in the country contributed £10 but they don't. This is a business and my concern is what is best for Williams Engineering and its employees."

Everywhere in Formula One things were coming to a head, either over drivers or money. There were creditors around some teams, bailiffs at another and drivers had their managers in attendance. Brabham failed to show, succumbing to the financial waves which had finally sunk them. The boss of the Andrea Moda team, Andrea Sassetti, was arrested for fraud and Lotus was granted a court injunction ordering a recently-departed employee to return data to them. Elf were considering legal action over the fuel regulations. Fun and games it was not, and after two days of sunshine, the weather closed in to match the prevailing mood.

Not that Mansell's driving betrayed any sense of let-down or anger. He is far too professional, competitive and committed to let his standards slip. When the work started, Mansell was right up there as usual.

Spa, as it is known, is a marvellous high-speed scenic circuit, swooping through the trees and up and down hills. It includes the two most spectacular stretches, Blanchimont and Eau Rouge. Blanchimont is a 190mph sweeping left-hander, Eau Rouge a roller-coaster run down from the hairpin above the pits with a nasty little twist as it starts to climb up the hill on the other side.

After the Hungaroring, this is a leap from a 50cc moped to a 500cc motorbike. Spa has speed, history, views, good vantage points and, above all, width, so that cars can pass each other or at least have a go. McLaren held the franchise on success here. They had won the previous five races, Ayrton Senna enjoying four straight victories.

Mansell was the last man before that run to succeed, in 1986 in a Williams Honda.

The length of the course, 4.3 miles, in this region means that it can be fine in one area, pouring with rain in another. Goodyear arrived with the 2350 Eagle Radial, warning that a circuit like this would require power and that the fuel changes to pump blend could have more dramatic effect than in Hungary, and could influence tyre performance.

The practice session offered the unusual sight of Perry McCarthy in the Moda car – Brabham's absence meant no pre-qualifying. It was not long, however, before Blanchimont had claimed its first victim, Erik Comas, who had a heavy smash after sliding off. Senna was first on the scene and stopped to help, and the practice session was stopped for a long time while repairs were made to the barrier. "The corner where Comas crashed is one of the nastiest on any circuit in the world," said Mansell. "It is very fast, not nice at all." Comas was fine but took no further part in the weekend. It was a warning to others, but this is not a sport in which the participants dwell on the dangers.

When the session got going again, Mansell was quickest, Patrese second. Even if neither of them had a future with Williams, they were not about to let the team or themselves down. Just to show how things can change in one season, the race statistics for 1991 had Senna first and Roberto Moreno with the fastest lap on 1 minute 55 seconds. On this Friday morning the same Moreno, now in a Moda, was 30th.

In the qualifying session Mansell's only complaint was a soft brake pedal problem but it looked as if he had hardly used it on the eighth lap as he came round in 1 minute 50.545 seconds, setting the highest speed at

193mph. Senna took second, but he was 2.198 seconds behind with Schumacher third and Patrese fourth. The Brazilian's main thrust of the day came after practice when he threw more light on some of the goings-on behind the scenes. He announced: "My negotiations with Williams are over. I will not be going there next year. Renault and Williams wanted me and three times we were close to signing but it came to nothing. The reason is that Alain Prost, who has been signed for many months, has a clause in his contract which allows him to veto me. He cannot cope with me. He doesn't want to take me on in the same team. The most likely option is that I will now take a sabbatical."

This was revealing, for it showed that Williams Renault had planned to oust Mansell and go for a Senna–Prost team. If Prost had quit in protest, Mansell would have partnered Senna. They could not lose.

Mansell's hand seemed to have been strengthened by Senna's announcement, but now the Englishman planned to erase his rival from the record books. "I am going flat out to get the ninth win to beat Senna's record of eight in a season," he confirmed. "After that we will see what happens. I can also give the team the constructors' Championship they are desperate to have."

Fortunes were mixed for other British drivers. Lotus confirmed that they had re-signed Johnny Herbert, the man many expected to be another World Champion, but inspired rumours suggested that Martin Brundle was about to be squeezed out of Benetton Ford to make room for Patrese. It was, said the chatterers, the Italian connection. The team was run by Italians and sponsored by Benetton, and they would prefer Patrese.

Overnight it rained and the wet weather continued into Saturday, wrecking the chances of improved positions on the grid – not that it stops drivers trying. Just before the end of the morning session Gerhard Berger stepped from a massive shunt after his car aquaplaned at Eau Rouge. Berger is a driver with perspective and humour, and his comment was: "You don't realise how fast you are going in these things until you stop!" Mansell, who had had a spin himself, said: "There was a river coming across the circuit at Eau Rouge and I have great sympathy for drivers who had accidents, especially Gerhard."

Patrese did not bother to enter the monsoon after lunch, one of eight drivers to stay dry in favour of having engine work done in the pits. "We have worked on a different wing setting because if it is a dry race tomorrow we want the facility to come into the pits to change things. I am happy with how things have gone."

Practice starts are normally not allowed but both Senna and Mansell had been spotted doing them. Mansell explained: "We got permission to do practice starts. When Ayrton and I are off the line it will be the driver who has the best computer on board who gets the best start. Once you drop the clutch it is down to the computer and the software who gets the best traction, and away you go. If there is one thing that disappoints me about technology it is that. I used to get really good starts, but now it is all down to the computers. Now the boffins are looking at the read-outs and if one is better than another they will make adjustments."

He insisted that his motivation was as strong as ever. "I want to win as many races as possible this season. I amazed myself yesterday. Maybe because I am a little more relaxed I felt I was going slower in the car, but in fact I was going quicker. Perhaps it is a threshold you reach when you win a World Championship, I don't know."

He did not want to talk of contract negotiations. "It is a good question, but I cannot add to anything I have said earlier. I think everyone should toddle off to Frank Williams and ask him. When you find out, please tell me." But he did manage an oblique swipe at both his critics and Williams when he was asked if he really was relaxed. "I am absolutely relaxed. No one who wants to be stubborn with me can say anything that could make me rise to it. It doesn't matter at all because we have won the World Championship, and those people who say those things are making themselves seem even more foolish."

That evening, Bernard Dudot, Renault's technical mastermind, insisted that the French company did want Mansell. He was an integral part of the team. "He has been very important in his attitude and his technical feedback for us," said Dudot. "I enjoy working with Nigel and he has done much to help us achieve so much success." It seemed another step towards clearing the path to a 1993 contract but Mansell, who had gone off to play golf as the weather improved after the test, responded with some scepticism the next morning.

He had run well in the warm-up, the weather had improved and he was in fine form as he sat outside the Williams motorhome with some reporters. "It is nice to hear that they want me but it doesn't ring true, does it, when someone else has been signed up for months. If they are saying that Prost is not signed up, then keep the team as it is. Today I am even more speechless after what I have learned over the past few days. I haven't even asked any questions, I have just been listening. And, having the inside track, I know that certain things fit in with what I already know. My strategy of just staying quiet, saying nothing, has worked. I am getting a picture now."

He revealed that all weekend, he and Frank Williams

had exchanged just five words. "Nothing has been mentioned this weekend about anything." And he added with a laugh: "I have said two words. Frank has said three and two of those were 'good morning'. I can't tell you what the others were."

If he was feeling bad, Mansell pointed out, think how his team-mate Patrese was feeling, having been kicked out. He even had a thought for Senna: "He has made his offer of driving for free, though a way would have been found round that by Senna's sponsors, and he has been rejected. He has had to swallow that bitter pill. He's had his face slapped. Yet they still say that there is no contract in place for Prost. If that is the case, why did they not sign Senna when they had the chance?"

He finished a cup of tea and rose to leave the covered awning area coupled to the motorhome. Then he paused, wondering how much more of his off-track torment to offer. "Gentlemen, I am just as bewildered and frustrated as you are. I don't think that being the new World Champion and winning 26 races for the Williams team, even if it is what I have been paid to do, counts for anything these days. The team doing as well as it has with Riccardo has made everyone extremely happy, yet they have to destroy the good feeling, goodwill and everything else. It is mind-boggling for any blue chip company. They don't need to do that, but they have deemed to do that."

Yet he still had a job to do on the track which required his full attention. "Yes, my motivation is dwindling a bit now, but I just have to get on with it." He was struggling with a stomach bug which had caused diarrhoea and had had a broken night, but his humour was high in spite of this and assorted other problems.

He had been loaned a motorbike to ride between his

hotel near Spa and the track and loved the run on the country road in the morning. That morning two policemen had stopped him after they recognised the bike as being local. He signed a few autographs. Then, at the gate, a 'jobsworth' had refused him entry to the track. He told the Champion that he was at the wrong entrance, did not have the proper sticker. "Do you know who I am?" Mansell had to say eventually, laughing all the while. "It was really funny. He said: 'I know who you are, and I don't care', but eventually we sorted it out." It says much for the man that he laughed it off and did not have the buffoon fired.

He then returned to his contract problems. "I thought that when you made it, you might actually be given a smoother ride. Instead they have pulled the carpet out from under us. Whatever you might feel for me, add at least half again for Riccardo. He's a gentleman. I feel really sorry that a family unit has been broken up." Off he went to lunch, pondering whether the McLarens had been on full tanks for their morning outing. If that were the case, he said, they were fast, very fast.

Heavy clouds rolled back over the track and mist shrouded the hilltops as the race began, but most drivers went off on slicks. Mansell got his technological start but Senna whipped past on the first lap. At the end of the second lap, however, the impatient Williams cars finally forced their way past the slower McLaren. But it was raining heavily and, one hour later, Mansell was in for wet tyres.

With Alesi and Schumacher, who had also been in for tyres, Mansell quickly carved his way back through the field. On lap eight, he and Alesi collided as they both went into La Source. Mansell drove on, but the Ferrari went out immediately with a puncture and suspension trouble.

The weather brightened and the racing line dried, forcing drivers to head in for slicks again. Senna went first, but the key change was when Schumacher took a trip across the verge, damaged his tyres and was lucky to survive.

Brundle went past and the German went in for tyres. When he came out, Brundle had to go in and Mansell went a lap later. Schumacher held the lead now, by six seconds on lap 34 from Mansell. A battle was on, with Mansell shaving time off the gap. By the 38th, it was down to a sliver over three seconds.

Suddenly, the clocks showed a 15.1 second gap. Red Five, said Mansell later, had lost the left bank of the exhaust, and the car's power dropped by 1400 revs. The fight for first was over and Mansell was just happy to finish second. Exactly a year after his debut for Jordan, which led to his controversial departure to Benetton, Michael Schumacher had become the first German since Jochen Mass in 1975 to win a Grand Prix. He cried tears of joy. It should also have been a night of delight for Williams Renault, for Mansell and Patrese, who finished third, had given them the constructors' World Championship.

Instead, the off-track events seemed to catch up with them. Frank Williams was nowhere to be seen, there was little jollity in the air and Mansell did not hang around long. He was gracious in defeat, congratulating Schumacher with the words: "This is a fantastic win for Formula One. I was looking forward to a real, great battle at the end but, like Riccardo, I had a big problem."

It turned out to be an electronic glitch, but Mansell was not too concerned. "I am going back now to think about what I know, put all the pieces of the jigsaw together. As I have said today, I thank the Williams team for all their help. This should have been the greatest year in motor racing history for them. For me it has been great.

"Right now, I am going home to relax and decide what is right for Nigel Mansell and his family. I am not going to wait any longer. When I spoke on the Isle of Man, I knew something that was definite – unfortunately, what I knew then was not correct. The goalposts moved, things changed and Ayrton Senna has cast new light on matters this weekend. I have not been upset and I am not upset now. I am very relaxed. The biggest problem is not understanding it all." He roared off on his bike to do his thinking.

Martin Brundle headed home with more points, having gained fourth place. It was his seventh points finish in eight races. As Mansell sat in the Isle of Man contemplating his future, Brundle's was decided by Benetton. Four days later he was sacked.

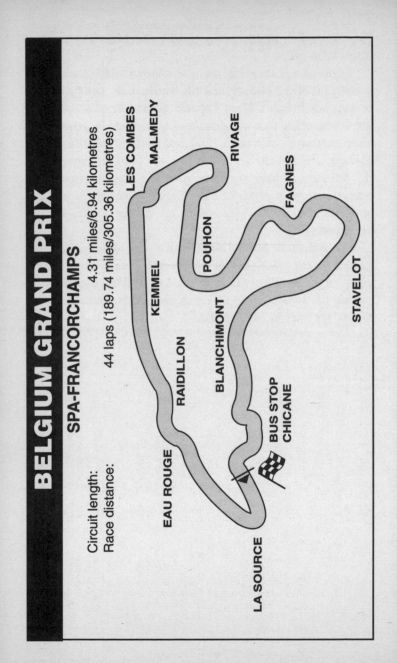

1992 – BELGIAN GRAND PRIX – SPA
RACE CLASSIFICATION AFTER 44 LAPS
(306.856 km = 190.671 mls)

Pos	Nr	Driver		Team Make	Make	Total Time	km/h	mph	Diff
1	19	M. SCHUMACHER	GER	CAMEL BENETTON FORD	BENETTON FORD	1:36'10.721	191.429	118.948	
2	5	N. MANSELL	GBR	CANON WILLIAMS TEAM	WILLIAMS RENAULT	1:36'47.316	190.222	118.199	36.595
3	6	R. PATRESE	ITA	CANON WILLIAMS TEAM	WILLIAMS RENAULT	1:36'54.618	189.984	118.050	43.897
4	20	M. BRUNDLE	GBR	CAMEL BENETTON FORD	BENETTON FORD	1:36'56.780	189.913	118.006	46.059
5	1	A. SENNA	BRA	HONDA MARLBORO McLAREN	McLAREN HONDA	1:37'19.090	189.187	117.556	1:08.369
6	11	M. HAKKINEN	FIN	TEAM CASTROL LOTUS	LOTUS FORD	1:37'20.751	189.133	117.522	1'10.030
7	21	J. LEHTO	FIN	SCUDERIA ITALIA	BMS DALLARA FERRARI	1:37'48.958	188.224	116.957	1'38.237
8	4	A. DE CESARIS	ITA	TYRRELL	TYRRELL ILMOR	1:36'58.425	185.544	115.292	1 LAP
9	10	A. SUZUKI	JPN	FOOTWORK MUGEN-HONDA	FOOTWORK MUGEN-HONDA	1:36'59.659	185.505	115.267	1 LAP
10	14	E. VAN DE POELE	BEL	FONDMETAL F1	FONDMETAL FORD	1:37'33.147	184.444	114.607	1 LAP
11	16	K. WENDLINGER	AUT	MARCH F.1	MARCH ILMOR	1:37'37.077	184.320	114.531	1 LAP
12	17	E. NASPETTI	ITA	MARCH F.1	MARCH ILMOR	1:37'58.775	183.639	114.108	1 LAP
13	12	J. HERBERT	GBR	TEAM CASTROL LOTUS	LOTUS FORD	1:33'43.774	187.502	116.508	2 LAPS
14	33	M. GUGELMIN	BRA	SASOL JORDAN YAMAHA	JORDAN YAMAHA	1:35'30.931	182.090	113.145	2 LAPS
15	32	S. MODENA	ITA	SASOL JORDAN YAMAHA	JORDAN YAMAHA	1:37'08.859	180.905	112.409	2 LAPS
16	24	G. MORBIDELLI	ITA	MINARDI TEAM	MINARDI LAMBORGHINI	1:37'09.026	180.900	112.406	2 LAPS
17	30	U. KATAYAMA	JPN	CENTRAL PARK-VEN. LARR.	VENTURI LAMBORGHINI	1:37'48.633	179.679	111.647	2 LAPS
18	29	B. GACHOT	FRA	CENTRAL PARK-VEN. LARR.	VENTURI LAMBORGHINI	1:30'58.736	183.972	114.315	4 LAPS

NOT CLASSIFIED

Pos	Nr	Driver		Team Make	Make	Total Time	km/h	mph	COVERED
19	25	T. BOUTSEN	BEL	LIGIER GITANES BLONDES	LIGIER RENAULT	1:05'14.599	178.641	111.003	27 LAPS
20	28	I. CAPELLI	ITA	FERRARI	FERRARI	58'22.803	179.188	111.342	25 LAPS
21	15	G. TARQUINI	ITA	FONDMETAL F1	FONDMETAL FORD	58'28.508	178.897	111.161	25 LAPS
22	9	M. ALBORETO	ITA	FOOTWORK MUGEN-HONDA	FOOTWORK MUGEN-HONDA	46'54.726	178.353	110.848	20 LAPS
23	27	J. ALESI	FRA	FERRARI	FERRARI	16'30.135	177.496	110.291	7 LAPS
24	3	O. GROUILLARD	FRA	TYRRELL	TYRRELL ILMOR	2'23.952	174.408	108.372	1 LAP

FASTEST LAP: 19 M. SCHUMACHER – Lap 39 Time: 1'53.791 (220.636 km/h = 137.097 mph)

Italian Grand Prix

Monza

As omens go, the end-of-the-world atmosphere in the airliner carrying Nigel Mansell and a host of other Formula One people as it bumped and tossed through thunderstorms into Milan was more accurate than a nuclear clock. Everything was up in air, not just the few delayed jets which circled later while the worst of the storm swept over northern Italy. The lure of Monza and the Italian Grand Prix is one of the strongest on the circuit for romance, emotion and tradition, but once more the race was secondary to the battles raging in the motorhomes and boardrooms.

Mansell had arrived in Monza early in the week and Wednesday, by which time the weather had become more typical, was a marvellous day for him. He played in a pro-am golf tournament and won. That evening he was greeted by the Monza Ferrari Club, which claims to be the oldest, who presented him with a gold watch to commemorate his World Championship.

Yet Thursday morning brought headlines such as NIGEL AXED BY WILLIAMS in the *Daily Express*. Mansell had spoken to some overseas journalists and had mentioned *that* telephone call after the Hungarian Grand Prix. This was not news, but it gave more credence to reports that he was considering offers to drive on the American Indycar circuit. The team, owned by Paul

Newman and Carl Haas, was believed to have made him a £3 million offer for 1993. It was a significant development, for a week earlier McLaren boss Ron Dennis had successfully completed a deal for 1993 with the reigning Indycar champion, Michael Andretti – from Newman Haas.

The American offer was lower than his worst deal with Williams, but there were advantages for Mansell. He would be able to operate from home in Florida, and a commercial future in the huge US motor sport market could develop. At the very worst, the Newman Haas offer might put some urgency into the Williams end of negotiations.

Yet again there had been no contact between Williams and Mansell since the previous race. By opening talks with Newman Haas, Mansell had put into operation the first part of the plan he had revealed in Belgium – to do what was right for him and his family.

While Mansell worked in one direction, his team-mate Riccardo Patrese had fixed himself up with Benetton Ford, who had dumped Briton Martin Brundle after his best-ever season. Brundle, sixth in the Championship, had been thanked for his 'excellent performance'. . . excellence had not been good enough, it seemed.

Mansell, sheltering from the rains at Monza, admitted that he had had exploratory talks with Newman Haas, adding: "I am pleased to say that some people are interested in my services. But these are early days." This was another barb directed at Frank Williams, but Mansell had been led to believe that their deadlock might soon be broken. "I understand that Frank is in Paris, presumably talking to Renault, and that he is coming here with an offer. My future may be sorted out this weekend. I have always been available and he knows where to find me."

Friday was cloudy but warm and drying, and even before the sound of snarling engines filled the air, more controversy erupted. This time it was caused by Honda, who announced that the sound of silence would settle over their engines in Formula One after the 1992 season. The announcement that ended one of the most successful partnerships in the history of Formula One was short and puzzling. Having won the Championship for five successive years with Williams and then McLaren, the Japanese company signed off without a mention of thanks to McLaren. The Honda withdrawal had been expected, but now the paddock buzzed with rumours of who would replace the power unit. It was vital – Senna's continuation with the team depended on it.

At last the scream of tortured metal filled the air and the brightly-coloured fans who had arrived early at the circuit settled down to enjoy the speed and action. The autodrome at Monza has changed little since the first Italian Grand Prix was held there 70 years ago. The track is the fastest on the calendar, the 1991 pole time averaging a twitch under 160mph. Here you enjoy a wonderful symphony of colours and emotions played by drivers and fans alike. Mansell had been the conductor in 1991, and despite his problems he was intent on leading again. He was still chasing his historic ninth win.

From experience, Goodyear knew that Monza was the hardest on tyres and had brought only one, compound B, the hardest. Soon Mansell and Patrese were giving the tyres a good work out, both finishing top of the morning practice session. Mansell had been asked not to talk about the contract situation and seemed optimistic.

The McLarens had arrived with their new active suspension for the first time but no decision had been made about running it in the race. Mansell was reasonably happy with his provisional pole time, set on his eighth lap, but he led Senna by just two tenths of a second and Jean Alesi was only four tenths behind in third. Patrese was fourth, and both Williams drivers complained of handling problems. Mansell warned: "We will have to go a lot quicker tomorrow to stay in front. We will have to sort out a few problems. The car was perfect for one lap and then it lost its power. The handling is not quite right, either. It has been hard work today, with a lot of oil on the track."

Any contract talk, he was asked? "I believe you need to be talking to one another to have negotiations," he replied with a smile. "I believe something will happen tonight." The mood was good, and Mansell stated: "I have said time and again that I am happy to stay with Williams to defend my title. I believe I deserve that, and it is what I hope to do. We have been close in the past but a lot of things have happened in the last few weeks.

"I just want equal treatment with anyone else who is in the team next year. I hear that Renault are really fed up with the way things have gone. In fact, I hear that there has been a major row between two leading sponsors. Things are not happy with Williams now. Alain Prost has not been officially announced and already the team has been destabilised.

"I recognise that Williams must satisfy its sponsors and work to a budget. I accepted that before, and I do now. This is not the biggest team in the world, but if they can afford to pay someone else, I am only seeking the same treatment. They know my position. I am not the one who has been moving the goalposts."

Mansell seemed ready to accept a cut in his salary, negotiated two years earlier when Frank Williams had been turned down by Ayrton Senna. The Englishman had been able to drive a hard bargain. Now he realised that commercial and political times had changed. After Hungary, Mansell had said that they were down to arguing over the number of bedrooms he would be allowed for each race in the coming season. "We need more because I want to take the family to as many races as possible," Mansell had said. "And we have already looked at taking travelling tutors with us to make sure that the children's education does not suffer."

Williams, too, now seemed to be moving towards a compromise solution. Mansell's salary, a closely-guarded secret, was reputed to be somewhere between £6 and £7 million a year. At its lowest, the most recent Williams offer after Senna's 'drive for nothing' claim was around £3.5 million; at its best, £5.5 million. Breaking his silence, Williams said: "I am optimistic about a successful outcome. By that I mean that Nigel stays with the team. The only deadline as far as we are concerned is mid-January, but I hope things are sorted out long before that. His re-signing is our priority. He is the only driver we are talking to at the moment."

Rumours abounded of a plot among the team bosses, led by Bernie Ecclestone, FISA's top man, to drive down the huge salaries. Only that afternoon Ron Dennis of McLaren had added credence to this by stating: "We are paying a very high percentage of costs in drivers' salaries. It is obvious from the comments of some drivers that money is secondary to winning, and so right now I think a better way to spend our money is on making a better racing car. Drivers will have to take a cut in salaries. You cannot continue to pay these kinds of sums in a recession." Ecclestone was later to confirm his view that times had changed. Mega-salaries had gone with Filofaxes and yuppies.

Mansell put his worries behind him and went off to take part in the event he had been eagerly looking forward to for weeks . . . a football match. The annual game between the reporters and the photographers who cover the Grand Prix circuit has taken on a new status with the backing of Camel. Mansell loves playing other sports but most are banned in his contract to ensure that he stays fit for racing. Football and golf have escaped and his enthusiasm is boundless. In 1992, the reporters became the All-Stars team and the top three drivers in the World Championship, Mansell, Patrese and Michael Schumacher, all turned out for them. Somehow, a couple of players from one of Italy's top clubs, Atalanta, also appeared.

Schumacher played well on the left wing, Patrese with skill in midfield, and Mansell in boots was like Mansell in cars. He played up front, a strong, courageous and reasonably quick striker. With his upper body strength and overall fitness he is difficult to move off the ball. His low golf handicap, around six when he is rusty, proves he has a good eye for the ball. He scored twice and set up two other goals in the All-Stars' 6-4 victory. For good measure, he was also booked. He loves the dressing-room banter and the after-match analysis, and he was tempted to join us for drinks and a meal. But there was the small matter of a meeting with Frank Williams late on Friday night.

If any problems arose at that meeting, they did not show up in Mansell's demeanour on Saturday morning when a bright, hot Italian day dawned. Mansell led the warm-up. "Problems?" he queried. "Just a bit stiff from the football, but it was worth it. Great night."

But the first hints of unrest were now permeating the paddock and his plans for an afternoon press conference, at which he had intended to reveal all, were put on ice. The day then took on an extraordinary air with one rumour climbing over another. Mansell, Prost and Senna were seen everywhere, as were team owners. "There is nothing I can say right now," said Mansell. "I have a lot of people to see."

At lunchtime, Mansell met the president of Elf, the French fuel company who are among Williams' main sponsors. Elf, he was assured, wanted him to stay.

Mansell received a fax in the garage from Ron Dennis, and soon afterwards the two men had a very public meeting outside the McLaren motorhome. Dennis insisted that it was a private meeting, adding: "Nigel explained the situation and his frustrations and I listened and explained my position." Could it be that two men who did not have a lot of empathy with one another were about to solve each other's problems? "Maybe we can find some common ground," said Dennis.

Amid all this, Mansell somehow managed to twice improve his Friday time, getting down to 1 minute 22.221 seconds, to increase his lead over Senna to six tenths of a second. Then he left the circuit for two hours to consider things and make telephone calls from his hotel. At 5.00pm he returned for another meeting with Frank Williams.

Two hours later, he and his friends from Williams, commercial director Sheridan Thynne and Peter Windsor, the team manager, went for supper at the Lotus motorhome with another old pal, Peter Collins. They stayed for almost a couple of hours and Mansell went back to his hotel to ponder the conversation.

First thing on Sunday morning, he called a press conference. Nothing is simple in Formula One: FISA had to give their permission for the conference to take place in their press room. Finally Mansell came in and took his place on the podium. While cameras and microphones were hurriedly set up by startled, half-awake media men, Mansell joked about a new book coming out the following week.

At the back of the scrum of reporters, Williams officials in their blue, red and yellow uniforms tried to squeeze through. Mansell had happened to mention on his way past the Williams motorhome that he was going to make an announcement.

"I have a statement here and it has taken many hours to decide on this. It has not been easy or taken lightly," he said. "Due to circumstances beyond my control . . ."

As he started his statement, Williams commercial manager Gary Crumpler suddenly forced his way through to whisper in Mansell's ear. "I have just been given a message which I am not at liberty to tell you – but it has tried to stop me doing what I am doing now," said Mansell.

"Due to circumstances beyond my control I have decided to retire from Formula One at the end of the season. I have made this decision with some regret – and some pause, as you have just noticed.

"Any relationship between a driver and a Formula One team is vital for success and partly dependent on money, because it defines how seriously the team and its backers take the driver. Those who know me well understand the importance of the human side and the mutual trust and goodwill and integrity and fair play that are the basis of all human relationships.

"All these issues have suffered in recent weeks. Looking back, I feel that relationships between me and the Canon Williams Renault team started to break down at the Hungarian Grand Prix. A deal was agreed with Frank

Williams before the race in front of a witness, and I have to say that at the time I felt very good about racing again with Williams in 1993. Having won the Championship, I was looking forward to defending the title with what I believe to be a very competitive car.

"However, three days after Hungary I was telephoned by a Williams director who said that he had been instructed to tell me that, because Senna would drive for 'nothing', I, the new World Champion, had to accept a massive reduction in remuneration from the figure agreed in Hungary, considerably less than I am receiving this year. If I did not, Senna was ready to sign that night. I rejected this offer and said that, if these were the terms, Williams had better go ahead and sign Senna.

"Since then, it is fair to say that relations with the team have not been good – and I refer here to the directors rather than to the scores of people behind the scenes at Williams. I have listened to many, many opinions, some well-meaning, some not, and we heard the public statements made by Senna in Belgium, and to say that I have been badly treated is, I think, a gross understatement.

"Of course, a team owner – any team owner – is free to choose whomever he likes to work for him. It is the lack of information and the sudden changes that I have found disappointing. It is difficult to put into words the sort of commitment you have to make in order to succeed in Formula One. I am aware of the criticisms made of my approach to racing. But I am the way I am because I believe in total sacrifice, a total ability to withstand pain and a total belief in myself and my ability.

"To have the motivation to win a World Championship you must in turn have those commitments back from the team. When I returned from Ferrari I did so with the belief that I had that motivation and that the team had the commitment. I don't think I was wrong. Now things are different. I no longer feel that the commitment from the team towards me for next year is there. There are many reasons for this.

"I have tried to give some idea of how I feel – other people will no doubt draw their own conclusions. For one thing, it is clear that Alain Prost has been committed to the team for months to drive for Williams. For another, I thought I had a deal when clearly I did not.

"Needless to say, I do not understand why these things have happened. Yet in recent weeks various key people have tried to smooth things over. I respect that and I thank them for their time. But now I realise that it is too late. To my mind it all comes down to fair play – or the lack of it. Money, the trigger for the problems after Hungary, is now no longer an issue for me. And just so you know, because I want you to know everything, I was told 'everything is agreed' just while I was sitting here now. Money is not the thing. As you can see, I have continued to sit here.

"I will always be grateful to the Williams team and to Renault for the support they have given me – and I hope will still give me – in 1992. I want to win the remaining races and I am sure that the FW15, from what I know about it, will do the job in 1993.

"As for myself, I know that I am not ready to retire completely. I still love my motor racing and I still want to win. So I may look at the Indycar World Series and see what opportunities are available, if any."

That was the official statement, but he added: "There is no disagreement between me and any of the sponsors. Frank Williams and I spoke minutes before coming here. I publicly thank him and Renault and all the associated sponsors. We have not fallen out. It was not a question of finance. I think I have demonstrated that in front of you, which was difficult.

"Now we are here to do a job and win this Grand Prix. I hope I can go into the race with a clear mind. Now I am relieved and I wish to enjoy my racing for the rest of the year and then retire from Formula One."

Yet it was clear that Williams and Mansell, while never having had a real raging row – perhaps it would have been better if they had – were as far apart as it was possible to be. Mansell felt cheated, wronged, and at the base of it, as he had admitted, was the question of how much he should be paid.

Williams, publicly spurned at the press conference, issued a curt and pointed statement: "Williams Grand Prix Engineering Limited deeply regrets Nigel Mansell's decision to retire from Formula One. Nigel has won 26 races for Williams, and our association has been extremely fruitful. Everyone at Williams thanks him for the remarkable efforts he has put in while in the cockpit and we wish him and his family a happy future in his retirement.

"It is noteworthy that despite the enormous support for both the team and Nigel from many British fans, we are still unable to raise any significant sponsorship from the UK. We are obviously aware of the disappointment that Nigel's retirement will generate in the UK, but Williams Grand Prix Engineering is an international company that operates on a global basis and must continue to do so."

The announcement caused uproar in the paddock. Public poses were struck by everyone from the British president of FISA, Max Mosley, who insisted it would make no difference to the popularity of Formula One, to Prost who 'regretted' Mansell's decision. Peter Collins of

Lotus, who had dined with Mansell the previous evening, now revealed that Mansell's mind had seemed pretty well made up then. Collins had worked with Mansell at the start of his racing career and his regret was real.

"His decision will take a lot out of motor racing. He is a very exciting driver to watch, a great driver, and maybe when he retires we will really appreciate him for what he was. I certainly did not try to talk him out of it. I am always happy to see drivers leave this sport in a healthy condition. But we are losing a major talent."

For two hours, the race almost lived up to the drama of the paddock. Mansell had secretly struck a deal with Patrese to help his team-mate win his national race, and for a while it seemed to be working perfectly. Mansell put his cares behind him, surged away from the grid in pole position and built up a lead of over 12 seconds by the 18th lap, by which time Patrese had climbed to second. Suddenly, the Italian was in front. Mansell, displaying great sportsmanship, had fulfilled his part of the bargain, slowing to allow Patrese past.

Now he would ride shotgun to hold Senna at bay, but after a few laps the Brazilian was left behind and the Williams cars pushed on. Mansell was never less than a fraction of a second behind while Senna slipped to 4.7 seconds adrift. On lap 39, Mansell set the fastest lap, 1 minute 26.119 seconds, to add to his nine previous quickest tours in the race. But three laps later he was out. Hydraulic failure locked up the gearbox and he cruised into the pits, acknowledging the roars of the crowd with what looked like farewell waves.

Patrese roared on, building a ten second lead with only six laps to run for his first Italian Grand Prix win, but on lap 48 the car slowed, crippled by hydraulic failure. He limped on but finished a sad fifth.

Senna swept to victory, and Martin Brundle's magnificent second place was all but swamped by Mansell's retirement plans.

Had Senna caused Mansell's problems, the winner was asked after the race? "It is no secret that I have tried very hard to get some deal with Williams. The situation is very complex. It is not nice, not clear either, but I don't think Nigel's position today or before that is the problem. The problem is somebody else. I don't think I was the cause. I have some sympathy with him because it seems that he does not want to stop now."

Former Champion James Hunt hoped that Mansell would change his mind but added that his demands for a high salary had been unrealistic.

Mansell left soon afterwards, saying: "I retired once before, two years ago, but this is different. There will be no change of heart this time. The environment is not right to carry on. I have been saying that I would make a decision which was right for Nigel Mansell and family. Now I have, and I believe it is the right one. Rosanne is also disappointed at how things have turned out over the past few weeks. I could have waited longer but there seemed no point. I had to make my own judgement, my own decision."

Five days later he made another huge decision about his future.

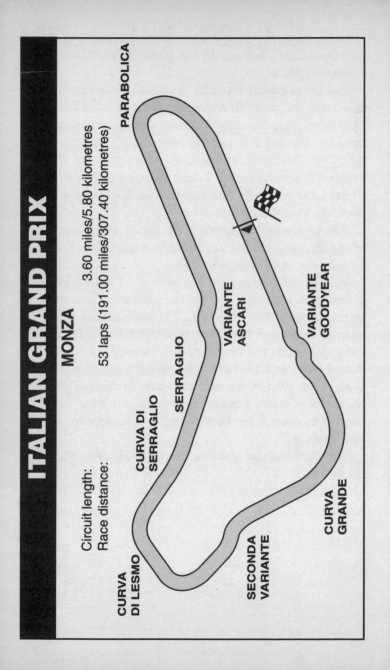

ITALIAN GRAND PRIX

MONZA

Circuit length: 3.60 miles/5.80 kilometres
Race distance: 53 laps (191.00 miles/307.40 kilometres)

PARABOLICA

CURVA DI LESMO

CURVA DI SERRAGLIO

SERRAGLIO

VARIANTE ASCARI

VARIANTE GOODYEAR

SECONDA VARIANTE

CURVA GRANDE

1992 – PIONEER ITALIAN GRAND PRIX – MONZA

RACE CLASSIFICATION AFTER 53 LAPS

(307.400 km = 191.009 mls)

Pos	Nr	Driver		Team Make	Make	Total Time	km/h	mph	Diff
1	1	A. SENNA	BRA	HONDA MARLBORO McLAREN	McLAREN HONDA	1:18'15.349	235.689	146.450	
2	20	M. BRUNDLE	GBR	CAMEL BENETTON FORD	BENETTON FORD	1:18'32.399	234.836	145.920	17.050
3	19	M. SCHUMACHER	GER	CAMEL BENETTON FORD	BENETTON FORD	1:18'39.722	234.471	145.694	24.373
4	2	G. BERGER	AUT	HONDA MARLBORO McLAREN	McLAREN HONDA	1:19'40.839	231.474	143.831	1'25.490
5	6	R. PATRESE	ITA	CANON WILLIAMS TEAM	WILLIAMS RENAULT	1:19'48.507	231.103	143.601	1'33.158
6	4	A. DE CESARIS	ITA	TYRRELL	TYRRELL ILMOR	1:18'30.332	230.506	143.230	1 LAP
7	9	M. ALBORETO	ITA	FOOTWORK MUGEN-HONDA	FOOTWORK MUGEN-HONDA	1:18'37.871	230.138	143.001	1 LAP
8	22	P. MARTINI	ITA	SCUDERIA ITALIA	BMS DALLARA FERRARI	1:19'37.524	227.264	141.215	1 LAP
9	30	U. KATAYAMA	JPN	CENTRAL PARK-VEN. LARR.	VENTURI LAMBORGHINI	1:16'54.952	226.221	140.567	3 LAPS
10	16	K. WENDLINGER	AUT	MARCH F.1	MARCH ILMOR	1:18'24.821	221.900	137.882	3 LAPS
11	21	J. LEHTO	FIN	SCUDERIA ITALIA	BMS DALLARA FERRARI	1:17'07.057	229.985	142.906	6 LAPS

NOT CLASSIFIED

Pos	Nr	Driver		Team Make	Make	Total Time	km/h	mph	COVERED
12	33	M. GUGELMIN	BRA	SASOL JORDAN YAMAHA	JORDAN YAMAHA	1:11'07.063	225.092	139.865	46 LAPS
13	5	N. MANSELL	GBR	CANON WILLIAMS TEAM	WILLIAMS RENAULT	1:00'21.431	236.393	146.888	41 LAPS
14	25	T. BOUTSEN	BEL	LIGIER GITANES BLONDES	LIGIER RENAULT	1:01'52.425	230.599	143.287	41 LAPS
15	26	E. COMAS	FRA	LIGIER GITANES BLONDES	LIGIER RENAULT	53'05.069	229.446	142.571	35 LAPS
16	15	G. TARQUINI	ITA	FONDMETAL F1	FONDMETAL FORD	51'26.445	202.952	126.108	30 LAPS
17	3	O. GROUILLARD	FRA	TYRRELL	TYRRELL ILMOR	41'33.985	217.676	135.257	26 LAPS
18	12	J. HERBERT	GBR	TEAM CASTROL LOTUS	LOTUS FORD	27'16.404	229.674	142.713	18 LAPS
19	17	E. NASPETTI	ITA	MARCH F.1	MARCH ILMOR	26'21.380	224.462	139.474	17 LAPS
20	27	J. ALESI	FRA	FERRARI	FERRARI	18'08.486	230.181	143.034	12 LAPS
21	28	I. CAPELLI	ITA	FERRARI	FERRARI	18'10.894	229.683	142.719	12 LAPS
22	24	G. MORBIDELLI	ITA	MINARDI TEAM	MINARDI LAMBORGHINI	18'27.817	226.175	140.538	12 LAPS
23	29	B. GACHOT	FRA	CENTRAL PARK-VEN. LARR.	VENTURI LAMBORGHINI	17'25.345	219.717	136.526	11 LAPS
24	11	M. HAKKINEN	FIN	TEAM CASTROL LOTUS	LOTUS FORD	7'44.568	224.725	139.638	5 LAPS
25	10	A. SUZUKI	JPN	FOOTWORK MUGEN-HONDA	FOOTWORK MUGEN-HONDA	3'21.295	207.457	128.908	2 LAPS

FASTEST LAP: 5 N. MANSELL – Lap 39 Time: 1'26.119 (242.455 km/h = 150.655 mph)

Portuguese Grand Prix

Estoril

Nigel Mansell, signed, sealed but not delivered, landed in Lisbon as an Indycar driver. A week earlier he had confirmed that his future lay with the American team part-owned by film star Paul Newman. He had agreed to a one-year deal worth around £3 million, give or take a fluctuation in sterling against the dollar.

The Newman Haas team were delighted: they had wanted Mansell as the perfect replacement for Michael Andretti, who was lined up with McLaren in Formula One for 1993. It was a swap, Champion for Champion, but the Americans were getting the better deal and Carl Haas was jubilant.

"Nigel will thrill the crowds with his all-out driving style. He is one of the top drivers and any time a driver of his calibre is available we have to be interested. We have known each other for a long time and I am extremely pleased that he is joining the team. He will create a lot of excitement and his aggressive style will please Indy fans. This will also give Indycar a shot in the arm at home and will get us publicity all over the world."

Mansell would be teaming up again with Mario Andretti, the man with whom he began his Formula One career in 1980. Now 52, Andretti, the 1978 World Champion, had no doubts about Mansell: "He will be a wow. The way he drives will really get the fans going over

215

here. It will be fantastic. Here the cars are pretty much the same. In a recent test the top 12 cars were separated by less than a second. It is the skill of the driver that counts rather than the technology of the car, and that should suit Nigel. He loves driving and he will enjoy it here. He will give Indycar a whole new presence in Europe."

Mansell's announcement was followed by a chorus of doubt in Europe. First off the grid was Derek Warwick, World Sportscar Champion, who warned: "Nigel is a fool. I am amazed and shocked by what he has done. He has got carried away with his own importance. Twice Williams have saved his career and he has got the best car in Formula One. I thought it was another bluff from Nigel when he said that he would be leaving Formula One.

"By doing so he has made the first mistake of his career – and the biggest. It is unbelievable that Nigel is not going to retain his World Championship. When Williams win the Formula One title again next year he will feel it, because he will know it should have been him again."

But Scotsman Jim Crawford, who lives and drives in the USA, countered: "The fans will be queuing up to see him. He is a great driver. But it may take him a year to make the change."

The great fear was how Mansell would cope with the short, concrete, oval tracks, barely a mile long, which have none of the big safety run-off areas strictly demanded in Formula One. Emerson Fittipaldi, twice Formula One World Champion, appeared in Portugal and offered to give Mansell any advice he needed.

"This is one of the great things about Indycar already," said Mansell. "Here is a driver who will be a big rival next year and yet here he is offering to give me help.

Emerson is offering to drive me round the circuits next season, to give me the tips I will need. That is so different to what I have been used to in Formula One. I really appreciate the help, and it is another reason why I am happy with my decision to race there next year. My team-mate next year, Mario Andretti, has made a similar offer. It seems that there is much more of a friendly attitude in Indycar."

Mansell had no qualms or doubts about his decision to quit Formula One and go for the US circuits. "I was impressed by the way they do business and it is a new challenge," he said. "I had no doubts once we sorted out the details. There were none of the problems I have had in negotiations in Formula One. It was straightforward, and I can't wait to start racing there next year."

Between the races, Mansell had opted to stick to his schedule of public engagements and sponsors' support work while the arguments raged about his decision. Labatt's, one of the major sponsors, were less than impressed by it while Camel, another major backer, were publicly outspoken over the way the deal had been handled.

Before making his decision, Mansell had gone to the Southampton International Boat Show to appear on the stand of Sunseekers, two of whose powerful and luxurious motorcruisers he owns. He was delighted at the reception he was given by the boat show spectators. Williams had cancelled a scheduled press conference that day and Mansell said: "It is an admission of guilt. They are worried about facing the press."

Speculation was high that he might be talked out of the plan to quit or lured by another Formula One team, but he was adamant: "Anyone who is under any illusion that I will change my mind is wrong. I just need some space and time now to decide my future. A lot of people have been in touch, including Newman Haas. I have been getting lots of advice and now I need to listen to my heart. It is the fans I feel for. I am as disappointed as anyone at not getting the chance to defend the title, but it was not my doing."

Then he was off to blow away his troubles, taking the wheel of a motorcruiser for an exhilarating 30 minute thrill ride around the Southampton waters. He has plenty of experience of piloting his own cruiser around the waters off Florida, and he soon had the boat swooping around. The Sunseeker was fitted with two 680 horsepower diesel engines. Mansell's touch had it carving white water patterns on the greenish surface at 50 knots.

"I hope I didn't see you hanging on," he joked as he headed back to the dock. "I feel almost human again after that." His fix of speed had set him up for the day.

But his parting shot was telling. "I just hope it all dies down now. The decision is made and I sincerely hope that nothing else is said by any party and we can all get on with our lives."

Just three days after his announcement, Mansell attended the launch of a book, *Mansell and Williams*, commemorating his title win. Coincidentally, it was held in Renault's central London showroom. Mansell was in good spirits, but the irony of the situation was not lost on him. "We had hoped it would all fit in but here we are," said Mansell as the guests arrived. Frank Williams was not there.

All week, Frank Williams had found himself at the end of a torrent of criticism. The *Sun*, typically, had run a 'Save Our Nige' campaign. They organised an outing to the company's Didcot factory to demonstrate. Williams, at his most perverse, finally spoke about Mansell to the *Sun* and then granted the BBC an interview, making comments which angered Mansell.

The team owner said that talks with Mansell had started as early as the second Grand Prix in Mexico, and that both sides had been close by Spain in May. "After that things ground on a bit," he said. "It was always a problem convincing Nigel that he could work with Alain Prost. Things changed because our circumstances changed, and we are in a recession. That had to be addressed." He talked in the past tense of Senna joining the team. "I would have tried, but it would have been very difficult managing Prost and Senna," he conceded. And his message to the supporters who had been bussed to Didcot to protest was simple: "They should have been demonstrating outside Nigel's house."

It was enough to have Mansell putting his side of the story once again at the book launch. In a tiny office in the car showroom, he stood with his wife Rosanne, a couple of lawyers and his surprise guest, Sheridan Thynne. Mansell announced that Thynne was the Williams director who had been told to telephone him after Hungary with the 'take it or leave it' ultimatum.

"Sheridan resigned soon afterwards and he is here tonight as an old friend and colleague," said Mansell. "I did not want to say any more but the public is being misled and I cannot stand back and let this happen. I was ready to sign a deal in Hungary and I had a witness, my wife Rosanne, but the goalposts were moved. The offer changed, it was nothing like the one originally made. I have always wanted to defend my World Championship but the opportunity was not afforded me as conditions constantly changed."

Which of the drivers did Mansell expect would fill

his seat at Williams, Martin Brundle or Damon Hill? "Brundle has the experience, but Damon knows the car very well through all his test work and he would offer some continuity," came the reply.

In Paris, Prost was denying that he had a contract with Williams at all, and therefore denying the veto clause used against Ayrton Senna. He was merely 50 to 70 per cent sure of driving again in 1993. "It saddens me to hear of Mansell's decision to retire as much as hearing that in England I am blamed for it," said the three-times World Champion. "Frank Williams told me repeatedly that he wanted to keep Mansell to team him up with me. Mansell started off very high. Williams does not have a bottomless budget. If I drive one of its cars, I will be more poorly paid than I have been in the past. I was prepared, if we were in the same team, to give up part of my salary to him."

Senna, who had supposedly given up on any hopes of a Williams drive, had made a last ditch attempt, his lawyers meeting team officials to try to find a way into a car.

By the time of the Portuguese Grand Prix, Mansell had decided to keep the job as short and professional as possible to minimise the hassle. He opted to fly out on the Thursday morning with most of the Grand Prix set, mechanics, public relations people and team managers, on a scheduled flight. He was relaxed and very laid back. "I am here to get my ninth win of the season and the world record. That is my motivation," he said. "This weekend I can watch the others get on with it."

Sure enough, soon the scurryings between the motor-homes made them as frantic as a rabbit warren with a stoat inside. Williams might make a decision or two at last; McLaren might announce a driver; Footwork were talking; one of the new teams for 1993, Pacific Racing, were much in evidence. Engine company bosses were also around and agents, managers and drivers were looking for seats. Mark Blundell, Damon Hill and Perry McCarthy kept a high profile.

Mansell, with two victories at Estoril, felt confident that this, his final race in Europe in Formula One, would provide the victory he craved. On Friday morning he was almost denied the chance when his car suffered a sudden hydraulic failure. So much depends on the hydraulic pump that the suspension failed and the gearbox jammed, as it had done in Monza.

This time he was moving at high speed, around 165mph, and went dancing and spinning into the gravel run-off area without hitting anyone or anything. Mansell was shaken, and admitted: "It was a big, big moment. Everything just went so quickly, there was nothing I could do. It was pretty nasty."

By lunchtime the warm-up had the Williams cars firmly in the one-two positions with Mansell 1.6 seconds faster than the third placed McLaren. The end-of-term feeling continued as the Honda press liaison man announced: "As this is the last European event of the season it also marks the last event for the Honda motorhome. In a budget-saving exercise, we have decided to burn the bus and claim the insurance rather than take it back to England. As firm believers that every cloud has a silver lining, we will be using the heat from the fire to cook up some traditional tempura prawns and vegetables. Join us."

It was that kind of weekend. The night before, Formula One's own rock band, the Pit Stop Boogie Boys, comprising mechanics, journalists, caterers, even team owner Eddie Jordan, had played in the local town square.

On the track, everyone danced to Mansell's tune. In

the first qualifying session, he set a standard no one could match. His time of 1 minute 13.041 seconds was six tenths ahead of Patrese and over two seconds quicker than Senna. The Brazilian had proved that anything Mansell could do, he could match, even in the disaster department. His rear wing flew off and the car went on its own high-speed journey, careering through a run-off area.

Torrential rain turned the track environs to mud on Saturday as Formula One woke to find that Indycar was now planning a New York race on the same day as the British Grand Prix. The heat was increasing. Mansell was unhappy with his car at lunch on Saturday. "Don't even ask me," he implored. He remained on pole in the second qualifying session but was still in doleful mood about the problems.

The new RS4 engine, he revealed, was rougher with the new fuel, brought in after FISA had cracked down on special blends. "The vibration of the engine is about eight times more than it was with the RS3, and I think this is causing the hydraulic problem, which is quite serious. When the pump shears there is no pressure to the suspension or to the gearbox. So there has been a big transition since Hungary [his last win] and the use of the new fuel. What we do have is better aerodynamics through the corners. During the winter we tested for seven straight days here, and we have come with basically the same set-up."

Mansell added: "My motivation is as high as ever. It is to get away as quickly as I can. If that means getting pole and winning the race as early as I can so that I can get home, that's what I will do. I am disappointed to see how people have used my situation to their own ends. They write things which suit them, not about how it is.

222

I am also amused, because I know a lot of what is going on now, even within the Williams team.

"I am satisfied, too, to see a lot of people very embarrassed. I just feel very sorry about the circumstances in which it all happened. But I am just getting on with my life. I am very happy and comfortable now. I am starting a new career and I will look forward instead of back. I would like to remind everyone that it is history. I am out of it, and it is nice to just watch the amazing things that are going on.

"Now I know that these races are the last in my Formula One career, I can go out and enjoy them. I look to Japan, just like Australia, as a race I would dearly like to win. I haven't won at either of those circuits, and if I had to trade anything this weekend, I would trade a win here for wins in Japan and Australia."

Mansell spoke of the challenge ahead in the USA, but he rounded on the critics who suggested that his aggressive style would be his downfall on the tight oval circuits. "I read a lot of things about what a lot of people are saying about Indycar. I don't know how they qualify to comment, because they have never driven at the ovals themselves. I think only of the people who have been any good on ovals.

"Emerson Fittipaldi is one of them, and so is my team-mate, Mario Andretti. Both have offered to help me, without my having to ask, and that is very refreshing. I can honestly say that in all the 12 years of my Formula One career, I have had no assistance at all, other than from the late, great Gilles Villeneuve and Colin Chapman. No one else springs to mind."

The warm-up on Sunday morning was in drying, sunny conditions and went by in another blaze of Mansell domination. He headed onto the grid for his 29th pole start.

By that time, surprise, surprise, the Canon Williams Renault team had been "happy to announce that Alain Prost will be driving one of our Williams Renaults in the 1993 World Championship."

Mansell wore the look of a man who could not help saying "I told you so", but he took his vengeance out on the brakes at the first corner, where Patrese looked like getting in first off the green light. But Red Five was gone, following the tactics which had won Mansell the British Grand Prix, building up a big, early lead to deny the others a target. Get the race won early, he had said, get home early. He had not been joking. He set up the seven fastest laps on eight of the first ten trips round the Estoril circuit. After two laps he was four seconds ahead of Patrese. By the time ten had gone, he was 8.8 seconds ahead.

Maybe in Mansell's mind were memories of the same race a year earlier, when he had hurried in for a tyre change and was sent out with a rear wheel hanging off. It disappeared within yards of the garage and he was disqualified after the mechanics had to work on it illegally in the pit lane. When he chose to go in for tyres this time, he had a lead of over 20 seconds. He already knew that Patrese had suffered a fairly disastrous pit stop when the rear jack had broken. Mansell's stop on lap 29 was not sensational but it was good enough, at just under ten seconds, to put him back in the lead by almost 3 seconds from Senna.

After 40 laps his charge had pulled that to 12 seconds. The big battle to entertain the fans was Patrese's struggle to pass Berger for third. There was nothing at stake except pride, but that is still *the* motivating factor. For half a dozen laps they had jousted, Berger holding on with sheer driving skill, but on lap 43 they swept round the top bend into the pit straight. Berger kept more to the middle as he intended a pit stop. Normally, a hand would be raised to show an intention, but the Austrian claimed afterwards that the G-forces on the last bend had made this impossible.

Whatever the reason, it led to the luckiest escape of the season so far from the most spectacular of crashes. Patrese's front right wheel caught the left rear tyre of Berger's McLaren, and in a fraction of a second he was climbing straight up like a rocket at take-off.

The car seemed to halt in mid-air, and for a long time everyone was able to consider the possibilities of it falling backwards onto the track. Instead it belly-flopped on the track in front of the pits. Two wheels flew off along with a hail of debris, yet amazingly Patrese stepped from the wreckage 200 yards from the impact spot and no one else was injured. Berger said later that it had been a misunderstanding and was exonerated by the stewards after a Williams protest. Patrese, who said he could see the sky as he took off, insisted: "I could have been killed. I had no warning that he was going to the pits."

Senna had to make no fewer than four pit stops, and with Mansell howling round, setting new lap records on 38, 56 and 57 by a second (although Senna eventually topped these on 66), there was no doubt this time. Mansell had his ninth win of the season, erasing Senna's 1988 record and giving him yet another landmark in the season.

The refreshing trait of honesty which upsets so many people who prefer modesty and understatement was again obvious after the race. Was he surprised to have pulled out such a huge gap at the start? "No, not really. I know how much I was pushing. I was 'qualifying' in the opening laps and I enjoyed it. I was feeling very fit this weekend so I just made a break. I was optimistic but not confident at the start, and outbraking Riccardo into the first bend was good. I am delighted to have the ninth win. It adds to an extraordinary year."

Now that Mansell had the five opening wins sequence, he had become Britain's most successful race-winning driver and World Champion and had the best haul of victories in one season.

But for once he was upstaged on the platform as Senna, who had shown his brilliance by battling back to take second, launched a scathing attack on Prost for keeping him out of the Williams team. Mansell could only sit and smile as the Brazilian pounded the Frenchman with whom he has twice had high-speed tangles. "If he wants to be sporting, he must be prepared to race anybody under any conditions on equal terms. Now the way he wants to win the Championship is by having everything laid on for him before he starts."

Mansell could not resist nodding and saying "yes" as Senna continued: "It is like going for a 100 metre sprint and he has running shoes while everyone else has to use lead shoes. That is the way he wants to race. It is not racing and it is bad for all of us." Warming to his subject, Senna later added: "I do not accept being vetoed by anyone in the way that this has been done. In my opinion, we had two fantastic World Championships last year and this year, and two very bad ones in 1989 and 1990. They were a consequence of the unbelievable politics going on and bad behaviour by some people. I think we are now coming back to the same situation again.

"It is impossible to accept somebody joining a team in February with a signed contract vetoing myself – and him, too," he declared, pointing at Mansell. "Eventually they changed their minds as far as Nigel was concerned but stayed with the veto on myself. I think that if Prost wants to be World Champion and maybe win another he should be sporting. The way he is doing it, he is acting like a coward."

Senna had already suggested that he might drive, even in a competitive car, to show Prost who was boss. Get your ringside seats for 1993.

Mansell could afford to smile, grab his case and dash to the airport for the Sunday night flight home. The squabbling was history for the history-maker.

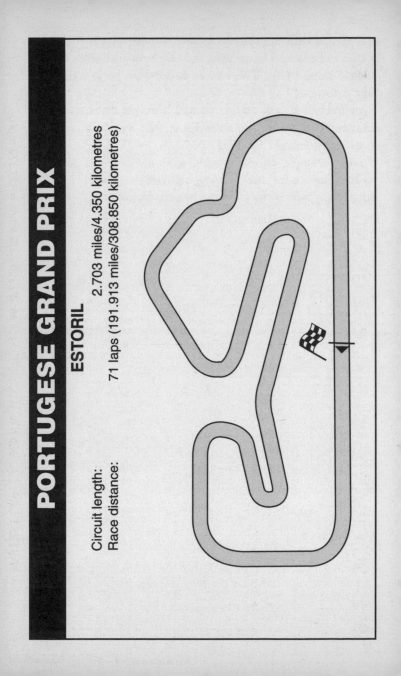

PORTUGESE GRAND PRIX

ESTORIL

Circuit length: 2.703 miles/4.350 kilometres
Race distance: 71 laps (191.913 miles/308.850 kilometres)

1992 – SG GIGANTE PORTUGUESE GRAND PRIX – ESTORIL
RACE CLASSIFICATION AFTER 71 LAPS
(308.850 km = 191.910 mls)

Pos	Nr	Driver		Team Make	Make	Total Time	km/h	mph	Diff
1	5	N. MANSELL	GBR	CANON WILLIAMS TEAM	WILLIAMS RENAULT	1:34:43.659	195.521	121.491	
2	2	G. BERGER	AUT	HONDA MARLBORO McLAREN	McLAREN HONDA	1:35:21.192	194.239	120.694	37.467
3	1	A. SENNA	BRA	HONDA MARLBORO McLAREN	McLAREN HONDA	1:35:09.845	191.984	119.293	1 LAP
4	20	M. BRUNDLE	GBR	CAMEL BENETTON FORD	BENETTON FORD	1:35:12.391	191.899	119.240	1 LAP
5	11	M. HAKKINEN	FIN	TEAM CASTROL LOTUS	LOTUS FORD	1:35:37.373	191.063	118.721	1 LAP
6	9	M. ALBORETO	ITA	FOOTWORK MUGEN-HONDA	FOOTWORK MUGEN-HONDA	1:35:55.630	190.457	118.344	1 LAP
7	19	M. SCHUMACHER	GER	CAMEL BENETTON FORD	BENETTON FORD	1:34:47.316	189.991	118.055	2 LAPS
8	25	T. BOUTSEN	BEL	LIGIER GITANES BLONDES	LIGIER RENAULT	1:35:28.932	188.611	117.197	2 LAPS
9	4	A. DE CESARIS	ITA	TYRRELL	TYRRELL ILMOR	1:35:35.862	188.383	117.056	2 LAPS
10	10	A. SUZUKI	JPN	FOOTWORK MUGEN-HONDA	FOOTWORK MUGEN-HONDA	1:34:49.557	187.164	116.298	3 LAPS
11	17	E. NASPETTI	ITA	MARCH F.1	MARCH ILMOR	1:35:10.368	186.482	115.874	3 LAPS
12	23	C. FITTIPALDI	BRA	MINARDI TEAM	MINARDI LAMBORGHINI	1:35:10.539	186.476	115.871	3 LAPS
13	32	S. MODENA	ITA	SASOL JORDAN YAMAHA	JORDAN YAMAHA	1:35:24.492	186.022	115.589	3 LAPS
14	24	G. MORBIDELLI	ITA	MINARDI TEAM	MINARDI LAMBORGHINI	1:35:53.396	185.087	115.008	3 LAPS

NOT CLASSIFIED

Pos	Nr	Driver		Team Make	Make	Total Time	km/h	mph	COVERED
15	21	J. LEHTO	FIN	SCUDERIA ITALIA	BMS DALLARA FERRARI	1:11:48.422	185.372	115.185	51 LAPS
16	16	K. WENDLINGER	AUT	MARCH F.1	MARCH ILMOR	1:07:28.120	185.686	115.380	48 LAPS
17	26	E. COMAS	FRA	LIGIER GITANES BLONDES	LIGIER RENAULT	1:05:02.661	188.594	117.187	47 LAPS
18	30	U. KATAYAMA	JPN	CENTRAL PARK-VEN. LARR.	VENTURI LAMBORGHINI	1:05:26.391	183.466	114.001	45 LAPS
19	6	R. PATRESE	ITA	CANON WILLIAMS TEAM	WILLIAMS RENAULT	58:15.378	192.428	118.570	43 LAPS
20	22	P. MARTINI	ITA	SCUDERIA ITALIA	BMS DALLARA FERRARI	1:00:26.797	185.719	115.401	43 LAPS
21	28	I. CAPELLI	ITA	FERRARI	FERRARI	48:17.366	183.767	114.187	34 LAPS
22	3	O. GROUILLARD	FRA	TYRRELL	TYRRELL ILMOR	37:54.250	185.916	115.523	27 LAPS
23	29	B. GACHOT	FRA	CENTRAL PARK-VEN. LARR.	VENTURI LAMBORGHINI	35:47.906	182.279	113.263	25 LAPS
24	33	M. GUGELMIN	BRA	SASOL JORDAN YAMAHA	JORDAN YAMAHA	26:58.151	183.877	114.256	19 LAPS
25	27	J. ALESI	FRA	FERRARI	FERRARI	16:38.943	188.110	116.892	12 LAPS
26	12	J. HERBERT	GBR	TEAM CASTROL LOTUS	LOTUS FORD	5:51.554	89.090	55.358	2 LAPS

FASTEST LAP: 1 A. SENNA – Lap 66 Time: 1'16.272 (205.318 km/h = 127.579 mph)

Japanese Grand Prix

Suzuka

Even as Mansell was switching from driver mode to his role as dad back at home with his family in Clearwater, soaking up some Florida sunshine, Alain Prost was eagerly settling into Red Five in rainy Portugal. Off came Mansell's insignia, including the Union Jack, and on went the French tricolour and Prost's name. It must have seemed as odd to the Williams mechanics as it did to Mansell that while he jetted across the Atlantic someone else was striding into the garage in the familiar blue racing suit and slipping behind the wheel of the car they had prepared all year for the Englishman.

The Williams team had stayed on in Estoril for the official test session, hoping for decent weather after their success in the Portuguese Grand Prix, for a dual reason. Prost, having been confirmed as their new driver, could finally try out the supercar, and the team had their first opportunity to run the new, narrow tyres. The Estoril track is a Williams favourite. They had spent a week there in the build-up to the season, and Mansell felt that had been the basis for their domination in 1992.

Now they were to launch a new era at the same venue with the French three-times World Champion, who was re-starting his career after a season out. They were already setting up the car for 1993 with new aerodynamic settings after testing out with the slimline Goodyear tyres.

Riccardo Patrese, who would also no longer be a Williams man in the 1993 season, was absent, so the team's test driver, Damon Hill, was on duty. The weekend held extra significance for him. There was still a vacancy for the second driver's seat at Williams, and despite a queue of eager applicants, Frank Williams was in no hurry to fill the job. Hill had strong hopes that he might at last get the meaty Formula One drive he had longed for since the days when he had watched his famous father Graham conquer the world, twice becoming World Champion. Hill junior had proved himself as he fought his way through the ranks of motor sport and with Brabham, who had given him his first drive at top level in their lifeless car. He had done well, managing to nurse the Brabham to a finish, albeit last place in 13th position, in Hungary. Many others had not lasted long enough to see the chequered flag that day and Hill's ability as a test driver was not in question.

It is no good for the team if the test driver does not take the machinery to the limits of endurance. They need to find out how the various components, particularly the innovative gadgetry, react under pressure. The driver has to be prepared to push himself when there is no one else around to inspire competitive fervour. Hill had been found to be extremely capable for Williams, and the team owner and Mansell had both acknowledged their debt to him. The World Champion had even gone as far as to say that he hoped Hill would get the drive.

"Damon deserves it. He knows the car and he can provide the continuity needed for the team next season," said Mansell. "Martin Brundle is obviously another contender, but I hope Damon gets it, honestly. He has earned the drive." Hill, an amiable young man, had smiled when told of Mansell's seal of approval. "That's great," he said, before adding with a laugh: "But in view of the situation between Frank and Nigel at the moment, maybe it is not so good to get a recommendation."

It was on the Tuesday following the Grand Prix that Prost ventured out, although because of rain he was on the normal wet tyres. Mansell's engineer, David Brown, now had extensive discussions with Prost, explaining the intricacies of the machine the Frenchman was taking over. Prost concentrated on getting to grips with the FW14B, coming to terms with its idiosyncrasies, getting the feel of the active suspension and the power of the Renault engine. When he had spent a couple of days bumping and bruising around the circuit after a year out, he was soon seeing the physiotherapist.

His view of the car was not troubled. "It is the best car I have ever driven," he said. "It does not have a weak point and that makes it more difficult for me – the car is so good that I cannot push it hard enough because I am not in my best condition. I cannot take it to its full potential, but it is getting better every day." Prost had tried active ride with Renault and Ferrari in previous years, but was not used to anything as sophisticated as the system which now made the Williams car the supreme car everyone wanted. At Estoril he merely concentrated on coming to grips with what he felt was a fantastic package of engine ride and handling.

Prost also confirmed that he had spoken to Williams as early as November 1991 and that talks had rolled on for months. It also became clear that he *did* have an exclusion clause in his contract which had allowed him to veto Ayrton Senna and he admitted that there was no way he could have worked with the Brazilian. After Senna's outburst just a few days earlier, that possibility looked about as probable as Stirling Moss making a comeback with Ferrari. Prost had also insisted that he would not return as Number Two. "Equal Number One? No problem. The plans were always to have myself and Mansell," said the 33-year-old Frenchman. It would never happen now. The lead-up of denials, politics, shifting positions and adjustable figures had driven the other half of the dream team, Mansell, 3000 miles away.

Meanwhile Hill, already confident with the car, had startled other teams and interested parties at Estoril by powering round the track on the narrow tyres in 1 minute 14.19 seconds, just a second slower than Mansell's Grand Prix pole position time of the previous week. A second faster than Prost, Hill was the quickest of the 22 drivers on the three-day test.

Back on the Isle of Man, people had not forgotten their local hero, even if he had taken himself off to Florida. Senna Street was to be renamed Mansell Street, it was reported.

Soon the teams were at Silverstone for another official test session, with Michael Schumacher trying out active suspension and traction control on the Camel Benetton Ford for the first time. Benetton had supplied a nice touch by giving Perry McCarthy a test drive the previous week, providing the British driver with some much needed cash and a boost to his morale.

About the same time, it was confirmed that McCarthy's previous team Andrea Moda, had been thrown out of Formula One for bringing the sport into disrepute after team owner Andrea Sassetti was arrested for alleged forgery.

Ferrari also tried active suspension in Italy but the driver, Nicola Larini, was also new, replacing the sacked Ivan Capelli for the last two Grands Prix. At Silverstone Schumacher was fastest driver but, interestingly, McLaren's test driver, Mark Blundell, was second quickest. Like Hill, he boosted his hopes of a drive in his team's empty seat if Senna stuck to his threat to depart.

Another British driver, World Sportscar Champion Derek Warwick, turned up again, driving for Footwork, but by now drivers were everywhere in their search for a car. Al Unser Jr denied that he was moving from Indycar with Michael Andretti to Formula One.

Mansell had not been idle. He went to look at Indycar racing for the first time since making his decision to race in that series in 1993. He was as enthusiastic as Prost had been about the Williams car. Mansell had already been welcomed by his new boss, 67-year-old film star Paul Newman, co-owner of the team with Carl Haas. Newman, a car racing fanatic, was as excited about the coming of Mansell as he is about a new film. They had met only once, but Newman was impressed by Mansell's style, enjoyed his humour and loved his competitive edge.

Newman looked forward to another meeting and predicted: "Nigel will love it over here. It is very close racing." It was a view that Mansell was soon confirming after he spectated at the Laguna circuit in mid-October. He spoke with one of Indycar's most famous men, Roger Penske, the owner of a rival team. "I have said it before, but over here it seems that everyone is one big family," said Mansell. "It is the single most impressive thing I have noticed over here, the way people co-operate. They seem to want to make it the best for everyone, to put on a good show. Yet everyone is so competitive, they all want to win – it is the best of both worlds.

"I think your racing is totally refreshing," he told American journalists during the weekend. "It accommodates sheer competitiveness, it provides the spectacle which entertains the crowd. I think Formula One is losing sight of that and I was going into the space age there. I am sitting here as probably the most experienced Formula One driver as far as the technology, the computers, the active suspension, automatic gearbox and traction control variables are concerned.

"What I would say to you, gentlemen, is that it takes tens of millions of dollars to get to where I have just left Formula One. And I think that is entirely wrong. You have a formula which, in my opinion, and it is only a personal opinion, is fantastic. Why? Because everybody can compete more or less on the same level, whether they have a $50 million budget, which no one has, or a $10 million budget.

"It is fantastic, and we must not lose sight of that. I have no regrets about leaving Formula One. If I had been afforded the chance to defend my Championship in the manner I wanted, then perhaps I would not be sitting here. But because that was not afforded me, I am delighted that Carl and I have got together. As he said, he's excited, I am excited and the world's press is excited. I know my country is also excited, because the television rights have gone up five times. I wish I had bought them."

It was vintage Mansell – relaxed, confident, chatty, straightforward. But he insisted, in case anyone should think differently, that he was not coming for a quiet escape from the Grand Prix jungle. "I am very highly motivated for 1993," said Mansell, who had told Carl Haas while watching a qualifying session that he wished he could race there and then. "I retired for the right reasons in 1990 and I 'unretired' for the right reasons, which culminated in my winning the World Championship. I did not want to end my Formula One career, or my driving career. This is going to be an incredible challenge."

It was exactly what the Americans wanted to hear. They have long cherished the notion that their own Indycar series is the equal of the Grand Prix circus, and now Mansell had arrived to give it the stamp of approval they wanted. In the American sports world, where spectacle is everything, hype is vital and winners are to be revered, Mansell was just what was wanted.

Back in Europe, everything was going on very much as usual, with rumour outbidding rumour, but there was one definite piece of news which left Martin Brundle astonished and disappointed. Brundle had been widely tipped to win the race for the Williams seat and had had talks with Frank Williams in Portugal and in the fortnight after the race. Suddenly he was out of the frame. A draft contract for two years had even been drawn up, and a bewildered Brundle said: "It just needed to be signed. Everything had been fixed up and then Frank phoned to say it was all off. I am baffled, but despite this, I am not giving up. I am still hopeful of getting the drive."

Now it was suggested that Williams had failed to get Patrese back. The Italian had signed for Benetton as he had not been offered a contract for 1993 by the World Championship team. It was also suggested that Williams now had his sights set on the Team Lotus men, Johnny Herbert and Mika Haakinen, two young and very talented drivers. Peter Collins, the Lotus boss, firmly quashed any idea of either driver leaving, but was particularly vehement that Herbert would stay.

There were also reports of Ferrari making a huge bid to buy Mansell out of his contract with Newman Haas but Mansell, his American bosses and the Italian team soon flattened such talk. Senna, too, got involved, saying that he had turned down an offer of around £15 million from Ferrari to drive for them. "I still dream of driving for them one day," he said. "At the moment it is 50-50 whether I race or take a sabbatical next year." Meanwhile his boss at McLaren, Ron Dennis, was hopeful that he had now found an engine to replace the Honda for the new season, saying that he was close to a deal. He was trying to buy the Ligier team's Renault V10 engines in a highly complicated deal.

Mansell, divorced from the cares of Grand Prix, breezed into Suzuka from Florida and was promptly hit by pit gossip which suggested that he had been asked to make a u-turn and go back to Williams. Had a secret meeting taken place in Japan between the two men to attempt a reconciliation? Williams was said to be having regrets, hence the long delay in putting in a new driver. Mansell killed off the reports swiftly. "I am racing Indycars next season and I am glad to be out of Formula One. They have made me very welcome and I am looking forward to next season," he confirmed.

Mansell had more immediate concerns. He had never won in Japan and was anxious to add this scalp on his last visit. "It is a really good circuit which most of us like as it is very testing," he said. He had crashed in qualifying in 1987 while still chasing the world title, failed to finish in the following three years and crashed again in 1991.

Suzuka is a tight circuit, yet another where overtaking is extremely limited. There were other factors to consider on Friday, the first day of qualifying. Honda, bowing out at the end of the season, wanted a final flourish at home. Renault were as keen not to let it happen. If Honda produced a slightly hotter engine for qualifying, Renault did even better. It was warm and sunny and the lucky 120,000 fans of the six million who had applied for tickets settled down to watch another Mansell blitz.

Early in the morning warm-up, the Englishman set

the fastest time of 1 minute 42.9 seconds and then sliced another two seconds off that. He squeezed into the 1.30s and went off to lunch happy. The afternoon session was merely another parade for Red Five, but there were some spicy moments. On an early lap on his first set of tyres, Mansell went off line, lost his rhythm and dropped a wheel over the kerb. The spin did not put him off, for he finished clearly fastest with a time of 1 minute 37.360 seconds. Senna tried everything to catch up with some superb driving near the end, but his engine was not up to the task.

Saturday was not the day spectators, drivers, television or those attending the circuit's funfair had hoped for. It poured in monsoon fashion and only eight drivers ventured out. Mansell, as ever unable to resist a chance at the wheel, went round, had a spin and went home again. So bad was the weather that the medical helicopter could not have flown and the session was brought to a halt.

Never one to miss an opportunity, Mansell used the pole press conference to put a few thoughts on record. He was concerned that there was no one to take on Prost in the coming season. "This year we have worked on Williams' reliability," he said, "and I forecast that if Frank does not have comparable driver in the other car, Alain Prost will win all 16 races. We have perfected the car and Renault's engine is getting stronger. The FW15 is developing and its anti-locking brakes will take away skill from the driver.

"A puppet can drive the car and win everything, and that looks like what will happen. The way Formula One is going, they should stop all technology. Anti-lock braking may get to the stage where all the driver has to do is be brave round corners, and committed. You have power," he told the press, "and you can help to get a decent driver in the car. Damon Hill would be my choice to beat Prost, but other than that I believe that you should say let the two World Champions be together. Put Ayrton in the other car, and you will have an exciting year."

This begged several questions. Mansell's critics had said all year that anyone could have driven the car to the Championship. It did not mean that he was a puppet. Surely it was his own driving, vibrant, skilful and brave, which had won the title. Patrese had never quite managed the same times or results with the same machinery.

Others wondered if Mansell was making a subtle plea to be asked back to compete with Prost. It seemed unlikely. He was more concerned that there would be a big accident in the race if the rain continued but his fears evaporated with the puddles when Sunday dawned bright and warm again. Warm-up provided another small problem when he went over a kerb and damaged the underside of the car, the tray. He had had to back off quickly behind Thierry Boutsen on a corner, which caused the kerb collision.

Tactics would be crucial, with carefully timed tyre changes. Disaster struck Senna on the third lap of the race when he cruised to a halt with a dead engine. He sat gazing at the rest of the field going round, contemplating the season and his future. If anything was going to drive him into a sabbatical year, it was the McLaren, particularly now that the Renault engine deal seemed to have cooled.

While Senna strolled back to the pits, waving at the crowds, Mansell went on in his usual way at the front, having opened a three second gap over second-placed Patrese by the end of the first lap. His lead was 10 seconds when he ran over some debris from Mauricio Gugelmin's car and had to pit for tyres. But he stayed at the front and built a 20 second lead. Suddenly he was slowing, and at the chicane he stopped. Patrese shot past, and just as quickly Mansell was behind him on lap 36. No one quite knew what had happened for soon Mansell was right on Patrese's tail.

Even Patrese was unsure, but Mansell had decided to let his team-mate through to build his points difference over Senna and win his first Grand Prix of the season. He planned a one-two, as he had in Monza when they both broke down. This time Patrese did take the chequered flag but Mansell did not. His race finished in spectacular fashion on lap 45 when his engine went up in flames.

Gerhard Berger had nursed his McLaren to second place to provide some honour but the best drive of the day came from Martin Brundle, who had spent Saturday in bed with food poisoning. Weak and still suffering, Brundle had had to start from 13th on the grid but he drove bravely to finish in third place. "It was very tough. I just had to pace myself to get through," said Brundle, adding with a smile. "I don't think a result like this does my P45 chances any harm at all."

Patrese, too, was happy. "I have to thank Nigel for helping me today. I think in the end I deserved this win as I have pushed hard all season."

Mansell found himself under attack during the race from Britain's previous World Champion, James Hunt, who challenged: "Stay in Formula One and prove you are a worthy Champion by taking on Alain Prost. Running away to America does you no credit at all. You would earn great respect even if you failed to beat Prost, which I doubt."

Mansell, heading straight to Australia to meet up with his sister and friends, retaliated by saying that Hunt, previously a McLaren driver, had certain affinities and had a problem because he was not the current Champion but the last one. And he added: "The truth is that the negotiations with Williams were handled abysmally. They accept that now. There was nothing to make me think about staying there in what was being offered.

"Therefore I cannot see how anyone can accuse me of running away. That is absurd. You must realise that my first choice was to defend the World Championship, but in the manner in which I won it. I don't believe, as I have said all along, that I was offered a sensible chance of defending it in the same way."

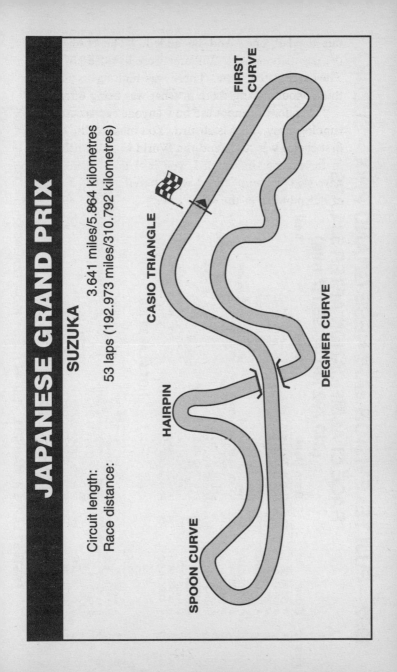

1992 – FUJI TELEVISION JAPANESE GRAND PRIX – SUZUKA

RACE CLASSIFICATION AFTER 53 LAPS
(310.792 km = 193.117 mls)

Pos	Nr	Driver		Team Make	Make	Total Time	km/h	mph	Diff
1	6	R. PATRESE	ITA	CANON WILLIAMS TEAM	WILLIAMS RENAULT	1:33'09.553	200.168	124.379	
2	2	G. BERGER	AUT	HONDA MARLBORO McLAREN	McLAREN HONDA	1:33'23.282	199.678	124.074	13.729
3	20	M. BRUNDLE	GBR	CAMEL BENETTON FORD	BENETTON FORD	1:34'25.056	197.500	122.721	1'15.503
4	4	A. DE CESARIS	ITA	TYRRELL	TYRRELL ILMOR	1:33'36.423	195.452	121.448	1 LAP
5	27	J. ALESI	FRA	FERRARI	FERRARI	1:33'49.236	195.007	121.172	1 LAP
6	23	C. FITTIPALDI	BRA	MINARDI TEAM	MINARDI LAMBORGHINI	1:33'50.341	194.969	121.148	1 LAP
7	32	S. MODENA	ITA	SASOL JORDAN YAMAHA	JORDAN YAMAHA	1:33'57.562	194.719	120.993	1 LAP
8	10	A. SUZUKI	JPN	FOOTWORK MUGEN-HONDA	FOOTWORK MUGEN-HONDA	1:34'05.613	194.441	120.820	1 LAP
9	21	J. LEHTO	FIN	SCUDERIA ITALIA	BMS DALLARA FERRARI	1:34'13.243	194.179	120.657	1 LAP
10	22	P. MARTINI	ITA	SCUDERIA ITALIA	BMS DALLARA FERRARI	1:34'14.551	194.134	120.629	1 LAP
11	30	U. KATAYAMA	JPN	CENTRAL PARK-VEN. LARR.	VENTURI LAMBORGHINI	1:34'24.637	193.788	120.415	1 LAP
12	28	N. LARINI	ITA	FERRARI	FERRARI	1:35'01.430	192.538	119.637	1 LAP
13	17	E. NASPETTI	ITA	MARCH F.1	MARCH ILMOR	1:33'20.392	192.242	119.454	2 LAPS
14	24	G. MORBIDELLI	ITA	MINARDI TEAM	MINARDI LAMBORGHINI	1:33'26.270	192.040	119.328	2 LAPS
15	9	M. ALBORETO	ITA	FOOTWORK MUGEN-HONDA	FOOTWORK MUGEN-HONDA	1:34'05.215	190.716	118.505	2 LAPS

NOT CLASSIFIED

Pos	Nr	Driver		Team Make	Make	Total Time	km/h	mph	COVERED
16	5	N. MANSELL	GBR	CANON WILLIAMS TEAM	WILLIAMS RENAULT	1:17'03.534	200.898	124.832	44 LAPS
17	11	M. HAKKINEN	FIN	TEAM CASTROL LOTUS	LOTUS FORD	1:17'50.450	198.880	123.578	44 LAPS
18	29	B. GACHOT	FRA	CENTRAL PARK-VEN. LARR.	VENTURI LAMBORGHINI	1:10'47.039	193.854	120.455	39 LAPS
19	26	E. COMAS	FRA	LIGIER GITANES BLONDES	LIGIER RENAULT	1:04'51.671	195.282	121.343	36 LAPS
20	16	J. LAMMERS	HOL	MARCH F.1	MARCH ILMOR	50'34.992	187.803	116.695	27 LAPS
21	33	M. GUGELMIN	BRA	SASOL JORDAN YAMAHA	JORDAN YAMAHA	40'27.801	191.296	118.866	22 LAPS
22	12	J. HERBERT	GBR	TEAM CASTROL LOTUS	LOTUS FORD	27'01.775	195.253	121.324	15 LAPS
23	19	M. SCHUMACHER	GER	CAMEL BENETTON FORD	BENETTON FORD	23'51.735	191.680	119.105	13 LAPS
24	3	O. GROUILLARD	FRA	TYRRELL	TYRRELL ILMOR	11'17.129	187.058	116.232	6 LAPS
25	25	T. BOUTSEN	BEL	LIGIER GITANES BLONDES	LIGIER RENAULT	6'07.140	172.499	107.186	3 LAPS
26	1	A. SENNA	BRA	HONDA MARLBORO McLAREN	McLAREN HONDA	3'37.487	194.130	120.627	2 LAPS

FASTEST LAP: 5 N. MANSELL – Lap 44 Time: 1'40.646 (209.749 Km/h = 130.332 mph)

Australian Grand Prix

Adelaide

Race 16, Adelaide, and Nigel Mansell's last race in Formula One – or was it? Even before the entire Grand Prix circus had arrived in Adelaide for one of its favourite events, the Australian Grand Prix, the rumours were spreading.

The story was that FISA, the governing body, and FOCA, the teams' own association, were so concerned about losing their star attraction that they were making moves to keep Mansell. With Ayrton Senna also warning that he would take a year out unless he found a competitive car, which seemed increasingly unlikely as McLaren continued to search for engines, the sport as a spectacle was under threat.

Williams Renault had Alain Prost back but, as Mansell had said earlier in the year, the Frenchman is a chauffeur, a highly polished driver, tactically astute, a winner – but not of the same school of aggression as Mansell or Senna. Mansell, of course, had his contract in place with the American Indycar team of Newman-Haas, but in Formula One the only certainty is that nothing is certain.

A highly complicated deal, the like of which could only be struck in Formula One, could see Mansell's contract bought out. Williams would then, with the backing of their multi-national sponsors, have their man back. That would put two great drivers up against each other in identical equipment in 1993, providing the drama to satisfy the needs of the television companies who had paid fortunes or, in some cases, were waiting to pay on delivery.

It was part theory, part speculation, but even Mansell had to admit: "Yes, I know of moves to do this. I am not party to it. All this does is cause complications. At this moment nothing has changed and I don't see anything changing."

His contract negotiations with Williams still rankled. The wrangling had cost him the chance to defend the title, and as Mansell stood at the door of the garage after the Friday morning warm-up session in Adelaide, he again reviewed the situation. "It is a bit of a compliment but it is a little bit frustrating and annoying, too. The job could have been done in the first place. Everybody appreciates now that it was messed up from start to finish. No matter how people apportion blame, I am not the management of the team, I am not a mega-sponsor of the world controlling things. They should know how to behave and they did not behave very well.

"What we all have to do is to be big enough to get on with our lives. I have my own family to take care of. They cannot do anything without my co-operation. I have made a commitment to the American side of racing and those who know me realise that if I give a commitment I will fulfil it. There is no way I would let anyone down in America."

But there was a report that Newman Haas had asked for £10 million to release him. What if it were true that they might sell if someone matched their scare-away figure? "Well, that would hurt, too," admitted Mansell honestly. "I am then put in a situation I am not controlling. Perhaps

I will go fishing and golfing. Senna says they need both of us? I think they would forget us both in about a week.

"I have tried to keep my head down this season and have fulfilled my dream of winning the World Championship. I don't think I could go back. An awful lot of bad things have been said. I am really happy to be out of it. What makes me laugh is that they changed their minds. They had me one minute, they agreed everything, then they did not want me, which was fine for three weeks, but then a month later they wanted me again.

"Well, I am sorry, but we are human beings and in that time we had decided to do something else. That's business. At least I have sorted out my future – I think – although I cannot control what other people do."

It was an extraordinary start to a dramatic race week-end, and gossip was fuelled by the absence of the two top men in motor sport, Max Moseley, president of FISA, and Bernie Ecclestone, boss of FOCA, who were both elsewhere on other business.

After lunch on the warm, sunny Friday, Mansell went out to silence his critics who, as usual, were suggesting that he might not be 'up' for this race. He was playing too much golf, it was his last Grand Prix, his mind was elsewhere. On the 18th lap of Adelaide's demanding circuit, which encompasses four of the city's streets, he delivered his answer. A time of 1 minute 13.732 seconds in the closing minutes put him on provisional pole, although Ayrton Senna split the Williams cars with his time, which was just 0.470 seconds behind Mansell.

The McLaren cars, their team boss Ron Dennis admitted, were less disadvantaged on this type of street circuit. It made for some closer racing, but it is interesting to look at the number of problems that sophisticated Formula One cars throw up: Ferrari had wrong gear ratios, acute oversteer and were trying an active suspension unit on one car. Thierry Boutsen's Ligier had engine vibrations, Martin Brundle complained of oversteer and understeer in his Benetton, Christian Fittipaldi blew his Minardi's engine after over-revving at 18000 rpm. There were broken alternators, water leaks, clutch problems, electronic failures. And, of course, there were human failings too, with cars spinning off on the dusty track – but that is what the spectators love.

Mansell headed back to the golf course. He had been made a temporary honorary member of the exclusive Royal Adelaide Club and was due to play in the South Australian Open the following week. He had won a pro-am in midweek with a par 73, costing team owner Eddie Jordan a $100 bet in aid of charity. Twice he had played 36 holes in a day and now he was off for a different kind of driving lesson.

The week had begun with an abortive fishing trip. Mansell loves fishing and when the opportunity arose to fish from a boat on the Murray River it was too good to miss. But on the flooded river there were no bites. The local paper reported that Mansell had stormed off but Grand Prix photographer John Townsend, who was with him, saw it differently. "The boat owner would not take us where we wanted to go. It was a waste of time for Nigel. And when it was suggested that for a publicity picture he could just hook on a fish which was conveniently in a tank on the boat, he decided to go."

Adelaide really buzzes for the Grand Prix. The city puts on a festival of entertainment and the best support events for the crowds on the track and in the air. Fortunately for Gerhard Berger, the traffic policeman who stopped him after he drove his hire car through a red light was caught up in the mood and he let the Austrian off with a warning. All over the town there seemed to be Grand Prix parties or receptions while Adelaide's movers headed for the Grand Prix Ball. Hindley Street in the city centre was sealed off and jazz bands played from balconies and doorways as thousands partied the night away.

On Saturday the weather was even hotter, perfect for those spectators who were hanging around nursing head-aches but not so good for the drivers who were looking for quicker times. The heat made tyre grip less certain and only two improved. Senna was quickest of the day, but his time was not faster than in the previous session and Mansell had his 14th pole position of the season, a remarkable record. "That's fantastic, it means a lot," he said. "I congratulate Renault for the last two races – we've had qualifying engines and I have no doubt that if we had not had one here, I would not be on pole. I like that record, it's one that helps you win races because at a lot of circuits, including here, it is very, very important to start at the front.

"Senna's time was very good today. They have im-proved by half a second over yesterday. It's going to be a tough race. At some circuits like this the active suspension is not an advantage at all. Over the whole lap, I'm talking about. If you look at the start and finish line speeds I am not particularly quick. The main problem we have with active on a circuit like this is traction, turning into slow corners and getting the power down, and the car's not very good for this. Fortunately, the majority of circuits are medium to high speed."

The question of Mansell's future arose again at the pole press conference. Was this his last Grand Prix? He was a little upset, he said, because he had been told that Bernie Ecclestone was in the US to try to buy his contract. "I cannot pass comment," said Mansell. "As far as I am aware, I start testing for the Indy series in early January. That's it. What I can't say to you, what I can't control, is what the powers that be might be doing."

Senna was not forthcoming about his future plans except to insist that it was important to be competitive. He explained with some style how he needed the motivation for his goals. And he stressed: "Nigel will be away from Formula One and with the possibility that I would do a similar thing, the balance of change to Formula One, with the return of Prost and the cost of it, is out of the question. Not a single person will benefit. Everybody is going to lose, and lose a lot."

The spectre of Prost was everywhere, even if the man himself had stayed away. Patrese was already tipping the French three-times Champion as 1993 favourite but wondered whether Prost's style, similar to his own, would suit the car. Mansell, he conceded, had driven fantastically well to win the title but the Williams, while efficient and quick, was not easy to feel through the steering wheel or the backside. He was taking his expertise to Benetton in 1993 to help them set up their active suspension, but he was worried about the arrival of the new Williams car and Renault engine combination. Mansell later revealed that the Williams FW15 for 1993 was estimated to be 10 per cent quicker!

The hunt for better engines was on in other teams, too. Tyrrell switched to Yamaha, who had been with Jordan, and two days later Jordan announced a deal with British race engine specialist firm Brian Hart Ltd, who would supply a V10 unit. V12s were bad news with their extra weight, fuel penalties and size.

The element most drivers feared in Adelaide was rain, which had fallen in torrents in previous years, washing out races. When Sunday dawned, forecasts of heavy showers cast as much of a gloom as the grey clouds. Mansell had problems in the warm-up, trying both his race car and the back-up, and it was Patrese who was fastest. Mansell was second and Senna and Berger third and fourth.

The McLaren drivers, however, were optimistic about their chances of success as they compared their times and performances with those of the Williams men. There was much at stake for a last race with the Championship already won. Mansell should have won the title here in 1986 but at almost 200mph, with two thirds of the race gone, a tyre had exploded. He had been lucky to survive and had had to wait another six years for glory.

Mansell had never won the Australian Grand Prix, one of only three venues where he had yet to record a win (the others were Monte Carlo and Japan). He also wanted to be the first driver to break into double figures in a season with his tenth win. Moreover, he was keen to win because he likes the city and the people – and they like him. 'Mansell is fair dinkum' proclaimed one banner while another, in poorer taste, said 'Senna Sucks'. But before the day was out, these complementary emotions were to be highlighted.

Red Five had an engine change between warm-up and the race. Renault also had a special reason for wanting more success: their big rivals, Honda, were to quit after Australia and desperately wanted to go out on a high. The drivers went for their last briefing of the year, shook hands and wished each other well for the future, and had a 'class of '92' photograph taken. Mansell and Senna sat together.

Around the small paddock – of course, no motorhomes or elaborate motorised offices had been shipped to Adelaide – there was an end-of-term feeling. The drivers concentrated on the job in hand. The 100,000 crowd was down on the previous year, but the race is given a state subsidy of around $4 million and the event is guaranteed for the city until 1996. It brings in $30 million, about £12 million, which explains why so many cities are desperate for a Grand Prix race.

Mansell had to return to the pits after the formation lap to have leaves and debris, which could have blocked the radiator, removed from the sidepods of his car. By now it was windy and there were spots of rain in the air. The final parade – lifeguards, rescue boats and a navy band – was a fate-tempter for the race, which had been shortened by rain a year earlier.

When Mansell weaved his way through the stationary cars already assembled on the grid, which was packed with mechanics, media and guests, he was given a huge cheer by the crowd in the stand. Normally he left the car while his team made their last-minute adjustments and checks. He would stand at the side, chatting to his personal engineer, David Brown, have a drink of water and enjoy the frenetic scene. But on this, his final day, he remained in the cramped monocoque for those 15 minutes and there were few words for anyone.

Often his eyes were closed as if in contemplation. Brown gave him an occasional word about the car and then Peter Collins, the boss of Team Lotus, appeared. Collins was one of the men who had originally helped Mansell into Formula One 13 years and 180 Grands Prix earlier. They had both advanced successfully and now Collins was there to wish his friend good luck in his last race. Mansell may have allowed a few thoughts from years gone by to drift into his mind as he sat there, 12,000 miles from the Midlands, where he had first started with a kart. He had not had much money but he had battled on and made his start in Austria in 1980 in a Lotus in courageous fashion.

Fuel had poured into his seat as the tank was topped up on the grid and he had driven in searing pain for 40 laps as the corrosive mixture burned his skin, refusing to quit until the Lotus car cracked before he did. Perhaps he thought of that, or of the time in 1978 when he and his wife had sold everything they possessed to allow him five races in Formula Three.

It was an audacious gamble but he survived, just as he had in a series of crashes, including one which had paralysed him. He had been told he might not drive again, and that he would be on his back for six months. Within a week he discharged himself and was driving again within seven.

In 1980, as a rookie driver trying to get a Formula One drive, he met the illustrious Colin Chapman of Lotus cars after the world's top team had had a terrible race. "You know what the problem was," said Mansell. "I wasn't driving for you." Chapman had looked at him and walked out without a word. Mansell feared the worst, but soon he was test driving. His cheeky confidence had paid off.

It was poignant, then, in Adelaide when Peter Collins, the man who had introduced him to Chapman and given him his start, came up to the grid to wish him luck. Now the cocky, headstrong young man was a multi-millionaire who had delighted in making a host of sceptics eat their words. He had turned down Enzo Ferrari in 1986 and the great man had returned to take him to Italy two years later. He was World Champion, a record-breaker with five straight wins at the start of 1992, ten victories and 14 pole positions in the season, and Britain's most successful race-winner. Now, reluctantly, after the collapse of his contract negotiations, he was on his way to America. The last leg of his Formula One adventure had arrived and he was out to claim career win number 31.

Both Mansell and Senna were aware of the importance of reaching the first corner in the lead. Adelaide is a tight track for overtaking. Whoever led was likely to control the race. Earlier that weekend Mansell had complained once again that too much of the driving had been taken away from the driver by computers. Nonetheless, this time his software was better than Senna's and when red turned to green he was off and first to the bend. Behind them some did not survive the crush – three cars touched and two went out.

At the front, Senna tucked in behind Mansell. He slipped past at the hairpin but ran wide and the Englishman darted back inside to regain the lead. They charged on, and it was obvious that Senna was out to enjoy what might be his last outing for a long while. He lost tenths of a second instead of the chunks of time more usual on quicker circuits.

They wound it up, trading fastest laps as they raced round, and by the 18th lap they already had the backmarkers in sight. Both men slipped past the traffic, but the slight delay allowed Senna to sit right on the tail of Red Five once again. Round they came, locked together, until suddenly, Senna went slamming into the back of the Williams. His car reared up, the front left wheel flew off and in a flurry of debris both cars careered off, onto the grass and out.

Mansell sat for a few seconds, his arms over his helmet, and then climbed out and began to run across the track, dodging a passing car. Behind him, Senna climbed out and walked back to the pits, to more than a few jeers.

Mansell had run to escape his own anger. After a similar incident in Belgium in 1987 he had hunted down

Senna in the pits and had pinned him to a wall while explaining his point of view. This time Mansell headed for the pits, changed, and when Frank Williams told him that they would not be protesting about the incident, he went to the clerk of the course's office amid a throng of reporters and television crews.

It was a short, angry visit. They refused to hear his complaint. They had looked at the incident and decided that it was a sporting accident. Mansell, with wife Rosanne at his side, held an instant press conference while he waited for his children to be brought to the vehicle which would take him out of the Formula One paddock for the last time. His hot anger had become cold fury, and the stewards were his first target: "They are gutless," he said.

Around him Formula One life went on. The cars thundered past, occasionally blanking out Mansell's angry words, hurting eardrums. Mansell's team-mate, Riccardo Patrese, in his last race for Williams, held the lead until the 51st lap when his car broke down. Senna's team-mate, Gerhard Berger, leaving for Ferrari in 1993, took over at the front and held off Michael Schumacher's Benetton for his second win of the season. Behind them came Britain's Martin Brundle, another victim of Formula One's ruthlessness. He had scored his 11th points win in the last 12 races, but was looking for a drive for the next season.

By the time they were spraying champagne for the last time in 1992, Mansell was already back in his luxury hotel with Rosanne and their three children. He had come up the hard way, starting with little, surviving on self-belief, determination and, ultimately, talent. He had not endeared himself to everyone. For some his complaints were moans, delivered in a flat, Midlands

255

accent. To millions he was a genuine hero, self-made, given to the odd wrong word, but with few airs and graces. His skills earned him fortunes, mansions, an OBE, and a huge following.

Many would have quit, allowed themselves to be quelled. It was five years before he was a winner. He was leaving the sport at the top of his form now and it was a loss for him that he could not defend his title. It was a bigger loss to Formula One, who were making efforts to win him back. The Italians, who took to him in a big way, had dubbed him *Il Leone* for his aggressive, fearless driving, but in fact he is much more a British bulldog. There was plenty of bite in his remarks.

The furious World Champion admitted. "If I had confronted Senna I would have flattened him. I am disgusted with the whole thing. I am glad I am rid of all this. There would have been a big fight and that would not have been the way to finish my Formula One career. I ran across the track to avoid him."

But Senna claimed: "He braked earlier than he should have. I never expected it. He's always complaining. It is normal for him. It would have been better if he had not run away. Even if he was not happy, he should have come across and shaken hands and let it go. We were never quite in agreement on occasions but that is not a reason for him to run away and complain. More than ever this was the opportunity to shake hands and say goodbye in a good way."

Mansell said: "I wonder what he would have said if the roles had been reversed? And what would the stewards have done then? It seems that certain people can get away with anything. That's been amply demonstrated here. I have been fined thousands for less. There is a rule for one and a rule for another. There are people in the pit lane so biased it is not true. These are appalling standards and I am glad I am out of it. Any doubts I had about leaving have been wiped away. I'm glad to be out. I am looking forward to the US – that should be a good year with fair racing."

The next morning he gazed out from his luxury suite in Adelaide after a busy night looking after his son, who had an earache, and his daughter, who also felt unwell. "It is great to be able to sit and talk about my Formula One career," he said, hinting at the dangers he always recognised but never allowed to intimidate him. Sitting with Rosanne, he said: "We came back from retirement saying that we would do whatever it took to win. We kept our side of the bargain, lifting the team out of the doldrums and into the forefront of Formula One.

"It was team effort and we fulfilled our dreams. We changed our lifestyle to accomplish that, but unfortunately, as soon as Williams got success, I was not wanted. But I've got the title, my family and I am looking forward to racing in the United States. It has been a fantastic year."

The partnership with Red Five, last seen broken and bruised like a tired warhorse, was finished . . . but it would never be forgotten.

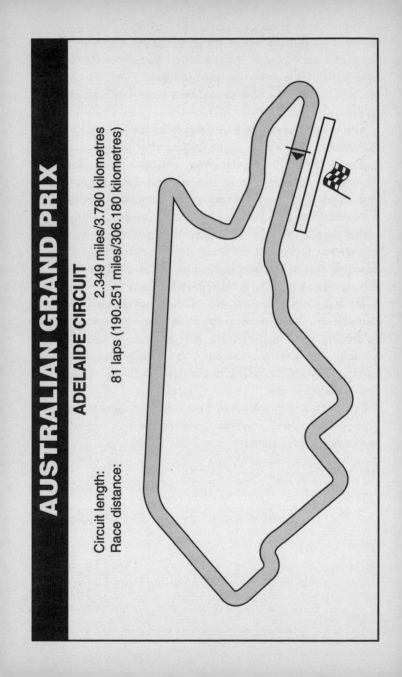

AUSTRALIAN GRAND PRIX

ADELAIDE CIRCUIT

Circuit length: 2.349 miles/3.780 kilometres
Race distance: 81 laps (190.251 miles/306.180 kilometres)

1992 – AUSTRALIAN GRAND PRIX – ADELAIDE

RACE CLASSIFICATION AFTER 81 LAPS

(306.180 km = 190.251 mls)

Pos	Nr	Driver		Team Make	Make	Total Time	km/h	mph	Diff
1	2	G. BERGER	AUT	HONDA MARLBORO McLAREN	McLAREN HONDA	1:46'54.788	171.829	106.770	
2	19	M. SCHUMACHER	GER	CAMEL BENETTON FORD	BENETTON FORD	1:46'55.527	171.809	106.757	0.741
3	20	M. BRUNDLE	GBR	CAMEL BENETTON FORD	BENETTON FORD	1:47'28.942	170.391	106.878	54.156
4	27	J. ALESI	FRA	FERRARI	FERRARI	1:47'31.593	168.740	104.850	1 LAP
5	25	T. BOUTSEN	BEL	LIGIER GITANES BLONDES	LIGIER RENAULT	1:47'51.171	168.220	104.633	1 LAP
6	32	S. MODENA	ITA	SASOL JORDAN YAMAHA	JORDAN YAMAHA	1:48'02.179	167.944	104.355	1 LAP
7	11	M. HAKKINEN	FIN	TEAM CASTROL LOTUS	LOTUS FORD	1:48'16.288	167.570	104.120	1 LAP
8	10	A. SUZUKI	JPN	FOOTWORK MUGEN-HONDA	FOOTWORK MUGEN-HONDA	1:49'03.350	167.363	103.995	2 LAPS
9	23	C. FITTIPALDI	BRA	MINARDI TEAM	MINARDI LAMBORGHINI	1:49'04.3'0	167.338	103.979	2 LAPS
10	24	G. MORBIDELLI	ITA	MINARDI TEAM	MINARDI LAMBORGHINI	1:47'17.281	167.001	103.770	2 LAPS
11	28	N. LARINI	ITA	FERRARI	FERRARI	1:47'18.1'5	166.973	103.756	2 LAPS
12	16	J. LAMMERS	HOL	MARCH F.1	MARCH ILMOR	1:48'06.134	166.645	101.584	3 LAPS
13	12	J. HERBERT	GBR	TEAM CASTROL LOTUS	LOTUS FORD	1:47'06.199	168.054	101.317	4 LAPS

NOT CLASSIFIED

Pos	Nr	Driver		Team Make	Make	Total Time	km/h	mph	COVERED
14	21	J. LEHTO	FIN	SCUDERIA ITALIA	BMS DALLARA FERRARI	1:35'28.539	166.283	100.324	70 LAPS
15	17	E. NASPETTI	ITA	MARCH F.1	MARCH ILMOR	1:15'53.518	162.227	100.803	55 LAPS
16	29	B. GACHOT	FRA	CENTRAL PARK-VEN. LARR.	VENTURI LAMBORGHINI	1:09'44.49'6	165.852	103.958	51 LAPS
17	6	R. PATRESE	ITA	CANON WILLIAMS TEAM	WILLIAMS RENAULT	1:08'26.875	170.702	100.070	50 LAPS
18	30	U. KATAYAMA	JPN	CENTRAL PARK-VEN. LARR.	VENTURI LAMBORGHINI	50 20.017	157.708	97.995	35 LAPS
19	4	A. DE CESARIS	ITA	TYRRELL	TYRRELL ILMOR	38 44.179	155.550	102.850	28 LAPS
20	5	N. MANSELL	GBR	CANON WILLIAMS TEAM	WILLIAMS RENAULT	23 47.913	171.840	106.590	18 LAPS
21	1	A. SENNA	BRA	HONDA MARLBORO McLAREN	McLAREN HONDA	23 40.351	171.857	106.483	18 LAPS
22	33	M. GUGELMIN	BRA	SASOL JORDAN YAMAHA	JORDAN YAMAHA	10 08.856	158.451	97.214	7 LAPS
23	26	E. COMAS	FRA	LIGIER GITANES BLONDES	LIGIER RENAULT	6 62.364	154.477	95.687	4 LAPS

FASTEST LAP: 19 M. SCHUMACHER – Lap 68 Time:1'16.078 (178.889 km/h = 111.144 mph)

Mansell's Future

Nigel Mansell left Formula One to face squarely the most merciless and dangerous examination of his life in America in front of the world's largest sporting attendance, half a million spectators. The centrepiece of the Indycar season, in which Mansell was to drive for the team which bore the name of film star Paul Newman, is the Indianapolis 500 mile race in May. It is super-fast – the speeds are much greater than those of Formula One – and is hemmed in by solid walls. It is potentially very, very dangerous.

Why did Mansell decide to go there? The questions tumbled hard and in bewildering profusion. Was he risking his life to an unacceptable degree? What was this Indycar racing, anyway? Wasn't it the one where they drove round and round oval circuits until they made themselves dizzy? Indy was where they had horrendous, monstrous crashes, wasn't it? The questions did not stop there. They served to open up a direct comparison between Formula One and Indy. Which was better? Which faster? Which demanded more skill, which carried more prestige? How similar were the cars – or how different?

Many, many people in Britain were suddenly and understandably curious when Mansell announced that he'd fallen out with Williams, was retiring from Formula

One after 12 years which had culminated in the World Championship, and was going Indy. There were precedents. Mario Andretti came from Indy to Formula One and won the Championship with Lotus before returning to Indy. Emerson Fittipaldi, twice World Champion, was still driving Indycars.

Others had cross-fertilised between the two: Eddie Cheever, Danny Sullivan (once of Tyrrell), Derek Daly, Stefan Johansson and, most notably, Nelson Piquet, three-times Formula One World Champion. Piquet went there at the end of 1991 to join a team called Menard. Practising for the Indianapolis 500 he crashed at more than 200mph, the car flipping and smashing itself. Piquet was extremely fortunate to escape with no more than severe leg and ankle injuries. It could have been – and for a dreadful instant looked as if it was – much, much worse.

If a driver of Piquet's experience – 204 Grands Prix from 1978 – could do this, what might happen to a charger like Mansell who, while a very experienced driver himself, drives on the cutting edge of risk? Questions, questions, questions.

Formula One, in many ways an extremely insular activity, regarded Indycar racing as something drivers retired to, a domestic American championship of no great relevance or even significance. There were whole dynasties of drivers whose names were known only slightly, as if they came from fables: A.J. Foyt, several Unsers, a lot of Andrettis, Bobby Rahal, Rick Mears, Gordon Johncock. Who were those guys? Were they any good?

Michael Andretti, son of Mario, announced during 1992 that he was departing Indy for Marlboro McLaren in Formula One which, of course, prompted many, many people in America to become suddenly and understandably curious about Grand Prix racing. Senna, Prost, Mansell, who were those guys? Were they any good . . . ? Because Indycar was so strong in the United States, Formula One never really sunk deep roots there although it had tried hard enough.

Between 1959 and 1991 the United States Grand Prix – sometimes labelled the United States Grand Prix East, sometimes the United States Grand Prix West – wandered between the unlovely and unloved Watkins Glen circuit in upstate New York, the extremely unlovely Detroit, Long Beach, Las Vegas (a circuit built partly in a car park), Dallas and finally Phoenix. It was at Phoenix that the wandering finally stopped in 1991, and Grand Prix racing has not been back since, nor was it scheduled to go again in 1993. Watkins Glen apart, these were street circuits, and while they demonstrated how nimble a Formula One car was and emphasised its precise handling qualities, the average speeds were inevitably slow in the context of narrow, tight, artificial circuits lined by concrete blocks. To Americans, nurtured and suckled on lap after lap at over 230mph at Indianapolis, it seemed very slow. That last Grand Prix at Phoenix, on 10 March 1991, had a fastest lap of 95.936mph.

This needs exploring. The Indycars continued to use Long Beach – they replaced Formula One there in the early 1980s – and in their race in April 1991 the average winning speed was only 81.195mph (recorded by Al Unser Jr). American supporters, however, fully understood that Indycars had a wide range, and when these same cars went to Indianapolis Rick Mears won with an average speed of 176.457mph. The fastest lap in qualifying was 224.468mph, a mind-boggling statistic even on an oval circuit containing only curved corners – there are no chicanes or anything remotely like them.

The real point was that Indycar supporters never did see Formula One cars going through their full range: not just the nip and tuck of Detroit, Vegas, Phoenix or Monaco, but the majestic sweep of Spa, the scorching speeds of Silverstone, the fearsome straight in Portugal, the balance between fast and slow at Monza. Yet because every Formula One circuit has real corners and chicanes the cars could never be set up for total speed. If you asked engineers and designers the most simple question, namely how fast their cars could be made to go in a straight line on a piece of straight track, they would reply that they didn't know. It has never been necessary, because they're setting the car up for optimum speed through the corners and chicanes as well as the straights, which is another kind of balance, well expressed by the varying demands of Monza. The absolute potential top speed of a Formula One car is conjectural and nobody bothers much about it. It didn't help Indycar supporters to understand, though.

The worlds of Indy and Formula One have always been divided, either virtually or completely. The modern era of Formula One began in 1950 and from then until 1960 the Indianapolis 500 counted as a round of the World Championship in order, it was thought, to make the Championship truly of the world. This was an artificial device, since the Indycar drivers ignored all the Grands Prix and the Grand Prix drivers ignored Indy. There were only a couple of examples of drivers competing in both.

After 1960 Colin Chapman of Lotus nursed powerful ambitions of winning Indianapolis, though strictly as a one-off, with Jim Clark. In 1963 Clark came second in the race and earned more than $50,000 for his trouble

– not so bad, he would say cryptically, for turning left 800 times, which is what you do on an oval. A year later he took pole, thus mortifying the American media, who anticipated endless soul-baring interviews with him as part of their wall-to-wall coverage (excuse the pun). American drivers were suckled and nurtured on giving interviews and didn't refuse. Clark, meanwhile, was at the airport trying to catch a plane to get to Monaco for the Grand Prix there. The Indianapolis 500 race meeting, as we shall see, is spread over a month from first practice through qualifying to the race itself, affording Clark enough time to commute across the Atlantic. Chapman and Clark decided to dispense with commuting the following year, 1965, when Clark missed Monaco and won Indianapolis.

Clark may well be relevant to Mansell, apart from the obvious historical connections of Lotus and Chapman, because while Mansell is not by nature shy as Clark was, they are both in subtly different ways extremely 'British' figures. Clark came to loathe Indianapolis because of the incessant interviews which he regarded as intrusions, symptoms of the cheerleader mentality, the gigantic showmanship and the rest of it. Before flying there for one of those races in the 1960s he became so depressed that he telephoned a journalist friend from the departure lounge at Heathrow and invited him for a drink. Journalists being reasonably intrepid, the summoned friend managed to get through to the departure lounge with neither passport nor airline ticket – it simply had not crossed Clark's innocent mind that this might pose a problem – and found Clark drinking brandy and talking about not going to Indianapolis.

Clark went, of course, and it might well be that Mansell will revel in the razzmatazz, the adoration, the attention, the microphones, the whole big deal; but if he doesn't he'll have an extremely awkward time and he won't be flying away from it after just one race as Clark did. The big deal will be Mansell's daily diet.

Before we leave the 1960s, it might be interesting to note that in 1966 Graham Hill won the Indianapolis 500 from Clark amid some potent confusion over the number of laps covered and who had covered more. Both thought they had won. No matter: a British one-two proved that it could be done. Thereafter the Americans reconquered America, Foyt in 1967, Bobby Unser in 1968, Mario Andretti in 1969, Al Unser in 1970 and so on and so on. Indycars did not need Formula One, Formula One did not need Indycars, and that was the real separation of the worlds. Hence all those questions when Mansell decided to go there and Michael Andretti decided to come here.

Mansell's own supporters, holding images of Piquet's crash so vividly in their minds, immediately feared for Mansell. A British motor racing magazine carried a graphic photograph of Piquet crashing on their front cover, the car battered and upside down and Piquet's helmet grinding the surface of the track; and ghastly film clips of it appeared on British television, the car suddenly twitching loose, ramming the wall, thrashing, disintegrating. The wall? Yes, the wall. That seems to be – and is – a stark difference between the worlds. The walls have long gone from high-speed Formula One circuits and have been replaced by sand traps, run-off areas, armco, tyre walls. Walls remain only at the street circuits where speeds are much slower. Moreover, even people with the most casual interest in motor sport must have seen across the years plenty of television clips from Indianapolis with cars thundering against the wall which runs round the outside of the oval, bouncing and bounding back into the path of packs of cars travelling at over 200mph. Some of those clips are not for persons of a nervous disposition.

Other events in 1992 compounded the fears over Mansell. A driver called Jovy Marcello died when his car hit the wall at Indianapolis in the run-up to the race. In the race itself there were 13 crashes, Michael Andretti's brother Jeff being among the most seriously injured. He hit the wall head on and required eight hours of surgery on his legs. It is true that Marcello was the first driver to die in an Indycar since 1982, and the Indycar fraternity have pointed out, in the relative and important discussions on comparative safety which accompanied Mansell's announcement, that three Formula One drivers have been killed since 1982: Gilles Villeneuve and Riccardo Paletti in 1982 and Elio de Angelis in 1986.

Scant consolation any of this, because any man's life is a human life. But you have to be as dispassionate as you can about safety or you simply couldn't discuss it sensibly. The Formula One 16-race calendar which Mansell has left has taken deliberate and severe steps to protect the drivers and the crowd. (An airborne car did get into the crowd in the early 1980s, mercifully killing no one.) Some new tracks, notably the Hungaroring and South Africa, seem neutered to the point of eliminating virtually all risk, which makes perfect sense in one way, but is a violation of the essential nature of man-to-man combat in hot cars in another.

Formula One drivers have themselves become extremely safety conscious. Twice in his career Alain Prost stopped during races because he judged that lashing rain had made conditions unacceptably dangerous, and Niki Lauda did the same at Mount Fuji, Japan in 1976, thereby forfeiting the Championship to Hunt. In the 1980s, when Spa had been relaid and the surface of the track began to break up, it was Lauda to whom the other drivers looked for a verdict on whether the race should take place. Lauda said no, and the race was postponed.

This is in no sense a critical comparison with Indycars, just an examination of the way Formula One evolved (Indianapolis is famous for its advanced and efficient medical facilities). Nor does it disturb the basic and ever-present spectre that danger can never be completely eliminated. Martin Donnelly's crash in Spain where, under tremendous and destructive forces, the car was torn to pieces and he lay on the track proved that. Gerhard Berger's crash at Imola, when his Ferrari became a fireball, proved that. Riccardo Patrese's collision with Berger and subsequent launching into the air in Portugal in 1992 proved that. The latter was what they call a motor racing 'accident' – meaning that whatever you do, however you arrange every precaution, there will always be combinations of circumstances which defeat you. This may be pilot error, to use an apt expression – the driver making a genuine mistake – or more likely a mechanical failure. Something on the car breaks and in an instant the car becomes a wild animal.

The faster you are travelling the wilder the animal becomes, and the less time you have to tame it. That is simple logic. At Indianapolis, to seize upon an entirely relevant comparison, the slowest speed in a corner has been calculated at around 210mph, and you don't need a degree in ballistics to know that from 210mph to the wall is essentially no time-gap whatsoever in which to catch and tame the animal. These are the film clips the British have seen, the film clips they remembered with such clarity and apprehension when they contemplated Mansell going there.

However, this popular perception – fantastic, flat out speed round and round and round, occasional split seconds of horror – is as misleading about Indycars as Detroit was about the full range of Formula One cars. Of the 16 Indycar rounds per season, only two are on super speedways. Four are on ovals which measure a mile and the remainder on circuits which would be familiar to Formula One, streets and roads. It is here that Nigel Mansell is expected to be immediately comfortable and extremely formidable. This leads only to more and more questions. What exactly does Mansell face? What are the cars really like? What new techniques will he have to learn and then master? How will he acclimatise to another culture, to the openness of America, after the laboured secrecy of the enclosed, tinted-glass, air-conditioned Formula One motorhomes where drivers spend so much of their time?

He will certainly face a shock in the paddock, an area which in Formula One resembles a fortress. In Indycar the general public can, for a modest amount, buy tickets to go into the paddock and they expect to see the drivers, and perhaps talk to them. An Indycar driver who ignores the general public is considered a very naughty man and will be told about it. An American journalist suggested that Mansell would have to show himself or hire a press agent, but the latter would not be very popular. In theory, and no doubt in practice, the openness ought to worry Mansell less than some of the other exponents of Formula One, who are virtually invisible people before they get into their cars and after they get out of them. If Mansell didn't cultivate mass adoration at Silverstone and the British Grand Prix each year, he certainly embraced it, and has always spoken of the fans and his bond with them. At Silverstone he habitually made himself as accessible as anyone could without being completely overwhelmed.

That, at least, has been some sort of preparation, although clearly the adulation will not be coming at him on the same scale or with the same fervour. Initially, there will be curiosity, and if he starts to win races a great deal more than curiosity, but he will remain a foreigner. The British are not the only chauvinistic nation on earth.

The voracious American press will be different. Americans are by inclination more open, as becomes apparent whenever one of their policemen is interviewed on television talking about a crime. He imparts as much information as he can. A British policeman in the same circumstances imparts the minimum. And most of the British spy books written – the factual ones, not fiction – are researched in the Library of Congress, Washington DC, because there freedom of information is regarded as an enrichment of society, not a threat to it. How will Mansell cope with the demands of a press attuned precisely to this? The demands are always going to be heavy. Indianapolis actively sells and promotes the 500 race: there are hour-long documentaries covering its history (including the crashes), every team manager and driver is interviewed at length and in depth. They are expected to be perceptive, eloquent and interesting.

Mansell has had a difficult relationship with certain sections of the British press for historical reasons. Many Formula One journalists have covered his career virtually from the beginning in Formula Ford 1600, and the specialist writers in the motoring magazines feel free to criticise him as they judge the occasion demands – as well as to lard on their praise. Mansell has always found criticism awkward, and the fact that the specialists know him so well – and he knows them – sharpened that. The popular press has been much kinder, and forgivably so. During the Formula One season, which stretches from March to November, and particularly before and after the races themselves, journalists have to look for a story and invariably that story has been Mansell, whatever he has done.

In every respect America will be different. He is going there as a stranger, their journalists will be only vaguely, if at all, aware of his early struggles; unaware of the schisms which have grown between Mansell and many other people in Formula One; unaware of people's perception of him as a multi-millionaire who moans. Mansell can handle the press adroitly when needs must, charm them, make little jokes and be what America treasures so warmly: candid. He will take a colossal advantage with him. He speaks English, so that at no stage will he encounter the difficulties he did at Ferrari, where he didn't know what people around him were actually saying. And of course Americans do love the accent (they won't know it's Birmingham), and they do think the way we speak is quaint. To charm them would be no difficult matter. If Nigel Mansell is not exactly a Laurence Olivier Americans might well think he is; or Michael Caine, anyway.

The car he will drive, and the cars he'll race against, could pass at a distance for the same as those in Formula One. There are, on closer inspection, profound differences and in trying to explain them several American journalists draw the comparison between apples and oranges. One journalist offered a variation on the theme and went for Coca-Cola and Pepsi, but you get the general idea. Specifically, an Indycar is considerably heavier. It could have a turbo-charged engine (long since banned in

Formula One) and be fuelled by methanol, a combination of carbon, hydrogen and oxygen (Formula One is supposed to run on ordinary garage forecourt pump fuel, although this is a controversial subject). A Formula One car does four miles to the gallon, an Indycar 1.8 miles. An Indycar generates about 725 brake horsepower with a Chevrolet turbo engine, a Formula One car – say the Honda V10 – about 670 brake horsepower. An Indycar's top speed is 235mph, the top speed Formula One cars reach is around 202mph.

The extra weight of an Indycar (40 per cent more) is for safety. Cheever said: "If you had a big accident at Indianapolis in a Formula One car, there would be nothing left at all. They would just sweep up the pieces with a broom." This extra weight makes the cockpit area – the survival cell – strong enough to hit the wall without destroying itself and, furthermore, strong enough to hit the wall several times on the theory that at speeds of over 200mph the car will rotate back into it. This does not prevent criticism within Indycar that the detachable front nose of the cars – generally the first part to take an impact – ought to be incorporated as a rigid part of the chassis. As someone pointed out, if the nose cone gets ripped off there's not much left to protect the driver's feet.

There have also been tentative talks about ways of restraining speed, something with which Formula One, and Mansell, are familiar. Formula One circuits have been deliberately doctored to achieve this and Silverstone, once driven virtually flat out, is a good example. A chicane was constructed there just after the Daily Express Bridge, and when the cars outgrew even that the track was extensively modified with a new, twisty 'complex' of corners in place of the chicane.

Mansell spent most of his Formula One career using

special qualifying tyres which were made to last a single flying lap, two if you were very, very lucky. These do not exist at Indy.

Actually driving an Indycar magnifies the differences. Races involve a couple of pit stops for fuel and tyres and this alters a driver's tactics. He must select the best moment to stop by reading the position of all the other cars, whether they've stopped, when they are likely to stop, what advantages can be exploited as a result. Formula One cars no longer stop for fuel (like turbos, long since banned) and rarely stop twice for tyres. Indeed, it is becoming standard practice to run through on one set, although a single tyre stop remains the norm at present.

The uncertainties of an Indycar race are compounded by the yellow flag system, again something virtually unknown to Mansell. It works like this: if there is an incident, even a minor incident, yellow flags are waved. A 'pace' car – an ordinary road-going vehicle, usually with a celebrity on board (not that that matters) – comes out onto the circuit and the racers have to line up behind it and tour at slow speed until the incident has been cleared away. Then the pace car peels away and they set off again at full bore. The races then become a chess match because the racers do not retain whatever lead they had before the arrival of the pace car. Mario Andretti intitially thought this unfair but now, significantly, says that it makes the races more interesting and that things tend to even themselves out: you have a big lead in one race and lose it behind the pace car, you're a long way behind in the next but gain the lead behind the pace car.

Every waving of the yellow flags creates what is virtually a new race, with the front, midfield and backfield runners bunching. The manipulation of opportunities offered by the yellow flags is almost an art form – and a gamble, because no driver has any idea how many yellow flags there will be in a race or when they will be waved. To take one obvious scenario: when yellow flags are waved early in the race the leaders often dive into the pits for tyres and fuel rather than waste time following the pace car. By doing this they remove themselves from the queue and as they do so each car behind moves up a place, the leaders having to join the tail of the queue when their pit stop is over. By gambling and staying put, a driver may gain half a dozen places in the queue, and when the pace car has gone and the race is on again, he won't have to slog and scheme his way past those half dozen cars. They are behind him.

The driver's chances may then depend on further yellow flags and how they coincide with the pit stops he will eventually have to make before his fuel runs out or his tyres become too worn. The early gamble of staying out may give him a clear advantage. On the other hand, if further yellow flags come at the wrong time for him . . . Andretti's judgement about this is centred on the glorious uncertainty it brings to the race, and the public like to see that. No processional races here, unlike those everyone saw throughout 1992 with Williams and Mansell, when one car vanished into the distance and circulated comfortably half a lap ahead of the others and far out of their reach, the race essentially having been settled a few minutes after it had started. Imagine that Mansell and his rivals in Formula One had had to make the two pit stops, and that there had been the queuing behind the pace car after several yellows. If he'd made the wrong moves in the chess games, Mansell would still have won a host of races – there is no way any rules would have prevented that – but the wins would have been infinitely more exciting. The uncertainty factor would have held interest right to the end.

To those who say it's artificial, Indycar people respond crisply, "So what? This is racing *and* entertainment, buddy, what else should it be? Hey, we're parading something wonderful here, step right in and feast yourselves on it. We ain't got no guy who paralyses the races and leaves everybody yawning." A sports columnist, Rene Fagnan, has written: "Indycar racing is entertainment whilst Formula One claims to be the most advanced form of motor racing in the world. In fact nobody denies that Indycar rules are first and foremost designed to give a good show with heavy use of pace cars, yellow flags and pit stops. The mentality of Formula One is drastically different, but Indycars prove that technology and show can go very well together."

One aspect of this difference in mentality is internal politics, which are rife in Formula One but almost absent in Indycar. This makes for a more relaxed atmosphere there and more concentration on the races themselves. Paradoxically, Mansell might have to take some time adjusting to this because, like everyone else in Formula One, he has spent years watching his front as well as his back. Prost once said that you never know if the hand slapping your back has a dagger in it. Johansson, long versed in the ways of Formula One but now enjoying himself in Indycar, insists that the absence of politics does not dilute the intensity of the racing but makes life more straightforward, easier, more pleasurable.

Politics are largely about money as well as rampant personal ambition, and Formula One needs almost endless amounts of money. Prost, who was poised to buy the Ligier Formula One team, estimated that he needed a minimum of £50 million a year to get it into the big league, that is in a position to win races and championships. This would not include the engine. Compare Indycars to that. A chassis costs £211,000, and even when you've added the electronics, fuel pump, turbo-charger and exhaust manifold you're still going to have a lot of change from the cost of the same operation in Formula One.

Nobody is saying what Formula One engine budgets are but Honda, if the rumours are true, had no budget: their policy was spend whatever you have to spend to make a winning engine. Their outlay must have been many hundreds of millions of dollars. Indycars? A new engine costs £80,000 and a used engine a mere £21,000. Most engines are rebuilt after 500 miles of racing at the fantastically cheap price of £14,000. Fantastically cheap? Ask anyone in Formula One and they wouldn't believe it possible.

The real question which hovers over Mansell is beyond even these matters. It concerns very directly not the car he is to drive or its power, but his own style of racing, forged and hardened on the Grand Prix circuit since 1980 and thus now second nature to him. Mansell is a driver's driver, a raw combatant of chance, which is how he was able to bring a race to life in an outrageous moment. Once in Mexico he overtook Berger on the outside in a tight corner where geometry and gravity decreed that such a manoeuvre was not possible; another time, rounding the right-hand spoon of a corner to reach the straight at the Hungaroring, he saw a momentary gap left by Senna and, by a combination of reflexes, intuition and instinctive car control, he thrust himself into – and through – the gap. You can still do these things on Indycar's street and road circuits but don't ever try it on the super-fast ovals. That is quite literally courting disaster.

Traditionally, to overtake in Formula One you either

burst past on the straight or pursue the driver in front towards a corner, move inside and alongside, brake later than he does and seize the advantage. This naturally leads to disputes about whether you were alongside or not, but that apart it works pretty well. On an oval, where the driver in front is reaching for the corner at maximum speed, it doesn't work at all. There, the driver in front is on the limit, with nothing in reserve; he can't alter the line he is on to make space for you because if he tried that any alteration would be likely to pitch the car out of control. In fact, the driver in front will be negotiating the corner as smoothly as he can, nursing the steering wheel. Even lifting his foot off the accelerator – if done suddenly – could destabilise the car. You use the brakes with extreme caution, caressing not plunging them.

Emerson Fittipaldi emphasised that this is a new technique to a Formula One driver, one which he must explore slowly, painstakingly and with an open mind. Far from outbraking into corners and darting about in heroic ways you ease the car round, foot hard on the accelerator, knowing that if anything goes wrong you'll have to respond faster because the car is going faster, and if you over-respond . . .

No one who watches Grand Prix racing on BBC Television can have missed James Hunt talking about the 'hole in the air' which the car in front punches, and how it helps and hinders. It drags a following car along but also creates turbulence. This is sharply accentuated in Indycar, particularly if there are five or six cars running together and you're tail-end Charlie. The air-flow alters constantly and from instant to instant, buffeting the driver to the point where he can't always see clearly, and directly affecting the aerodynamic performance of the car. Mansell already knows about G-forces and what is termed the

9-G snapover – 4.5G in one corner and a second later 4.5G the other way in the next corner at Silverstone – and although Indycars don't pull the same degree of G-force – around 4.0 – the air buffeting is another matter.

The central concern remains how Mansell will harness his bravery while all this is going on. None ever doubted the bravery of Mansell, which sometimes expresses itself in an impetuous way, sometimes in the most creative way, but exists deep within him, a profound element of the man. Might this self-same bravery lead him towards the impetuous on an oval circuit? Might his red blood propel him to try some Formula One overtaking? This is what alarms the people who understand Indycars – that at his age, newly crowned World Champion, and at a very advanced stage of his career, he might find the waiting and learning difficult.

Certainly any culture shocks with the American way of life will diminish naturally. Mansell already has a house in Florida and intends to live there. This will minimise the commuting to races: for the majority of the 16 Indycar rounds he can hop on a plane and be there the same day. He has Greg Norman, a close friend, as a neighbour, and Florida is not exactly bereft of golf courses. He has business interests, notably a Ferrari dealership in England, to supervise, so he won't have to worry about filling his time. And his children growing up in America and acquiring American ways can only help the familiarisation.

The fact that Paul Newman is directly involved in the team will remove some of the pressure, particularly at the Indianapolis 500 which Newman habitually attends, attracting, understandably, a great deal of attention. However interested the media are in Mansell, the presence of Newman will generate interest of its own; and

Newman is no dilettante in racing. He contested the Le Mans 24 hour sportscar race in a Porsche as part of a three-driver team, and at one stage they nearly took the lead. Carl Haas, who runs the team, is a man who calls a spade a spade – and no back-chat, thank you, especially if he's paying a driver $7 million, as he is paying Mansell: the highest fee in Indycar. Mansell, Haas has said, will be fully expected to do his share of promotional work for the team's sponsor, K-Mart, a national chain of discount general stores with an extremely aggressive marketing strategy. They have hourly special offers announced over tannoys in every shop.

Of more significance, Mansell is to partner Mario Andretti, the number one Lotus driver when Mansell made his Grand Prix debut in Austria in 1980. Andretti is vastly experienced – he began racing in the early 1960s – and is the sort of fellow to impart relevant advice in pithy one-liners if necessary. Andretti is a master at condensing situations into a handful of penetrating words. The great comfort is that Andretti has been Formula One World Champion himself and truly understands the undercurrents of both disciplines, and how and why both disciplines operate. Andretti is very much at home in Indianapolis for the 500, which is as much a part of American mythology as a motor race, a gigantic technicolour extravaganza complete with echoing fanfares. Indianapolis is a town in mid-state Indiana south of Chicago, and the circuit is about five miles from the town centre. The circuit has sold itself and the race hard and takes care to make prices affordable.

The schedule for the 500 for May 1993 demonstrates how much more than just a race it is: there is practice from 8 to 14 May and 17 to 21 May from 11.00am to 6.00pm; qualifying on 15 and 16, 22 and 23 May;

final practice on the 27th, complete with a pit stop competition; the race on Sunday, 30 May. If you go to Grand Prix racing, the prices at Indianapolis defy credulity: admission to practice sessions is £3, £6 for qualifying, £12 on race day. The selling does not stop there: admission to the Hall of Fame is 60p and a track tour is the same price. The organisers' description of the latter runs: "A memorable ride around the track in an official vehicle is available when the track is not being used for racing or is closed due to inclement weather." You are recommended to allow an hour and a half for the Hall of Fame and the tour, a total bargain at £1.20 – especially if it's raining. They want spectators to come and enjoy themselves.

Race day attendance is reaching towards half a million, making it the best-attended sporting event in the world. That is partly due to the fact that the race track is long so that you can get more people round it than, say, you can pack into a football stadium. But to picture the full scope of Indianapolis you must imagine five Wembley Stadiums side by side, and all full. Final Indy qualifying, incidentally, boasts the second largest attendance for any world sporting event.

How will Mansell cope with all that? It is the final question, and it is the big one. We do at least have a form guide to help anticipate how he will fare. He has known karts and the separate demands of single seaters, mastering the tiny Formula Ford 1600s and Formula Three and sampling Formula Two before reaching Formula One. There he had to master skirts on the side of the cars, which made them cling; then cars minus skirts, non-turbo engines, turbo engines and non-turbo engines again; then he had to master the electronic revolution resulting in many aspects of Formula One becoming computer driven.

He has known three Formula One teams, each of them a different sort of operation: Lotus in decline, Williams at the summit, the frantic, frenetic atmosphere surrounding everything at Ferrari. Taken together, it is enough to suggest, and suggest strongly, that he will master Indycar. The Indycar people look forward to it. They feel that Mansell will bring a global audience with him.

Nor will he be going into exile. FISA, the world's governing body, and CART, who run Indycar, spent the latter part of 1992 healing their long-standing feud with a sequence of compromises, and the result was that both bodies felt that together they could promote motor racing worldwide.

It made – or at least seemed to make – for the perfect way to begin another career, another life.

Can Nigel Mansell win the 1993 Indycar Championship? As he prepares to contest it, the question is not as far-fetched as it might seem.

Of the sixteen rounds from March to October, the nature of ten of the tracks is familiar: streets (like Monaco) or roads (like Spa).

The other six, all ovals, will involve alterations to his driving technique – but of sixteen rounds, ten seems a good number to be comfortable with. The schedule:

March 21	Surfers Paradise, Queensland, Australia (street)
April 4	Phoenix (oval)
April 18	Long Beach, California (Street)
May 30	Indianapolis, Indiana (oval)
June 6	Milwaukee (oval)
June 13	Detroit (street)
June 27	Portland, Oregon (road)
July 11	Cleveland, Ohio (street)
July 18	Toronto (street)
August 1	Michigan (oval)
August 8	New England – Loudon, New Hampshire (oval)
August 22	Elkhart Lake, Wisconsin (road)
August 29	Vancouver (road)
September 12	Mid-Ohio – Lexington (road)
September 19	Nazareth, Pennyslvania (oval)
October 3	Laguna Seca, California (road)

The History of Formula One

King George VI, hatless, arms classically behind his back, moved along the line of drivers smiling benignly. He paused, spoke a word or two, moved on. It was 13 May 1950: a bright, crisp, clear day at Silverstone. Within a few minutes the modern era of Formula One racing would be launched. Across the decades before 1950, Grands Prix had been run as individual events. Now, beginning at Silverstone, the races counted towards the World Championship – the very same World Championship as that won by a certain Nigel Mansell at Hungary on 16 August 1992.

From a very gentlemanly and yet deeply dangerous activity Formula One grew into a billion-dollar industry with a global television audience bettered only by the Olympics and the soccer World Cup. It grew from Stirling Moss buying his own driving gloves for a fiver to salaries of ten million dollars and more. The cars, metallic beasts in 1950, evolved into rockets using the space-age technology of NASA – the American space agency which knows a great deal about rockets. A strange and difficult Italian, Giuseppe Farina, set fastest lap at Silverstone in 1950 in an Alfa Romeo, covering 2.920 miles in 1 minute 50.6 seconds.

By 1992 the circuit had been lengthened to 3.247 miles and doctored at several places to restrain the speed of the cars. Mansell covered this in 1 minute 22.539 seconds. Farina's average speed was 95.060mph; Mansell's 141.633mph.

In terms of overt, raw glamour – men risking their lives in the most sophisticated and costly cars that could be built – Formula One ascended to a place almost unique among all sports. Nowhere else did such amounts of money and danger come together. Formula One generated enough money to float Third World economies and swallowed money on that scale, too. It plucked unlikely people from unlikely places and thrust superstardom upon them: Keke Rosberg from frozen Finland, Mansell from sleepy Upton-on-Severn, Alain Prost from a cabinetmakers in a small, obscure French town . . .

Along the way Formula One professionalised itself, deliberately cultivated its own image, spread the glamour as thick as it could. Those first cars that thundered round Silverstone in 1950 had no roll-bars, the drivers did not wear crash helmets; discussions on safety were regarded – if they took place at all – as cissy.

Mike Hawthorn, a great hero and the first British World Champion, drove wearing a bow tie and once, on his slowing-down lap after a Grand Prix at Silverstone, stopped to accept a pint of beer offered from the crowd. These days each driver has flame-proof overalls, an oxygen supply in case of fire and three seat belts which hold him absolutely rigid. The cars are made of kevlar, a bonded material which is pliable but stronger than steel. The pits hum with computers receiving information from the cars as they go round – and extremely detailed information, too, covering every aspect of the car's performance. The gentlemanly pastime has become high-tech, and yet its essential character remains undiluted.

Racers accept risks, however diminished. Motor racing could never be completely safe anyway; it never has been and never will be. This, then, is the story of the evolution of Formula One, the story which began when the first flag fell unleashing 21 cars at Silverstone on 13 May 1950.

The man who slotted his car onto the front row of the grid as the Grenadier Guards played and King George watched closely somehow looked already old. He was nearly 40 and came from an obscure town in the depths of Argentina. His face was serene and becalmed and sanguine and would always remain so, whatever fate brought.

He was called Juan-Mañuel Fangio, and all subsequent drivers who laid claim to greatness would be judged against him. That led to an immediate paradox. Fangio did not win the British Grand Prix at Silverstone – an oil leak stopped him on lap 62 – nor did he win the 1950 Championship. Farina, a political economist from Turin, won both: Silverstone from another Italian, Luigi Fagioli, by 2.6 seconds, the Championship from Fangio by 30 points to 27. Then, as now, you needed the right car and the right car was an Alfa Romeo. At Silverstone Alfas filled the whole of the front row of the grid (it was four abreast) and an Alfa won every one of the six rounds which constituted the Championship.

The cars were either 1500cc supercharged or 4500cc if they weren't, and no weight limit yet applied. In fact weight limits were not introduced until 1961. Farina remains a little-known and controversial figure. Enzo Ferrari, the Italian who went on to make the cars against which all others would be measured, likened him to a 'highly-strung thoroughbred'.

Farina crashed a great deal in his career and died in 1966 when, travelling to watch the French Grand Prix, his car plunged off the road and struck two telegraph poles. But his place in history is safe as the very first World Champion and thus, in a sense, the founder of an imperial and imperious dynasty leading all the way to the boy from Upton-on-Severn.

Another Italian, Alberto Ascari, finished fifth in the 1950 Championship with 11 points, and he, like Farina, remains obscure and controversial. Between them he and Fangio won every Championship from 1951 to 1957 inclusive. Fangio, born in the town of Balcarce 200 miles from Buenos Aires, had trained as a mechanic before he began driving competitively before the Second World War. After he won a race in 1949 the crowd yelled at him: "Go to Europe, Juan, go and race them there!"

Fangio did.

His main rival in 1951 was Ascari, a man wracked by superstitions but a superb driver who liked to dominate races from the front. Ascari had what all the consummate drivers have had: the inborn facility to find more speed when he needed it without sacrificing any of his car control.

It was a tight Championship, and as drivers were able to count only their four best finishes from the seven races Fangio totalled 37 (31 counting), Ascari 28 (25 counting). At the end of 1951 Alfa Romeo withdrew from Grand Prix racing, leaving the Ferrari team in splendid isolation. In an echo of the Williams Renault superiority of today, that alarmed many people. Clearly Ferrari would have paralysed the 1952 season, rendering it extremely boring. So, to broaden the scope and allow more entrants, the Formula One Championship was reduced to Formula Two specifications. That meant a maximum of 2000ccs for cars with compressors, 2500ccs for cars without.

But near-tragedy struck early on disturbing all the

calculations. In a pre-season race at Monza, Fangio made a mistake in a Maserati, was thrown out and broke his neck. He didn't race again in 1952, leaving Ascari to bestride the season in, inevitably, a Ferrari.

While Ascari was winning the second race of 1952, the Belgian Grand Prix, a young, fresh-faced chap from Surrey was bringing a Cooper Bristol into fourth place on his debut. He was called Mike Hawthorn and – again like many consummate drivers – he was good immediately. A year later he joined Ferrari and at the French Grand Prix in Reims held off Fangio (by one second) to become the first Briton to win a race. He would have to wait a lot longer for the Championship; until Fangio had gone, in fact.

Ascari took the Championship in 1953 and in 1954 Formula One returned to being Formula One (1750ccs with compressor, 2500ccs without). And Fangio moved towards immortality. To qualify and evaluate his achievements is extremely difficult because they lie beyond statistics, however monumental the statistics themselves. Fangio took the Championship in 1954, 1955, 1956 and 1957 – and no man has come remotely near to duplicating this.

Fangio had a complete range of skills, including patience when necessary. The level of his skills was so high that he plundered race after race, year after year. None was better than the race in which he won the 1957 Championship. It was held at the Nürburgring, the most fearsome and feared circuit in the world: 14.150 miles of track in the countryside, all hills and bumps and jumps and ravines and trees.

Fangio was in a Maserati, Hawthorn and another Briton, Peter Collins, in Ferraris. The background is simple enough. Fangio was to make a pit stop for tyres and fuel, the Ferraris were not. What Fangio needed was a lead so great that he could afford the time the pit stop would take. He got that lead, but the pit stop went terribly wrong and lasted almost a minute. From this disaster Fangio constructed a stunning assault, climaxing in a new lap record of 9 minutes 17.4 seconds. It may well have been the greatest lap ever driven. He himself felt that finally he had probed and solved every mystery of the Nürburgring. The sharp comparison, and the only real comparison, with that lap is the qualifying time set by Fangio himself. He had taken pole position with 9 minutes 25.6 seconds. To go eight seconds quicker in the race defies credulity. He beat Hawthorn by 3.6 seconds and Hawthorn was so intoxicated by the pace and splendour of the race that he hugged Fangio as if he'd won it himself.

A neat, organised Briton finished fifth that year at the Nürburgring. In a sense his career lay in the shadows of Fangio's virtually throughout the 1950s, and yet his name too became synonymous with speed. Stirling Moss was without question the best driver never to win the Championship. He came second in 1955, 1956 and 1957. Approaching 1958 Moss reasoned that with Fangio retired his time had come. Moss drove a Vanwall, Hawthorn a Ferrari once again and by the last race of the season, Morocco, Moss had to win and set fastest lap, while Hawthorn needed only to come second. Hawthorn, restraining himself and judging it nicely, did come second.

In that race another Briton, Stuart Lewis-Evans, crashed and subsequently died of his injuries. Death was no stranger to motor racing in the 1950s. Peter Collins died at the Nürburgring in 1958 when his car swerved off, Hawthorn himself died in a road crash in

1959. Ascari had gone, killed in testing at Monza in 1955 when, as it would seem, he wasn't wearing his lucky crash helmet – his superstitions would not normally have allowed him to step into a car without it.

The fatality list is monstrously long: a Frenchman, Jean Behra, killed on the Avus circuit in Berlin; Italian Eugenio Castellotti, killed testing a Ferrari; Fagioli killed at Monaco; Fangio's friend and fellow countryman Onofre Marimon killed at the Nürburgring. Worse even than all of this, at the 1955 Le Mans sportscar race Hawthorn was involved in a crash which killed 78 people.

Deep controversy still surrounds the accident but, briefly, Hawthorn overtook a slower car and headed for the pits. The slower car had to brake hard and spun. A Mercedes, driven by Frenchman Pierre Levegh, struck it, was launched and parts of it bored into the crowd. The *Daily Express* understandably made this their main front page story the following day under the headline RACE CASUALTIES OVER 150, and the motoring correspondent, Basil Cardew, quoted Hawthorn as saying that it was the "most tragic day of my life."

And in 1961 at Monza, Jim Clark and a German, Wolfgang von Trips, collided. Von Trips' Ferrari vaulted into the crowd, killing him and 13 spectators. Phil Hill (also Ferrari) won that race to become the first American Champion – a bitter sweet victory, as he would say. Desperately bitter sweet.

Astonishingly, real steps towards making motor racing safer were not taken for several years, until a canny and perceptive Scotsman, Jackie Stewart, said, in essence: enough is enough. On the track a decisive shift took place in the late 1950s. The days of Italian domination – already unbalanced by the return of Mercedes to Formula One before they withdrew in the aftermath of Le Mans – were drawing to a close. A small team founded by a restless genius entered Grand Prix racing in 1958. The man was Colin Chapman and the team was Lotus. Within a couple of years Chapman had hired a quiet Scotsman, Jim Clark, and soon enough people were speaking of Clark in direct comparison to Fangio.

By then, too, a taciturn and aggressive Australian, Jack Brabham, had proved that your birthplace need be no constraint to a successful career. He journeyed to Britain and won the Championship in 1959 and 1960. To do it in 1959 he had to physically push his car over the line at the Sebring circuit, Florida, after it ran out of petrol.

Britain was becoming the centre of Formula One and British drivers were poised to become its core. Graham Hill, a Londoner with a reputation as a *bon viveur* away from the track but dogged when he drove a racing car, took the Championship in 1962, Clark in 1963 – and with a breathtaking 73 points (54 counting) against Hill's 29.

John Surtees became the only man to win Championships on two wheels and four. He had already taken the 500cc bike title in 1956, 1958, 1959 and 1960 and, in a Ferrari, added the car Championship in 1964, Hill coming second, Clark third. Clark responded by touching invincibility in 1965. He won the opener, the South African Grand Prix, missed Monaco so that he could win the Indy 500 (Mansell's next stop), won Belgium, France, Silverstone and Holland and secured the title at the Nürburgring. During that German Grand Prix Clark set fastest lap at 8 minutes 24.1 seconds. Thus can the speed of progress be measured: less than ten years before Fangio had recorded 9 minutes 17.4 seconds, widely, and rightly, regarded as a miraculous feat.

As in the case of Fangio, a finite evaluation of Clark's ability is elusive, although many have tried to make one. He had what is called natural talent. He could instinctively feel what any car could be made to do. He didn't have to think about it. There are revealing stories of how, if he had some mechanical problem, his lap times would inevitably slow down but within a few laps he'd be back up to the same speed as before. He'd simply compensated in his driving for whatever was wrong with the car, driving round the problem, as they say in the trade. Few can do this.

Clark adored the act of driving and competed in a host of different classes: saloons, sportscars – he even tried the RAC Rally in a Cortina and was quick until he crashed it. Clark, shy but never reclusive, found himself with what ought to have been a decisive advantage in 1967. A company called Cosworth produced a racing engine for Ford. From its debut in the third race of the season, Holland, the Cosworth ushered in a complete new era. It was to become the workhorse of Formula One, and its most potent package. Yet in a squeeze of a Championship the rugged New Zealander Denny Hulme, who died of a heart attack in late 1992 in a race in Australia, won with 51 points from Brabham on 46. Clark was third with 41.

What might Clark have done with the Cosworth in 1968? We'll never know. He won the opener in South Africa, beating Graham Hill (also Lotus) by 25.3 seconds, but was killed in a Formula Two race at Hockenheim, Germany. His car suddenly veered off the track, pitching him amongst trees.

Many feel that Colin Chapman never really recovered from this; certainly it changed him, hardened him, made him sometimes difficult with his drivers. One, the American Mario Andretti, said that working with Chapman "wasn't no trip to Paris." Clark and Chapman had been more than driver and team manager – they complemented each other perfectly. Chapman made outstanding cars, and Clark drove them outstandingly.

Hill, finding himself in the midst of a shattered team, produced one of the great feats, and one which is still perhaps underestimated. He hauled himself and the team to the Championship. Young Jackie Stewart finished in second place to Hill. He wouldn't be second for long. Stewart was to become much more than the leading exponent of driving a racing car in the late 1960s and early 1970s. He rationalised the art by dissecting each facet of it; he drew conclusions and applied them. He became and remains one of the most eloquent of all sportspeople with a gift for rendering the extremely complex into simple terms.

If that had been the sum of it Stewart would have taken his place in the dynasty as . . . well, as just another leading exponent. Stewart's enduring contribution lies elsewhere. He began to rationalise the whole matter of safety. This began at Spa, a circuit similar to the Nürburgring, although not quite as savage. The perennial problem at Spa, an extremely fast place with minimal protection, was the wet weather. By a climatic quirk there could be rain on parts of the circuit while other parts remained dry, and the drivers moved from one to the other without warning. Even Clark loathed the place, and the tough motorcycle fraternity raced there with extreme trepidation. Spa could kill, and did kill.

In a wet Grand Prix there cars slid and skipped off – one came to rest straddling a wall – and the ambulance taking Stewart to hospital got lost. Somehow, until then, death was something that just happened. Stewart was initially vilified for insisting on proper precautions to minimise danger. Some said that motor racing had always been a macho thing, and that the safer it got the less macho it would be. Some said that a generation whose thinking had been governed by the War, when death was commonplace, had missed the mood of the new times.

Whatever the case, motor racing could not go on as it was, accepting the deaths which occurred and regarding coverage in the popular press of those deaths as sensationalist outbursts. Stewart's contribution, reinforced by the clarity of his logic and expressed with his eloquence, provided the impetus. In time the Nürburgring ceased to host Grands Prix and Spa, subjected to a drivers' boycott, hosted no more, either, until it had been transformed into the circuit we know today.

Stewart's role in the important matter of safety was so central that even 20 years later he became the first holder of the Labatt's Safety Award.

The early 1970s were as good a time as any to consider human preservation. Speeds continued to rise and Farina's 95.060mph at Silverstone in 1950 seemed almost stately. 121.118mph was recorded there by Denny Hulme in 1967, 129.606 by Stewart in 1969, 131.880 by Stewart again in 1971. An ambitious Englishman, James Hunt, increased this to 134.061 in 1973. (Silverstone, incidentally, alternated with Brands Hatch as the venue for the British Grand Prix.) Thereafter a chicane was added to Silverstone just after the Daily Express Bridge to deliberately slow the cars, and it did, briefly. The chicane was so tight that the drivers had to brake heavily in front of it and thread carefully through before accelerating away.

But even with the chicane the Swiss Clay Regazzoni lapped at 130.345mph in 1975, and by 1979 Regazzoni had taken it to 141.871 – and it kept rising. Keke Rosberg of Finland covered the 2.932 miles in 1 minute 5.591 seconds during qualifying in 1985, breaking the fabled

160mph barrier (specifically Rosberg averaged 160.938). By then, of course, safety was well established and cars were able to withstand enormous impacts. The crowds no longer sat along the rim of tracks with, perhaps, only straw bales between them and the cars. Ambulances did not get lost; tracks had extensive on-site medical facilities and helicopters to whisk the injured to hospitals and Formula One had its own resident doctor, Professor Syd Watkins.

Ironically, Stewart's greatest race was at the Nürburgring in a thunderstorm in 1968. With water running in rivers and rivulets across the track and visibility virtually non-existent, Stewart started from the third row of the grid. As he had planned, he took the lead quickly to escape the spray being thrown up by the other cars and won by more than four minutes. To his talents, then, must be added another: bravery.

Stewart spanned two distinct generations. In the 1970s a new one came through, led by Niki Lauda, a toothy Austrian and a very competitive man. He won the Championship in a Ferrari in 1975 and then almost died in a fireball at the Nürburgring a year later. Lauda was so badly burned that he was given the Last Rites. He did not die and, defying mortality, was back racing within weeks – back in time, in fact, to resume his struggle with Hunt (McLaren). Lauda was so pragmatic that he couldn't understand what all the fuss was about, or if he could he disregarded it. Few human beings have understood the mechanisms of their own mind better than Niki Lauda.

The decisive race was the last, at Mount Fuji, Japan. Lauda went into the race three points ahead of Hunt. Heavy rain fell, drowning the circuit, and amidst the ensuing chaos the start was delayed. When the race did begin Lauda judged the conditions too dangerous and withdrew on lap three. At that moment the Championship shifted towards Hunt, who needed only to come in fourth.

Hunt led as the rain slackened and stopped and the track started to dry. A dry track shreds grooved wet-weather tyres because they overheat. Hunt waited for the team to signal him in to change tyres; the team waited for Hunt to make the decision himself because they felt he was in a better position to judge. On lap 68, and with only five laps left, Hunt's front left tyre disintegrated completely. Entirely by chance he happened to be near the pits so that instead of having to slog all the way round he was able to come in straight away. Because the tyre had disintegrated the suspension of the car was so low that the jack wouldn't go underneath. A mechanic had to bodily lift the car so that the jack could be moved into place.

Hunt rejoined the race but had no idea where he was in it. Because of the rain and so many tyre stops lap charts resembled mazes. Hunt drove ferociously, overtaking any car he found amid the lingering spray. He finished third, but he didn't know that. He was absolutely convinced that he'd finished a lot lower, that the Championship had been plucked from him, that everything had been in vain. The team surrounded the car to acclaim him. He emerged from the cockpit in a towering rage and wouldn't believe he'd made it, wouldn't believe the forest of splayed hands around him, all with three fingers held up for third place. Hunt accepted the truth only when the officials had confirmed it.

Hunt's image before this victory, that of the typical public schoolboy, was deceptive. Hunt was in no sense a devil-may-care gung-ho chappie. He was an iron racer who was sometimes physically sick before a race as the tension claimed him. He was not dissimilar to Graham Hill: both concentrated on putting mind over matter.

Who could have known, as the Grand Prix circus dispersed on the evening of 24 October 1976, that the dynasty of Hawthorn, Clark, Hill, Surtees, Stewart and now Hunt would not be continued until the Hungaroring, 16 August 1992? A ridiculous notion . . .

The remainder of the 1970s belonged to others: Brazilian Emerson Fittipaldi (a man who clearly enjoyed himself); the articulate and witty Andretti; the careful South African Jody Scheckter. Scheckter rationed out the Championship in 1979 by allowing his team-mate at Ferrari, Gilles Villeneuve, to blaze away in qualifying and rap out fastest laps while Scheckter himself gathered points. He knew full well that this season of 1979 was divided. Up to Monaco there were seven races and a driver could count only his four best finishes. After Monaco there were eight races and, again, only the best four counted.

Scheckter reasoned that consistency was everything. If you had a bad first half you couldn't make up for it in the second – the four-finish rule prevented that. Scheckter was consistent and finished four points clear of Villeneuve, a man destined never to be Champion.

Paradoxically Villeneuve – who won no more than six races in his Grand Prix career – demands inclusion among the great for his style, his bravado and his enormous speed. He was in many ways a natural, innocent man captivated by racing and expressing himself through that. He said he really felt alive only at the wheel. His ethos touched spectators, struck profound chords in them; and it was also his epitaph. The memory of Villeneuve endures.

Like Lotus so long before, another small team were

poised to become big and powerful. For years Frank Williams had been struggling for money (the team used a local phone box when their own phone was cut off, the bills unpaid). The Williams team seemed to be going nowhere. But Frank Williams had many virtues which were not apparent, including fearsome willpower. He secured major sponsorship from Saudi Airlines and hired a blunt, rugged Australian, Alan Jones. Regazzoni joined Jones and won the 1979 British Grand Prix at Silverstone – Williams' first. After that Jones put together a strong run and won Germany, Austria, Holland and Canada for third place in the Championship. Within a few months Williams had become a leading team and went from strength to strength until Mansell joined them, left for Ferrari, retired from racing altogether, and then returned once again.

Williams and his brilliant designer, Patrick Head, became a force of the 1980s and Jones gave notice of what was to come by taking the Championship in 1980. His five victories that year might easily have been six – he was beaten by 0.82 of a second by Jean-Pierre Jabouille (Renault turbo) in Austria. Both Jones and Jabouille, incidentally, lapped car number 43, a backmarker with a debutant driver named Nigel Mansell feeling his way round.

The 1980s were a time of radical change. Colin Chapman invented 'skirts', an idea so basic that it represented a genuine coup. Thin strips were put down each side of the car and trailed along the ground. Air flowing at the car could not escape through these skirts but only through the rear, and this compressed air sucked the car to the surface of the track. The faster you drove the greater the suction. It allowed alarming cornering speeds and the cars had virtually no suspensions, giving the driver a hammering. In time cornering speeds became so great that circuits couldn't cope.

Speed, speed, speed.

Turbo engines, introduced by Renault in 1977 to general scepticism, recycled power to produce more and more of it. In qualifying, these 1980s drivers would have more than a thousand horsepower under their accelerator pedal, an amount difficult to imagine, never mind harness smoothly. Before the end of the 1980s skirts and turbos were banned, but while they existed drivers had to learn entirely new techniques. One example will suffice. With skirts a car went exactly where it was pointed in cornering – there was no drift any more, no need to fine tune through a corner as Clark had done – but if the driver wasn't absolutely accurate in his pointing he was in a lot of trouble, and fast. Put another way, he was helpless, a passenger. Worse, if the suction was broken by a car leaving the ground during an accident, the skirts had an opposite effect, turning the car into an aeroplane by forcing it up, up, up.

There would be other dramas. The Constructors' Association, who sought to professionalise the sport, went into combat with the governing body, FISA. There would be re-fuelling during races, which terrified many because with all that fuel down the pit lane a fire could become a holocaust. The laws, sometimes applied savagely to curb all this, mirrored the evolution of the sport.

The minimum weight of any car, 575 kilograms in 1980, was progressively reduced to 540 by 1983, where it stayed until 1988. A fuel restriction was introduced in 1984 (220 litres), and progressively reduced to 150. Turbo-charged engines were restricted to 1500cc in 1987 before being banned altogether in 1989. In their time turbos made exacting demands on each driver. He had a boost button which, when turned up, made the car go faster – but the downside was that it guzzled fuel. The trick was to use the boost sparingly, at crucial moments, itself almost an art form.

But, in a sense, whatever the law-makers decided technology drove the sport. The high-tech era was at hand, requiring drivers to learn yet another set of skills: how to co-habit with computers, read computer print-outs and exploit a car whose mechanisms were pre-programmed.

The 1980s produced four genuinely outstanding drivers: Nelson Piquet and Ayrton Senna from Brazil, Alain Prost from France and Nigel Mansell. Piquet, Champion in 1981, had an almost telepathic understanding with Brabham designer Gordon Murray, himself a radical innovator (he convulsed Formula One by suddenly putting an enormous fan on the back of one of his cars). Piquet was a curious ad-mix of the casual, the laid-back and the urgent. He was completely indifferent to what people wrote about him (and perhaps to what they thought about him) and spent a lot of his time fishing, beyond the reach of telephones. In a car he'd match anybody for speed.

Keke Rosberg won the Championship for Williams in 1982, setting a record unlikely ever to be equalled: he won only one race. The Williams had no turbo engine, so Rosberg got there on consistency, and this in a season in which no man established domination. For once, the consistency and the single win was enough. It was very different from the route taken by Mansell ten years later.

But 1982 was savage, unremittingly savage – Villeneuve was killed in qualifying at Zolder; a young Italian, Riccardo Paletti, killed at the start of the Canadian Grand Prix; Frenchman Didier Pironi crippled in a crash in the rain at Hockenheim.

Lauda was lured from retirement by Ron Dennis of McLaren. Partnering Prost – who had been fired by Renault at the tail end of 1983 – Lauda won the 1984 Championship by half a point from his team-mate. It was a day laden with emotion because everybody in the world knew about Lauda and his return from the dead in 1976. The reminders remained in the scorch marks still visible about his head, the tufts of hair, the places where his hair would never grow again.

At Estoril, the last race, Lauda needed only to finish second to take the Championship even if Prost won. The emotional atmosphere deepened when Lauda's wife Marlene came to the race, breaking the habit of a lifetime. Whatever she felt she masked behind a regal smile. Moreover Lauda, who had had a nightmare in qualifying – nothing had gone right – started from the sixth row of the grid. As the race unfolded, Prost leading, Lauda became trapped behind the midfield runners. He abandoned his normal and fabled caution, turned the boost button up and went for it. Knowing eyes along the pit lane saw Lauda get as near as he had ever got to taking real risks, flinging the car into gaps, fleeing across the edge of certainty. It was hypnotic, and when Lauda did come in second the world surrendered to him.

Poor Prost. He squarely faced a desperate quirk of fate, one which had cost him his first Championship. He had led the Monaco Grand Prix early in the season but the race had been stopped in a thunderstorm and only half points were awarded. If it had gone the distance and Prost had taken nine points instead of four and a half, he would have become the first French Champion.

As it happened, when that Monaco Grand Prix was stopped Senna, then with the little British Toleman team, was poised to catch and overtake Prost to win the race himself. Senna's car-control in these conditions confirmed what many suspected: here was a man who might hoist himself to the level at which comparisons might be made with Fangio and Clark. So, although he had to wait for his first win, it was not for long. He was a man in an extreme hurry to grab whatever motor sport offered, but principally the Championship. Nor did he intend to win it only once. Senna's pursuit of the title became so intense, particularly when he was competing with Prost, that fissures were created in Formula One which threatened to break it apart.

Prost, Champion in 1985 and 1986, made himself into one of the great tacticians. He read the whole of a race, his thinking projected far, far ahead of the rush and surge for the first corner, the jostle for places. Before his temporary retirement in 1992 he won more races than any other man, 44. Although he was a thinker, when he needed to be fast he was, often blindingly so. From 1981 he set fastest lap 35 times which, to make a direct comparison, was more often than Mansell had done from 1980 right up to his total domination in 1992.

Honda, who had made their own Formula One cars in the 1960s, returned, but only as engine suppliers. Only? Their engine took Piquet to the Championship in 1987 – Piquet was now with Williams – and when Honda moved to Marlboro McLaren they gripped Formula One tight. Senna came to McLaren via Lotus, whom he'd joined from Toleman. At first he and Prost co-existed peacefully enough and, superficially, seemed the ideal team-mates. Senna was hungry, a chance-taker; Prost mature, measured.

Senna won the Championship in 1988, an achievement so emotional for him – he had sacrificed his marriage and consecrated his whole adult life to this goal – that he dissolved into tears. An openly religious man, Senna had an aura approaching the mysterious wreathed around him. Nobody knew his depths, nobody knew how far he'd go to get what he wanted.

The fissure opened in 1989 when, Prost claimed, Senna broke an 'accord' they had established between themselves. Because the Marlboro McLaren Honda was so superior they decided not to contest the first corner of the races and thus risk crashing into each other. Whoever reached the first corner first got it. At Imola Prost was away fast but Senna overtook him before the first corner. Opinions are sharply divided about the rights and wrongs of this – specifically whether Senna had broken the accord – but whatever happened had happened, and after that their relationship was bleak, chilled, formal.

At the chicane in Japan, a race Senna needed to win to keep his Championship hopes alive, he and Prost collided. Senna tried to sling-shot through on the inside approaching the chicane; Prost, following the racing line, cut across him and both cars went off, locked together. Senna resumed the race but was disqualified because marshals had given his car a push and he'd rejoined the race from the escape road, thus missing out the chicane.

A year later Prost, now with Ferrari, found himself back in Japan in the Championship, jousting with Senna again. Senna took pole but was bitterly upset that officials wouldn't let him move out to the other side of the track where the surface of the track was cleaner and would offer him a better start. Senna subsequently confessed that he had decided to go flat out to capture the first corner, and tough if anybody got in his way. Prost got in his way and they crashed, ending up in the dusty run-off area. Senna had his second Championship because Prost had failed to finish.

Japan decided the 1991 Championship, too. Mansell needed to win. Senna and his McLaren team-mate, Gerhard Berger, adopted a very effective plan. Berger set off hard while Senna lingered, holding up Mansell. As every lap went by Berger moved further and further ahead. Mansell absolutely had to catch and overtake him, but first he had to get past Senna. Mansell backed off to catch his breath, and approaching the notorious Turn One where Senna and Prost had crashed the year before he felt the brake pedal go soft. The Williams skipped across the kerbing, spun and sank into the run-off area, beached.

Mansell would have to wait another year. Might he have to wait forever? It was a disturbing and unavoidable question. The answer was very decisive indeed . . .

THE EVOLUTION OF GRAND PRIX SCORING

1950–1959: 8 points for 1st place; 6 for 2nd; 4 for 3rd, 3 for 4th; 2 for 5th; 1 point for fastest lap.
1960: 8 points for 1st place, then 6, 4, 3, 2, and 1 point for 6th place. No points for fastest lap.
1961–1990: 9 points for 1st place, then 6, 4, 3, 2, 1.
1991 onwards: 10 points for 1st place, then 6, 4, 3, 2, 1.

Note: From 1950 to 1980 a driver could count a varying number of his best finishes – lowest four in the early 1950s, highest 13 finishes out of 15 in 1973 and 1974. It then settled as 11 best finishes to count out of 16 races until 1991, when all finishes counted.

THE MOST SUCCESSFUL DRIVERS

Most Championships: 5 (Juan-Mañuel Fangio)
Most wins: 44 (Alain Prost)
Most points: 699½ (Alain Prost)
Youngest winner: Bruce McLaren, aged 22
Oldest winner: Luigi Fagioli, aged 53
Most successful country: Britain (7 Champions: Mike Hawthorn, Graham Hill, Jim Clark, John Surtees, James Hunt and Nigel Mansell)
Driver with the highest winning ratio: Fangio (24 wins from 51 races)